Love, Lies, and Murder

A Novel by Keyaira Kinslow

Prologue

The story you are about to read will not be a happy one. It contains love, lies, and, most importantly, murder. You will laugh and cry, but more importantly, you will come out a new person. So, without further ado, sit back, relax, and enjoy the show.

When I was one year old, my father left me. I know what comes to your mind when I say that: a sad, one-year-old boy, pleading over the middle-aged man while grabbing his suitcase and raincoat and begging him. Only to find his father disappear forever into the rain.

No.

That's not what happened.

According to my mother, it was something less selfish. It was a car, two of them, crashing into one another. One of those cars was a brown Cadillac with white streaks on the side.

But as good as it looked, it was no match for the vehicle that hit it. From the words of my mother, it flipped over twelve times, causing all kinds of glass, tires, and metal to fall right off. According to the policemen, the car was in the form of a ball, a big, metal ball, curved and arched in every way.

It wasn't long before the police arrived at our house, giving my mother the news. Most people leave when something traumatic happens, but Mom and we stayed in that apartment with all the memories of Dad. Or Mom's memories of him. I was just a baby at the time, so I didn't really know much about Dad, except that he liked to paint. While I never saw any of his work I didn't need to. He loved me, and that's all that mattered. At least, that's what Mom says.

The days soon bled into years, and the house became nothing but an empty, hollow shell of memories of my father that slowly faded with each passing day. At least that's what my mom says.

But it would be many years before I figured out what that meant.

My name is Dominic Mitchell, and I have a story to tell.

Part

1

Chapter 1:

Seventeen Years Later

Every night, I have the same dream. I'm standing in front of a door with my eyes glued to the doorknob, waiting patiently for it to turn. I'm also holding a yellow toy racing car, one my mother brought for me on my fifth birthday. I continue guarding the door, waiting patiently for my old man to walk right in.

It isn't long until, suddenly, the doorknob twists, causing my eyes to widen in anticipation. Before I know it, the door swings wide open, revealing a man in silhouette standing over me. The worst part about this dream was that I could never make out what the man looked like, all except he had what looked to be a briefcase and trench coat.

If only he would just walk through; only then could I see him. Unfortunately, I don't. I never do. Before I can do or say anything to him, he fades into thin air, and before I know it, I'm awake, and I hear a knock at my door.

"Dominic! Dominic! Wake up!", said my mother's voice behind the door.

"Huh, what-what?", I say, rising from my pillow.

"Dominic, get up! It's time for school!"

With my brain now in focus, I put my hand through my hair, letting out an annoyed grunt. By the looks of it, you could tell I hate mornings, especially on the first day back at school. But that's not the only thing I hated.

Just one more year and I would get my freedom.

Just one more year.

Lost in thought, the knock at the door was heard again, bringing me back to reality. "Yeah?"

"Dominic, are you up yet?"

"Yeah, I am!"

"Well, hurry up! The bus will be here any minute!"

"Okay, okay! Geez!", I say, annoyed, before hopping out of my bed and into my jeans, pulling them up to my waist.

Not long after, I slip on my shirt, jacket, sneakers, and sketchers. As for my hair, there was not much to do there but comb and brush what little hair I had. That is the great thing about being a guy; you never have to worry about hair the way girls do.

Speaking of girls, one of them was on my ass this morning, doing their best to make my day a living hell. But not today because today was different. Today was new. Today was my day!

With these words of encouragement, I made my bed, grabbed my backpack, and headed straight out the door.

#

When I entered the kitchen, I expected nothing but a normal morning. That is, until I turned to the left,_-my eyes widening at the sight of an alien with green goo leaning in the back of her chair. Its hair was in pink curls with cucumbers over her eyes, while a convertible fan blew on her face.

"Um, Mom?", I say, confused.

Hearing this, the cumbered-faced alien raised her head, her cucumbers falling from her face before speaking. "Dominic?", she laughed taking a cucumber from her eye. "Is that you?"

I nodded. "Yeah, what are you doing?"

Mom looked up at the cucumber in her hand before speaking. "Oh, I'm just masking myself."

"Masking?"

"Avocado", she said pointing to her face. "It's good for the pores."

I raised my brow in confusion. "O-kay. Well, are you ready to go?"

"Mm-hm", she nodded, switching the fan off, before she turned her eyes back to me. "The mask is dry now."

\#

I sat beside Mom in the car, my eyes gazing out at the streetlights sitting beside her. Only, I couldn't get the satisfaction of listening in silence as my mother was humming to herself. I turned to her with my eyes full of irritation as she continued humming. "Do you have to do that?", I said making Mom turn her eyes in confusion. "Do what, baby?"

"Hum that song. It's so annoying."

"What do you mean? I used to hum this to you all the time when you were young."

"Yeah, when I was five, not seventeen, going on eighteen!"

"I don't see any difference, Dominic. Besides, it's not like I'm humming it to you. I'm humming for me."

"You always do."

Mom rolled her eyes. "So, are you ready for your first day back at school?"

"Yeah, I'm real excited."

"What are you most excited about?"

"Everything, really!" I laughed. "Prom, homecoming, and of course, graduation! I can't wait to experience them all!"

"I'm sure you can't, but you have to work for them, remember?"

I nodded. "Right, I know, Mom. Just like you always say, work comes first."

"Yes"

Mom and I end up looking back to the road before speaking. "Hey, Mom? Don't you have to work today?"

She shook her head. "No, that's Sue, baby."

"Right, I forgot", I said raising my hand up to the back of my neck, rubbing it profusely. "Well, I was just wondering, if you're not too busy, after school, could we run down to the thrift shop. My jeans are starting to shrink, and I don't think they can last the whole year."

"Hmm", Mom said looking down at my high-watered blue jeans going past my ankles. "Oh, yeah. You need some more pants", Mom looked up from my jeans to me. "Yeah, we can run by there today."

I smile. "Thanks, Mom"

Mom continued to look at the road before suddenly stopping at a large building where hundreds of students paraded their way to and from the building. It wasn't ng before she pulled into the driveway, stopping dead at the front door. "Alright, baby, this is your stop"

"Yep!", I swung my backpack on my back before raising my hand. "See you later, Mom!"

"Dominic!", Mom called, making my head spin. "Yeah?"

"You got your lunch money with you?"

I nodded in reply. "Always"

"Five bucks?"

"Mm-hm!"

She grins. "Good. Wouldn't want it getting lost."

"I will!", I was just about to make my way into the bus when my mom shouted these words: "I love you!"

Within seconds, every student burst out in laughter, making my stomach churn in embarrassment. Even the bus driver was having a laugh, making my embarrassment heighten. "Dominic, did you hear me?"

I did. I just didn't want to repeat it back, but I had to. After all, she was my mother.

With a quick sigh, I turned back to my mother, my eyes full of humiliation, before answering. "I love you too, Mom! See you after school."

The students continued to laugh, their fingers pointing right at me as I made my way onto the bus. My eyes lowered in humiliation as they judged.

Perfect.

Before I knew it, Mom droves away, leaving me annoyed. With nothing left but my dignity, I took off my backpack and walked straight into the bus.

#

As I walk through the valley of the shadow of death
I take a look at my life and realize there's nothin' left
'Cause I've been blastin' and laughin' so long that
Even my momma thinks that my mind is gone

Gangsta's Paradise, one of my all-time favorite songs, joyfully, played through my iPhone my eyes closed shut as I let the sweet tune of Coolio flood my senses.

But I ain't never crossed a man that didn't deserve it
Me be treated like a punk, you know that's unheard of
You better watch how you talkin' and where you walkin'
Or you and your homies might be lined in chalk
I really hate to trip, but I gotta Loc

It blasted through my headphones, making everything around me become entirely tuned out. Everything like this: "Summit High!", said the bus driver before the door slid wide open.

Within minutes, all the students marched their way from their seats and off the bus, their smiles worn with happiness as they stood. As for me, my mind was lost in the serenity of my headphones, not noticing a single student leaving the yellow vehicle. Soon, the last kid got off, giving the bus driver one final nod before hopping off.

Thinking it wasn't the last one, the bus driver turned his head around to find his bus completely empty. That is until he looked far in the back and found a pair of headphones bopping up and down. Seeing this, the bus driver lets out an annoyed sigh before rising from his seat and making his way down the line of leather seats, his arms crossed as he finds me, bobbing my head up and down, my eyes closed shut as I look hummed "Gangsta's Paradise" to myself.

Irritated, the bus driver folds his arms, giving me a stern scowl. "Kid?", I continue to bop my head back and forth. "Kid!"

I still wasn't listening, for I was too stuck in my music to hear him or anything else. With his eyes rolling in the back of his head, the bus driver raised his hands over my head and snatched my headphones off, causing me to whip my head around in confusion. "What the heck, man!"

"Don't give me that! You heard me call your name, yet you continued to listen to that devil box!"

"Devil box?", I scoff. "It's called an iPhone."

"I don't care what it's called! When people are callin' ya name, you should be listenin'. Not have these here, headphones lodged in ya ear!"

"Alright, I get it! Now, can I please have me my iPhone back?"

"Do you promise to open your ears next time?"

"Yes! Come on, I got to get to class! The school bell could ring any minute!"

With his brow raised, the bus driver's hands slowly handed me my iPhone. "Thanks", I said as I rose from my seat and out of the bus.

As soon as I was out, I gazed up at the large building with a whole sea of students making their way through the doors. It wasn't long until I spotted the sign that sat above the ginormous building: **Summit High.**

Seeing this, I look down at the quote found below: **"Where Knowledge is Power."**

With my eyes big and wide, I put my Walkman in my pocket, take a deep breath and speak. "A new year, new me"

With that, I make my way towards the school, melting in with the students as they enter the school building.

As for the bus driver, he watched from behind, his gaze very annoyed. "I hope he makes it to graduation", he said.

With these words, the bus driver lowered his lever, making the door close shut before driving off down the road.

A shiny, white BMW comes in right behind it, stopping right at the front of Summit High. Once stopped, a man in a black and white tuxedo made his way out of the car and quickly to the door, opening it wide. He held a red carpet which he quickly fanned out onto the concrete floor. Once done, he opened the car door. "We have arrived, Ms. Griffin."

With that said, a polished, white slipper with a red bow is placed down on the red carpet. "Thank you, Barry", answered a young girl with black, silk-pressed hair, glowing skin and emerald, green eyes. She looked up at the school, her eyes full of confusion as the large yet very small building presented itself. "Barry, I thought you said this was a private school?"

"It is, madame", Barry said, his hands behind his back. "Finest in St. Petersburg"

"But it's small", she said, turning to him.

"Small but big with brilliance!"

The young girl scoffed before turning her head up to the building where a couple of words were ingrained in the stone that read: **"Knowledge is Power."**

"Knowledge is Power?", she said covering her eyes with her sunglasses. "We'll see about that."

With that said, the young girl made her way to the building along with the rest of the students, ready to start the new year with a clean slate.

\#

I walked through the halls of Summit High, where several students chattered, mainly about their Summer. Everywhere I looked, there were students high fiving, hugging each other, and gossiping happily.

"How was your Summer?"

"Girl, my Summer was wild! We went to a Water Park and…"

…. My Summer was great! I've never had more fun in my life…

…. My Summer was fine but too short!"

Hearing this, I took a bite from my cinnamon bun. By the looks of it, I made it to the cafeteria on time, getting myself something delicious.

The sound of lockers opening and closing was heard as several students made their way through the halls, including nerds, hippies, goths, even the jocks and the cheerleaders. I turned to the left to find a jock pulling a blonde-haired cheerleader in his arms, quickly kissing by the lockers, wrestling with each other as they fought for dominance.

I rolled my eyes, disgusted by the sight of the two "love birds", "It won't last", I said to myself, annoyed any high school romances last?

With my cinnamon bun all gone, I roll it into a ball and throw it in the trash can. Afterward, I make my way to a set of lockers, one of which is mine flipping the combination. It isn't long before the doors of my locker open wide.

Standing before me was a set of textbooks. I reached my hand into it, pulling the books right out of my locker before sliding them into my backpack and zipping it shut.

Then I put my backpack over my shoulder and was seconds from closing the locker when suddenly, I got this tingly feeling in the back of my head. Without a second thought, I brought my hand up to the back of my head and my eyes to the pink locker set a few feet from me. That's when I saw her the light-skinned girl with freckles and beautiful hazel-brown eyes who was retrieving all kinds of schoolbooks from her locker.

My shining star, my angel, Nomi Scott.

I instinctively hid behind my locker, making sure Nomi didn't notice me. Nomi Scott wasn't just any girl. For three years, I've had the biggest crush on her, bigger than any guy in this school. Well, probably not any guy, but I knew for certain that I was that guy. The guy for her.

"Man, are you still stalkin' that girl?"

I turn my head to the light-skinned boy staring back at me. "Amari, what the hell?", I said to him. "You scared the crap out of me."

"Not as much as you're about to scare that girl if you keep staring at her like that."

"I'm not stalking. I'm just watching from a distance."

"So, stalking."

I scoffed, rolling my eyes as Nomi left her locker and went down the hallways. "Aw, man', I said, putting my back to the lockers in disappointment. "She's gone, again."

Amari shrugged. "I don't know why you don't just make a move, man."

"You know why I can't do that."

"Why? It's not like she's dating anyone."

"But what if she is?"

"I don't know why you don't just use your psychic powers on her."

I face him, my eyes giving off a lime-green hue. "My powers don't work like that."

"What do you mean? Can't you read minds?"

"No, I…", I pause, my eyes shifting away from him. "It's more of a feeling I get, like, in the back of my head."

"So, like intuition?"

"Yeah, exactly, intuition. But it depends on the person."

He nodded. "Gotcha."

I sighed, hoisting my backpack on my shoulders. "Any who, I gotta get to class, man. See ya."

"Alright, I'll still see you at lunch today, right?"

"Yeah."

#

A vacuum moved across a fluffy, white carpet. This vacuum belonged to none other than Joana Mitchell herself, who, as happened, was fixing up the living room. The vacuum was very loud, drowning out all the sound in the house. All except a loud knock.

Joana looked up from the vacuum to find a strange silhouette standing before the door. Confused, Joana turned off the vacuum, her eyes still glued to the door. "Who could that be?", she said, putting her vacuum to the side, and walked towards the door.

Joana sat with her eyelashes on her bathroom sink before running out the door.

The knocking grew even more as Joana made her way out of the living room, turning straight past a corner where her door was. Without a second thought, Joana grabbed the doorknob and opened the door wide. "Hello?", she said, her smile warm and welcoming to the bald man standing before her. "Mr. Winslow?", she said widening the door a few inches. "I didn't expect you to be here today."

The bald man didn't smile as he just stood there with a cold, strict face, making Joana very nervous. "I don't have any money on me right now."

"I know you don't. That's not what I'm here for."

"You're not?", she asked. "Then what are you here for?"

"This", he said, holding out a piece of paper. She took it and brought it to her eyes. To her surprise, she found the scariest word written in big, bold red letters: EVICTION.

Joana's eyes grew big and wide. "An eviction notice?", she said looking up to Mr. Winslow. "I don't understand?"

"You should. You haven't paid your rent in two months. Therefore, you're evicted. I expect you to be out in thirty days. Good day, ma'am"

"What?", Joana said as Mr. Winslow walked off. "No! Mr. Winslow! Wait!", she said running out her door and down the hall, where she grabbed Mr. Winslow's hand. "Please, you have to give me more time!"

"I gave you enough, for two months! Your time's up, you're out! Good day, Mrs. Mitchell"

"No, no! Mr. Winslow, please, I can't be kicked out of this apartment now. My son just started school today, it's his first day back! If you kick us out, he won't have a school to go to!"

"You should've thought of that earlier."

"Mr. Winslow, please."

"What's done is done, Mitchell. No ifs, ands, or buts about it. Either pay up or move out!"

With these words, Mr. Winslow walked down the hall, leaving Joanna in utter despair. Before she knew it, her back was against the door to her apartment, her eyes full of worry. "What am I going to tell Dominic?"

#

School dragged on, the teachers spoke nonsense, especially on the first day back, and the clocks all felt like they were going backwards. For most of the day, I was a zombie, a walking corpse dying to leave this god-forsaken place that was Summit High. It wasn't until the school bell rang that the zombie phase finally ended. Not because it was time to go home but because of something even better: lunchtime.

For many students, this was their favorite "class" of the day, as it was for me. After a long day of migraines and headaches from teachers and superintendents, lunch was the only time where I could get away from all of that.

Everywhere you looked, there were students walking left and right, making their way to the line of students. I held my blue lunch tray in my hands, my eyes looking down at the display of chocolate, vanilla, and strawberry milk. I lifted my arm, waving my hands above the three dairy cartons before choosing the chocolate. "Perfect choice"

Always the right choice.

It wasn't long before I found myself standing before the lunch ladies, their giant spoons plopping down a set of mashed potatoes, "meatloaf" or "contraband meat" as many kids at Summit High called it, all with a side of regenerated broccoli.

Yum.

With a quick sigh, I made it out of the lunch line and to the millions of seats that had already been taken. "Ah, come on!", I said, annoyed. There was a fork being waved in the distance. "Dom!", said a voice, causing me to look straight ahead. "Hey, Dom! Over here!", shouted my dread-headed friend Amari Jenkins.

Nodding, I made my way straight to the table. "Hey, Mar. What's up?", I said, holding my fist out.

"Ah, nothing much!?", he fists pump me, grinning. "Just trying to get through these classes. Can you believe what they put me in this year?"

"Where?", I said, picking up my broccoli.

"In home-economics!"

"Home-economics? You?"

"That's what I said, but apparently, they thought I could cook! Do I look like I know how to cook?!"

I shrugged. "Well, that class will teach you how. Work hard enough, and you'll probably come out as a world-class chef!"

Amari scoffs. "Or burn the whole school down."

I laughed. "Do that, and you'll be doing the whole school a favor."

"Yeah, especially the teachers", Amari laughed while I chuckled and broke into a laugh, making me almost choke on my food.

"Look, it's her!", shouted a student, pointing in the distance, along with several other students in the cafeteria. Following this voice, I turned to the left, to find three young girls walking through the cafeteria hall. One was blonde, the other brunette, and in the center, a girl with ginger hair. They were dressed in shiny, lavish clothing but not as lavish as the girl in front, who wore a white fur coat with black polka dots, that went perfectly well with her Michael Kors purse, and white Gucci boots. Not to mention her lavish, silk-pressed ginger hair, sunglasses and magnificently glowing white skin.

Speaking of glowing, she and the girls shone brightly as they walked, blinding all the students with a single stare, especially the two boys who sat at the table, laughing until the three glamourous girls stopped dead in their tracks.

Eyeing them, the girls remove their sunglasses. "Hello, boys", the ginger-haired girl said smirking. "I don't mean to be rude, but I'm afraid you're sitting at my table."

Amari scoffed. "I'm sorry, *your* table?"

"Yes", she said, extending her hands out to the two other girls behind her.

"Says who? Your father?"

"Actually, yes. He made it especially for me."

"Yeah, right. Come back when you're done lying", Amari said, rolling his eyes.

"It's not a lie! My father really made that table for me. My name's written right on it."

"Where?", I asked.

"Under the seat"

Confused, Amari and I dunk our heads under the table where, to our surprise, find a large and glamorous note: **Property of Amanda Griffin**.

"Amanda Griffin?", I say, raising my head up from the table.

"Of course."

Amari shrugged. "So? Is that supposed to make us rise from our seats faster because bossing us around isn't going to work?"

"I don't boss people around!"

"Is that what you tell your minions?", he said, eyeing the two girls next to Amanda.

"Your daddy's little girl, a rich, entitled brat who thinks she can just boss everyone around", Amari chuckled. "I see why you have them, right? Your minions"

"Minions?", she said, shocked. "These are my ride or die girls"

"Then I'm sure they'll be more than happy to go to another seat because Dominic and I aren't going anywhere."

"Look, man, maybe we should leave."

Amari looks my way, my brows raised. "What?"

"We're wasting enough time as it is. Let's just get up and let her have her seat."

"Absolutely not!"

"Dude, come on!"

"Yes, Amari, go!"

My words were suddenly cut off as the bell rang, making me sigh in disappointment. "Great."

Amanda sighed. "You've got to be kidding me."

"Tell me about it", I said.

"You stay out of this!", she snapped.

I paused, my face wide with shock. "Excuse me?"

"You heard me. Thanks to your idiot friend over here."

"Excuse me?"

"I have no choice but to go to class starving! So, thanks a lot!"

"Ok, listen, you bi-"

"Amari!", I said, taking Amari by the shoulder. "It's not worth it."

"It most definitely isn't", Amanda said, putting her sunglasses back over her eyes. "Let's go girls. See ya, boys."

"Good riddance!", Amari said. "You okay, man?"

"I'm fine", I replied. "Come on, let's get to class."

#

The Eviction notice sat on the table with the big, red words staring up the ceiling. Joana stared right at the words; her eyes full of worry.

Thirty days, that's all you get.

Joana let out a heavy sigh and slowly rubbed her eyes before gazing up at a pair of blue jeans, their price tags very visible. She had made a run to the thrift shop, to buy her son his pair of jeans. She smiled at seeing this, happy that her son would have a new set of jeans when she came home. That and the other thing quickly made Joana's smile disappear.

She was scared, scared of what she was going to do and what she was going to tell him but not just what, but also when and how. She needed an elaborate way to tell him so it wouldn't hurt his feelings.

With her head held low, Joana took a sip of her wine before letting out a heavy sigh. Then, the sound of the door opening came through, making Joana raise her head, looking quite curious. "Jo-Jo, I'm home!"

Joana rose from her seat to a curly-haired blonde woman in a pink uniform entering the kitchen. "Hey, Sue."

"Hey!", Sue put her purse on the kitchen table before loosening her bow, causing her curly blonde hair to fall all the way down her shoulders. "How was work?", she said as she took a seat. "It was fine. Although some old guy kept flirting with me."

"That's nice."

Sue raised her brow. "Nice? Me getting flirted on by some old guy. Nice"

"I didn't mean it like that, Sue. I'm just swamped now."

"Swamped?", Sue said, approaching the table, where there was a set of mail with the words written in red. "What is that?"

Joana sighed. "*This* is an eviction notice. Mr. Winslow came by, to give me this paper."

"What do you mean? Didn't you pay the rent?"

"I did, but…", she sighed. "I could only pay half."

"Half? Why would you pay half?"

"Well, you remember last month? You didn't have the money to pay rent, so I did it for you. I just thought I would be able to pay for the whole thing. I guess I wasn't."

"Jo!"

"I'm sorry, Sue. I didn't mean for this to happen."

Sue sat beside Joana; her head hung low. "Does Dominic know?"

"No", she shook her head. "Just you and I."

Sue sighed again. "You need to tell him."

"I know, but how?"

Sue looked around the room before looking at the refrigerator. She sat there for a good minute before a sudden thought came to mind. "I think I have an idea."

#

I stood beside Amari, rubbing his arms as we walked home from school. Gym class was rough, and my body was aching from the many agonizing exercises we were given. And for someone who isn't athletic, it only made things much more difficult than it needed to be.

"Man, my muscles are killing me!", Amari whined, massaging his arms. "I've never been so sore in my life!"

I shrugged. "Well, you can't blame 'em. Coach made us do like fifty push-ups."

"Felt like a hundred. It's our first day back at school, the only thing we should be doing is introducing ourselves. I guess this Coach Bryan guy is different."

"Tough, that's what he was."

Amari nodded. "How long 'till the bus arrives? I don't want to be at school longer than I already am."

"It'll be here soon. Just be patient."

"I don't have any patience."

I made a soft chuckle, eyeing Amari before the two of us were left in silence. That is, until Amari spoke up. "How's your mom?"

"She's fine. Yours?"

"Still sucks."

"Sorry, man."

"It's fine. There are worse mothers."

"If only mine would let us hang out more."

"I know how your mom feels about me. Thinks I'm a-"

"Bad influence", I nodded. "Yeah, I know. But you're not."

"I know. I just wish she could see that."

"She will-Just give her a chance."

"If only I could say the same for my mom."

Speaking of Mom, her car pulled up before me, making me smile. "Well, that's my mom. You okay walking home by yourself?"

"I'll be fine, man. See you at school tomorrow?"

"See ya, man."

"See ya."

I made my way into the car, placing my backpack on the floor. "How was school, honey?"

"It was good, mo-woah!", I said with wide eyes as the woman that sat in the driver's seat wasn't my mom but my aunt or as I call her. "Aunt Sue?"

She smiled at me. "Hey there, buddy boy. How was school?"

It was good. Where's Mom?"

"Oh, your mother had some shopping to do. So, she asked me to pick you up."

"Oh. Is it those pair of jeans I asked her to get me?"

She nodded. "Yes, and something else."

"Something else? Like what?"

"You'll see."

When we returned home, Aunt Sue and I were already out of the car and up the front door.

Without a single thought, I turned my eyes to the house and made my way right through the door. "Mom, I'm home!" I entered the living room and shut the door behind me. "Mom, are you here?"

"I'm in the kitchen, Dominic!"

Hearing this, I walked through the living room, passing through the hallway before turning a corner and entering the kitchen. As soon as I do, my eyes widen in shock. "Woah!"

Sitting on the kitchen table, I find a display of fried chicken, cornbread, and macaroni and cheese, all with a large bowl of mashed potatoes. It was like a dream come true, one I did not want to wake up from it. "Is it too much?", Mom said standing before me in an apron, her smile big and bright. "I thought this would be too much food for you", she laughed. "But it was a lot to go through. So, I guess it doesn't matter. Um, what do you think?"

With my eyes wide and my smile big and bright, I said. "Mom, I think it's great. This is a big surprise!"

"That's not the only surprise."

"What do you mean?"

She pointed to her left. "Look what I got for you in your room", she said happily.

Hearing this, I quickly make my way down the end of the hallway, making Mom and Aunt Sue smile happily. I burst open in my bed, entering the room. To my surprise, there was a pair of blue jeans lying on my bed, their price tags visible.

"My new jeans!", I said, making my way to them, bringing them up to my eyes as I smiled. "That's why she made the dinner!", I hugged my jeans. "She wanted to surprise me with the new jeans! This is the best day of my-", Dominic's words are quickly cut off as he finds a strange piece of paper lying on the bed, where the blue jeans were.

"Huh?", I said, making my way to the bed and lowering the jeans as I approached the paper. "What's this?"

I quickly turned the paper over to find a set of big, red words. As soon as I see it, my eyes are big and wide.

#

Mom was in the kitchen, setting up the table, her smile big and bright as Aunt Sue helped with the plates. The sound of my footsteps filled the kitchen. "Hey, baby. Come and sit down. I want you to tell me everything about your first day back at school and- ", Mom's words were quickly cut off by the look on my face. "Dominic, what's wrong?"

"You tell me", I said holding Eviction notice, making mom's eyes widen in shock. "What was this doing on my bed?"

"Dominic, I can explain."

"Can you? 'Cause by the looks of it, my new jeans weren't the only surprise I was getting. I mean, is this true. Are we getting kicked out?"

Mom stood there, her eyes wide and her voice silent. That's when Aunt Sue stepped in for her. "Um, Dominic. The landlord came by today asking your mother for rent money, money that she…didn't have. So, he gave me this eviction notice", she sighed, her face full of distress as she turned to Joana.

"We made this dinner to tell you", Joana stated. "I thought it would be nice for you to have a good meal so you wouldn't be as angry, and you would understand."

"Understand? Why would a dinner possibly make me understand that we're getting kicked out?! If anything, this ruins the dinner!"

"Dominic!", Aunt Sue snapped. "Don't talk to your mother like that, she's going through enough already."

I paused, taking my eyes away from Aunt Sue and Mom. "Ok, I'm sorry. This just doesn't seem real."

"Well, believe it 'cause it is."

"Look, Dominic. We're just as surprised as you are about this."

"Do you know how many days we have?"

"Thirty", Mom said. "He gave me thirty days."

"Thirty days, that's it?"

"Yes. That's all he could give us, and we're lucky to have that."

I frowned. "Lucky? No, we're not lucky!"

"Dominic, calm down."

"We're getting kicked out in thirty days. That's not something to be lucky about! It's just bullshit!"

"Watch your tone, young man! Don't forget who I am to you!"

"Whatever! I don't care anymore, Mom! I don't care about anything anymore!", I said, making my way out of the kitchen and down the hall.

"Dominic!", Mom called out as I turned the corner. My head was completely turned away from her as She approached. "Dominic, get back here!"

"Don't you at least want to eat something?!"

"Lost my appetite!"

Mom called me several more times, but I couldn't hear her. I was too far down the hall.

Soon, I was at my door, shutting it right behind me.

"Dominic!", Mom made her way up to my door, knocking. "Dominic!"

Mom's voice was drowned out by my pair of headphones, my iPhone resting on my stomach as I listened to the lyrics of "Gangsta's Paradise."

With a sad sigh, Mom took her hand from the door and headed down the hall, her head held low. "You okay, Jo?", Aunt Sue asked.

"Yeah.", Mom nodded.

"This boy, what are we going to do with him?"

Joana shook her head. "I don't know."

"Do you want to eat something?"

"No, I just want to go to bed."

"Okay", Sue nods.

The last dish, a white plate, was rinsed under the faucet and placed up on the dish rack, beside the rest of the dishes, water trickling off. Joana squeezed out her rag, placing it over the faucet. She sighed, looking around the entire kitchen. The whole area was now nice and clean, especially the table, the one where the incident occurred.

This is made Joana eyes lower in sadness, her arms severely crossed as she did.

Within seconds, she poured herself a glass of red wine into a glass cup, the red liquid rising all the way to the top, until the very last drop. Putting the bottle to the side, Joana took the glass cup to her hand before raising it up to her lips, the sweet yet bitter taste of alcohol bringing her serene tranquilness as she sipped.

There was a white piece of paper sitting on the table that upon seeing it. Joana took the glass cup from her two lips and brought it up to her eyes.

It was as clear as day, the words written in blood red, big and wide: EVICTED. It taunted her with annoyance. It was also a reminder of what she had to do, of what she *should've* done but didn't, and now, she was at a dead end.

Now, she was going to lose her house.

Her home.

Her life.

Maybe, just maybe, her son as well.

With her hand now on her forehead, Joana brought the glass of wine up to her lips and drank until the very last drop.

Joana lay in bed, her face flat on her pillow as she slept. Only she wasn't sleeping at all.

Through the soft fabric of her pillow, the sounds of sniffling were heard, growing louder and louder as she did. Sitting next to her was a small photo, consisting of three figures.

Joana lifted her eyes red from the tears that ran down her cheeks. She spotted the photo sitting across from her. With her eyes a bit blurry, she reached for the photo over the bed, taking it in her hands before bringing it up to her eyes, making the three figures even clearer: Joana, holding onto her baby son, Dominic, and a young, black, curly-haired man with luscious hazel brown eyes smiling back at Joana, whose eyes were full of nothing but sadness. "Oh, Otto", Joana said in a sad tone. "If only you were here right now, you'd know what to do."

With nothing more to say, Joana brought the photo to her chest, her arms crisscrossed before falling out on her bed and into a drunken stupor.

Chapter 2:

The Rift

"Amari, Amari!"

"Huh, what?", he said, rising from the sheets of his bed and to the door.
"Amari!"

His head popped right up from bed, before turning his eyes to the door.
"Yeah?"

"For God's sake! How many times do I have to call your damn name! Get
the hell out of bed now, Amari! I won't tell you again!"

"Sure thing Mom", he muttered.

Not long after, he slipped into some sweatpants and a shirt, all with a grey hoodie to hide his dreads. Lastly, he made his bed, putting his pillows wherever he could before heading out of his room, with his blinds closed, leaving it in utter darkness.

That's the way he liked it.

#

Two strawberry pop tarts, both with multi-colored sprinkles, popped right out of the toaster. He smiled proudly at them before bringing his hand to what would be his breakfast. That is, until two hands snatch them from view, causing him to whip his head back in shock. "Hey!"

Standing over him, were two boys, his twin brothers, Tony and Zane, much taller than Amari, laughing right in his face as they each held one strawberry pop-tart in their hands. "Hey, give it back!"

"Sorry, bro. First come, first serve", answered Tony.

He jumped high in the air, his hand stretched out as he tried to grab the pop tart with his brothers raising it higher in the air, making it harder to reach. "Almost got it!", said Zane. "Almost there!"

"Come on, you can do it, Mar Mar!"

"Don't call me that!", shouted before suddenly slipping and falling right on the floor, making Tony and Zane bust out laughing, their hands pointing at him as they did.

With a grunt, he stood up and dust himself off. "You guys' suck!"

"And *you* are way too short for us!", Zane laughed. "I mean, you couldn't even grab the damn pop tart without falling!"

"Without tripping!"

"Good one!", Zane said high-fiving Tony.

"Zane, Tony! Can you please stop harassing your brother for five minutes and look at me! I need your opinion on something", said a voice, a woman in a sparkly red dress, high heels, and long, luxurious hair standing at the doorway with her hands on her hips. "So, what do you think?"

Amari smiled, admiring his mother, *stepmother*. "I think you look goo-"

"I wasn't speaking to you", she said, shooting him a cold, scolded look. "Boys, how do I look?"

"Look hot, Mom!", said Zane.

"Smokin'!", Tony said last, making her smile happily. "Oh, thank you, boys!", she said, approaching them, and giving them kisses on their faces. "It's nice to know I have two loving, supportive sons!", she said while Amari lowered his head, disappointed.

"Alright, get to school, you two. Mama's got a date!", she said as she gave each of the twins a kiss on the cheek goodbye.

Zane and Tony took a bite from their strawberry pop tarts, their smiles visible. "See ya, Mom!"

"Bye, Mom!"

Amari sucked his teeth.

He shifted his eyes to the left, his feet slowly moving. "Um, hey, Mom"

His stepmother, Gwendolyn, turned from, her eyes full of disgust. "What do you want?"

He lowered his eyes to the floor, his hands rubbing against his knuckles before speaking. "I just wanted to ask you for some money for lunch today. I ran out a few days ago. Could you give me more?"

She scoffed, raising her brow. "*More?*"

"Yeah, I mean, I need to eat."

"Eat? By the looks of it, you eat too much", She looked him up and down. "Well, not too much, considering how short you are."

Amari grunted a bit, his hands clenched. "Could you not bring that up?"

"I most definitely will. It's the truth, just like how I'm not giving you any money for lunch."

"But you gave Tony and Zane money?"

"I only give money to good boys, you know, ones that actually came from me."

His eyes widened in shock before falling to the floor in shame. "Now, get your ass on that bus, boy. Derek is coming over, and I won't have it ruined by the likes of you."

"Okay, Mom", Amari said turning away from her.

"Don't call me that."

With his eyes to the floor, he put his hoodie over his head and walked out of the kitchen, leaving the house.

\#

He walked outside, his eyes completely puzzled as he made his way down the driveway all the way up to the front lawn. Suddenly, he stopped, as he realized something. His stepbrothers weren't outside next to me. He turned to the left to see Tony and Zane already on the bus down the road, munching on their strawberry pop tarts as they laughed. "Looks like someone's walking to school!"

"Walkies!"

"Shit!", he said sprinting up to the yellow bus that made its way further down the road. "Wait! Stop!"

But the bus just kept going, down, down, down the road, without warning.

The wheels on the bus screeched, stopping dead a few feet from Amari's grasp. "Oh!", he gasped, getting back on my feet, racing towards the bus, stopping dead in front of the door that split in two as soon as he did. "Thank you so much for stopping!"

"No problem, young man", the bus driver said with a warm, loving smile.

He give her a quick grin before walking to the back of the bus, where his brothers already were. "You got lucky this time", said Tony, making Zane nod. "Yeah, but you still have us to deal with."

"I'm not afraid of you guys."

"Or so you think", they both said.

The bus driver looked in the mirror, eyeing the two young men in the mirror who were mocking the young man. Irritated, the bus driver grabbed her microphone and raised it to her lips. "We will now be leaving for

Summit High. I advise *all* students to keep their hands and arms to themselves."

Hearing this, Tony and Zane left Amari, making him smile happily. Amari turned to the bus driver. *"Thank you"*, he mouthed.

She winked at him, making him smile. Without a second thought, the bus driver put her microphone back on the handle and pressed the gas, sending the bus all the way down the road.

\#

The door to my bedroom was closed shut, and a "DO NOT DISTURB: THAT MEANS YOU, MOM" sign in red was taped to the wooden surface. By the looks of it, I was still mad at her from last night, and if she had ever thought of communicating with me, she'd see this sign and know.

But I still had school, which meant I'd still have to face her.

But not today!

I opened the door and peeked, looking left and right, there was not a woman in sight.

Perfect.

Without a second thought, I busted out my bedroom door, my feet moving as fast as light as I turned a corner. Before I knew it, I was in the kitchen, my eyes big and wide. However, before I could make my way out, a voice called me. "Dominic?"

I whipped my head to find Mom standing behind me in her pink server's outfit and white apron. "I was wondering when you would leave your room. I was worried you wouldn't leave, especially with that sign you left on your door."

My eyes shifted to the left, feeling a sense of shame before speaking. "I was just going to catch the bus."

"That's what I wanted to talk to you about. Instead of taking the bus to school, what if you ride in the car with me?"

"Ride to school with you?"

Mom nodded. "Yes, would you, please. Just for today?"

Hearing this, I clenched my fists before speaking. "I guess I can. Sure"

Mom smiled. "Great!", I let out a heavy sigh as Mom let out her keys, jingling them in her hands. "Alright, let's go!"

A blue Ford van stood outside our garage. It was large and shiny, but as amazing as it looked on the outside, the real trouble was happening on the inside. Mom twisted the key in the van repeatedly. "Come on, come on! This always happens!", she said in frustration.

I watched as my mother struggled with getting the car to start in anger. "These damned keys!"

Not the keys, the engine. It's been messed up for a while now and my mother couldn't fix it because she didn't have the money to pay for it. I could fix it either as I didn't even have a job.

Sighing, I turned to my mother, my mouth seconds from convincing her that I could just walk to school until: *"Rumm!!!"*

The car engine started running, bringing my mother happiness. "Oh, thank God!", she said, praising the one above. "I was worried. I thought this was its last day. Never mind that, let's be on our way"

With her foot on the gas, the car exited the garage, going all the way down the white pavement hill before making its way down the road.

I stared out the window, my eyes watching several other houses go by. There were neighbors making out the trash and others just sitting out on the porch with cigars in their mouths, enjoying their morning. It was nice people watching as it meant I didn't have to see Mom.

My mother, on the other hand, had her eyes on me and my new pair of blue jeans. "I see you're wearing the new jeans I bought you. They look good on you."

"Thanks", I muttered, my eyes glued to the open road.

Expecting to hear more, Mom just sighed and turned to face the open road. "I know you're still angry from last night"

"Of course, I'm still angry. What did you think that I wasn't?"

Mom sighed. "Look, baby, I know things are scary right now, but I assure you I have everything under control."

I scoffed. "Control? Will that be before or after we're out on the streets?"

She sighed again. "I'm just saying you shouldn't worry so much about this. The bills will get taken care of."

"By the looks of it, you're not doing such a good job. I mean if you couldn't pay the bills before, what makes you think you can do it now! Believe me, if I could, I'd do a better job at keeping up with the bills. Much better than you ever could!"

Mom grunted, hitting the brakes as the blue Ford van stopped, in the middle of a red light. As soon as it did Mom whipped her head back over to me. "I'm not going to sit here and let you talk to me this way!"

"I have an ample right to talk to you this way! We only have thirty, twenty-nine more days before the rent of yours is due, and you're sitting here complimenting my jeans like everything's just A-okay, like you're not scared at all!"

"You think I'm not scared? You think I'm not worried about the idea that you and I could be living on the streets next month because I am! You're not the only one who hates being in this situation!"

"Well, maybe if you'd been more responsible, we wouldn't be in this mess!"

Mom grunted her eyes full of fire as she turned to me. "And maybe if you hadn't been born, I wouldn't have to worry about having another mouth to feed!"

My eyes widened in shock, hearing this, followed by the sound of my heart breaking as well. "Dominic, I-I didn't mean it like that. I-DOMINIC!", Mom shouted as I popped the front seat lock and jumped right out of the car door. "DOMINIC!", Mom took off her seat belt, hopping right out of the car.

I was a few feet into the street as I ran past several cars that stopped and beeped at me. The horns startled me, making my eyes turn bright green. All the cars were surrounding me, blocking any chance of exit. Scared out of my mind, I cuffed my ears and fell straight to my knees. For a moment, the world was quiet.

"Dominic Arsenio Mitchell!"

"Oh no" I said, raising my head, my eyes wide open to see my mother standing over me, her eyes fueled with fire. "What the hell were you thinking?! Running out in the road like that!"

"I'm sorry, Mom. I was just-"

"I don't want to hear it!", she shouted, taking my hand. "We're going back to the car now!"

"No!", I shout jerking my hand away.

"Dominic!", she protested. "Get back in that damn car!"

My hands made a fist, and my eyes turned bright green again. With all my rage boiling inside me, I looked to my mother and said the question that would give her a certain perspective on my life. "Why don't you talk about him?"

Mom paused, confused. "Who?"

"My father. Why don't you talk about him?"

Mom looked around the road before glancing back at me. "I don't want to talk about this right now?"

"No, I want to talk about this now. What kind of powers did he have? Was he just like me?"

"I'm not having this conversation with you!"

"Just tell me! Yes or no?"

"Yes!", she snapped. "Is this why you're acting out?"

I lowered my head, my eyes lazily looking at her. "It's just you never talk about him."

"What is there to say? Your father was just like you! End of story! Now, get your ass in the car! Now!"

With nothing else to say, I walked my way back to the car, leaving my mother frustrated.

#

I sat in my first period worried, my mind completely gone as I stared out at the large window in our class, revealing the set of school buses backing up in the driveway.

A large window stood next to me, revealing the outside where the school buses were found. I stared out at these school buses, my hand on my chin as I did. My English instructor, Mr. Wilton, was giving the class a lecture.

Another day, another dollar.

That's what those say when they have a job, when their lives are hanging by a thread, and when their lives are just peaches and cream. As for mine, it was another day, another migraine!

A big ass one at that!

"Mr. Mitchell? Mr. Mitchell!", said Mr. Wilton.

"What?", I shouted.

A group of students burst out laughing as I gazed up at my teacher, Mr. Wilton, who stood over me, his arms crossed as he scolded me. "Something on your mind, Mr. Mitchell?"

"No", I said, looking straight at him. "Was there something I missed?"

"As a matter of fact, there was. If you weren't stuck in your little fantasy world, you would know that we're now on the fourth chapter of Beowulf."

"Beowulf?"

"The Epic Poem?", I shook my head, making Mr. Wilton sigh. "The great warrior, defender of Hrothgar? The man who became a legend. Does any of that ring a bell to you?"

I looked down to the floor, a small smile forming across my lips. "Actually, it does", I said, raising my head. "Yeah, I remember now. It's the one about that guy who killed that monster, what was his name? Gernall? Girdal?"

"Grendal?"

I snapped my fingers. "Grendal, yes! Yes, the one who conquered Herot?"

"Conquered? Grendal didn't conquer Herot, he was killed by Beowulf. Well, until his mother came and-" Mr. Wilton gasped, covering his mouth. "Shoot, I just spoiled the next chapter!"

Hearing this, a couple of students turned to one another, whispering certain words like "The next chapter?" and "Chapter five?" before turning the pages in their books, making Mr. Wilton whip his head around. "STOP THAT!", he shouted, making the entire class stand still.

"It's fine, Mr. Wilton", I said. "They were going to find out eventually. Just like how Beowulf isn't really a hero."

Mr. Wilton cocked an eyebrow. "What?"

"Think about it. If Beowulf was such a hero, then why didn't he give any of his riches to the citizens? I mean, a giant monster attacks Herot, leaving the city in ruins, but as soon as he's defeated, Beowulf just leaves the citizens out in the dirt. Meanwhile, he gets thrown this huge party in the castle, *the castle*, giving him all kinds of food like smoked turkey, ham, and pig! He literally ate like a King while the rest of the citizens likely starved to death! That's not a hero, that's a selfish coward and it would've been best if he got eaten by Grendal, not the starving citizens who will spend the rest of their days on the streets!"

Mr. Wilton and every other student in the class went silent.

"I don't know what book you were reading, but it's not Beowulf. Please, go to the library and get the right book."

"What? Wh-"

"Now, Mitchell!"

With a quick grunt, I grabbed my backpack and left Mr. Wilton's literature class, seconds before the bell rang.

#

Horror.

Fiction.

Science-Fiction.

Fantasy.

Non-fiction.

These were all the genres of books I went through as I walked through the aisles of the library. Our library was very big, nothing but towers of books rising above your head. Every corner you turned, a new row of books could be found. This would be a dream come true for bookworms, but for me, it was like going through a maze, one that, if I was all alone, wouldn't be able to escape. Luckily, I wasn't, as there were several other students who were "trapped" as well. Or, in this case, in need of a book. Many of the kids I found were standing in the aisles, their backs, lazily against the walls reading, others scanning through rows like me, and those who, instead of reading, were making out in the farthest part of the library, the quietest part.

I usually roll my eyes at people like that, knowing deep in my heart that it won't last. I mean, do any high school couples do? Turning a corner, I found another aisle of books, but they weren't just any 'ole books. Looking above the library, I found a sign with a specific genre was found.

Poetry.

"There it is", I said happily before making my way down the aisle, my eyes scanning through each book:

Macbeth, Hamlet, Romeo and Juliet…

The list went on for miles! It wasn't until I passed Homer's *The Odessey* that I saw it. "Beowulf", I say before grabbing the cover. "Finally"

However, as soon as I pulled it off the shelf, a set of dust and cobwebs presented itself with nothing but the book title visible. "Uh, eww", I said, blowing the dust off the book, along with the cobwebs I snatched and pricked from my fingers. "So much dust."

With the book now clean, I held it across my chest and walked through the book aisle, but as soon as I turned a corner: "Oof!", I smacked right dab, into a girl with shades on, one I was very familiar with. "Watch where you're go=", said the ginger-head girl, her facial expression dimming. "Oh, it's *you*", she says in disgust.

I looked at the girl, my eyes full of shock, before speaking. "Hey, I know you. You're that girl from the cafeteria? The one from yesterday, right?"

The girl folded her arms and nodded. "Yes, and your friends with that troublemaker, I presume?"

My eyes lowered in anger. "Amari's not a troublemaker."

"That's not what I saw from his rude behavior at lunch yesterday. I mean, what idiot refuses to give up his seat?"

I scoffed, rolling my eyes. "He's not an idiot. Don't talk about my friend like that."

"I can talk about him any way I want. Speaking of which, where is he?"

I shrugged. "I don't know. Where are your "Ride or Die" girls of yours? Aren't they around?"

"Actually, they are"

Saying this, Amanda looked over her shoulders, her finger extended out to a pair of girls gathering books from the History section. "They're getting books for me, for my history homework."

"You have homework?"

"Yes"

"But it's the second day of school? Don't we get homework until like, next week?"

Amanda shook her head. "Not my history teacher. He likes to start the moment we walk through the doors."

I scoffed. "I'm guessing you get tests the day before", I laughed, making Amanda shoot me an annoyed look. "Don't get sensitive. I was just joking."

"I don't like your jokes."

"Well, I don't like how you talk about my friend. Guess that makes us even."

Amanda scoffed. "Touché"

Lost in thought, I looked down at my book, remembering my task. "Oh, yeah", I said, putting my book up to my chest. "I must get my book checked out. Have fun with history", I said, making my way past Amanda.

The two girls made their way towards Amanda, smiling. "We have your textbooks, Ms. Griffin."

"All for your history class."

"Is there anything else you need?"

"No", she said with a smile. "Not a thing", Amanda watched me leave the librarian at the desk before making my way through the doors and out of the library.

\#

"I can't believe this!", Joana said as she rode down a road, her eyes full of rage. "I take my son to his first day of school, getting him there on time but when I need to be somewhere, two cars want to clash into one another, leaving me in traffic and late to work! Great, just great!"

With an angry grunt, Joana turned her steering wheel to the left before entering the parking lot, the one that led to a restaurant, a diner with a big, red sign that read: MARTEY'S CAFETERIA.

On good days, Joana would be very happy to see this place, but this was not a good day. With her face balling up, Joana pulled her car into the parking lot, shutting the engine off.

On the inside of the diner, everything was loud. Everywhere was filled with people sitting in chairs while men, women, and children of all types waited patiently for a table. The tables were full of many of which were parties, making those who waited feel very irritated. But not as irritating as those in the kitchen. In the kitchen, were cooks, bussers, dishwashers, and waitresses. Cooks shouting orders, bussers wiping and sweeping, dishwashers washing, and waitresses serving. Yes, sire, all the employees were doing their part to represent the brand Martey's Cafeteria.

As for Sue Anne, she stood out in the back, her arms folded as she looked at the door before her and down at her wristwatch. "Where the hell were you, Jo?"

On the outside of the kitchen, several people still waited impatiently. Luckily, for Joana, she didn't have to worry about that, for she was a waitress, not a customer. Sue Anne was speaking to her co-worker and best friend. Sue Anne was waiting for her to respond. By the look of her face, her patience was running thin.

Joana happily made her way through the door and into the kitchen.

"It's about time. Do you have any idea what time it is?", Sue said.

"I'm sorry, Sue", Joana said, walking through the dining hall with Sue Anne following behind. "Sorry, doesn't cut it. This isn't the last time I've stuck up for you, Joana, and I'm running out of good excuses. Speaking of which, I hope you have an even better one to prove why you were late. So, whatever it is, spill it out now!"

Joana slammed her purse down on the counter, making Sue's eyes widen in shock. "My car broke down in the middle of the road. I had to walk the whole way here. You happy?"

Sue raised her brow, her arms crossed. "I just saw your car pulled up outside."

She sighed. "On our way to school, Dominic and I had a fight."

"A fight? About what?"

"I don't know. At first, he was mad about the eviction notice, but then…he asked me something."

"Asked you about what?"

Joana glanced back at a few men before bringing her friend close. "His father."

Sue pulled away from Joana, her eyes big and wide. "Really?"

"Yeah, just out of nowhere."

"But why?"

"I don't know. He was probably just curious."

"Or maybe it's something else."

Joana gave Sue a look. "No, Sue, that's not it."

"But what if it is?"

"You don't know that."

"Well, Dominic could. I mean, it's not like you talk about him a lot. You may have been able to get away with it when he was younger, but not now. Not anymore."

Joana shrugged. "So, what do you want me to do?"

"Tell him about his father. Just tell him enough so he'll know."

"Okay", Joana nodded.

"Okay", Sue said, tying her apron around her waist. "Come on, let's serve these brats!"

Sue Anne made her way out of the kitchen, her friend following behind her.

#

The hours ticked away, bringing in a whole new swarm of people. It was afternoon, and everyone in the kitchen was, as before, very busy. Everywhere one looked, there were customers in their seats, being served friendly meals with friendly faces. As for Joana Mitchell, she wore a knot with such a friendly face.

She was irritated not by her job but by the people, the customers. Well, one of them, that is. "Here you go, three sirloin steaks with the works, a Caesar salad", she said, placing the lunch onto the table, where three middle-aged men sat, their eyes all looking up at her. "Thanks, cutie"

Joana stopped before placing a small cup of Caesar dressing. "Here's your dressing, sir. Enjoy", Joana said before turning her head, but as soon as she does, one of the boys looked down at her rear end and said: "I'd sure like to cut that cake!"

Joana stopped dead and center. "What did you say?!", she shouted while the young boy and his friends laughed.

Irritated, Joana shoots a bird at them before storming away. "You think this is funny! Just wait until I come over there and-"

"Joana!"

I was her co-worker and friend, Sue, looking at her. "What are you doing?"

"Dealing with these damn teenagers!"

Sue looked over her friend's shoulder, where the three men were still laughing. Sue sighed. "Okay, first you came to work late, and now you're shouting at the customers! Whatever's bothering you, you need to spill it now!"

Joana lets out a deep sigh. "Sue, I-"

Sue nodded at Joana. "Yes?"

Letting out another sigh, Joana looked at Sue Anne. "It's the eviction"

"How?", she asked. "I decided to work for the money."

"Work for it? Here?"

"That's the thing: I decided to ask the boss for a raise."

"A raise? Joanna. Mr. Wilson doesn't give his employers a raise. What makes you think he would give one to you?"

"I must try, Sue. I got a kid to feed."

Sue sighed. "I know."

"I gotta do what I gotta do, even if it means, doing things I don't want to do."

Sue nodded. "I understand. I'll deal with the customers; you deal with Mr. Simpson."

Joana smiled. "Thanks, Sue"

"No problem. Now go"

With these words, Joana turned her head and made her way down the hallway, passing all her fellow workers.

\#

I had a pepperoni pizza sitting on my tray. I sighed. Soon, a young boy with dreads came running toward me in the distance.

"Dom! Hey, Dom!", said a voice, making me raise my head from my slice of cheese pizza to the young boy with dreads approaching my table. "Amari?", I said as he sat across from me. "You're here?"

Amari scoffed. "Uh, yeah. Why wouldn't I be?"

"Okay, this is crazy. Dude, you were gone for most of the day until now. I swear you're literally like a ghost, man."

"A ghost?", Amari laughed. "That's something you don't hear every day from your best friend?"

"Where were you?"

"Chill, Dom. I was in my classes. I mean, it is school."

"But I didn't see you at the lockers after them, and you're always at the lockers."

Amari bit into his pizza before speaking. "I got held up."

"Where?"

"With schoolwork."

"Oh", I sighed, taking a bite of my pepperoni. "Ok"

"You okay, Dom?"

I sighed, shaking my head. "No"

"What is it?"

"I don't think you want to hear this."

"If it's important, then you probably should say something."

I looked up from my tray, my eyes full of regret. "Are you sure?"

He nodded. "I'm sure"

"Okay. Hear me out.

"I'm all ears."

So, for about two minutes, I tell Amari about everything that had been happening with me and the eviction.

"No way! You've got to be joking!", Amari exclaimed across the lunch table, his eyes big and wide as he spoke. "You have to be lying, man!"

I shook my head. "I'm not. Everything I'm saying is one hundred percent true."

Amari sat back in his seat, his hand on his forehead. "I can't believe this."

"Don't be upset, man."

"I'm not sad, I'm pissed, really, really pissed!"

"So am I! I could get thrown out on the streets, the streets, Mar!"

Amari sighed. "This is crazy! They can't just kick you out of your own house!"

"Tell that to the landlord. If Mom doesn't pay off this eviction in the next twenty-nine days, we will!"

"That's how long you have?"

"It was yesterday, but now it's down to twenty-nine."

"How's ya Mom's goin' to earn money in twenty-nine days?!"

"I don't know!", I buried my face into my hands. "I don't know how we're going to get through this. I'm scared, man."

"So am I. Who's going to go to prom with me? Who's going to sit by me at graduation? Who Dom?"

"Until Mom can come up with the money, you'll have to find someone else. You'll have to find a new best friend."

"Screw that! That is not happening!"

"By the looks of it, it is."

"No, this is your year, man. I can't go through it alone."

"And I don't want you to. I want us to graduate with each other. I want us to be happy in our last year of high school. I guess that won't be happening now."

Amari frowned, shaking his head. "No, it will happen. You and I will graduate together."

I scoffed. "And just how do you know that?"

"Because I'm going to help you. I'm going to help you get the money you need."

"How?"

"I don't know, but I'll think of something."

I lowered my eyes in sadness. "That's what Mom said."

Amari brought his hand up to my shoulder. "Look, I know things aren't good right now, but I promise you they will with a little help. Besides, it's the least I can do for all the things you've done for me."

"I guess it wouldn't hurt to have some help."

Amari nods. "All help is good help, Dom."

\#

The bell rang, sending a sea of students to head to class, along with Amari. He made his way through the hallway, before turning to his left and entering his World Literature class, where they were. The students sat in their seats, laughing and throwing paper balls at one another.

Typical high school students.

With a quick sigh, Amari sat in his seat, his bookbag placed beside him. He looked down at his desk, his mind racing as he thought about Dominic. In a few weeks, his best friend could be kicked out of his house. He'd considered having him and his mother move in with him and his family, but we all know how that would work out.

That wasn't a good idea.

Amari sighed. He wished there was something he could do to help. He just didn't know how. Dominic was his best friend the last thing he wanted was to see him end up on the street. He needed help, he needed a sign, he needed-

"Good morning, students", said a young woman entering the classroom.

Amari raised his head to find a young, black woman in a yellow sundress walking toward her desk, her purse placed atop the wooden surface. "My name is Ms. Wilkins. Welcome to your first day of World Literature class."

Amari looked the young black woman standing before her, analyzing her face, which looked strangely familiar. "Now, before we begin, why don't we start getting to know each other. "I'll choose first", Ms. Wilkins raised her hand, her eyes searching for a certain student. That's when she found the young boy sitting in the center of the classroom. "You", she said, pointing.

Amari looked around the room before facing his teacher. "Me?"

She nodded. "Yes, you. What's your name?"

Amari shifted in his seat. "Um, Amari. Amari Jenkins."

She grinned. "Amari. That's a charming name."

"Thank you", he smiled. "My mom picked it out for me."

"Did she? Well, she had good taste."

Amari made a soft chuckle before answering. "She did."

Soon, the bell rang, and the students made their way out of the class, all except Amari. For he was busy packing his things into his backpack. "Remember to read chapters 1-4 tonight for homework, Amari."

"I will, Ms. Wilkins", he nodded, putting his bookbag over his shoulders. "See you, Wednesday."

Amari left his desk and walked straight towards the door, but before he could take a step out, Ms. Wilkins stopped him. "I noticed how those boys were treating you, back on the bus. They were disrespectful."

Amari turned his head back and his attention to Ms. Wilkins. "How do you know about that?"

She grinned. "I know a lot more than you think, A.J.', she winked at him.

"A.J.?", Amari's eyes widened in shock, looking at the young woman's face. "I haven't been called that in years. Wait a minute", he gasped. "Ms. Wilkins, that's right? My fifth-grade English teacher!"

She smiled. "I knew you'd remember."

"Oh my gosh!", Amari ran up to her, his eyes wide with joy as he wrapped his arms around her waist. "I can't believe it. It's been so long."

"Eight years, but who's counting", she laughed. "I'm so glad to see you again, Amari."

"Me too. So, when did you become a bus driver?"

"A good year ago. I needed extra money to pay off my car insurance. So, here I am. Teaching and driving students to school."

"Whatever pays the bills, I guess."

"Yes."

Amari and Ms. Wilkins remained in silence before Amari shrugged his shoulders and spoke. "Well, I should get to my next period. See you, later."

"Hold on, Amari."

Amari whipped his eyes back, facing his teacher. "Yes?"

"If those boys ever mess with you again, don't be afraid to talk to someone."

"I can take care of myself, Ms. Wilkins. I'm not a child."

"I know. I just don't like to see children being abused, especially by people like those boys."

"Those boys are my brothers, actually."

"Oh, really?"

"Yeah", he rubbed the back of his neck, feeling quite nervous. "Look, I really gotta go, Ms. Wilkins. Bye."

"Amari, wait!"

"Yes?"

He stopped to see Ms. Wilkins's scribbling on a piece of paper. As soon as she was done, she handed the paper to him. "Here, take this."

Amari took the card, peering down at the numbers written on the paper. "Ms. Wilkins, is this-"

"My phone number. I thought it would be nice for us to, you know, catch up. If there's anything you need. Give me a call."

"Thank you, Ms. Wilkins."

"You're welcome. Get onto class now."

"I will. Bye."

Ms. Wilkins watched her student leave the classroom, all alone with her thoughts. "Goodbye, A.J."

\#

Joana stood in front of a brown door; her eyes filled with fear as she saw a small sign above that read: Mr. Simpson. Or should she say, Martey Simpson.

Seeing this, Joana's hand began to tremble, the cold fear running through her veins, muscles, and every bone in her body. She was scared, scared of the reaction she would get if she told him what she needed. She feared the consequences that would come with it. But she knew the consequences she would face if she didn't get the money in time. At that moment, it didn't matter what the boss would say to her what mattered was that she got the money.

She had to do what she had to do.

With that, Joana took a deep breath and knocked on the door with nothing but confidence. "Um, Mr. Simpson?"

"Come in", said a voice.

Without a second thought, Joana grabbed the doorknob and opened the door wide, having her head poke out. In a room was a bald, white man with a lit cigar in his mouth, counting a set of crisp, dollar bills. "Twenty, Thirty, Forty…", he counted as each ten-dollar bill displaced from his fingers. "Sixty, seventy, eight", Joana watched nervously as Mr. Simpson continued, clearing her throat. "Um, Mr. Simpson?"

Mr. Simpson looked up from his money and at Joana. "Oh, it's you."

"What Cha waitin' for? Go on, sit down."

Joana nodded "Actually, there is", she said making her way to Simpson's desk.

"Well, don't keep me waiting. Go on."

Joana took a deep breath before speaking. "Well, you know that my paycheck doesn't come in 'till next week, right?"

"Yes", Mr. Simpson said, to look at her. "Why do you ask?"

Joana rubbed her fingers together. "Well, I was wondering if you could pay me in advance?"

Mr. Simpson's smile quickly melted, his expression falling flat. "What? You want me to give you a raise?"

Y-yes, just this once. Is that okay?"

Hearing this, Mr. Simpson took the cigar from his mouth before blowing a set of smoke from his mouth. "No, not. Do you have any idea how many employees I have I can't just stop and give you a raise. I mean, doesn't your kind get enough money from us?", he scoffed. "Just this once."

Joana lowered her eyes. "I…I just thought that since you give everyone else here a raise, you could give me one, too."

"Yeah, everyone who's not you. Now get the hell out of my office."

Hearing this, Joana speaks. "Mr. Simpson, pleas-"

"Now!"

Joana lowered her head. "Yes, sir."

With that, Joana rose from her seat and made her way towards the door, but before he could grab the doorknob, Mr. Simpson muttered a bad word: "Damn, negro."

Joana's eyes shot wide open when she heard this, but instead of reacting, she twisted the doorknob and walked out, leaving Mr. Simpson with a laugh and his money, which he continued to count.

#

The school bell rang all through the halls of Summit High, causing a whole sea of students to flood out of the classrooms and onto the buses. I was the first to get on, my backpack propped up my shoulders as I walked up behind the students who were entering the bus.

But before I could enter, my name was called. "Dom, wait up!"

Hearing this, my head turned back to find my friend, Amari, running up to me with a big, happy smile. "Amari?", I said as he approached. "Hey, man", he said, out of breath.

"What are you doing here?"

"What do you mean? I'm riding with you."

"You are?"

"Yeah, did you think you were riding home alone?"

"But isn't your house like a few blocks from here?"

"Dom, it's a bus. I'll just tell the bus driver to bring me home. Besides, with the situation you're in right now, you need a friend."

Hearing this, a happy smile forms across my lips. "Thanks, man. This eviction notice has been hard on me."

"I'm glad you told me. I couldn't imagine being in that situation. No matter what happens, I want you to know, I'll be there for you every step of the way."

I smile happily. "I'm lucky to have a friend like you, Amari. I couldn't ask for anyone better to keep my secrets."

"Yeah...", Amari's face quickly fell flat as he thought of another friend before nodding, "Same here, man."

"Oye!", said a voice, making Amari and I turn our heads, where the bus driver angrily presented himself. "Are you ladies getting on or what?"

With these words, Amari and I entered the bus, the door closing behind us.

#

The sunset over St. Mora, bringing in the cool breath of the evening. A few buildings away was the restaurant, Martey's, were standing outside a white woman with long, blonde hair and a cigarette in her mouth.

Standing behind her were two glass doors, both reflecting nothing, but the dining room. That is, until a woman in a pink skirt and apron burst out of the doors, her eyes full of fear as she did. "Come on, Sue!", she said, making the blonde woman take her cigarette out of her mouth. "Let's go!", Joana said, passing by her.

Sue watched in confusion as her friend made her way to the car, her head constantly turning back to the restaurant. "Sue!", Joana shouted making Sue whip her head back. "What Cha, waitin' around for? Come on!"

Sue flicked her cigarette away and made her way towards her white truck, taking her keys out of her pockets and pressing a button, which made the lights flick with a quick "beep-beep" noise.

The two ladies made their way into the truck, with Joana slamming the door shut before putting her seat belt on. "Joana, are you okay?"

Joana didn't listen, her eyes were glued to the glass window, where Martey, a.k.a. Mr. Simpson, stood. "Joana!"

"Hm, what?", she said, whipping her head back. "What did you say, Sue?"

Sue blinked, her eyes full of confusion. "I asked if you were, okay? You seem shaken up?"

"Wha…", Joana brought her hand up to her face. "No, I'm just tired, is all."

Sue cocked an eyebrow. "Are you sure? You were turning your head to the restaurant real suspicious like"

"I was just seeing if there were no other customers left in the dining room. It's just been a rough day. I just need some rest, that's all. Don't worry."

Sue gave her friend a confused look before slowly nodding her head. "Okay, then I guess we should go", she said, twisting her keys and starting the engine. "Let's go home."

Joana nodded. "Yes, let's go."

With these words, the truck went out of the restaurant's parking lot and down the road, disappearing in the distance.

#

Amari bobbed his head to the music as he listened, his eyes looking left and right, finding nothing but the shadows of trees and cell lines. As for cell lines, they were just like trees. He remembered the first time he'd climbed a tree. His brother got his kite stuck up in it and had asked him to get it.

Being the generous sibling, Amari climbed the tree, his hand reaching hard before grabbing the kite and dropping it straight down to his brother. It wasn't long until he dropped, too, straight on the ground, arm first. Before he knew it, he was rushed to the hospital, where his arm was put back in place.

Which, in fact, was dumb as it could've easily been put back in place by his father, who slapped him right across the face, his eyes full of rage at the medical bill that he had no choice but to pay for.

It was unfair but not as unfair as him leaving his mother for another woman and putting all the blame on him. It wasn't long before she would buy all kinds of wine bottles, drinking herself into a stupor. While she was there, Amari's brothers, Tony and Zane, were there to torment him with all kinds of torture. Every time he walked out of the house, he would get punched. Or when he was eating dinner, his brothers would come and take it away from him. For they, which his brothers believed, he did not deserve.

Then again, there was hardly any food in the fridge anyway. By the looks of it, his life was a complete nightmare.

With this thought in mind, Amari found a light, a bright one. Bright enough to make him stop front and center in front of a house, his house. Seeing this, he let out a sigh. "Home Sweet Home", he said.

He didn't mean that in a good way.

He removed his earphones, his music still jamming through, before making his way up, the steps, to the door, and inside the house. His pride was small, but his courage high.

"Hey, I'm home!", he said, entering the house. "Anybody home?", he shut the door straight behind him before a lone, figure exited from the house and into the living room. "Just us"

To his surprise, he found his brothers, standing next to the TV, their arms folded as he did. "Welcome home, little bro", answered Tony.

"Where's Mom?", Amari asked.

"Out with her boyfriend", Zane said.

"Boyfriend?"

"Yeah, Johnathan. You know, the bodybuilder?"

"I don't remember anything about Mom dating a bodybuilder?"

"Well, maybe if you were home more often, you'd know."

"Well, I'm home now. So, you don't have to keep any more secrets from me", Amari made to walk past his brothers but was held back by Tony. "Hey, where do you think you're going?"

"To bed? Where else?"

"No, you're not. Not until you play our favorite game."

"Yeah, hot potato!", Tony grabbed hold of Amari's backpack. Hey!", he shouted as Tony lifted his backpack in the air. "Catch, Amari!", he said as he threw Amari's backpack straight to Zane, laughing playfully as they did.

"Stop!", he said, trying his best to reach for his backpack. "I said stop!"

"If you want it, you have to catch it!"

Fed up, he charged straight toward Tony, trying his best to push him, but he quickly failed once Zane grabbed hold of the back of his shirt and threw him to the floor, his brothers laughing at him. "You're so pathetic!"

"You nothing but a weakling!", Tony said before throwing the backpack onto his brother's body, causing him to laugh hysterically. "What are you doing on the floor? Get up!"

Amari rose from the floor, took his backpack, and went down the hallway, his brothers still laughing as he did.

Before long, he busted through his bedroom, his backpack flying in the air before falling into a corner. Enraged, he hopped right into bed before putting his head on his pillow and shouting right into it. "Mmmmm!!!", he cried. "Mmmmmmmm!!!!!"

He continued to do this, eventually taking his face from his pillow and letting out a deep sigh. "I hate those guys! I swear, once graduation hits, I'm out of here!"

Saying this, his eyes turned to the left, where his dresser stood. Atop it stood a framed photo of two young boys, their eyes big and bright as they held each other.

Amari reached for the dresser and picked up the framed photo. He smiled at it, his fist rustling in his hair as he laughed. On the photo was: "Brotha's for Life."

Seeing this, his once happy smile lowered into a sad frown as a memory came flooding back to the surface.

If there's anything you need, anything at all. Give me a call.

"Aw, Dom", he said in a sad tone. "What am I going to do when you're on the streets?", he let out a sad sigh. "If only there was some way, I could help you and your mom. That way, we could go to graduation together."

Saying this, his eyes widened. "Hol' up."

He looked in his pockets, pulling out a white card, one with a phone number written on it. "Ms. Wilkins."

With his iPhone in his hand, Amari dialed a few numbers before bringing the phone to his ear. The phone rang for a few minutes until suddenly, a voice came through. "Hello?"

"Ms. Wilkins?"

A small gasp went through the phone. "A.J., is that you?"

"Yeah, it's me. How are you?"

"I'm doing well. What about you?"

"I'm…alright", he said in a weird tone, one that Ms. Wilkins quickly noticed. "Is something wrong?"

He rubbed the back of his neck, sighing. "I'm just having some issues at home, that's all."

"What kind of issues? Is it your brothers? Are they messing with you again?"

"It's a lot more than that. I don't think you'd want to hear it."

"There is nothing that I wouldn't want to hear from you."

"Are you sure?"

"Of course, I am. Go on, let's hear it."

With his eyes looking to the ceiling, Amari took a deep breath and spoke. "It's about a friend of mine. His name is Dominic."

#

By the time they arrived at the house, the stars were already out. Underneath it, stood a brown trailer house, and the lights shone brightly through the window.

Within seconds, a white truck approached the front of the house, stopping at the dead center before stopping. On the side were two women, Joana and Sue, one wide awake and the other asleep. Well, not asleep, just resting.

Seeing the house, Sue turned her eyes back to the left. "Joana?", she said, reaching over to her shoulder. "Joana, wake up." Hearing this, Joana's eyes shot wide open before turning over to Sue. "Wake up, we're here", Sue said. "What?", Joana said, rubbing her eyes.

"We're here"

"Oh", Sue nodded, turning back to the house. "The lights are on. He must be home."

"Yeah", she said, grabbing her purse. "I should get inside." "Joana, wait!", Sue said, taking Joana's arm, as she turned around. "What?"

"Nothing, I just...", Sue's words trail off before answering, "Are you really, sure you're, okay? I know I already asked you, but I just feel like you're keeping something from me, and I'm not letting you go until you say what it is that's bothering you. Please, Joanna.

Joana let out a deep breath. "You really want to know?"

Sue nodded.

Joana lets out a deep breath before speaking. "*You* are way too white for me!"

Sue's eyes widened in shock as Joana grabbed her purse, hopping out the door before slamming it shut, leaving her in dismay. "Too white?"

#

The door to Joana's house opened wide, the door slamming shut before leaning against it before sliding down to the floor. She looked down at her purse, with nothing but a dark, empty room.

Seeing this, Joana looked up to the sky and let out a deep breath.

Within a few moments, Joana was upstairs in the kitchen, her eyes looking up everywhere before finding a boy standing over the sink, the sound of dishes clashing together.

Joana's eyes widened. "Dominic?"

"Mom?"

Joana was about to open her mouth until the dreadful feeling of earlier this morning came hurdling back. As for me, I rubbed the back of my neck before speaking. "I was just washing some of the dishes. They have been here since this morning. So, I just thought it would be a good distraction."

Joana nodded. "That's good". "It's getting late. I should go to bed", I said, making my way out of the kitchen. "Night, Mom."

"Dominic, wait!"

I stopped in the middle of the hallway. "I just wanted to tell you I'm sorry for what I said to you, this morning. I didn't mean any of it", she said.

Hearing this, I turned back to her, my eyebrows lifted. "That's your excuse?"

Joana's face fell flat. "What?"

"That's your excuse for getting the eviction notice? As if that's not your first excuse for all the other things you've done?"

"What? Dominic, I'm apologizing for hurting you today and about you being a waste of my life!"

"Yeah, but you only think that because of the eviction notice! None of these feelings would've come to the surface if it weren't for you being an irresponsible parent!"

"Irresponsible?!"

"Yeah, if you just paid the eviction notice instead of using it to buy groceries, then we wouldn't be in this situation!"

"What are you talking about? I didn't spend the rent money on groceries!"

"Well, whatever it was, it was on something useless!"

"Paying for your semester was nothing useless!"

My eyes widened in shock before answering. "What did you say?"

Mom lets out an annoyed sigh, making her way to the kitchen table before sitting.

Seeing this, I quickly came up to her. "You used the rent money to pay for my semester, the one for school?"

Mom looked up at me, her eyes full of sadness, before nodding.

My eyes lower in sadness, my shame quickly rising. "Mom, I'm so sorry. I had no idea you did that for me."

"Well, I did. I mean, I didn't really have a choice. It was either pay rent or school, and I chose school. I chose what was most important."

"My education?"

Mom shook her head. "Your future", Mom let out another sigh, her fingers combing through her hair before speaking. "Look, Dominic. I know what I did seemed selfish, but believe me, it wasn't. I was only doing what was best for you. That's what good mothers want, the best for their children. I thought that if I paid the money for your school, I would eventually pay the rent. I thought I would have more time to do so, but the landlord came early. Which explains why we're in the situation we are now", Mom sighed one final time, her head drooping to the floor before speaking. "I'm sorry, Dominic. I was just trying to do what was best for you. That's all I ever wanted for you, but now, with the eviction notice, that dream is dead."

"No", I said, kneeling before her, taking her face. "No, that's not true, Mom. You didn't do anything wrong. It wasn't right for me to put so much pressure on you. If there's anyone to blame, it's me, okay? *Me* and no one else."

Mom shook her head, her eyes hanging low as I kneeled before her. "Mom, what was my father like? Please, I need to know."

With these words, Mom looked at me and sighed. "Your father was an artist. He had these paintings that were very…pragmatic."

"He was an artist?"

"Mm-hm."

"Did he keep any of his paintings? Any here?"

Mom swayed her head back and forth. "There were a few, but that was before…"

I looked into the pain in Mom's eyes and knew. "Before he died?"

She nodded. "I gave them away, the paintings", she sighed, bringing her hand to her face. "Things were a lot better when your father was here. The bills got paid, the house was stable, and everything was perfect. But now that he's gone, everything's bad, *I'm* bad! I'm a bad parent!"

"No", I said softly. "Mom, that's not true, you're a great parent. What I said was dumb! I've been putting all this crap on you like I pay the bills in this house when I don't! You've been doing everything in your power to raise me, and I've been taking it all for granted. I know things have been hard since Dad left, but if he was here right now, he wouldn't want to see you suffering", I put my hands on Mom's shoulders. "*I* don't want to see you suffer, Mom."

Hearing this, a small yet happy smile forms across her lips. "Oh, Dom", she said, pulling me in for a hug. "Thank you"

I smiled, my jaw straight. "You're welcome, Mom. Don't worry about the eviction notice, it'll get done."

Mom nodded. "I know. I love you, Dom."

I smiled, my face buried in Mom's rose-scented perfume. "I love you too, Mom."

Suddenly, I heard a door opening wide, accompanied by my mother's name being called. "Joana?"

Mom and I watch as Aunt Sue enters the kitchen, her eyes full of concern but soon melted by the look of Dominic and Joana. "Oh, hey, Aunt Sue."

"Hey, Dominic. Everything, alright?"

"Yeah. We were just talking."

"About what?"

I shrugged. "Just stuff. Personal stuff."

Sue nods, before brushing her hair, making my eyes glow bright green. "Are you okay?", I asked, my eyes full of concern, indicating my little "superpower"

She nodded. "I'm fine, Dominic. I just need a moment alone with your mother."

I could tell she was anxious. "I just didn't know why. I wanted to ask her, but I shrugged it off.

"Okay", I said before facing mom. "I'm going to take a shower. "Okay, Mom?"

"Okay."

Aunt Sue watched as I walked down the hallway, leaving her and Mom alone in silence. It wasn't long before she faced Mom. "Did you tell him?"

Joana nodded. "I told him enough."

She sighed. "We don't have much time, Jo-Jo. He's bound to find out sooner or later."

She nodded. "I know."

Sue faced Joana with concern. "Are you sure there's nothing you want to talk to me about? About work?"

She shakes her head. "No. I just want to go to bed."

Before she could say anything else, Sue watched Joana go down the hallway, leaving her all alone. As for Joana, she stood before her son's door, where she noticed the Keep Out sign was removed. She smiled, happy to see her son's anger had diminished. Without a second thought, Joana opened the door to her son's bedroom.

She Dominic, nestled under the covers, sound asleep in bed. Mom smiled and shut the door. That is, until my eyes shot wide open, glowing bright green.

Meanwhile, Mom made her way inside her room, switching on the light. She then turned to face a small, narrow door standing in the corner of the bedroom.

Without a second thought, Joana walked towards the door and twisted the doorknob wide open and to a room full of designer clothes. On the right was a set of dresses, skirts, and high heels on the floor. Yet, on the left, there was nothing, nothing but wired hangers, swaying back and forth.

Joana quickly passed them because she didn't care for them. All she cared about was the purple box sitting up on the shelf above her head. Seeing this, Joana reached right up to it, the box sliding to her before bringing it down to her eyes.

Without thinking, Joana knelt to the floor, her eyes glued to the box before opening it wide. There was a set of paintbrushes. Joana's eyes welled up at the sight of this, her tears becoming visible before wiping them away. "No", she says to herself. "No tears. There are more important things than that right now."

Important things, there were, and it was found in the purse, which she reached right into, pulling out a set of crisps, dollar bills.

A whole handful.

Joana took the paintbrushes from the box and put them outside. As for the money, it was put right in the box, equally separated from tens to twenties. Seeing this, Joana grabbed hold of the cardboard top, but before she could bring it to the box, she turned to the set of paintbrushes and said: "I'm sorry, Otto, but it's for the best", Joana turned back to the box, her eyes full of determination. "No matter what it takes."

With these words, Joana puts the top over the money, leaving it in utter darkness.

Chapter 3: Help Wanted

You have seven days to pay rent. If you don't, you're out!

My eyes widened in shock; my head was beading with sweat. I turned to the left, to the window with the sunlight peeking from the blinds. Letting out a deep breath, I rose from my bed, with nothing but my pillow and a very thin sheet covering my body, my body that was still in my day clothes.

Wiping the crust out of my eyes, I let out a yawn and pulled the covers from me and onto the bed where my thicker sheets were found. But I didn't pay any mind for I had something else on my mind.

Before I knew it, my bedroom door opened wide, and I found myself in the hallway. I looked left and right, finding nothing but an empty hall.

A *quiet* hall. "Mom?", I call out.

The door to Mom's bedroom opened, revealing nothing but an empty bed, untouched. Confused, I closed the door and made my way down the hall. "Mom!"

Before I knew it, I found myself in the kitchen, which, to my surprise, was completely in place. It was empty, just like the bedroom, with no one in sight.

Just me and an empty kitchen.

She couldn't have stayed out all night, right?

Anxious, I made my way to the door in the corner of the house, passing the refrigerator, where there was a small note next to a set of alphabet letters. My eyes quickly caught this, stopping me dead at the note before making my way to it.

Left to get a new job, I'll be back soon.

Love, Mom.

I lowered the note before letting out a small sigh of relief. "Well, I guess I should get ready for school."

\#

I stood outside of the bus stop, my eyes staring mindlessly at the road. I was alone, as today, Mom wasn't here to stand beside me and watch me.

It was lonely, which made me sad.

That is, until another thought came up, making my sad façade quickly crumble into a mad spell.

Amari.

But not just Amari: *The deadline.*

Amari and the deadline.

Within seconds, the mad spell quickly turned to a sense of fear.

Seven days, they only had seven days to pay that eviction notice. Mom was already looking for a new job. By the time she was done, she would already be on the street.

If only she had more time, things would be different.

If only Amari hadn't done what he did, things would be easier! But it wasn't things were bad, and things were worse.

Things were awful, and there was nothing he could do about it. My whole life was crumbling by the minute. Who knows just how long before we were on the streets for good.

I didn't know what I could do was hope.

"Oye!", said a voice. Raising my head, I found the bus driver looking right at me from inside the yellow school bus. "Ya getting' on or what, boy?!"

Now, out of my head, I grabbed my backpack and run straight into the bus, but before I could make it to the last step, I turned my head back to the empty bus stop. Sad, I took my eyes to the sky before speaking. "I love you, Mom."

#

A hospital, thousands of windows beaming with the morning sun shining down on it. Down below, was a parking lot full of cars, all at rest. Even the white truck, at the end of the corner was found parked at the end of the parking lot.

On the inside, was two women, sitting in the two front seats, one applying lip gloss and the other staring down at a piece of paper, her eyes full of confusion.

"Sue, are you sure this place is hiring?"

Sue, who was sitting at the left of the truck, gave Joana a quick nod. "Yeah, hospitals are always looking for new nurses. They're desperate for people"

Hearing this, Joana looked down at her resume. "Are they racist?"

Sue turned her eyes back to Joana in confusion. "What? No, why would you think that?"

"Have you forgotten about last night already?"

"What, of course not! Joana, you know I haven't forgotten. Why do you think I quit working at Martey's?"

Hearing this, Joana let out a sigh. "I know. I'm sorry."

Sue placed her hand on her shoulder. "It's fine. I know this is a rough time for you."

Joana nodded, looking down at the resume in her hands before taking a deep breath. "I just want this to be over."

"I know, and it will. You just need to have faith. Besides, with your bachelor's degree in nursing, you'll get the job in no time."

"Yeah, but there weren't that many nursing slots open for me then. So, I had no choice but to work for that racist jackass."

"Yes, but not today. Because today, things will work out."

Joana nodded, a smile forming. "Yeah, you're right. Things will work out."

Sue put her hand on Joana's shoulder and smiled. "It will. Now go get this job."

"Right", Joana grabbed her resume before popping open the door. "Well, wish me luck."

"You got this girl!", Sue said, giving Joana a quick thumbs up.

Joana did the same before slamming the door shut, leaving Sue with a genuine, happy smile. "You can do this, Jo-Jo."

\#

Literature sucked, especially with the boring lecture of Macbeth. As much as I liked he epic poem, the story is basic from greedy peasants to kings and knowing witches, the list goes on for miles.

I wasn't really listening as I had much more important things to think about than school: the eviction.

I was scared, terrified. While other students had worries about upcoming tests, I was the one who had to sit with the dreadful thought of living on the streets next week. Could you imagine me living on the streets, in boxes, begging for spare change.

I would give anything just to be able to worry about simple school stuff again, but I couldn't.

And I hated it.

Soon, the school bell rang, and I made my way out of the second period, heading for third, but not before I headed for the lockers. I unlocked the lock, making the "pop" sound before opening it wide.

I unzipped my backpack, grabbed a handful of books from it and went into my locker. I do this for the next minute, stacking book after book atop one another, but as soon as I do, my eyes turn straight to the left, where another locker, one with a devil sticker, was found.

It's right there, all the hate comes flooding straight back. *That* and all the sadness. Yes, I was sad, sad that, of all the things going on, I still longed to have someone to talk to about it.

That's where Amari came in, but he was gone. He was gone, and it was all my fault.

Stay the hell away from me.

I sighed, shutting my locker shut.

Even though he made our situation worse, it still would have been nice to have him here, to be nearby. Even if he didn't deserve it.

I just needed someone.

I needed some hope.

But hope wasn't going to help me. Believe me, I've tried praying. From the moment I got on the bus, from the moment I came to school, I've done nothing but pray to God. Mom always said that with God, you can get through anything.

With God, you can triumph over adversity.

But when your days away from living on the streets, God wasn't something that felt like what I needed.

I didn't need God.

I didn't need prayer.

And I certainly didn't need hope.

Hope wasn't going to get me out of this hole I was in. What I needed was a miracle.

What I needed was: "Hello, Dominic"

Hearing this, I whipped my head back from the locker to see a young girl with long, curly hair and golden hooped earrings, especially the lavish white dress she was wearing over her blue jeans. "Amanda?"

"Yes", she smiled.

"Hey", I half smile at her. "Were you standing there the whole time?"

Amanda laughed. "No. I just got here. I saw you standing by yourself at the locker. So, I just thought I'd come by."

I raised my eyebrows. "For what?"

"To talk."

I brought my backpack over my shoulder before shaking my head. "I'm sorry, but I don't need someone to talk to."

"Wait!", Amanda said, grabbing my arm, causing me to whip my head back, wide-eyed. "Sorry, I just", Amanda lowered her eyes to the floor before gazing back up at mine. "I just wanted to say I'm sorry for what I said about your friend, um, Amari, was it?"

I nodded. "Yeah, that's his name", I shifted my eyes to the left. "Amari."

"Look, I know you think I'm just some snobby, rich girl, but I'm quite decent once you get to know me."

With these words, I broke my arm away from Amanda's grip, leaving her in confusion. "It's okay, Griffin. It's fine, everything's fine. With you anyways."

"With me?", she said, shaking her head a bit in confusion. "What about your friend?"

"We're not talking to each other right now"

I made my way down the hallway, my backpack opened wide from the back, catching Amanda's attention. "Hey, you're-", Amanda's words were cut off as a small yet black and white composition notebook lay on the floor.

Without a second thought, Amanda grabbed the notebook from the floor and up to her eyes before gazing back up at the hallway, which was now empty.

Confused, Amanda looked back down at the notebook and brought it up to her chest before turning her head and walking down the hallway.

#

The hospital stood in the place, the sunlight now much lower down the windows, with a much darker red-orange hue. As for the parking lot, it was much bare now, with only a few cars parked, especially the white Ford truck, where the young blonde-haired woman was sitting in her car, looking left and right in confusion. "Where is she?", said Sue, looking out the window. "It shouldn't take that long for an interview."

Sue looked out the window, the giant hospital standing proud and tall before gazing down at the two doors, standing completely still. That is, until the doors split wide, revealing a curly, black-haired woman making her way out. "There she is", Sue said, looking away from the window and back into her seat, waiting for her friend.

She did this for a few minutes until a small "knock, knock" was heard, causing Sue to turn her eyes back with a smile as her friend, Joana, gave her a quick wave, a half-smile presented on her face.

Smiling, Sue popped the lock and opened the car door, causing Joana to slide right in. "Hey, girl!", she said happily.

"Hey", Joana said in a sad tone, closing the door behind her with a sigh.

Sue quickly noticed her change in demeanor. "How did it go?"

Joana wiped her eyes a bit before sniffling. "It was fine."

Sue raised a brow. "Fine? Fine, as in good?"

"No", she said, shaking her head. "Fine, as in bad, terrible, awful!"

"Awful? Did you get the job?"

"No, Sue! Did you not hear what I just said!", Joana let out an annoyed sigh before putting her face in her hands and speaking. "They said I wasn't experienced enough to be a nurse. That I was inadequate."

"Inadequate? Why would they think that?"

Joana scoffed. "I don't know, probably the same reason why I got fired from my last job: because everyone in this shit town is racist!"

"Joana, you can't use racism for every bad thing that happens to you!"

"I can, and I will!", Joana folded her arms, letting out an angry sigh. "You don't know what it's like, Sue. You don't know what it's like to be a single black woman who gets treated like shit by assholes that you have no choice but to work with! That's exactly how I felt back at Marty's! How I've felt ever since my husband…left us! As if *that* wasn't enough to make my life worse! My whole life has been filled with nothing but disappointment, and it's only going to get worse until I'm on the streets!", Joana put her face in her hands, sobbing hard.

Sue watched in sadness and a bit of shame as her best friend cried her eyes out. She turned her eyes back to the window where St. Mora Hospital stood in the afternoon light. Without a second thought, Sue popped the lock of her car, raising Joana's head bit before hopping out of the car. "Sue?", Joana said, confused. "Sue, where are you going?"

Sue turned back to Joana and said, "You'll see."

Confused, Sue slammed the door of her car shut, leaving Joana in confusion as Sue made her way to the hospital.

#

Summit High stood big and tall, the sun beaming on it before falling on the windows. On the inside, there was a library, where several students were found gathering books from the bookshelves, their eyes glued to the pages.

On the far left of the library, a row of students was found sitting at a table, their eyes peering down at books from all kinds of genres. At the very end, a girl with braided red hair and emerald, green eyes, eyes that peered down at the composition notebook that lay flat open on the wooden surface.

Amanda flipped through a few pages, many of which had several paragraphs written in them, all with cursive handwriting. "For a quiet guy, he sure knows how to write well."

Amanda flipped another page, and that's where she found the dates.

November 14, 2006

October 31, 2007

December 25, 2009...

The list went on for miles, making Amanda even more intrigued to read the paragraphs.

She started with the first date:

November 14, only twelve days 'till Thanksgiving. Besides, Christmas was my favorite time of year as we got to eat a whole feast of food. But for Mom's sake, it was a day of being thankful for what we had. For me, it was not going to bed hungry, every day of every year, I slept with a full belly. If that wasn't thankful, I didn't know what was.

Amanda chuckled a bit before flipping to the next page, to the next date:

"Happy Halloween!" is what people who celebrated the day would say. As for me, I didn't, I couldn't, thanks to my mom. Being a fully-fledged Christian, Mom didn't believe in celebrating anything that didn't have anything to do with God. In her eyes, Halloween, was a day that she called: "The Day of the Devil!"

That line was nothing but bullshit to me, as Halloween had nothing to do with that. It was all little boys and girls dressed in costumes and getting candy for FREE! If I could celebrate Halloween, I would go to the biggest houses in town and stuff my bag full of those sugary treats!

Unfortunately, I had no choice but to spend my Halloween indoors, watching thousands of kids gorge themselves on Kit Kats, Three Musketeers, Reese's Cups, and all the other great candy in the world, all from my bedroom window.

It was a sad time for me, that is, until, Amari, my best friend, sneaks me a few mini-Snickers and Milk Duds under his desk at school. We'd share them during lunch, with me tossing a few chocolate milk duds into each other's mouth, along with a few Skittles.

So, yes, Halloween was a sad time, but only when Amari was with me. Things were always better when my bro was around. Always.

"Aw", Amanda said with a happy smile before flipping to a third page where the final page was found.

Christmas. They say it's the happiest time of year, when families and friends come together and celebrate being together. But not for us, not this year, because this year would be the fourteenth birthday without Dad.

Amanda's eyes pull straight back from the notebook/diary before speaking. "Your father?", she pulled back to the notebook.

I know that sounds silly, especially since I have never met him. I mean, I was just a baby when it happened, and ever since then, Mom hasn't been the same. There are days when she is fine and days when she isn't, with Christmas being one of them.

Christmas was Dad's favorite holiday, and not because of God but because of the "feeling in the air", From what my mom says, Christmas was a magical time when Dad was around, and when he was around, everything was better.

But ever since the "incident", the magic faded without warning. Now, Mom spends Christmas alone in her room, with a bottle of wine at her side. It wasn't long before I found her in a drunk stupor. Before I know it, I'm spending Christmas alone, with no presents, no special dinner, just me and putting my mom to bed.

As sad as I thought Halloween was, I'm starting to rethink that situation: with no mother or father, Christmas is the worst day of the year, that being this year! Let's just pray that New Year's will be better for now, that's all there is.

For those who have better lives, have a merry Christmas and a happy, joyous new year.

The words stopped right at the last line of the book, making Amanda very confused. "Is that it?"

Amanda flipped through a few more pages, ones that were empty the more she did. "Huh, I guess it is."

Now, back to the original page, Amanda's eyes lowered in sadness. She felt bad for Dominic. "For a sweet guy, he sure has a sad life", Amanda looked down at the empty pages and smiled. "Maybe, I could do something to help him."

Amanda looked down at the notebook and smiled. "I *will* do something about it. Starting with the notebook."

With these words, Amanda closed the book shut before rising from her seat and heading out the library door.

\#

The hospital stood in the place, the sunlight now much lower down the windows, with a much darker red-orange hue. As for the parking lot, it was much bare now, with only a few cars parked, especially the white Ford truck. "Where is she?", Joana said, looking out the window. "It's been awfully long."

Joana looked out the window at the giant hospital standing proud and tall before gazing down at the two doors, standing completely still. That is, until the doors split wide, revealing a white, blonde-haired woman making her way out. "There she is", Joana said, looking away from the window and back into her seat, waiting for her friend.

Smiling, Joana popped the lock and opened the car door, causing Sue to slide right in. "Um, hey, Sue", she said before her eyes widened in shock at Sue, whose lipstick was smeared along with her hair being messy and out. "Hey, girl."

Confused, Joana opened her mouth. "Sue, what happened to you?"

"That's not important right now. Let's go."

With that, Sue fastened her seat belt and hit the brakes, causing the car to come out of the parking lot, her eyes right on the road. As for Joana, her eyes were right on Sue, but before she could speak, Sue did it for her. "I talked with Dr. Truman, and he said you can start tomorrow."

"Tomorrow? For what?"

"For the nurse job. That's what you wanted, right?"

Joana nodded. "Y-yes", she blinked, sitting up more in the car seat. "What did you say to him?"

"Oh, I have my ways."

Meanwhile, inside St. Mora Hospital, a middle-aged man in a white coat is found in his office, rocking back and forth in a corner, his eyes wide with fear as if he's seen a monster. Not to mention, his entire office was filled with sheets of paper scattered everywhere on the ground. "I'll give her the job", he murmured. "I'll give her the job."

Within seconds, the door opened, revealing a young nurse with a coffee cup in her hand. "Dr. Truman, I have your coffee for yo-"

"LEAVE ME ALONE!", Dr. Truman shouted, causing the nurse to sprint right out of the room, the coffee mug breaking into pieces.

Sue smiled happily at her "achievement" before turning back to Joana. "Shall we go then?"

Joana smiled. "Um, sure."

With these words, the two girls make their way down the road and into the setting sun. "Seriously, Sue, what did you say?"

"Some things are left better unsaid, Joana."

#

At the cafeteria, there were thousands of students sitting in rows, their mouths stuffed with various supplies of meat, vegetables, and grains. As for me, I came to lunch with a cheeseburger with a side of curly fries. I wasn't a fan of curly fries, but it was the only thing I had to eat.

Before I knew it, my butt was in the seat, and my lunch was on the table, but before I could dig in, my eyes were on my backpack that sat on the floor, my backpack that was wide open. "What?", I say in confusion. "What's my bag doing open?"

I searched through my backpack and found all my binders, but one thing was missing.

"Hey, where's my notebook?", I said, searching through my backpack. "It couldn't have dropped out of my bag, could it?"

"Looking for this?", said a voice, waving a small notebook over my eyes.

I gazed up to find a red-haired white girl, her emerald, green eyes gazing down at me. "Sorry for not giving back to you sooner. I lost you in the hallway."

Confused, I raised my eyebrow. "Amanda? You took my notebook?"

"Well, yeah, but don't worry, I only read a few pages."

"Pages?"

"Yeah but listen-", Amanda's words were quickly cut off as I snatched my notebook right from her hands. "What did you do with my notebook?"

"Did you write in it?"

"What, no? I would never do that!", she explained as I flipped through several pages in my notebook before finding one with paragraphs, *my* paragraphs.

Nothing written.

Nothing changed.

"I'm sorry if this makes you upset, but I was only trying to help."

Hearing this, I looked up from my notebook. "I don't want your help. Whatever it is you want from me, I want you to stop now!"

"Want from you? I don't want anything."

"Then why are you being so clingy, why are you snooping around in my notebook?! Are you spying on me?"

"What, no! I just-"

"Just what? What were you trying to do?!"

"I WAS JUST TRYING TO FIGURE YOU OUT!", Amanda shouted, making the whole cafeteria go silent.

As for me, I rose from my seat, my eyes full of anger. "I don't need you to figure me out. You think you're a decent person, but you're just a nosey creep, a snobby rich girl!"

With these words, Amanda's eyes widened in shock, that is, until two balls of fire rose into her eyes, making her sadness quickly turn to anger. "I was just trying to help you."

"I don't need your help, you're not my girlfriend."

Amanda scoffed, rolling her eyes. "You know what, screw you. You wanna be alone. Then be alone! Asshole!", Amanda shouted from across the table before she grabbed her purse and left the cafeteria.

As for me, I sat back down in my seat with my notebook thrown back in my backpack.

\#

As the sun set on St. Mora, the stars rose, with the giant, bright moon rising behind them. Underneath, the city shone bright, the giant skyscraper buildings glowing with their immense light, creating an even bigger light show than before.

In the farther parts of the city, there was a quiet neighborhood of Wayward Fern, where several lights glowed brightly through their windows. As for the Mitchell home, its lights were off, leaving a display of darkness.

For many people, this house would stand out from everyone else's homes. As for the white Ford truck parked outside the home, it was but a hollow shell of darkness. "The lights are off. You might want to head in now."

"Thanks, Sue", said Joana, grabbing her purse over her shoulder, but before she could make her way out of the car, she caught Sue rubbing her eyes with a tissue paper.

"You okay, Sue?"

"What?", Sue said, turning her eyes back to Joana in confusion. "Oh, it's nothing. I just had something in my eye."

Joana raised a brow. "And what would that be?"

"Oh, nothing, just some dust."

"Some dust or some tears?"

Sue's eyes solely shift from Joana to her hands before letting out a sad sigh. "Sue, what's wrong?"

Letting out another sigh, Sue took her eyes from the floor and back to Joana. "I haven't told you why I came out of the hospital looking like this, did I?"

Joana shook her head. "No, you didn't."

Sue wiped another of her eyes before speaking. "After I talked to Dr. Truman, I went to the bathroom to cry."

"Cry? Why. Did he do something to you?"

Sue shook her head. "No. I just got triggered, is all."

"By what?"

Sue looked into Joana's eyes. "By what you said about me."

Joana raised a brow. "Wait, are you talking about that racist crap. Sue, I was upset. I didn't mean to hurt you.

"No, not from that. It wasn't the racist thing that hurt me."

"It wasn't? Then what was?"

Sue sighed; this time even harder before speaking. "A few years back, years before I met you, I had a miscarriage."

Joana's eyes widened in shock at these words. "A miscarriage?"

Sue nodded. "I was twenty-one when it happened. I was in the delivery room, trying to give birth to my baby but…", Sue grabbed hold of her mouth, her eyes starting to well up. Joana takes her hand. "It's okay, Sue. It's okay."

Sue takes a deep breath. "My baby, my daughter, was f-", Joana's eyes were filled with not just shock but immense horror. "The doctors said he was dead, he was dead, and I couldn't even hold him." Sue took her face in her hands, sobbing.

Joana pulled Sue straight in for a hug. "It's alright, Sue", Joana said, now sobbing. "I had no idea."

Sue sniffed. "It's alright, Joana. It's not your fault."

"I know. That's why I want you to come stay with me, you and Dominic."

"What?", Joana pulled away from Sue, confused. "You want me to stay with you?"

"Just in case this whole eviction notice thing doesn't work out. I know what it's like to lose a child, Joana. The last thing I want is for you to suffer like mine. So, what do you say?"

"Yes. Of course, that would be great. Sue, thank you!"

Sue smiled. "You're welcome. Now get inside the house. I'm sure he's waiting for you."

"Right", Joana turned her eyes back to the door, but before she could make her way out, she grabbed Sue and pulled her back in for another embrace. "I love you, girl."

Sue smiled, squeezing Joana tight. "I love you too. Now go."

With these words, Joana popped open the door to her truck and headed out, shutting the door right behind Sue, who was smiling happily.

#

Joana made her way through her front door, her eyes full of happiness as she walked through her living room to her kitchen and soon down the hallway, where thousands of photos of her and Dominic sat.

It wasn't long before she saw a door with a "Keep Out" sign. Joana twisted the doorknob, opening it wide, where she found me lying under the covers with nothing but my forehead peeking out.

Smiling, Joana made her way to the bed, kneeling to kiss my forehead. "Things are looking up for us, baby."

With these words, Joana rose from the bed before heading out of her son's bedroom, the door shutting right behind her.

As soon as she was gone, my eyes popped right open, causing me to raise my head from my pillow.

Things are looking up for us.

What did she mean by that? Did something happen. Something good? Related to the eviction?

I didn't know what, but something was happening. I just hoped it wouldn't be the last. With these words, I rested my head back on my pillow and looked at the ceiling. My mind raced back to a memory, one that was now becoming clear as it rose to the surface.

I was in the cafeteria, my eyes looking down at my journal. I flipped through many of the pages. That is, until I find one on the left, one with a giant yet poorly drawn pumpkin on the left. Seeing this, I looked down to find the large paragraph below. *That* and the date: October 31, 1997.

Without a second thought, I brought my journal up to me and said: *Halloween was my favorite time of the year. But none as special as the one spent with my best friend, Amari, who would sneak candy from his brothers for me.*

He had a whole bag of Kit-Kats, Snicker bars, and even my personal favorite, Reese's cups! We spent the whole night gorging ourselves with the various delights of chocolates, and we spent the next morning vomiting it all up.

It was the best Halloween ever, and it was all thanks to Amari.

My best friend. Forever.

Reading this, a tear fell on the "r" of *forever*. My eyes welled up with loads of them as I wiped with the sleeve of my jacket. "Shit. There I go again", I said, lying on my bed, wiping my eyes. "These damn tears", I sniffed a few more times before taking my hand away from my eyes and looking back up to the ceiling.

Chapter 4: The
Bully

*A group of students were gathered in the cafeteria, their hands all raised
as they shouted one great word: "FIGHT! FIGHT! FIGHT!"*

They kept saying it, loud and clear: "FIGHT! FIGHT! FIGHT!"

*Behind the crowd, behind the rowdy kids, were two kids, one boy and a
girl, their fists raised and their eyes locked. "What are you waiting for,
Dom?", answered the redhead holding her fists up. "Come on, make your
move!"*

Scared, the thick, wavy-haired boy looked to the red head with fear. "Um, I don't think I can?"

"Why not?"

"Well, for starters, you're a girl. I can't fight a girl!"

"Don't worry, you won't have to. Just let me throw a punch, fall, and cry like a baby. You know, to make me look good."

"There is no way in hell, I'm doing that!"

"You don't have to just sit still and look: PRETTY!"

With these words, I'm knocked right in the nose, causing me to fall on the cafeteria floor, now blacked out.

"Oooohhhhh!!!!", echoed the entire students.

"Y-ES!", said Amanda, her arms raised in joy. "I AM VICTORIOUS AND IT ONLY TOOK ONE PUNCH!"

Amanda laughed happily as I lay on the ground unconscious, my nose now bleeding out.

#

"Gah!", I shouted, my head beading with sweat as I rose from my pillow and woke from my dream, my strange, confusing dream.

I put my hand to my sweaty forehead. "Ugh, geez! That's one dream I'll never forget."

Saying this, I turned my eyes up to my clock that sat on my dresser, the time read: 6:30. With my nightmare now gone from my head, I said, "Time for school, again."

The school bell rang loudly through Summit High's hallway, where hundreds of students made their way through. As for me, I made my way to the lockers, my backpack held behind my back. That is, until I looked up to see a young man with dreads standing at his locker, grabbing a set of books from it.

"Amari?", I said in shock. "Hey, Amari!"

Amari turned his eyes around in shock before gasping heavily at me. "Hey, Amari, wait, Amari!", I shouted as Amari shut his locker and sprinted down the hallway, hitting a few students before turning a corner. "AMARI!", I called out, failing to run after him as he was already down the hall.

With a heavy sigh, I lowered my head in disappointment. "Well, I guess that's that."

I made my way back to the lockers, but before I could take a step: "Oof!"

I bumped into someone, knocking their books right on the floor. "Oh my gosh! I'm so sorry!", I said as the mysterious person knelt to the ground. "No, no! It's fine. I ju-", Amanda's words quickly stopped as we looked at each other. "Oh", she said in an annoyed tone. "It's you again."

"I didn't realize you were here."

"Well, I am", she scoffed. "What did you think. My Ride or Die" girls go to class for me?"

"Well, they get *homework* for you. So, I wouldn't be so surprised."

Amanda grunted. "You're just mad because you don't have someone to help you out with your studies."

"No, I'm mad because I have a person who likes to snoop in my business!"

"Oh, don't tell me you're still mad about me being in your journal"

"I am! In fact, I don't even know why I'm talking to you right now! If anything, you'll probably go right back and snoop!"

"I am not a snoop, and you know it!"

"Yeah, okay!"

As we both went at each other, the bell rang. "Finally!", I said, shaking my head. "I must go to class now. Enjoy having your minions go there for you, snoop!"

"I go to class by myself, dickhead!"

With a sad sigh, I lifted my backpack over my shoulder and made my way down the hallway, my head held low.

A few miles away, far from Summit High, the hospital, Clear Waters Hospital, stood proud and tall in the morning light, the sun hitting the windows, the windows that several patients stared through, desperately longing for the outside.

Unfortunately, they were stuck in hospital beds, sick, their eyes glued to the TV screens they had. As for the employees, they were up and running, a fleet of nurses, doctors, and respiratory therapists pacing the bleached tile floors of the hospital.

Speaking of employees, there were two nurses sitting at a desk, their eyes peering down at the telephones that sat below them, dead and still.

Much like Sue and Joana, who, in this case, had absolutely nothing to do. "This is not fun", said Joana, sighing.

Sue sighed, her head nodding. "I know, girl. Mondays are always the slowest."

"No, I mean this job: nursing. It's not as fun as I thought it would be."

"What do you mean? Nursing is a great job."

"Yeah, for *you*. You get to check the patient's heart rate and check monitors. Meanwhile, I'm sitting here waiting for the phone to ring from random people."

"Random people? Joana, those *people* aren't just people, they're in desperate need of help from people who could help them, and that someone is you. Sure, it's not checking patients, but it's just as important as any other job."

"Well, it doesn't feel like it."

"It does for *them*. Each call you make, is a beacon of hope."

With her hand on her cheek, Joana let out a sigh. "I guess you're right. Besides, it could be worse", she laughed. "One of the phone calls could be about my son."

"Yeah, hopefully it won't come to that."

"Yeah, *hopefully*"

The telephone rang, breaking them out of the awkward silence. "Telephone!", Joana said, reaching her hand to the phone handle and bringing it up to her ear. "Hello?", Joana answered, listening to the voice, the copper coil wrapping around her fingers as she nodded. "Mm-hm, uh-huh", Sue watched, confused. "Okay, a paramedic will arrive soon. Yes, you're welcome, goodbye."

Joana put the telephone back on the handle. "What did they say?", Sue asked.

Joana turned to Sue. "It was a mother she said her daughter was attacked by a donkey."

Sue raised a brow. "A- a donkey?"

Joana nodded. "Yeah, the kid was taken to a petting zoo for her sweet sixteen birthday. There, she wanted to ride the donkey, but as soon as she got on, she realized the donkey was too slow for her. Fed up with this, the girl does the stupid thing and slaps it on its ass."

"It's ass?"

"Yes, she slaps the *ass's* ass! Once she did, the donkey kicked the sand and she went flying in the air, hitting the ground hard. Thanks to me, she's on her way right now with a broken arm and fractured rib!"

Sue raised a brow and slowly smiled. "Thanks to *you*"

Joana nodded. "Yep, thanks to me."

The two women stared at each other for two short seconds before bursting out in laughter, causing several others to turn their heads as they do. "Okay, that has got to be one of the funniest stories I've ever heard!"

"I know, right?", Joana cackled, holding onto her stomach. "Truly priceless!"

#

After a whole hour spent in the library reading, the school bell rang, and the hallway was now full of a sea of students. Everywhere you looked, there were students making their way into their classes, some saying goodbye to their boyfriends and girlfriends as they "parted ways".

For them, their classes would be Art or Math, Theatre, and some Music, but for me, it was French. Of all the languages out there, French was my least favorite. I never understood French and the strange sounds my teacher, Ms. Yael, made. For most people, French was supposed to be the "language of love" Unfortunately, it was difficult to see it that way as I always struggled with pronunciation. Mostly because the words didn't sound the way they appeared. It was weird.

Unlike languages like Spanish, where you hear words like: "luna", "mas" and "Martes", French was "vingt" (vunt), "rouge" (rooj), and "bonne" (bun).

Okay, only some of the words sounded like each other, but still, French, is a tough subject.

Today and I would have no choice but to endure the entire *conference*.

Lecture, I mean.

I turned the corner and made my way to French class, where there were several other students, repeating phrases to one another.

I sighed, knowing deep in my heart that I would never get to that level. I would need someone with extraordinary French skills to teach him.

I just hoped he/she existed.

Annoyed, I made my way to a desk and sat right down before dropping my backpack on the floor. But as soon as I did, a mysterious person in an orange and black striped jumpsuit made its way past me, its eyes glancing at me before turning away.

I gazed back at her, my eyes following her as she made her way to the back of the class, but before I could say anything: "Bonjour, la classe!", I heard as my eyes looked up to the young blonde lady making her way into class.

"BONJOUR, MADEMOISELLE YAEL!", the class chimed in, their posture tall and proud.

"Ooh, bon travail, classe! Bon!", Ms, Yael said before turning her head and digging straight into her purse. "I hope you all have studied because today we will be having a pop quiz."

The class let out an irritated sigh. "Now, now, classe. Zhis is no physical quiz, for today I will be grading you all on pronunciazion."

"But before we do that. I'd like to introduce our new student to the class."

"New student?", I scoffed. "I wonder who that could be."

"Ms. Griffin, could you stand up for the class, please?"

"Of course, Ms. Yael."

"Hello, everyone! I'm Amanda, *Amanda Griffin,* and I'm your new student", A small gasp escaped from her as her eyes met mine.

"Mrs. Griffin, are you okay?"

Amanda smirked, her eyes looking right at me. "Yes, Ms. Yael", she said, turning back to the teacher. "Everything's just fine."

"Well, you can sit down now. We have to get started."

"Yes, of course", Amanda sat, her eyes shifting back to me.

Confused, angry, and a bit scared, I turn my eyes back to Ms. Yael.

Yet, little did I know, the mysterious girl, sat at her desk, continued to look at me, her eyes full of anger.

"Alright, classe. We will now begin our exam. Be prepared, for I will be picking you one by one", Ms. Yael said, writing on the board with her piece of chalk. "Let us begin with Parker

A big-headed boy, with headphones on is found jamming his head to whatever song he was listening. "Y-yeah."

Ms. Yael looked at Parker, her arms folded. "I hope that music you were listening to had something to do with Edith Piaf, monsieur?'

-"Parker took his headphones off, shaking his head. "No"

"Then I suggest you open your ears and tell me what: "Thank you" in French means?"

"Thank you?", Parker's eyes opened wide. "Oh, that means, Merci, right?"

Ms. Yael nodded, her smile present. "Corriger", she said turning to point at another person. "Johnnathan, how do you zay: "Green" in French?"

"Vert", answered an overweight boy in glasses.

"How is zit said en feminine?"

"Verte"

"Corriger, Raine: Vot"

"Chaude o chaud!"

"Carlos: Cold"

"Froide o froid"

"Dominic!"

"No!", I shouted, shocked.

The class, including Ms. Yael, turned their heads, looking directly at. I quickly cleared her throat. "I, um, I mean, yes! Yes, tell me the question?"

Ms. Yael continued to look at me with an evil smirk across her face. "I see that you are hesitant."

"Yes, he is!", said the strange voice. When I turned to look, it was the redhead. "He's afraid of being called on. It's obvious he doesn't understand French."

"That's not true", I said with my eyes wide open.

"Yes, it is! Admit it, you suck at French!"

"No, I don't!"

"Arrête!"

Amanda and I turned to Ms. Yael. "None of that! Mademoiselle, this isn't your time to speak! Now sit back down in your seat."

Hearing this, Amanda let out a sigh before slouching in her seat, her arms crossed. "Fine."

"That's what I thought", Ms. Yael turned to me. "Dominic, since time is now short, I will ask you a sentence."

I make a quick lump in my throat. "Dominic, how do you say: *Where's the bathroom?*"

"The bathroom?"

"Yes"

Blinking, I make another gulp before speaking.

Shit! I thought, fearful. *And it's a long one, too.*

I hated long answers.

This was the main reason why I hated coming to Ms. Yael's class because she did shit like this to me but because of less time, thanks to *Amanda*, it's worse!

But there was nothing I could do now. All I could do was open my mouth and make words.

And make I did. "Aoi me...el lune"

"I'm sorry, what was that?"

I grunted my palms now sweating. "Aoi me es lune."

Amanda giggled a bit as Ms. Yael shook her head in confusion. "Um, no, Dominic. That's not it, the word i-"

"Oui est la salle de bain!", blurted Amanda. "That's what he meant, Ms. Yael. See, I told you he didn't know French."

My hands clenched into a fist. Even Tiger Girl from behind me had angry eyes for her.

"Mademoiselle!", Ms. Yael said stumping her feet. "Hey, I'm just being honest. I mean, I said it perfectly.

You should've gotten me to speak for him."

"You just did. In fact, you interrupted him and since you did, I'm giving you a cero for this exam!"

"Wait, what? A c*ero,* as in a *zero*?"

"Yes, what were you expecting an A?"

She scoffed. "Uh, yeah! All my other teachers do!"

Ms. Yael folded her arms. "Well, I'm not *those* teachers. *I* am different."

"Different!", Amanda slammed her hands on the desk. "Lady, do you know who my father is? Do you have any idea what he could do to you?"

"Whatever it is, I'm sure it won't be as bad as what he would do to you when he finds out the grade you will receive on your report card, madame."

Ms. Yael's little taunt is what made everyone in the class laugh at her, making Amanda rather embarrassed before the bell rang. "Ooh! That's the bell! Remember to read Chapters neuf et dix tonight! Au revoir!", Ms. Yael said, making her way out, her purse hanging by her side before spotting me rising from my seat. "Dominic", I hear, my eyes turning to her making her way to me. "Yes?"

Ms. Yael puts a hand on my shoulder. "I've decided to give you an eighty, a *quatre-vingt* for trying."

Hearing this, I smiled. "Really? Thanks."

"Ah-ah-ah! In French."

"Right, sorry: Merci, mademoiselle. Merci", I said to Ms. Yael's delight without the sudden realization that Amanda was watching from behind, her eyes fuming with fire.

"I hope to see you in class next week. Au revoir."

"Au revoir, Ms. Yael."

Ms. Yael made one final wave before passing Amanda's seat, her eyes full of annoyance, much to Amanda's dislike, before leaving class.

Once Ms. Yael was gone, Amanda turned her eyes back to me, my backpack now up to my shoulder, as Amanda made her way to me. "You're lucky you got a B it's the grade for those who are second best."

Hearing this, I lifted my backpack up to my shoulders before speaking. "Oh, then I guess *ceros* are for winners. If it is, then congratulations, Amanda!", I sighed, making my way past Amanda before. "You got anything else you want to put on your hate list?"

Amanda grunted, sucking her teeth before making her way out of class, her back turned as she headed out.

Yet, as soon as she did, a shadow approached behind me. "Are you okay?"

Hearing this, I turned my head around to find the young girl in the tiger-themed suit, her hood covering her face. Confused, I said, "Um, yeah. Who are you?"

Saying this, the girl unveiled her tiger hood, revealing a light-skinned girl with hazel brown eyes and freckles. My eyes widened seeing her before speaking. "Wait a second: Nomi, Nomi Scott?"

The girl blinked, confused. "You know me?"

Of course, I knew her. Nomi Scott, the girl I've had a crush on for years, was standing here, talking to me face-to-face.

"Yeah, I've seen you! I mean, I've seen you a lot in the hallway", I put his hands on the back of his neck, my face flushed with red.

Nomi chuckled a bit. "I've seen you there too, in the hallway, I mean."

I nodded. "Yeah"

Hearing this, Nomi's bright, joyous smile quickly fell to shame. "Hey, I'm sorry."

I raise my head, looking at her, confused. "Sorry? What are you sorry for?"

"For Amanda. Everyone knows how big of a jerk she can be, especially when it comes to getting her way. Believe me, I know. Don't let her walk all over you like that. You don't deserve that, especially for a good guy like yourself, okay?"

Hearing this, my face became even more flushed with red. "Don't worry, I won't."

"Good", she smiled at me before turning her head back. "Well, it was nice meeting you, Dominic. Bye."

My eyes lit up with joy hearing this.

She said my name.

SHE SAID MY NAME!

Nomi made her way out of French class, her eyes gazing out at the empty hallway as she did. It wasn't long before she got a strange feeling that something was near, something bad. Feeling this, Nomi turned her head to the left, to a set of lockers.

Yet, little did she know, a girl, a redhead, stood behind one of them, her emerald, green eyes full of envy-envy and greed.

With her fists clenched, Nomi muttered her name: "Amanda."

Saying this, Nomi put her Tiger hood back over her head before making her way down the hall.

As she did, Amanda came from behind the lockers, her eyes full of distress. "Nomi", Amanda muttered as she watched the young freckled-faced girl make her way down the hall, her pink Hello Kitty backpack bobbing up and down as she disappeared into the sea of students.

\#

A pair of sneakers are found walking down the hall, squeaking against the polished, white tile floor as they do. Panning up, we found Amari, with a big, bright smile as he made his way down the hallway, waving at students as he passed. "Hey, Josh!", he said, passing a blonde girl with glasses. "Hey, Stephanie!"

He turned to the left one final time before speaking. "Oh, hey-DOMINIC!"

A piece of paper with Dominic's name written in red hung on a locker, *Amari's* locker. "Oh, it's just a picture", Amari raised a brow. "Wait, why is it on my locker?"

Taking the paper off, Amari read: MEET ME IN THE BASKETBALL COURT BEFORE LUNCH! I NEED TO TALK TO YOU ASAP!, DOMINIC.

A small gasp escaped from Amari. "Oh shit", Amari said, looking at the words. "I can't believe this. Dominic, he wants to talk to me and after everything I did."

Amari looked at the paper one last time. "Well, he did try earlier, and I ran away from him. Maybe I shouldn't do that, especially when he's giving me a chance now."

Amari looked back down at the letter. "I guess I should take that chance, for an old friend."

With these words, Amari lowered the letter and looked out at the hallway.

#

I sat on the basketball court, my eyes sad and low as I peered down at my wristwatch. "Ugh! Where is he?", I said, annoyed. "It's almost twelve. Didn't he get my message?"

Confused, I looked up to the lights swinging above, the silence growing before speaking. "Maybe he did, he just doesn't want to come", I sighed. "Then again, I did say some pretty bad things to him. I wouldn't be here anyway."

Seeing that it was now two minutes from twelve, I rose from the bleachers, ready to leave the place until, above the bleachers, a door opened wide, revealing some light in from the darkness that was the gym.

It wasn't long before a figure made its way inside, the door shutting behind him. "Dom!", Amari called out, making me raise my head in surprise. "Amari?"

Amari gazed up at the bleachers, his eyes looking down at me before speaking. "Um, hey", I said, rubbing the back of my neck.

"Hey", Amari said, awkwardly. "I got your message, the one from my locker. It looked important."

I nodded. "Yeah, it was."

Amari nodded. There was an awkward silence afterward. "Do you want to sit down?"

"Yeah, sure."

With that, Amari made his way to the bleachers, sitting right down next to me. We sat for a few seconds, the silence becoming more awkward before I spoke. "Dom, if this is about the thing with the money, I really am sorry about that."

I shook my head in denial. "This isn't about the money, Mar."

"It's not", he said, confused. "Then what is it?"

Letting out a sigh, I gazed up at the light and speak. "I'm moving."

Amari's eyes widened. "Moving? To where?"

"To my mom's friend's house. Mom didn't have enough time to pay the eviction notice. So, she decided that I must move in with her. We also must move to a new school."

"School?", Amari said, now standing up. "Who said you were moving to a new school?"

"No", Amari said, shaking his head. "No, this isn't fair! You can't just move!"

"I know it's a lot to take in"

"Of course, it is! If it wasn't for me, you wouldn't even be in this mess! Ugh! I should've never taken that money from Ms. Wilkins!"

"Amari! It's just a few blocks away. We'll still live in St. Mora."

Amari paused, looking at me with a raised brow. "You're not?"

"No"

Amari let out a sigh of relief before speaking. "But you made it seem like you were going away!"

"Well, I'm not. I'm not going anywhere!"

With these words, Amari pulled me in for a tight hug before speaking. "I'm sorry, man. I'm so, so sorry! I never meant for any of this to happen! You're my best friend. There's no one who understands me like you do. Not even, Ms. Wilkins", he sighed. "After what she did to me, I cut her out of my life for good. He tried to take me away from you, I didn't realize it until you found out about the money. Dom, I know you hate me right now, but I want you to know that I will do whatever it takes to fix this."

"You don't need to make anything right for me, man. None of that matters anymore."

"Really?", he questioned.

"Yeah", I nodded. "Look, can we just put this whole thing behind us? Move on."

He smiled. "Sounds good to me."

With the fire distinguished and our rift now mended, a small rumble conjured in the pit of my stomach. "Damn"

"What is it?"

I touched the center of my stomach, facing Amari. "I'm starving. Like, really bad."

Amari let out a laugh. "Well, let's get to the cafeteria."

#

Amari dipped a French fry into a slab of ketchup, the red tomato sauce smeared against the plastic paper like a paintbrush, before lifting it and into his mouth, chewing softly as he did. I sat across from him, my mouth stuffed with a cheeseburger.

By the looks of it, we were having a good meal together. Just two boys sharing a meal together, just like old times.

Things could never be better.

That is, until *they* came.

Turning a corner, Amanda and her two "Ride or Die" girls were found behind her, walking in their casual "cool girls" walk. It wasn't long before they approached me and Amari, our mouths still stuffed with food, before turning our eyes to her.

She wore her shades, the same shades she had when she first encountered us. Only this time, she took them right off. "Hello, boys."

Amari rolled his eyes, accompanied by my grimacing face. We both looked at Amanda Griffin, who stared down at us with wide grins. "Hi."

"What do you want?", I speak. "Are you going to tell us to move, that we're sitting in the wrong seat?"

"Oh, no. I just thought I'd come and visit."

"Well, you're welcome is overstayed. Now leave."

Amanda grunt. "Can't yo-"

"Dom?", says Amari, making his way to the table with a tray in his hand. "Sorry, I'm late. I was getting some of that pudding for-", Amari's eyes lowered as she saw the girl standing before him. "What is she doing here?"

"Nothing, she was just leaving."

Amanda rolled her eyes. "I was just having a few words with him."

"Oh? Well, it seemed like you're all done now. So, shoo, shoo", Amari said, sitting down on the seat.

"I see you two are eating together. Must've patched things up."

"Yeah, we have. What's it to you?", I said.

"I hope you're happy and glad you have each other now because once graduation comes, it'll be the last time you'll ever see each other.

With these words, I slammed my hand against the table and made my way out of my seat, with Amari snatching my arm. "Dom, no!"

"No, Amari! She's been fooling with me all day, it's time I face her!"

Snatching my hand away, I turned from Amari and marched straight after Amanda, her girls making their way with her. "Hey, rich girl!"

Amanda gave a smile present. "Yes, peasant?"

"What's your problem?"

"What's *my* problem?! You're the one who's been taunting me!"

A group of students turned their heads to find the red-haired rich girl and the scruffy, curly-haired boy standing before each other.

"You started it back in the hallway!"

"That doesn't mean shit! You're just mad because I said it!"

"FIGHT, FIGHT, FIGHT!", shouted a crowd of students, surrounding Amanda and I as they chanted in unison. "What are they chanting about?"

"What do you think they're chanting about? They want us to fight!"

"Fight? You and me?"

"Yes!"

"But you're a girl, I can't hit a girl."

"Exactly!", Amanda brought her hand straight to my face, but before she could hit me, my head jerks the opposite direction, giving her nothing to punch but air. "Hold still!"

"No!"

"FIGHT, FIGHT, FIGHT!", the crowd cheered.

"Come on, everyone's waiting!"

"Well, they're going to have to wait a little longer because I'm not going to fight you! Plus, I'm getting a serious case of déjà vu right now!"

"Oh, really? Well, did your déjà vu predict you getting your teeth knocked out!", Amanda said, throwing a second punch, that I missed. "Maybe it did, but it didn't fix our problem!"

"The only problem was you seeing me as some self-absorbed thief when all I was trying to do was give you back your journal!"

"Give it a rest, will you! What I said, wasn't about you!"

"Then what is it? Just tell me!"

"Why are you so invested in my life right now! Are you that nosey, or are you just downright lonely? Do your parents not like you or something? I wouldn't be surprised since there's no one who likes to, let alone wants you!"

Amanda put her fist in the air and brought it right to my face, causing me to fall back in Amari's arms, his eyes wide with shock. "Oh shit, Dom!", Amari shouts, shaking me awake. "Dom, wake up!"

Scared, Amari looked up to Amanda and me. "He's out, *you* knocked him out!"

Several heads in the cafeteria turned to each other, whispering and gasping as they crowded Amanda and the two boys. As for her "Ride or Die" girls, they turned their heads and stormed out of the cafeteria, leaving Amanda all alone. "You guys, get back here!"

Amanda only had two words for this situation, and that was this: "Oh, crap."

#

An ambulance rode a few blocks down the road, all the way up to Summit High.

When I came again, I was in a hospital bed, hooked to a strange beeping machine. Confused, I turned to the left, where my mother sat next to me, her face buried in my hand that she held tight. "Mom?", I said, causing my mom to raise her eyes at me, mascara running down her face as she gaped. "You're awake!"

"Yeah, Mom, what are yo-", My words were quickly cut off as Mom pulled me in for a hug. "You scared me!"

"Wait, what?"

"I got a phone call today telling me that you got into a fight with some girl! I was so scared that you were covered in bruises or had your face swollen up!", Mom let out a sigh of relief. "At least now you're safe."

I nodded. "Yeah, I'm fine. Really, I'm fine, but that "fight" we had wasn't just a fight, it was just an argument."

Mom raised a brow. "An argument with who?"

"Amanda, that's the girl who, well, knocked me out", I said, rubbing the back of my neck. "So, I guess it kind of was a fight, one-sided if anything."

Mom blinked, in confusion. "Joana!", someone called.

Hearing this, Mom turned, her eyes full of disappointment. "I must go back to work. I'll come to check up on you later."

I nodded. "Okay, Mom. See you later."

With a slight kiss on my forehead, Mom took her hand away from my cheek, her back completely turned before leaving the room.

As for me, I lay back on the bed, my head resting on the soft, fluffy fabric of the pillow. But as soon as I do, a set of footsteps are heard, entering my room. "How are you feeling?"

I raised my brow. "Mom are you back already?", I said, raising my eyes up to the dizzy redhead with roses in her hands. "Mom? Oh no, it's me", she said.

I lowered my eyes in anger before speaking. "Amanda!", I said, shocked.

Amanda raised her hand and waved at me. "Hi, Dominic", she said, with a half-smile.

Chapter 5: Moving Day

I lied in my bed, my eyes gazing up at the ceiling.

Green eyes.

Frizzy hair.

Cherry red lips.

That's the first thing I remember.

That kiss.

That sudden, impulsive kiss.

It happened so fast, and I couldn't get it out of my head. Although it all happened yesterday, the thought still plagued my mind. I just wished there was something that could make me stop.

Luckily, my prayers were answered as there was a knock on my door. "Dominic, hurry up. The bus is almost here."

Hearing this, I raised my head up from my pillow before turning my eyes to the set of packed boxes that were in my empty room.

#

I made my way out of the house, with a large box in my arms before entering the parking lot, where Mom and Aunt Sue were stacking a set of boxes on the back of a U-Haul truck.

Seeing this, I quickly made my way up to them both, my smile big and present as I approached Mom. "Here you go, Mom", I said, handing the box to her. "This is the last box of clothes."

"Thank you, Dominic", Mom took, the box, shooting me a raised brow, much to my confusion. "What?"

Mom shook her head. "Nothing. It's just that you took a very long time to come out here. Is there something bothering you?"

"What?", my eyes lit up, shaking my head nervously. "Um, no."

Mom raised a brow. "Are you sure?"

"Yeah, I just…", I put my head behind my back, rubbing it simultaneously before turning back to the house. "Can't believe we're moving."

Hearing this, Mom's looked confused, making a sad frown. "I know, baby", Mom said, pulling me close. "It seems only yesterday your father and I moved into this house."

My head lowered in sadness, hearing these words. "You miss him. Don't you?"

Mom nodded. "Everyday"

I took Mom's hand. "It's going to be okay, Mom."

"I know. It's not every day you find good people to help you."

I lowered my head, my eyes peering down the ground. "Speaking of help, where's Aunt-I mean, Sue?"

"She's calling the movers. She and them'll be here soon."

Mom gazed up at the yellow bus making its way up the road in the distance, making her wipe a bit of her eyes before speaking. "You should get onto school. The bus will be here."

"What?", I said, looking in Mom's direction. "Oh, right", I said, lifting my bag over my shoulder before kissing Mom on the cheek. "See after school, Mom."

"I'll pick you up right after school!"

"Alright!", I waved, running straight towards the door.

#

The hallways of Junior High were flooded with students, with many of them hugging, high-fiving, and gossiping with one another.

Speaking of students, Amari and I were making our way to the lockers, our frowns low and dull as we made our way to the lockers. "Man, I can't believe you're leaving tomorrow", said Amari, making me nod. "Yeah, it seems so surreal. If only Mom had paid the eviction notice, none of this would've happened."

"Bet", Amari opened the locker that he had now approached.

I opened my locker as well, taking a set of books out. "What time are the movers coming?", Amari asked.

"Around eight. Mom and I already got the boxes packed."

Amari sighs in sadness, much to my dislike. "This sucks, man."

"I know, but this is just the way things are."

"Well, the way things are stinks. I mean, what am I going to do without you?"

"That's what I should say."

Amari laughed, easing his sadness. "I guess you're right."

Hearing this, I placed my hand on Amari's shoulder. "Hey, man. This ain't the end. You and I can still write letters. We can still communicate; we can make it work."

"I don't want it to work, Dom. I just want us to be together. I don't want us to be apart."

I sighed. "I know, man, but we don't have a choice. We're moving tomorrow, there's nothing we can do about this. I would need a miracle for that."

Hearing this, Amari looked up at his friend. "Do you believe in miracles?"

I blinked, my eyes low. "I do", I shake my head, "but not now."

With these words, Amari slammed his locker shut, his eyes full of fire. "Remind me to not be there for you when you move."

"Amari!", Dom called out as Amari made his way down the hallway alone. "Amari!", I called out again, but Amari was already too far down the hall.

With a deep sigh, I grabbed the rest of my books from the locker before closing it shut. Little did I know, I found a dizzy redhead, *the* dizzy redhead, her smile big and bright. "Hi, Dominic!"

"Oh!", I said, turning to Amanda in shock. "Um, hi Amanda", I said, confused, "Um, were you standing there the whole time?"

Amanda giggles, her smile big and bright. "Oh, not long."

I rubbed the back of my neck, feeling awkward because of the silence between Amanda and me. "Well, I should get to class. Wouldn't want to be late."

"Hold on, Dominic!", Amanda said, grabbing my arm, and bringing me back to the moment between us. "You're avoiding me."

Hearing this, I let out a heavy sigh before speaking. "Well, what do you expect? I mean, you just pulled me right in."

Amanda nodded. "Yeah, I know."

"Why did you do that? Do you like me?"

Amanda twisted her fingers from her hair before speaking. "Maybe", she says, her eyes gazing up from the floor. "What about you? Do you like me?"

Rubbing the back of my neck, I thought about yesterday's "incident" between Amanda and me, not just the incident but our talk, the deep conversation we had under the stars. That special, peaceful moment we had, just me and Amanda. Us and no one else.

Now, he had to sum it all up into one word. Only, they weren't "yes", it was: "No"

Amanda gave me a confused look. "What?"

"I mean, I like you, but not like that. I don't like you in that way, Amanda."

Amanda put her hair over her head. "So, you just see me as a friend?"

"That's how I'll kind of always see you", I looked back down at the force. "Especially when I move."

Amanda raised her head, her eyes lit up. "Move?"

"Yeah, my mom forgot to pay her eviction notice and now we have no choice but to leave for the country."

"The city? With the bugs and the trees?"

"Yeah."

"But that's not fair."

"Yeah, well, neither is life, but I don't think you understand, Amanda, coming from money."

Amanda widened her eyes in shock. She wanted to say something but quickly stopped. "Today is the last day you and I'll be able to see each other. I'm glad I got to know you. Goodbye, Amanda.", I reached my hand out to her, wanting her to shake goodbye.

She took my hand and shook it firmly.

As soon as I let go, I lifted my backpack over my shoulder before making my way down the hallway, leaving Amanda in utter sadness.

\#

Later that day, I was back home. My home, what was once a home thriving with love and happiness, was now an empty, hollow shell of boxes with furniture inside. Soon, the box is closed, and Aunt Sue, wearing a wide smile, used tape over it. "Alright, that's the last of 'em."

With these words, Sue turned her eyes back to the rest of the taped-up boxes. It isn't long before she realized she is all alone.

Joana, who was sitting in a small closet, was peering down a brown box.

Without thinking, Joana reached and pulled out a paintbrush, an old, dirty paintbrush covered in dry paint varying from blue to orange. Analyzing the brush, Joana ran her hand over the two initials on the brush: **O.M.**

Joana touched the letter, her fingers tracing against the wooden surface, but before she could do it anymore, she heard her name from behind her. "Joana?"

Shocked, Joana turned to see Sue Anne. "Oh, sorry, I didn't mean to scare you."

Joana shook her head. "You didn't scare me."

Sue raised a brow. "Are you sure? You got a little jumpy there. Are you okay?"

"Yeah, I was just looking at something."

"At what?"

"Oh, just some old belongings"

"Um, okay. Well, could you help me get some more stuff out to the car"

"Sure thing", Joana said, putting her "belongings" back in the blue box before closing it shut. "Don't you want to take the box with you?"

"Um, no. I decided to leave it here until tomorrow. Come on, let's go."

With these words, Joana made her way out of the closet, but before Sue could leave, she turned her eyes back to the box that sat on the front shelf. Concerned, Sue switched off the light, leaving the closet in total darkness.

#

Summit High's cafeteria was full of children, with many of them laughing, shouting and gossiping as teenagers do. I sat at a table in the farther part of the place, my eyes peering down at the cheeseburger and fries.

I wasn't eating it, not one bite.

As you can tell, I was upset.

I was moving, my best friend wanted nothing to do with me, and there was nothing I could do to change it.

My life was falling apart.

Things went from bad to worse in just a few days.

Of all the bad things that could happen, it couldn't have happened like on the day of my graduation. But no, it happened at the very start, the very beginning of my senior year and I hate it!

There was no worse time than it is now. I just wish I had someone to share my sorrows with.

I wish I had a miracle.

"Dom?", I heard, which caused me to turn my head back to see Amari, standing over me, his eyes sad and low. "Hey, can I sit here?"

Without a second thought, I nodded. "Yeah"

With these words, Amari, my best friend, sat across from me with his tray of spaghetti. The both of us were left in an awkward silence, with Amari poking his fork in his spaghetti. "I'm sorry, man", he said, making my eyes lit up. "Sorry? What are you sorry for?"

"For being stupid, for not being there when you need me, especially currently. I was being selfish and I'm sorry. Can you forgive me?"

"I already forgive you, man."

"Really? Even after everything I did?"

"Amari, you're my best friend. There's nothing that can make me too mad nor too sad to make me hate you, especially now. I'm just glad I get to have my best friend here with me."

With these words, Amari gave me a warm, happy smile and spoke. "I'm glad you're here too, man. Hey, why don't you and I do something today."

"Like what?"

"Like one last day, like to do whatever you and I want to do together."

"You mean like one last adventure."

Amari nodded. "Yeah. What do you want to do for your last day in St. Mora?"

I put my hand up to my chin, thinking long and hard. That is, until I looked far in the distance, and I saw Nomi, with her adorable freckles and brown eyes, making her way over to the table with her tray of hamburgers and fries. I smiled at her, my eyes full of rainbows. "Dom?", Amari said, causing me to look down. "You, okay?"

I smiled. "I know what I want to do?"

"Really? What is it?"

My face turned red. "I want to ask Nomi out."

Amari laughed. "No, seriously, what is it?"

I scoffed. "I'm serious, Mar. For my last day, I *want* to ask Nomi out, that's what I want."

Amari raised his brow. "Are you sure? I mean, what if she says no?"

"I don't care about that. I just want to get over this fear. After all, it is the only chance I get."

Amari smiled. "Yeah, this is the only chance. There's no better time than now. Okay, let's do it."

"Really? You want to do it?'

"Yeah, if this is what you want, then do it, man. I'll be right there beside you."

"Thanks, Amari", I said, smiling.

\#

Amanda sat in her class, her eyes gazing up to the ceiling as she looked out at the ceiling. As she was, her English teacher was teaching his students of the lecture of King Macbeth, a once poor peasant who stopped at nothing to get the one thing he needed most: power.

As for Amanda, she was not all ears for it. For her mind was elsewhere.

Somewhere.

In St. Mora, where a handsome, curly-haired boy awaited her.

Yet this was no ordinary boy, for this boy had problems.

Money problems.

Even when she wasn't paying attention to her instructor giving the lecture, it didn't mean she wasn't listening. Much like Macbeth, he had them, too, as he was poor and did whatever it took to get what he so rightfully deserved.

What Dominic deserved.

With this in mind, Amanda peered down into her notebook and wrote down something that would help her: **DAD.**

\#

Summit High's public library was filled with students, many of whom were found sitting at desks, their eyes glued to the pages of their books. Some of them stood and some waited patiently in a line just to order a book.

Yes, everyone was busy doing something, all except for the two boys who stood at the very center of the library, their eyes full of confusion as they looked left and right.

"You sure she's here?", I said, turning to a nodding Amari. "Yeah, they said she was."

"And who's *they*?"

"A few guys I met. I asked them if they were friends with Nomi Scott and if they knew where she was. Unfortunately, they were more acquaintances than friends, but they knew exactly where she was, and that was the castle of books. So, here we are."

"The library"

"Yeah"

"Are you sure she didn't leave the moment we got here?"

"What, no? From what those guys told me, Nomi loves the library, she would stay in the books all day when she had the time, and that time is now. So, no, man, we're not too late."

"Mm, okay", I nod, my eyes full of hope.

Amari turns his head to the left once more before a soft gasp leaves him, his eyes wide with shock before answering. "Dom, Dom!", Amari whispered.

"What, what?", I said, looking in Amari's direction. "There she is."

Looking far in the distance, I saw Nomi sitting all alone at a table, her eyes peering down at her book, all with a set of headphones covering her ears. "See?"

I nodded, smiling. "Yeah, I see her."

"Well, what are you waiting for? Go get her!"

With these words of encouragement, I took a deep breath and made my way across the room. Nomi's freckles grew the closer I got. It wasn't before I approached her that I saw she had not only headphones but glasses, *reading* glasses, I assumed. Probably to help her see the words on the book, whatever that was.

Coming up to her, I let out a small cough. "Um, excuse me, Nomi?"

Nomi didn't hear me, as her head slowly bobbed to the loud, booming music she was listening to. Seeing this, I brought my hand to the table and knocked on the wooden surface, alerting Nomi. "Hi", I said, causing Nomi to let out a small "oh" before taking off her headphones, her smile big and bright. "I remember you. It's Dominic, right?"

I nodded. "Yeah, Dominic, Dominic Mitchell."

"Right, Mitchell", Nomi said before making a confused look. "Is there something I can help you with?"

I put my hand behind my back, my face red a bit, before nodding. "Actually, there is", I turned my eyes back to Amari, his head peeking behind a bookshelf. He smiled and gave me two thumbs up, mouthing a quick: *You got this.*

"Um, Nomi, there's something I've been wanting to ask you for a minute now."

Nomi moved her book away from her before gazing up at me. "Okay, what is it?"

Exhaling, I looked at Nomi. "Um, I was wondering if you wanted to, I don't know, maybe see a movie with me tonight? Possibly?"

Hearing this, Nomi's eyes lit up, causing a small yet bashful smile to form. "Um, that's real sweet of you, but I already have plans to go to the movies with my boyfriend."

My face fell flat, disappointed even. "Oh, really?"

"Babe!", said a voice, causing Nomi to turn her head around and smile. "Hey!", Nomi said, wrapping her arms around what looked to be a buff jock.

It was at that moment; I knew what was happening. Soon, Nomi pulled away from the buff jock and turned back to me, looking quite embarrassed. "Oh, sorry. Where are my manners? Dominic, this is Paul, my boyfriend", Nomi turned to Paul. "Paul, this is Dominic, a friend from my French class."

A friend?

A sharp knife cut straight through my chest, causing me to fall right down on my knees before collapsing on the floor, bleeding out.

Just kidding, it was all in my head, but it sure as hell felt real. "Nice to meet you, man", answered Paul, reaching his hand out to me.

I quickly took his hand, squeezing it firmly. "Woah, strong grip", Paul said, pulling away. "Yeah. Well, I should probably get going now. It was nice talking to you, Nomi."

Nomi, with her boyfriend's arm grabbing her waist, made a half smile before nodding. "Nice talking with you too, Dom."

With that, I made one final nod. "Enjoy the movie, guys", I said, walking away but not before turning my head back to Nomi, whom to my surprise, was pulled right in for a kiss, which she quickly returned as I walked away.

It wasn't long before I walked past a bookshelf, where Amari's head quickly came up from behind. "So?", he said, eyeing me. "What happened?"

"See for yourself."

Amari turned to see my crush in the arms of a buff, heavyweight jock, making out. "Oh, shit", Amari said, turning back to me. "Sorry, man"

"It's okay", I sighed sadly. "I mean, as much as I like her, I can't help but think that she loves someone else."

Amari nodded. "Yeah"

I sighed again before Amari wrapped his arms around me. "Hey, don't sweat it, man. After all, you know what they say: there's plenty more fish in the sea"

I nodded, smiling a bit more. "Yeah, I guess you're right."

"The right girl will come. Just give it time."

With this said, the bell rang, causing the two boys to gaze up at the ceiling before laughing. "Looks like it's that time of day again, man."

"Yep. Race you to the bus!"

"No, you won't!"

A black telephone stood at the edge of the bed, inches away from the dizzy redhead that sat crisscrossed applesauce. Amanda looked at the phone nervously as she waited for the phone to ring. That is, until her bedroom door opened wide, causing her to jump in fear. Butler Barry with a tray of food in his hand. "Sorry to interrupt you, madam. I was just bringing your dinner up."

"You didn't interrupt anything, Barry. Just place the tray on my bed."

Barry nodded. "Indeed, madam."

Amanda's eyes remained glued to the telephone while her dinner rested next to her. She didn't take a bite of it as the only thing she bit was her nails. "Ms. Griffin are you alright?", Barry asked, concerned.

But Amanda just nodded. "Yeah, I'm fine."

"Are you sure? You seem nervous?"

Amanda continued to chew her nails before the realization kicked in, causing her to take her fingers from her mouth and sigh. "I *am* nervous", she said, now turning to Barry. "I'm waiting for a phone call from Dad. "Waiting for a phone call? Have you called him yet?"

"Yes, I sent him a message and everything, but that was two hours ago. I've been sitting here waiting since."

Hearing this, Barry laughed. "Now, madam, there's no need to fret over your father. You know he's a very busy man."

"I know. I just wish he would, you know, pick up. I really need him right now."

"I'm sure he knows that, dear."

"Does he? If he knew, he could at least pick up the phone to see if I'm here, let alone alive!", Amanda sighed. "And what about Mom? Where's *she* when I need her?"

With these words, Barry pulled Amanda in for a warm, embracing hug. "I know how you feel, dear. Growing up, my mother and father, weren't there for me, too."

Amanda looked up at Barry, confused. "Really?"

Barry nodded.

Suddenly, the phone rang loudly, causing Amanda to take the phone up to her ears. "Hello?", Amanda's eyes widened in shock. "It's Dad!", she said, turning to Barry. "It's Dad, go! Go, go, go! I want to be alone!", Amanda continued to push Barry before he rose from the bed to leave. "Alright, alright! I'm leaving!"

Barry made his way out the bedroom door, closing it shut. Or so she thought but the door opened with a crack, with Barry's head peeking from behind, his smile big and present as he listened.

"Dad? Is that you?"

"Yes, sweetheart. It's me."

Amanda laughed happily. "It's so good to hear your voice again."

"It's good to hear you too, sweetheart. Is there anything I can do for you?"

"Yes. Um, do you still have any of those vacation homes left?"

#

"Dominic, Dominic!", said a voice, causing my eyes to open. "Dominic, wake up!"

"Wha-what?", I said, opening my eyes. "Mom?"

"Dominic, put your clothes on right now."

"What, why?"

"No time to explain, the landlord wants us out now."

What do you mean? Where are the movers?"

Mom looked at me dead in the eye before speaking. "They didn't come."

Mom and I made our way out of the house, shocked. Sue Anne was outside. "Aunt Sue, what's going on?", I said before I'm pulled in for a quick, tight hug. "I'm so sorry, ya'll. I'm so sorry!"

"Sorry, what are you sorry for?"

"The movers, they said they never came to my house. They had all the furniture, but they never came", Sue let out a sad sigh. "I'm so sorry. I didn't mean for any of this to happen."

"Nobody did, Sue", said my mother approaching her. "Don't blame any of this on yourself, Sue. It's not your fault. Whatever happened was probably some misunderstanding."

"Exactly"

Approaching us was an obese, fat guy with a cigar hanging from the edge of his mouth. "You guys have been sitting here for a good minute. Thought you'd be at your new house by now."

A scoff left Mom, followed by a small snarl. "We were asshole, but the movers never came."

Mr. Winslow, the landlord raised his brow, confused. "What do you mean? Yes, they did."

Mom scoffed. "No, they didn't."

"No, they *did*. The girl told me."

"What girl?", said, Sue Anne.

"The *girl,* the kid, the red hair", my eyes lit up hearing this. "She came by the house this morning and told me to take your furniture to the house. Come to think of it, she gave me the address. Here, let me get it for you", Winslow's eyes lit up at these words before reaching into his pocket to pull out a thin sheet of paper, and hold it out to him. "Here"

Confused, Mom made her way up to Winslow, snatching the paper right from his hands. On it was written: **2678 Winstor Street.**

"What's it says?", asked Sue Anne, joining in. "Is it my address?"

Mom shook her head in denial. "No, it's someone else's."

"Someone else's, what do you mean?"

"I don't know!", Mom grunted. "Is this some kind of joke?"

"What, no! I'm not playing with you at all!"

"Don't you bullshit me!"

"I'm no-"

"Mom!", I said, causing Mom and Aunt Sue to turn their heads. "He's not kidding. That address is real."

"How do you know?", asked, Amari.

"Because I know who that girl was and whatever that house is, that's where she wants us to go."

Hearing this, Mom turned, her eyes back to Landlord Winslow, who shrugged. "Listen to the kid, Joana"

"Shut up. You're the reason we're in this whole mess in the first place", Mom said and turned her head back to me. "Alright, let's go. Wherever this house is, our stuff is there."

With a quick nod, Mom, Amari, Aunt Sue, and I all ran straight to Sue Anne's car, shutting the doors behind us. But before Mom could enter, she turned to look back at her apartment one last time. Mr. Winslow, all alone with his cigar, walked back to the apartment. "Finally, some peace and quiet."

\#

"Are we there yet?", Amari whined from the backseat.

"We get there when we get there, kid!", Joana said, in the front seat. "Speaking of which, I don't even know why you came?"

"He's just here to support me, Mom."

"Why? It's not even family."

"He is to me", I brought my iPhone out to pull a digital map. "Make a sharp left here!"

"Now?"

"Yes, now!"

Shifting back to the road, Mom turned her steering wheel, swerving her van to the left.

I jerked in the seat, along with Amari, whose body jumped. "Sorry!", Mom said, making me shake my head. "It's fine. We should be at Winstor Steet in-"

"There it is!"

"The street?"

"No, our furniture!"

Turning to the right, Mom swerved her way up the parking lot, a very white, clean parking lot with a pocket fence.

As soon as the car stopped, the car opened wide causing the four of us to exit, Mom being the first to exit.

"Hey!", Mom said, running up towards the buff men, retrieving boxes from the truck. "HEY!"

Hearing this, the men turned, their heads back, their brows raised high as the angry black woman made her way to them. "What do you think you're doing with our furniture!?"

"I'm sorry?"

"Our furniture! This is my son's stuff now give it back!", Mom said, grabbing the box from his hand.

That done, Mom stopped to look at where we were. There was a lovely garden which was flourishing with purple and pink flowers and in front of her was a large, two-story house, along with several other lavish homes sitting right next to each other.

Without a second thought, Mom popped the lock of her car. Aunt Sue, Amari and I made our way out of the van, our eyes wide with awe as we looked. "Wow, this house is beautiful. Whose house is this?"

"Yours", said a familiar voice. It was Amanda, Amanda Griffin speaking. "Amanda?"

Amanda smiled happily at me. "Hi, Dominic"

"What are you doing here?"

"Yeah, what are you doing here?", said Amari heading in.

Amanda scoffs at Amari's taunt before speaking. "I'm here to welcome you."

"Welcome me where?"

"My home?"

"Yes, it's my dad's, well, *one* of my dad's. It's his vacation home. I'm sorry I didn't tell you sooner, I wanted it to be a surprise."

"I'm sorry, who are you?", said my mom, confused.

Hearing this, I turned my eyes to Mom before speaking. "Mom, this is-"

"Amanda. I'm a friend of your son's", Amanda lowered her eyes in sadness. "I'm also the one who took your furniture."

"Wait, *you* took our furniture?"

"Yes, I'm sorry about that. I wanted to surprise you."

"Surprise us with this house?"

"Yes, the movers are setting everything up now. Until then, would you like a tour?"

I blinked in confusion. "Um, I don't think-"

"Yes, we would love a tour!" said my mom, her eyes wide with excitement.

With a quick nod, Amanda turned her head back to us. "Well, come on then."

Amanda opened the doors to the house while Mom, Amari, Aunt Sue, and I entered. The place was huge, with various sets of rooms, the first one being a room full of lavish furniture, and a set of our furniture was placed by the movers. "This is the living room, where you'll have an ample amount of entertainment to your liking." Mom, Amari, and Aunt Sue wore excited faces, their smiles big and wide as they walked through.

As for me, my eyes were wide with shock. I didn't know what to feel. At that moment, all I felt was overwhelmed.

Turning to the left, Amanda took us to a room where a stove, oven, and refrigerator were found. "And this was the kitchen. You'd make all kinds of meals for breakfast, lunch, and dinner."

"Wow, this is beautiful."

It sure was, but also too much.

"Let me show you your rooms. I'm sure you'll be very pleased with what's inside."

"Oh, you don't have to give us a tour of that. We can see it for ourselves."

Amanda blinked. "Oh, okay. Well, they're across the hall to your left."

"Thank you. Come on, Dom!"

I rubbed the back of my neck, my expression still very much overwhelmed. "Actually, Mom. I'll let you guys go. I need a minute to take everything in."

"Are you sure, Dom?" said Amari.

"Yeah, man. I'll see you guys later."

Mom gave me a quick nod before speaking. "Okay, baby. Take your time." Mom turned her eyes back to Amari and Aunt Sue, her smile big and wide. "Come on, y'all!"

As for me, I turned my eyes to Amanda, who took quick notice of my unsettling look. "Dominic?" Amanda asked in confusion. "Are you okay?"

I shook my head. "No, I need to speak with you now!"

"Okay, where do you wa-ahhh!" Amanda said as I took her arm, gripping it tight before taking her out of the kitchen, into the hallway, to the front door of the house.

Amanda and I stopped dead on the porch, my hand now loosened from Amanda before answering. "Whose house is this?"

"What do you mean? It's yours."

"I know that. I mean, how did you get the money? Did you buy this house, or did someone else do this? Answer me now."

Hearing this, Amanda took a deep breath and spoke. "Okay, you want the truth? Well, here it is. This house is my father's, well, his twelfth house. He owns many more. This was just the one I picked."

I raised my brow. "So, what is this like, some vacation home?"

Amanda nodded. "Yes, one of them. My Dad offered it to you. He said you could stay in it if you'd like."

I blinked. "Wait, he said that?"

"Yes, I asked him."

"You asked him? Why would you do that?"

Amanda fiddled with her fingers before speaking. "Because…because I didn't want you to go. Maybe I couldn't bear the thought of you suffering. I mean, it's the least I could do after being such a jerk."

Hearing this, my confused, overwhelmed face quickly turned soft, revealing a happy smile to form across my face. "You're not a jerk, Amanda."

"I'm not?" Amanda said, gazing up at me where I shook my head. "No, you're amazing. Thanks to you, I have a glorious house. I don't have to leave my best friend behind. You changed my life for the better, and for that, I say thank you."

Hearing this, a happy smile formed across Amanda's face, causing her cheeks to light up red. "You're welcome, Dominic."

I smiled very happily. "I'll also give you something."

"What?"

"This!" Taking her face, I leaned in and kissed her.

Shocked, Amanda pulled away from me, her face now red. "But I thought you didn't like me?"

I smiled, my eyes full of life. "That's because I didn't know what I wanted then. Now, I do. I want you, Amanda. That is, if you still want me?"

Hearing this, Amanda made one of the happiest smiles in the world and nodded. "Of course, I do. Come here, baby!"

With the pull of my waist, Amanda pulled me in for the long-awaited kiss. At that very moment, we were no longer friends or rivals.

We were lovers.

Best of both worlds.

Part

II

Chapter 6: The Secret

I walked hand in hand with Amanda in the halls of Summit High, our smiles visible from miles away.

Like when we walked down the hallway, hand in hand. As you would guess, many people judged or "booed" at us, but we didn't care.

There was nothing wrong with a guy and his girl holding hands. We did a lot.

I had always thought having a girlfriend would be too much of a hassle, but I realized it was fun. I had someone I could talk to and share my deepest secrets with. If anything, it was kind of like having a second-best friend.

With our hands still intertwined, Amanda and I turned a corner, but as soon as we did, we saw a boy with dreads descending the hallway; not long after, he raised his head and saw me. "Yo, Dom!"

Shocked, Amanda turned away from me, her back wholly turned as she hid behind one of the lockers. I gave a quick nod, mouthing a quick "Stay there" before nodding at Amari.

I turned back and found Amari approaching me. "Hey, man. I was looking for ya. Where you been?"

My eyes lit up in shock. "Oh, I was just catching up on some homework," I nodded.

"You were? Where?"

"The library. Yeah, I did a ton of work there now."

Amari shrugged his shoulders a bit before speaking. "Okay. Well, check it, man: there's this new arcade in town. It opens up tomorrow. You want to check it out?"

"Um…" I glanced back at Amanda, who was still very much hiding, before nodding. "Yeah, man. Yeah, sounds like fun."

Amari nodded, his smile big and bright. "Cool, I'll hit you up as soon—" Amari's words were quickly cut off as the school bell rang, causing Amari's eyes to roll in annoyance. "Looks like it's that time of day again."

I nodded. "Yep."

"Yeah…" Amari breathed before turning his eyes straight to me. "Alright, man. We'll talk about it more after class, okay?"

"Okay, man! See ya!"

With those words, Amari went down the hallway, his back completely turned as he headed to class.

"Is he gone?" asked Amanda, peeking her head out from behind the lockers.

I nodded. "Yeah."

Amanda mouthed a quick "Good" before making her way up to me. "You know you can't protect him forever."

"What are you talking about?" I turned to her, my brow raised.

"I'm talking about *us,* Dominic. You can't just keep hiding from me whenever you see your friend walk into the room. Sooner or later, you're going to have to tell him about this."

I sighed. "Amanda, you know I can't do that. Knowing Amari, he can be sensitive, especially when it comes to change. If I told him about us, he'd be two seconds from a nervous breakdown! Besides, I know how you feel about each other."

Amanda nodded. "I guess you're right."

My eyes shifted from Amanda to Amari, who was now making his way down the hallway. "I'll tell him when I'm ready. Until then, I will keep this a secret, for Amari."

#

A set of tomatoes sat on a cutting board, the sharp knife chopping them into little minced bits. Panning up, we found Joana cutting them, her smile big and happy as she hummed a sweet, somber tune of "Baby, be mine" before another white woman made her way over her.

"What are you humming there, Joana?", asked Sue, making her way past her with a basket of bread to her. "Oh, I was just humming a little song I used to sing back in the day."

"Really, what is it?"

"Oh, nothing serious. Well, it's kind of is being so darn happy!", Joana laughed.

"I bet you. If it weren't for that girl, you wouldn't be in this amazing house."

"Which is why we're throwing her this party to thank her."

"We sure are", Sue sat on the basket of rolls at the front counter. "Hm, I wonder if she'll like the food. Being a rich kid, I'd probably expect her to be stuck up about it."

"Stuck up", Joana scoffed "Maybe for getting dirty but not for food. No one can be stuck up for a hardy, good meal. Especially when it's made by the best!", Joana said, holding up the bowl of salad, with tomato toppings were found. "Besides, real dinner is better than no dinner."

"You got that right. I don't care how rich the kid is she had better be happy she's getting a meal."

"Exactly"

#

Amanda sat at the end of the stairs, her eyes looking lazily down at her pink, polished fingernails. She continued looking at them before the footsteps were heard from behind. "Amanda?", said a voice.

Turning her head, Amanda saw me standing above her in my casual black leather jacket, a white shirt, and blue jeans. "Are you okay?", I asked, concerned.

But Amanda just smiled. "Of course, I am."

I blink, confused. "Are you sure? I got a call from the principal's office saying you had an emergency and needed me to come immediately."

"There is, there is, but there isn't."

I raised my brow. "What do you mean?"

Without saying a word, Amanda took my hand and led me down the hall, the both of us becoming small little dots in the distance.

It wasn't long before we found ourselves standing before a small, narrow closet that Amanda quickly opened. We found a mop, a broomstick, and a shelf full of various cleaning products sitting above.

"The Janitor's closet?", I said, turning my eyes back to Amanda. "This is the emergency?"

"What? No, *this* is the surprise."

"Surprise? What's so surprising about the janitor's closet?"

"I'll show you."

With these words, Amanda pushed me straight into the closet, my back against the wall, as Amanda closed the door behind her. As soon as she did, Amanda grabbed hold of my face, her lips smacked right into mine as I leaned farther into the cleaning utensils behind me.

"Amanda!", I said, pulling away in shock. "What are you doing?"

"What do you mean? This is the surprise I was telling you about."

I gave Amanda a confused look before speaking. "Amanda, you pulled me out of a math class, the moment when I was taking one of the most difficult tests in history, all so you could have a make-out session with me?", I said in anger, one that was quickly short-lived as a momentous grin was found. "You're the best girlfriend I could ever have! Come here, you!"

I grabbed Amanda by the waist, her smile big and wide as I pulled her in for a kiss, continuing our make-out session.

That is, until the school bell rang, causing the dream to be a hellish nightmare. "Ugh, great!", Amanda said, annoyed. "That damn bell!"

"Hey, don't worry, babe. We'll have our time", I said, pulling her, my girlfriend, close. "When? This was the perfect time for us to make out. When are we going to get another chance like this?"

I glanced down. "Maybe at that new arcade."

"Arcade?", Amanda said, gazing up at me. "What arcade?"

"Oh, nothing. Just someplace I promised Amari we would go to after school."

"After school?", Amanda chuckled. "Aren't we supposed to attend that dinner party tonight?"

"I promised Mom I'd be home before then. Besides, it's not just a dinner party, it's a coming out party as well."

Amanda nodded. "I don't think you telling your mom about us is considered coming out?"

"It is when I tell her what girl I'm dating. Who just so happens to be the hottest girl in the school."

Amanda made a cute yet sexy smile before leaning into my lips, but before she could kiss me, the door to the janitor's closet opened, causing the both of us to turn our heads, our eyes wide as a fat yet very tall man stood before us. "What the hell are you two doing here?"

Without a second thought, Amanda and I ran out of the janitor's closet, our hands held tight as we ran down the hallway, leaving the janitor. "Yeah and stay out!"

\#

A slab of mashed potatoes, peas, and meatloaf was slammed down onto Amari's lunch tray, his eyes full of life as he gazed up at the wrinkly, old lunch lady seen before him, her eyes gazing right at him before answering. "What Cha smiling' for, boy? Can't ya see your holding' up the line?"

Amari nodded. "I do, but I see that you're missing something?"

"Oh, really?", the lady said, folding her arms. "And what's that?"

Taking his hand from his tray, Amari reached into his pocket and retrieved a red rose before handing it to the lunch lady. "For you, Mrs. Miller."

Mrs. Miller smiled happily as she retrieved the rose. "Oh, Amari. This is beautiful."

"I thought you could use something happy."

Mrs. Miller smiled happily, bringing the red flower to her. "Thank you."

"You're welcome", Amari brought his tray up to his chest and spoke. "You have a good day, ma'am."

With these words, Amari made his way to the lunch tables, leaving Ms. Miller with a big smile.

As for me, I had a huge frown on my face, my eyes full of terror as I watched my best friend make his way to the lunch table, sitting straight down in his seat before digging into his meal.

Standing in the distance, Amanda and I stood at the place, our eyes full of fear as we watched. "There he is", I said, standing next to Amanda.

"He's waiting for you. You should go before he sees us."

I sighed at those words. "I hate that we have to do this."

"I know, baby, but we don't have a choice", she turned to me. "Unless you're thinking about telling him.

"No, not yet. Not until I'm ready."

Amanda let out a quick sigh. "Then I guess we're sitting at separate tables."

I nodded. "I guess we are."

"See you afterwards"

"See you"

With these words, my girlfriend and I split, going in separate directions as I made my way down the tables.

Amari, who was sitting at the table, dug his face in the mashed potatoes with a mixture of his peas, nibbling them one by one, much to Amari's delight. "Mm, these potatoes are slamming'! Mrs. Miller really put her foot into this one."

"Whose foot?", said a voice, causing Amari to gaze up at me. "Hey, Dom! I was starting to worry."

"Worry?", I said, sitting down in my seat. "Yeah, you took a minute to come here, were you busy with something?"

"Um…", I looked to the left at Amanda, who was munching on the same mashed potatoes and peas, shooting me a quick wink before returning to her tray. "Yeah, just some homework."

"You've had a lot of homework lately?"

"You know me, I'm a studious student."

"Not to mention overachiever", Amari scoffed.

"Yep"

With the scoop of my spoon, I brought a set of mashed potatoes to my mouth, but Amari spoke up before I could eat. "So, what do you think is going to be at this new arcade?"

"What?"

"The arcade, the one we're going to after school?", Amari raised his brow. "You didn't forget, did you?"

"What, no? I just don't really think they'll be much."

"Why is that?"

"Well, it may be a new arcade, but the same stuff, the same games, the same prizes, and the same pizza."

"Hey, don't go against arcade pizza. Arcade pizza is the best pizza."

I laughed. "Tell that to Chuckie Cheese."

Amari tilted his head a bit before nodding. "Yeah, you might be right about."

"Besides, the only thing I'm actually interested in is just getting to spend time with you, Amari."

Amari smiled, his eyes big and bright. "Me too, man", Amari brought his hand up to me, shaping it into a fist. "Bros?"

Without a second thought, I raised my fist to Amari's, our knuckles touching. "Bros."

#

Meanwhile at home, the *new* home, stood proud and tall as the rest of the suburban homes that stood side by side with one another. Inside, a set of boxes were found, many of them opened wide. All except for the one where the curly-haired woman in pink sat.

Opening it wide, Joana found a set of items: a shaver, a two-comb, a two-sided brush, and hair gel. Confused, Joana lowers her eyes where she finds the box, with a set of words written in bold: **Hair Products.**

It wasn't long before Joana let out a scoff. "Dominic."

Joana reached for her hand and put it into the box, pulling out several of the hair products. Yet, it wasn't until she reached the hair gel that she found something else, something new.

Peering down, Joana noticed a brown journal on the bottom of the box. Confused, she reached into the box, retrieved the journal, and opened it wide.

She flipped through several pages, many of them blank. That is, until a set of words written in bold, black letters jumped at her, much to Joana's confusion.

Seeing this, Joana looked to find a date written on the top right corner of the journal: *December 25, 1996.*

Christmas Day the year before.

"Nineteen ninety-six", Joana said, lowering the journal. "That was last year. Why would Dominic keep a journal of last year?"

Christmas. They say it's the happiest time of year, when families and friends come together and celebrate being together. But not for us, not this year, because this year would be the fourteenth birthday without Dad.

I know that sounds silly, especially since I have never met him. I mean, I was just a baby when it happened, and ever since then, Mom hasn't been the same. There are days when she was fine and days when she wasn't, with Christmas being one of them.

Christmas was Dad's favorite holiday, and not because of God but because of the feeling in the air. From what my mom says, Christmas was a magical time when Dad was around, and when he was around, everything was better.

But ever since the "incident," the magic faded without warning. Now, Mom spends Christmas alone in her room, with a bottle of wine at her side. It wasn't long before I found her in a drunk stupor. Before I know it, I'm spending Christmas alone, with no presents, no special dinner, just me and putting my mom to bed.

As sad as I thought Halloween was, I'm starting to rethink that situation: with no mother or Father, Christmas is the worst day of the year, that being this year! Let's just pray that New Year's will be better for now; that's all there is.

For those who have better lives, have a merry Christmas and a happy, joyous new year.

A small tear fell on the "r" of year, followed by a few sniffles, her eyes full of sorrow as she sobbed. It wasn't long before the sound of footsteps entered the room, along with a dark shadow creeping up behind her. "Hey, Joana?"

Joana turned around to find Sue Anne standing at the door with a cookbook in her hand. "Do you know where I can find the whisk? I need it to make these brownies, and I can't seem to fi—" Sue Anne's words were quickly cut off as Sue Anne saw the tears running down Joana's face. "Hey, are you okay?"

Without saying anything, Joana rose from the floor and rushed to her best friend, hugging her tight as she sobbed. "Hey, hey! Joana, what's wrong?", she said, the cookbook now out of her hand and onto the floor.

Joana continued to sob. Not wanting to say anything anymore, Sue pulled Joana in for a hug, and they both fell to their knees as they embraced.

#

I sat in my class, my eyes full of boredom as I listened to my geography teacher, who showed us various slide shows of his adventures in the wild. He stood next to the board, a joystick in his hand, as he looked at the screen of the smiling man with a set of snakes surrounding him.

"And this is where I visited Cancun."

He flipped to another slide where he stood on a mountain. "And this was me at the Grand Canyon."

The third slide featured him in the mountains, completely covered in ice. "And this was me at Mount Everest."

Many students in the class watched in awe at the sight of this. As for me, my eyes were dull and sad as I gazed out at the window, thinking.

Thinking of Amari.

Was I doing the right thing?

Was keeping this secret from him worth it?

I mean, I'm only doing it to protect his feelings, but is that really the best thing to do? I know how he feels about Amanda, if I told him about us, all hell would break loose.

Or that's what I thought.

Maybe, it was just all in my head.

Maybe Amari would be a bit mature about Amanda and I dating.

And maybe, just maybe, Amanda and he could learn to be friends.

We *all* could be friends.

"Yeah, maybe we could."

The bell rang, causing me to snap out of my head and Mr. Duff out of his show. "Aw, man. I was just about to show you guys-", he said, annoyed.

"Curse that bell. Alright, have a great weekend. Study hard, and I'll see you guys on Monday."

Grabbing my backpack, I rose from my desk and made my way out of the class, along with several of my fellow classmates following behind me.

Passing a group of boys, I made my way to the lockers, where Amari had his back against the lockers and his arms folded. "Hey, there, Sophomore. Ready to have some fun?"

"You bet I am!", I said, high-fiving Amari before wrapping my hand around his neck.

Amari and I headed through the doors of Summit High down the stairs, and out to the road.

Yet, little did we know, a dizzy redhead was watching us, her head peeking from the door as we headed down the road.

#

In the farther part of St. Mora, far from the traffic and the loud horns, was an arcade with neon lights: *FUN ZONE!*

"Welcome to the Fun zone!", Amari said.

"Those lights are pretty large", I said.

"Yeah, well, the inside is just as big. Come on, let's go!"

"Alright!"

With these words, Amari and I ran through the doors, our hopes big and high. Yet, little did we know, a mysterious figure with red hair was found standing outside the area as the two boys went inside.

As I was saying, Amari and I had high hopes. We couldn't wait until we beat each other at Mario Bros, shot each other with laser tag, and jumped into the giant ball pit of Doom! It was going to be the best day ever!

Or so we thought, when we came through the doors, that our hopes were gone.

"Fun zone, here we are—", Amari's words were quickly cut off as his eyes grew big and wide, along with his smile.

Before his very eyes, Amari found a Fun-Zone, only there was nothing "fun" about it. Before the two of us, there were thousands of children, not teenagers, but children, ages 5-9, running around.

What we thought were countless rows of video games, turned out to be baby sets of basketball. As for the laser tag, it was nothing but plastic guns, with water shooting from them, the children laughing as they played with each other.

But that wasn't even the worst part. What we thought was the Ball Pit of Doom, turned out to be a small, kitty pool of colorful balls where a whole group of children jumped, their hands raised as they threw the balls at one another.

Amari and I witness all of this with nothing but angry frowns.

Our hopes were low, and our disappointments high.

"Is *this* an arcade? Is this Fun Zone?"

"I know I'm not trippin'? They said specifically that this place was for teenagers!"

"Do you see any teenagers, Amari?"

Amari nodded. "Yeah, us!"

"Exactly!", I let out an annoyed grunt before a young man in an orange dinosaur suit playfully made his way up to us. "Ho, ho, ho! Hey, there, kids! Welcome to Fun Zone! Where the fun is in the zone! What playful activities can I interest you in today?!"

Hearing this, Amari and I turn our heads to each other, our eyes full of anger before turning back. "Do we look like kids to you?"

"Ho-ho-ho!", said the playful dinosaur, his back arched as he held onto his tummy. "Oh, dear boys. Here at Fun Zone, age is just a number. Why, *all* children are welcome!"

"We're not kids!", said both Amari and me.

"Ho-ho-ho! You two are so funny!"

"And *you* are an annoying, loudmouth, idiot!", I said, stomping my foot. "Now take your jolliness and leave Barney!"

Hearing this, the orange dinosaur lowered its head, letting out sadness before sniffing. "Ho-ho…wahhhh!!!", the dinosaur turned its head and ran away in sobs, leaving Amari and me alone. "Woah, Dom. I had no idea you were so bossy?"

"Of course, I am. I *had* to be. Guy was getting on my last nerves. Someone had to tell him off."

Amari nods. "Yeah" he sighs before turning to me with sad eyes. "Hey, I'm sorry about all this man. I didn't know all of this would happen."

"Hey, man, this isn't your fault."

"Yes, it is. I always mess things up. Just like with the money?"

"Hey, none of that was your fault. You were tricked."

"But I still could've figured something out; I could've just…knew."

"*Could've, should've, would've.* What happens in the past *stays* in the past. Things are a lot better now; I have a new house, and I get to stay here with you. Things couldn't be better."

With these doubts now gone, Amari lets out a sigh and nods. "You're right. What was I thinking?"

"Just negative thinking. Now, come on, let's go down to the mall and catch a movie."

Amari nods. "Yeah, we can do that. Just let me take a shit first."

"Alright, I'll be right here when you come out."

"A'ight, be back in a gif."

With that, Amari made his way past me before making his way out of the place, leaving me all alone. Or so I thought, when the mysterious figure with red hair approached me from behind. "Hey there, cutie"

"What did you just say to—" My words were quickly cut off as my dizzy, redhead girlfriend was found smiling at me. "Amanda?"

Amanda smiled. "Hi, Dominic."

"What are you doing here?"

"Oh, I just came to visit my boyfriend. I heard the fun zone's a great place for a first date."

"Date?"

"Yeah, why else would I be here?"

"Amanda, we can't do this right now. Amari's in the bathroom waiting for me. If he catches us together, we're dead."

"Well then, maybe we should go somewhere quieter."

"Where?"

Without saying another word, Amanda took my hand and pulled me towards her, and both of us headed out. "Amanda where are we going?", I said before she stopped dead in front of the Fun Zone building. "Nowhere, this is the place."

"The place? Amanda, we're outside."

"I know. I want him to see us."

"What? Why would you want that?"

"Come on, Dominic. You know you can't keep this from him forever."

"Yes, I can. I just must keep hiding from you for the next three thousand years. He'll never find out!"

Amari stood over the bathroom sink, his eyes gazing down as he washed his hands. It wasn't long before the faucet shut off, his hands soaking wet before wiping them dry with the brown paper towels sitting in the basket.

Amari took the stuff in the trash can and turned to look at his reflection in the mirror. Seeing this, Amari smiled. "The past is the past. There's nothing you can change about that", Amari turned away from the mirror and went to the door. "From now on, the future will be the focus", he nodded. "Only the future."

With that, Amari grabbed the doorknob, opening it wide before making his way out. It wasn't long before Amari found his way back to the set of children running past his feet and legs, causing him to almost trip before picking himself back up.

But as soon as he looked up, he noticed the spot, the same spot where his best friend stood. Confused, Amari looked all around, his head turning at an almost 360-degree angle, but found nothing but toddlers running around.

Kids and only kids.

"Dom?", Amari said, confused. "Yo, Dom!"

Amari turned his eyes to the left before stopping dead at the window, the window where he found Dominic, his back turned as he, what looked to be him, talking to someone.

Seeing this, Amari's eyes lit up in shock.

Amanda sighed, crossing her arms, making Dominic upset. "I want to tell him, Amanda. but I'm just scared."

"Scared of what? Of his reaction?"

"No, I'm afraid that if Amari finds out about us, he'll try to break us up."

Amanda raised her brow. "Break us up? Why would he do that?"

"Because I know him, Mandy, you don't. I've been friends with him long enough to know how he feels about the people that come into my life", I sighed, taking Amanda's hands. "I don't want you to be taken away from me."

Amanda smiled happily before answering. "Oh, Dom" she said, bringing her hand over to my cheek, smiling. "No one is going to take me away from you. Not even Amari. It doesn't matter what he thinks, I love you, Dom, and if we have that, we have everything."

With these words, a warm, loving smile forms across my face before speaking. "Oh, Mandy"

Amanda smiled at that cute little nickname before leaning in to kiss me. I quickly kiss her back, my hands wrapping around her waist before pulling her in. It wasn't long before both of us were lost in each other's lips.

It was at that moment, there was no arcade; there were no fears.

There was no Amari.

There was just us.

Until it wasn't. "DOMINIC!"

Shocked, Amanda and I pulled away from each other; our eyes turned to the light-skinned boy in dread, his eyes wide in shock. "Amari!"

"What the hell is going on here?"

Amanda and I were frozen, our eyes wide with fear as my best friend waited for an answer. Unfortunately, we couldn't say anything.

All we could do was stand frozen.

And frozen we were.

Chapter 7: Secret Revealed

Amanda and I were still very much frozen. "Um, hello?", said Amari, bringing us back to reality. "I asked you two a question!"

I blink, the ice coming from me along with Amanda. "Amari, it's not what it looks like."

"Yes, it is," said Amanda, taking my hand in hers. "We're together, dickface! Either take it or leave it!"

"What?"

"Amanda!"

"No, Dom! I told you I wanted him to see us", she gripped my hand nicely and tightly. "Us, like this."

"No!", Amari said. "No, this can't be happening! This has got to be a joke!"

"It's not, asshole!"

"No, it's not! Dom?!", Amari said, turning to me. "Dom, is the snobby rich girl lying? Answer me!"

My eyes looked down to the concrete floor, their eyes full of sadness, before nodding. "Amanda"

"What?"

"Her name is Amanda!", I said now, looking at him. "And she's not lying. We're together."

Shocked, Amari turned to Amanda, her brow raised high before speaking. "And there's nothing you can do about it."

With these words, Amari clenches his fist and charges straight to Amanda, ready to attack. Or so he thought when I took him by the arm and slammed his body on the ground with full force. "Argh!", Amari grunts. "What the hell, Dom!"

"Don't hit my girlfriend!"

"Girlfriend?!"

"Yeah, what did you think we were friends?"

"More like his house pet, not friends! Ow!", Amari shouts as my hand slaps the side of his cheek. "What was that for?"

"For being a dick!"

"Oh, *I'm* the jerk? When you're sitting here rubbing faces with your girlfriend!"

Hearing this, I gazed up at Amanda, her eyes full of realization, while I closed my eyes, letting out a heavy sigh. "You're right."

"I am?"

I nodded. "Yeah. I shouldn't have kept this from you, not from my best friend. Look, I'll explain everything; just promise not to attack my girlfriend?"

"Only if she doesn't attack me."

"Even if I did, I would've had you on the ground faster than any other simp like you!"

"SIMP!"

"That's enough! Get up, Amari!"

Amari slowly picked himself up from the ground, rubbing his head. "Come on, let's go over here", I said to Amari. We stepped a few feet away from Amanda, our backs completely turned.

As soon as we were alone, I looked dead in my best friend's eyes and spoke. "Listen, I know this is all so sudden."

"Sudden?", Amari scoffed. "You're sitting here making all kinds of excuses! 'I got a lot of homework to do, bro, sorry'. Yeah, you had a lot of *homework* to do."

"I know, I know."

"I mean, why would you keep something like this from me? What, did you not trust me or something?"

"No, I just, I know you."

"*Know* me?"

"I know how you are. I didn't tell you about Amanda because I know how you feel about her. You hate her!"

"Of course, I do, and so did you!"

"What?"

"You hated her, man. From the very moment we met her, you hated her! Tell me how you went from *hate* to smoochy, smoochy!"

I laugh softly but quickly shake it off. "I didn't like Amanda at first, okay, I didn't. I hated it even more when she punched me in the face!", I shifted away a bit. "But then she apologized, she apologized, and I forgave her."

"You did?!"

"Well, not at first. I was angry, but she came back, pleading repeatedly until I finally said, gave up."

Amari raises his brow. "Wait, is that why she was at the hospital that day?"

"Yes, she even stayed the night at the hospital with me."

"She stayed the night?"

"Yes, look, Amari, I know you're upset."

"Of course, I'm upset! This is the same girl who punched, humiliated, and harassed you! How could you let her stay the night, let alone kiss you! Ew!"

"Maybe because she bought me and my mom a house! A house that was close to the school, preventing us from moving and leaving my best friend behind, remember?"

Amari's eyes lit up hearing this. "Oh, yeah. I forgot that."

"When Amanda bought me the house, I was so thrilled. I saw her in a different light. I realized that Amanda wasn't as bad as I thought that she was sweet. It wasn't long before I acted on it", I sighed. "Look, I know this is new for you, but I need you to get over this. Amanda and I are together, and you need to learn to live with that. If you can't, then you and I can't be friends. So, what's it going to be?", I said, my arms folded.

Hearing this, Amari turned to Amanda, her eyes gazing up at me. Then, Amari turned back to me and sighed. "Fine", he said.

#

My arms were still crossed as I stood between my best friend and girlfriend, their eyes locked with each other as they looked at each other. "Amanda, Amari had something to say to you."

"Does he know?", Amanda said, raising her brow and making Amari nod. "Yes, I do", Amari let out a heavy sigh before speaking. "I'm sorry for trying to attack you. I was being…well, a dick, okay. Dom and I talked things out, and I think that you and I can try to get along, okay?"

Amanda nods. "Okay, I forgive you."

Amari raises his brow high. "*You* forgive *me*?"

"Yeah, I mean, it's not my fault you have anger issues."

"Anger issues!"

"Amari"

"No, Dom, she's wrong! I do not have anger issues!"

"Uh, yes, you do! You've had them the moment you and I met!"

"You mean that argument back in the cafeteria?! If I don't recall, it was *you* who started the damn thing!"

"Stop it, both of you!", I shouted causing Amari and Amanda to turn to me. "We're not doing this, okay? All this back-and-forth nonsense, venting! This will not be a part of our relationship."

"Look, I'm sorry, man, but I can't do this with her."

"Yeah, we obviously hate each other too much!"

"You *hate* each other, or do you just not *like* each other."

Amari and Amanda glance at each other before turning to me. "Both!", they said.

I sigh. "Okay, you guys don't like each other. I can live with that, but what I can't live with is you two fussing with each other. I ask you: what can I do to make this relationship of ours work?"

Hearing this, my best friend and girlfriend turned to each other with a sinister smile. "Hold on a minute", Amari said. They whispered to each other, their heads peeking back to glance at me before going back to their little "discussion." After a few more seconds of whispering, Amari and Amanda turned back to me, their grins very visible as they approached me.

"So?", I said with a quick nod.

My best friend and girlfriend turned to each other before answering. "We decided to share you," Amanda said, making me very confused. "*Share me?*"

"Yes. We mean we want certain days with you, days where we can spend time with you. That way, we can both get what we want and still be happy."

I nod. "Oh, um, okay. So, what days do you want?"

"The week—"

"The weekend," Amari said, cutting Amanda off. "No, you get the weekend?"

"No, *you* get the weekend. Dom and I get the week."

"What?! You said I'd get the week!"

"I changed my mind."

"Well, change it back!"

"No. See Amanda, Dom and I have been together for much longer than you", Amari wrapped his arms around my shoulder. "That makes us life partners; you, on the other hand, just got here."

"That's bullshit!", Amanda said, taking my left arm. "I'm Dominic's girlfriend, I deserve to have the whole week with him!"

"No, I do! Dominic was my friend first; he's mine!", Amari said, pulling me back to him. "No, he's mine!", Amanda pulled.

"Mine!", Amari pulls.

"Mine!", Amanda again.

"Mine!", Amari also.

I spend the next few minutes being tugged by my best friend and girlfriend, their constant bickering continuing into one big blowout: "MIIIIIINNNNNNNEEEEEE!!!!!"

"E-NOUGH!", I shouted, causing Amanda and Amari to turn their heads back to me.

I yanked my arms away from the two of them, and a heavy sigh released from me before answering. "*I* am the boyfriend here. Therefore, I should be the one to decide."

Hearing this, Amari and Amanda turned to each other, nodding in agreement before turning to me. "That's fair."

With these words, I turn to Amari. "Amari"

"Yeah, man", Amari said with his head raised high. "As your friend, I think that it would be best if you and I get the weekend."

"What?", Amari said, shocked, making a sinister grin form on Amanda's face. "Why would you choose the weekend?"

"I'm sorry, man, but it's for the best."

"But I'm your best friend!"

"And Amanda's my girlfriend, and as that, I would like to be able to spend as much time as I can with her", I said, taking Amanda's hand in mine before speaking. "I just want you to understand."

Hearing this, Amari looks straight to me and Amanda and sighs with a quick nod. "I understand."

I smile, nodding as well. "Good"

The three of us all take a moment to stare at each other before I speak up. "So, you still up for the mall?"

Amari scoffs. "Nah, I'm over it. After finding out about all this, I need a mental break."

I blink. "Oh. Well, I guess that's fair", I said, rubbing the back of my neck in embarrassment.

"Don't worry, babe. We can still make this day last. We can have a whole day with each other."

"Just you and me?"

She nodded, squeezing my hand. "Just you and me."

I laugh, my face flustered with red. "Then what are we waiting for?"

Smiling, I turn my eyes back to Amari and speak. "See you tomorrow, Amari."

Amari watches as Amanda and I walk hand in hand with each other, our backs completely turned. That is, until Amanda turned to Amari, raising her hand up to her head and forming an "L", with her thumb and index figure as she stuck her tongue out.

"Did she just—" Amari said, shocked, before raising both of his hands, with two of his middle fingers shooting up to Amanda's shocked face, her eyes big and wide at Amari's hand gesture. "That's for you, bitch!"

Seeing this, Amanda lowered her hand, her eyes rolling before turning her head back. As for Amari, he lowers his hands, his arms now crossed, before speaking. "So, if that's how you want it, Amanda," Amari said with a sinister grin. "Then let the games begin."

\#

Griffin Manor stood proud and tall in the evening light, the birds whistling in the trees as they chirped. On the inside, Butler Barry sat in the library, his face completely buried in a book that was Moby Dick. Next to him stood a plate of tea and cookies. Or as he called it: Biscuits.

He flipped a page of his book once more, immersed in the wonders of his book before bringing his cup of tea to his lips. That is, until the sound of something ringing is heard. "Hm?", Barry said, raising his head as the ringing noise was heard. "Oh!", Barry rises from his chair, leaving his book behind on the desk.

On the inside of the kitchen was a black telephone sitting on the wall, ringing loudly as it sat against the cherry red wallpaper. "Griffin Residence. Who is this?", Barry gasped. "Oh, Ms. Griffin!", he said happily. "What a surprise. I had no idea it was you."

"Of course, it's me, deary" answered a short, brunette-haired woman, her back completely turned as she stared out an open ocean. "You sound quite tired, Barry. Have you gotten any rest?"

Barry nodded. "Y-yes. I got some earlier. Why do you ask?"

Ms. Griffin's cherry-red lips make a quick grin. "Oh, nothing. I just wanted to know, especially as I'll be coming home soon."

"Coming home? But don't you have your business trip?"

"The board is having a bit of a hiatus now. So, Robert and I'll be coming home a bit earlier."

"Really? You and Sir Griffin. Oh, that's wonderful news, I'm sure Amanda will be thrilled!"

"Amanda. I almost forgot about my daughter. How is she doing?"

Barry lowers his eyes in sadness. "She's…better."

Mrs. Griffin's brow is raised. "Better?"

"Well, she's better than before. She has a boyfriend now and—" A huge gasp leaves Barry, causing him to slap his hand on his forehead. "Oh, no! That was supposed to be our secret!"

"It's fine, Barry."

"It is? You're not mad about this?"

The brunette woman shook her head. "Of course not. If there's any secret she needs to keep, it should be addressed with me first."

"What do you mean?"

"What do you think?"

Hearing this, Barry lets out a deep sigh before speaking. "Forgive me, Amanda dear", Barry said, putting the phone back to his ear. "Alright, what do you want to eat?"

"Oh, just the usual."

#

ST. MORA MALL!

That's what the sign above the door read. Amanda and I stood below it, our eyes big and bright as we turned to each other, our smiles visible. "Shall we?", I said, holding my hand out.

Without a second thought, Amanda took my hand in hers, and we entered the mall as boyfriend and girlfriend. Yet little did we know, a mysterious figure in black followed us from behind, his smile big and present as he entered the steel doors.

Amanda and I stood in a line, thousands of kids waiting to get a movie ticket. There were hundreds of students, making the wait much longer, especially for Amanda. "What's taking so long?"

"What do you mean?", I said, turning to her.

"This line. I never had to wait this long for a ticket, not with this many people", Amanda brought her hand to her chin as she thought. "Then again, I don't remember ever having to wait in line for any movie."

I laugh. "Well, it looks like you'll need to have some patience."

"Patience?", Amanda scoffed. "I have no patience."

"You don't have a choice now, do you?"

Amanda crosses her arms, her eyes turning away from me in annoyance. "Don't worry, we're almost there. Besides…", I grabbed Amanda by the waist, causing her eyes to turn back to me as I smiled, "You have me with you. So, it's not all that bad now, is it?"

Amanda's annoyed look quickly turned cute and adorable. "No, I guess not", she said, her face turning red.

Saying this, Amanda brought her lips to mine, our arms wrapped around each other as we made out. Many kids watched in disgust, their eyes rolling as they watched. Some left, as they couldn't bear watching the boy and girl in their little make-out session.

"Next?", said a voice as Amanda and I continued kissing. "Next!"

Hearing this, Amanda and I's eyes pop open, finding the line in front of us to be gone, leaving us at the front of the line where the ticket man stood. "If you two want to make out, I'd suggest you do it somewhere that's not in public."

With these words, Amanda and I pulled away in embarrassment, our faces now flushed with red before speaking. "Y-yeah, sorry about that."

Amanda nods in agreement. "Yeah, sorry."

I approached the ticket stand, my wallet brought up to me before pulling out a thick wad of cash. "Two tickets for: 'Crocodile Man', please?"

Without another word, the ticket man took the twenty-dollar bill from me and brought it into the booth. I turned my back to Amanda, who smiled. "Here you are", the ticket man said, holding two Crocodile Man tickets. "Enjoy the movie."

"Thanks", I said, taking the tickets from him before holding my hand out to Amanda, my smile present. "Ready?"

Smiling, Amanda took my hand in mine and nodded. "Ready"

With these words, Amanda and I walk hand in hand to the theatre. As for the ticket man, he turned to look at the line. "Next!", he said.

The mysterious figure in black approached the ticket stand, his eyes turning to the couple in the distance. He had a sinister grin as he turned his attention back to the ticket stand. "I will have whatever *they're* having."

\#

A crowd of people burst out in laughter as a fluorescent screen presents a scrawny, white male running on a track, his face beaded with sweat as he desperately tried to run up to the muscular, toned black man. The man's very fit, muscular body gives him the speed and endurance to run farther and farther away from the scrawny, white male.

From the high-pitched laughter from the audience, the man had no chance of winning. That is, until a white piece of cloth is brought up to the man's face, causing him to fall straight to his knees, hitting the ground head first as the scrawny, white male stands over his back, huffing and puffing in his victory.

The audience lets out a few "oooooohhhhhhssss", in their shock before their laughter is brought back. As for Amanda and me, our laughs were just getting started. "I wasn't expecting that!", I said, laughing.

"Me neither!", Amanda laughed loudly. "That's one determined man!"

"Its Crocodile Man. What do you expect?", I wrap my arm around Amanda's neck, and both of us laugh as we huddled close together.

Yet, a few rows from us, the mysterious boy in black is found with a pair of binoculars over his eyes, his smile visible from view. "Target in sight", he said, lowering the binoculars from his eyes, his sinister, fiery eyes.

The boy put his binoculars away before retrieving a green 8-inch, high-pressure, plastic water gun. With his evil laugh, he brought the water gun up to his eyes, a grin presented as he aimed the gun directly at the redhead.

With the crowd lost in laughter, the boy placed his finger on the trigger and pulled it, causing a line of water to shoot out from the gun. Unfortunately, it was a fat guy who made his way behind Amanda. "Argh!", said the fat guy, rubbing his head. "Who did that?", he said, wiping his face. "Who threw water at me?"

Scared, the boy put his water gun away, his eyes shifting to the left as he whistled. "He did it!", answered a teenage blonde girl sitting next to him.

The boy quickly turned to her, his eyes full of anger as the fat guy made his way up to him. "No, no", he said. But just as quickly, a hand touched his shoulder, causing the fat guy to stop dead in his tracks. "Don't worry," said the superintendent. "I got this one."

Without a second thought, the boy was grabbed by the shirt and thrown straight out of the theatre, his head hitting first. Now outside the theatre, the boy took out his sunglasses and the hood over his head, revealing his face.

Amari.

"Those damn guards," Amari said, picking up his sunglasses, his eyes looking back to the doors. "Can't mind their own damn business!"

#

Soon after the movie, Amanda and I sat at the food court, where there was a frozen yogurt stand known as: **YOLO FROYO: BEST IN THE WORLD!**

Hundreds of people were sitting in their seats, eating all kinds of frozen yogurt, with various types of flavors: strawberry, chocolate, banana, and even green tea. Not to mention the toppings. For Amanda and I, it was all the toppings.

Served to us was a triple fudge swirl with M&M's and brownie bits, all with two red and white swirled straws in between us. "Here you go", said the man in the pink outfit, his nametag being Greg. "Enjoy."

"Thank you", I said, jabbing the straw in the froyo before the two of us drank from the straws together, smiling happily as we did.

Yet, little did we know, Amari was watching, not *stalking* from behind a bush, his eyes stuffed with the pair of binoculars where he found Amanda and me feeding each other frozen yogurt. Amari grunts in envy before taking the binoculars from his fiery, devilish eyes. "That should be me feeding him ice cream, not you."

Amari watches as Amanda wipes off a piece of chocolate sauce from the side of his lip, making Amari's anger grow. "Mmmmmmmmmm!!!!!", Amari grunts, lowering his binoculars from his eyes. He brought out a slingshot and a golf ball, one that he put right in between the sling, the rubber stretching out as he raised it to his eye. "You'll never enjoy food again, once your food goes to your mouth, this ball hits you right in th-"

"What are you doing?"

"Ah!", saying this, Amari accidentally released his golf ball from the sling, causing it to hit a lesbian couple's frozen yogurt with strawberries that once sat on the top and now on both of their faces, the glass container destroyed.

"Shit!", Amari said, shocked, before turning to the police guard, his stick raised high in the air. Without a second thought, Amari drops his slingshot before taking off, the police guard now chasing after him.

A bowling pin is brought down by a red bowling ball, knocking every single pin collapse to the ground as they are swept in by the woman. "Yes!", Dominic said in happiness. "Strike!"

Amanda comes right up to me, her arms wrapped around me as we jump up and down. Yet, in our celebration, Amari sat behind one of the bowling ball machines, his smile big and bright as Amanda made her way over to the machine.

This was the perfect opportunity.

Turning to the bowling balls, Amari took the green one, the ball almost slipping from his arms before placing it down on the ground. As soon as he does, he grabs another ball in the same color, only it was painted, before placing it on the bowling machine.

Amanda made his way toward the machine balls, with Amari hiding behind them. Amanda took the ball in her hand. That's when she stopped dead in confusion at the sudden weight of the ball, much to my dislike. "You okay, Mandy?"

Amanda nods. "Yeah", she looks down at the odd-looking ball before answering. "This ball is extra light."

Minding the weight, Amanda brings the "bowling ball" up to her eyes and throws it towards the bowling pin. Unfortunately, the ball was raised too high, hit the edge of the place, and bounced from it, rising high in the air.

Amanda and I watch the ball, their eyes following the green ball that fell right past the bowling machine, making a loud "bum" sound. "Ow!"

Amanda and Dom hear this and make their way to the bowling machine. Unfortunately, they find only the green "bowling ball". Confused, I take the ball in my hands before weighing it in his hands. "This is a dodgeball."

"A dodgeball?", Amanda said, confused. "What idiot would put a dodgeball here?"

"I don't know, but whoever it is. He got exactly what he deserved."

With these words, I put the dodgeball back in the machine and pulled Amanda by the waist. "Come on, let's play another game."

"Okay"

With that, Amanda and I take each other's hand and walk off. Yet, little did we know, Amari, with his hand over his injured head, turned to watch Amanda and I leave the arcade. "That's it. I'm done."

#

A teacup was scooted across a wooden table surface, Joana's eyes peering down. "Here, this should help."

Joana looks down at the tea, the hot steam warming her face as she brings it to her lips. "Thank you, Sue."

Sue nodded happily as Joana sipped the tea, the water warming her senses. "Mmm, this is good tea."

"I made it just the way you like it. Lavender and honey."

Joana smiled, nodding quickly. "It's how *he* made it, too."

"Who? Dominic?"

Joana shook her head, her eyes closed shut before humming a distinct tune to herself. "What's that?", Sue said with a raised brow. "What are you humming, Joana?"

Joana's eyes open, her humming now stopped before answering. "Oh, nothing. It's just a song that I used to sing. You know, when I was younger."

Sue blinks. "Sounds like it's more than just a song."

"Of course, it is. It was our song, after all."

"Our?"

"Otto and I", she said, smiling. "Otto and I would sing it together. A song of ours"

Sue frowns in sadness. "Is that why you were crying earlier today because of him?"

Joana nods. "Not just him, Dominic too. I had no idea he would write something like that in his journal."

"Write what? What did he write?"

Joana sighs, her fingertips touching her steaming teacup before turning to Sue. "It was about that day."

"What day?"

"Christmas Day, Christmas *Eve*. In his journal, Dominic wrote about him noticing me being upset, about me missing Frank."

Sue raises her brow. "Why would Dominic think that?"

"Because it's true. I did miss him. He said that things wouldn't have been the same without him here, and he was right. Things haven't been the same. I'm lonely, and so is Dominic", Joana sighed. "If only I had stopped him, if he hadn't left. He would still be here."

Feeling sorry for her friend, Sue brings her hand up to her, gripping her finger tight before answering. "You can't blame yourself, Joana. That wasn't your fault."

Joana nods. "I know. I just feel like it was."

"How? What about that day was your fault?"

With a quick sigh, Joana turned to her friend. "Because I had a feeling."

#

A car made its way up a hill, its headlights glowing big and bright before stopping dead. Inside the car was a boy and a girl, and only the girl looked confused. "Um, Dom? Where are we?", Amanda said, turning to me. "Take off your blindfold."

Hearing this, Amanda brings her hands up to her blindfold and snatches it right off. As soon as she does, a huge gasp leaves her, her eyes big and wide as she finds a whole set of city lights sitting below the hilltop. "Oh, Dominic", said Amanda. "This is beautiful."

"It's St. Mora, at night. I thought it'd be nice to let you see it from above. You know, as a last date. So, what do you think?"

"Aww, babe. This is the cherry on the top. Thank you", Amanda leans in to kiss my cheek. "You're welcome. So, what do we want to do now?"

With these words, Amanda pulled me by the waist and smiled. "I'll show you."

Hearing this, I leaned into my girlfriend, my lips inches from hers, but before the two of us could do anything else, I heard a sneeze, causing both our eyes to open. "What was that?", I said, confused. "Was that you, Amanda?"

Amanda shook her head. "No, that wasn't me?"

"I could've sworn I heard a sneeze."

"It was probably just the wind. Come on, let's get back to it", Amanda said, pulling me back in.

But as soon as she does, a bright light flashes in our faces. "NOT SO FAST YOU TWO!"

"Ah!", Amanda and I shout, our bodies frozen to the bright light. "YOU TWO ARE IN A WHOLE LOT OF TROUBLE!"

"For what?", I said in fear.

"Yeah, what did we do?"

"I SHOULD BE ASKING YOU THE SAME THING, MISSY! NOW, HANDS IN THE AIR!"

Following orders, Amanda and I raised our hands high in the air. "Who are you? What do you want?"

"THIS IS THE POLICE, AND YOU TWO ARE UNDER A-AH-AH-AHHHH-CHOOOO!!!", answers the silhouette figure, much to my confusion. "Hold on, I knew that sneeze sounded familiar. Amari, is that you?"

"Um, what?", answered the silhouette, his voice now normal. "NO, I'M THE CHIEF OF POLICE! ST. MORA'S FINEST!"

"Enough of the tricks, Amari, and lose that megaphone!"

"WHAT MEGAPHO-", Amari's words were quickly cut off as his megaphone and flashlight were taken from him. "Oh, yeah, that."

"Amari, what the hell are you doing here?"

"Yeah, you're ruining our date night!"

Amari scoffed. "*Your* date! This was supposed to be me and Dominic's day until you came in and ruined it!"

"*I* did!"

"Yes, *this* is your punishment or eight punishments. I mean, I've tried to do it back at the frozen yogurt zone."

"The frozen yogurt places?"

"That and the movie theatre!"

"THE MOVIE THEATRE!", Amanda and I turn to each other, our eyes full of anger, before turning back to Amari. "Why are you guys looking at me like that?"

Before he could say anything, Amari was grabbed by the arm, his flashlight falling on the ground as he screamed.

#

In the eastern part of St. Mora, a quiet yet very ghetto neighborhood was found, with nothing but the sound of dogs barking and owls howling. But that wasn't the only thing that was loud. Coming up in the distance, a limousine made its way up the road, stopping dead in front of Amari's house. "Home sweet home, Amari", I said butler Barry turning back to Amanda and I turned our heads to the back seat where Amari was duct-taped to, growling at us like some hungry wolf.

"By the look of your eyes, we can tell you've learned your lesson", I said, turning to Amanda. "Amanda, take the tape off him."

"Gladly", Amanda said before ripping the tape from Amari's mouth, causing a sharp grunt to leave him. "Thanks for ripping my damn skin off", Amari said, facing me. "And thanks for the ride home. Although, it wasn't much of one."

"You deserved it after trying to sabotage our night."

Amari turned to Amanda; his eyes lowered in shame. "Look, I'm sorry for ruining everything, okay", he shrugs. "I just can't stand the thought of you two being together."

"Why?", I asked.

He shrugged. "Oh, come on, Dom. She's rich, and you're…well, average. You're also the only friend I've ever had, and the fact that you're going out with my arch-nemesis is just pure evil!"

"Sounds to me, you're just jealous?"

He scoffed. "I'm not jealous", he said, making Amanda shoot him a look. "Ok, fine. I'm jealous, but only because I care. I just don't want to see you get your heart broken, man."

I let out a deep sigh. "I'm not going to get my heart broken, man, and no one, and I mean no one could ever replace you."

Amari raises his head, his eyes full of hope. "No one?"

I nod, my smile big and wide. "No one."

Amari exhales, letting out his relief. "Thanks, man. That makes me feel a whole lot better."

I hold Amari tight before speaking. "You're welcome, man."

Amanda watches with a smile as the two boys pull away from each other, their eyes now turning to her. "I guess I owe you an apology too, huh?"

"Yes", Amanda said, arms folded. "Go on."

Amari took his hand from his head. "I'm sorry for giving you such a hard time. I just wanted to know if the girl he got with was worthy enough of him", Amari looks down at Amanda's hands, which are intertwined with mine. Seeing this, Amari looks up to her and nods. "After tonight, I see that you are indeed."

Amanda smiled; her hand gripping tight with mine before nodding. "Well, I guess this makes us friends then."

Amari swayed his head a bit. "Ermmm, I wouldn't say that. I need a bit more time to get to know you before I can call you my "friend". So, for right now, let's just be acquaintances."

Amanda nods. "That'll work. Acquaintances it is", Amanda holds her hand out to Amari, his eyes full of promise, before taking it. "Acquaintance."

My smile is big and wide to these words before speaking. "Oh, I'm so glad you guys are finally in a good place. I guess this means no more fighting between you."

My girlfriend and best friend turn to each other, their smiles big and wide before bursting out into laughter, cackling as they did before shaking their heads. "No way, man."

"Yeah, no."

I roll my eyes, expecting this, before nodding. "Alright, well, if that's settled, then Amanda and I should get going. Mom will have a search party for us if we don't hurry back."

Amari nods. "Yeah, wouldn't want that."

"We sure wouldn't."

"Well, see ya man."

"Oh, really? You don't want to come? You know, sabotage anymore of our day?"

Amari shook his head. "Nah, I sabotaged enough of you guys today. The least I can do is step off."

Amanda smiled. "I'm impressed."

"You guys have fun. I'll see you later."

"See ya, Mar. Come on, babe", I said, taking my girlfriend's hand as the both of us headed for the limousine.

Within minutes, the car engine turned on, and the wheels turned at a rapid pace before driving down the road, leaving Amari with a happy grin that quickly turned sour. "Snobby rich bitch."

#

The limousine stopped dead in front of Mom and I's two-story house, the engine shutting off the moment we parked. Amanda watched as I took the keys from the hole, letting out a quick sigh before turning to her. "You ready?"

Amanda nods, her frown low. "What if they don't like me?"

"They'll love you. You want to know why?"

Amanda raises her brow. "Why?"

"Because *I* love you, Amanda, and if we have that, other people's opinions don't matter. Remember?"

Amanda nods. "Yes, I remember. Alright, let's do this."

"Okay"

With these words of encouragement, Amanda and I lean in for a quick kiss before pulling away.

#

A large salad bowl was placed on the table, alongside a basket of buttered rolls, grilled corn, and well-seasoned pork chops, all set by Joana Mitchell herself. "There we go", she said with a happy smile. "That's all of it."

"Not all of it", said Sue Anne, bringing a plate of pie to the table. "Um, Sue, what is that?", Joana said to Sue Anne's confusion. "It's a pie."

"Yes, but what kind?"

"Pumpkin"

"Pumpkin? Ew."

"Ew?"

"I hate pumpkin pie."

"What do you mean? Pumpkin pie has a perfect blend of sugar, cinnamon, and nutmeg."

"That's not what I taste when I eat it. It's all mushy and cold."

"It's pumpkin pie; it's supposed to be cold."

"And that's what makes it disgusting."

Sue scoffs. "I don't know what you're talking about, Joana. Pumpkin pie is the best kind of pie."

"Well, I beg to differ."

Sue rolls her eyes. "Whatever."

As soon as this was said, the sound of the doorbell rang, causing the women to look up from the table and to the woman. "Was that the door?"

"Yes, what do you think it was?", Joana said, taking off her apron. "I'll go answer it. You take care of the food."

"Alright, go!"

With these words, Joana made her way out of the kitchen, going past the hallway before making her way to the front door, where two silhouette figures stood. With nothing left, Joana fluffs her hair out before twisting the lock and opening the door. "Dominic"

"Hey, Mom."

Joana said, turning to the girl. "And Ms. Griffin. It's so nice to see you again."

"It's so nice to see you too, um, Mrs. Mitchell."

Joana laughed. "I like your compliment. Come in."

With that, Amanda and I follow Mom, the door shutting behind us as we make our way down the hallway.

#

Amanda, Mom, Aunt Sue, and I all sat around the dinner table, laughing happily as their plates were cleared. 'I mean, that's what she told me, that's what she told me!", said Aunt Sue, picking everyone's plate up. "Mm, this corn is really good, Mrs. Mitchell."

"Thank you. Sue Anne helped as well."

"Oh, well, thank you *both* for a wonderful dinner."

"You're welcome", answers Joana.

"Yeah, it's the least we could do for you after giving us this house. By the way, thank you."

"Oh, it was nothing."

I smiled happily at Mom before turning to Amanda, my eyes widening before answering. "Oh, Amanda."

Amanda turned to me, confused. "What?"

"You've got butter on your cheek."

Amanda raises a brow. "Where?", Amanda touches her face, trying to find the butter before I take the napkin in my hand. "No, no. Don't do that. Here."

Mom watches as I bring Amanda's face forward, gently wiping the cotton fabric on her cheek, and scooping the butter off before speaking. "There, all clean."

Amanda smiled, putting her hand to her face. "Thanks, ba-", Amanda stops herself. "I mean, Dominic."

"You're welcome, Amanda."

Joana continued to smile before Sue came back with another set of plates, much smaller than the others. "Who wants pie?"

"I do!", Amanda her hand raised in the air.

"What kind of pie is it, Aunt Sue?"

"Only the best kind"

"Apple?"

Sue scoffs. "What, no. It's pumpkin."

I raise my brow. "Pumpkin? Ew!"

"That's what I said", answered Joana. "Nobody likes pumpkin pie, Sue!"

"How do you like it if you don't try it?"

"I don't need to try it to know. One look says it all."

Sue scoffs. "Fine, suit yourself. I'm sure Ms. Griffin would love some of my world-famous pumpkin pie. "Would you, baby cakes?", Sue said with a bright smile as she brought the plate of pumpkin pie to Amanda. "Um, sure?"

"Really?", I said, turning to her. "Yeah, a little pie never hurt anybody."

"Oh, wonderful! Alright, here you go, miss", Sue said, taking a slice from her plate and onto Amanda's plate, a few crumbs sitting below it. "Enjoy."

Seeing this, Amanda picked up her fork and dug into her pie. Mom, Sue, and I watched as Amanda brought the piece of pie into her mouth, slowly munching it. "How is it?", I ask quickly, causing Amanda to turn her eyes to me. "It's actually good."

"It is?", Joana said, her brow raised. "Yeah, here, try some."

Without a second thought, Amanda scooped some of the pumpkin pie into her spoon before bringing it into my mouth as I chewed. "It's good, right?"

I nod. "Mm, yeah. Wow, this *is* good."

"IT IS!", Sue speaks, her smile big and wide. "Yeah, it's good. A perfect blend of sugar and cinnamon"

"Oh, I'm so glad you feel that way!", Sue said, turning to me and Mom. "See? Some people *do* like pumpkin pie."

Joana rubs her eyes, hearing this before answering. "Well, if they like it, then I guess I could give it a try."

"Good, finally."

"Yeah, yeah, yeah. Just give me some pie", Mom said, lifting her plate out.

\#

Soon, the dinner ended, and Amanda stood outside, our hands held as we waited for the ride. "I had a great time with you tonight, Dominic."

"Me too. Sorry, I didn't get the chance to tell Mom about us."

"It's fine, babe. There's always tomorrow."

I nod. "Yeah, there is."

Saying this, the black luxury limousine made its way up the road, stopping dead at our house before beeping. "That's Barry", Amanda said, turning to me. "See you at school tomorrow, Dominic."

"See you, babe."

With that, Amanda pulled in for a quick kiss, having no idea that Mom was watching from the house blinds, her smile big and bright before closing them shut. She turned to find Sue standing next to her, her arms crossed before speaking. "So?"

Joana nodded. "They're dating."

"I knew it!", Sue clears her throat before holding her hand out. "Now pay up."

With a quick grunt, Mom digs into her purse and pulls out a crisp, twenty-dollar bill into her hands, much to Sue Anne's liking. "Thank you."

\#

I make my way down the hallway, turning to the left as I make my way into my room, but not before saying goodbye to Aunt Sue as she left the house.

Before I knew it, I made my way into the room, ready to retire, but as soon as I opened the door, Mom was found sitting on my bed, her eyes full of sadness as she gazed down at the notebook in her hand.

"Mom?"

"Hey, baby."

"What are you doing here?", I asked.

"I need to talk to you. Can you shut the door"

Confused, I shut the door behind me, leaving me and Mom alone before answering. "Sit down."

Without a second thought, I sat on my bed, sitting next to Mom. "What is it?"

Mom looks down to the floor before speaking. "Earlier today, I was unpacking some of your things, but I found something."

"Found what?"

Sighing, Mom turned away from me before handing me a brown journal. "This"

"My journal!", I said, shocked, taking the journal in my hands. "Where did you find this?"

"It was in the box, with all your hair products."

"My hair products? I should've known to check there."

"It doesn't matter right now, Dominic. What matters is that I checked it."

"Checked it? What do you mean?"

"I mean, I read it, Dominic. I read your journal."

"You did?", I said, bringing my journal to my chest. "What did you read?"

Mom lowered her eyes. "Mom?"

Sighing, Mom raised her head and looked at me. "It was about your father."

"D-dad?", I lowered my eyes. "Mom, whatever you read in there, I didn't write it to offend you."

"I know. I know, baby. I wasn't offended by what you wrote, that's not the problem."

"It's not? Then what is the problem?"

Mom sighed. "It's been seventeen years since your father's passing, and I haven't been the same since."

I gazed up at Mom. "Do you miss him?"

Mom nodded. "Every day. Dominic, I know you're worried about me, but I want you to know that I cared for your father. It's just ever since he left, it felt like a piece of me was missing. I haven't felt the same since."

"Were you and Dad close?"

"Very, he would sing to you when you were a baby, almost every night."

"Really?"

Mom nodded. "He loved you with all his heart. He loved everything, people, plants, he loved everyone. You could say he was an angel."

I smiled. "I bet he was."

I looked back at my notebook. "I wish I knew more about him. Know who he was."

Mom smiled. "I think I can help you with that."

"What?", I turned to Mom, who was now up from my bed and down the hall. "Mom?", I called out, but she didn't answer back.

I had waited a few minutes when Mom came back into my room with a small, purple box in her hands. I watched as she sat on my bed, her eyes shifting towards me before handing the box to me. "What is this?"

"Open it"

I took the box from my mother's hand, taking off the top. To my surprise, I found a set of paintbrushes. Confused, I turned to Mom. "Paintbrushes?"

Mom nodded. "Yes"

"Dad collected paintbrushes?"

She laughed. "No, he was an artist. Your father was an artist."

"Really?"

"Mm-hm. He loved to paint. Would do it almost every day."

"Woah, I had no idea", I took one of the paintbrushes from the box, one with a coalition of blue, green, and yellow paint marks. I held it up to Mom before speaking. "Was this his favorite?"

Mom looked at the paintbrush and shook her head. "No", Mom reached into the box, pulling out another paintbrush, one with two letters carved into it. "*This* was his favorite."

I gazed up at the paintbrush with a thicker brush as it was placed in my hand, replacing the other brush. Seeing this, I bring the brush to my eyes, analyzing the two letters carved into the wooded paintbrush. "O.M.?", I said, turning to Mom.

"It's his initials. He wrote it specifically in this brush."

"Why?"

"Because this was the first brush he had ever made."

"Made?", I blinked. "Dad made his own brushes?"

She nodded. "All by hand."

"Woah", I said, tracing my hand against the wooden figure. "They're beautiful."

Mom smiled. "Not as beautiful as his paintings."

"He had paintings too?"

"Hundreds of them", Mom lowers her head in sadness. "That is, until he stopped."

"He stopped. Why?", Mom turned to me, her eyes serious. "Oh", my eyes shift away from me. "It was me."

"No, Dominic. It wasn't you. Your father wanted loved to paint, but it just didn't pay the bills. Your father had no choice but to give up painting to support us. It had nothing to do with you."

I nod, understanding things more before speaking. "I know. I just hoped I wasn't a regret, that Dad didn't regret having me."

"Your father did not regret you. He loved you more than anything in this entire world."

"Just as he loved you?"

Mom nods. "Just as he loved me."

With these words, I joined Mom in for a warm, embracing hug, my smile big and bright as I did. "I love you, Dominic."

"I love you too, Mom", I said, burying my face into Mom's face.

"Alright, enough of this sad talk; tell me about *her*."

"Her?", I said.

"You know what I'm talking about. I saw you holding her hand on the way in."

My eyes widened in shock. "Oh, you mean Amanda!", I laughed, rubbing the back of my head as my cheeks were flushed red. "Yeah, that was just a thing."

"Holding hands and feeding each other pie doesn't count as a 'thing"

I roll my eyes, my cheeks still glowing red as Mom folds her arms. "Come on, spit it out. I want to know everything."

Hearing this, I let out a sigh before answering. "Okay, get comfy. It's going to be a long story."

#

The limousine parked outside of the large mansion stood proud and tall in the misty night air. As for the residents of the home, they made their way inside the front door with nothing but laughter. "And then the mom made him some pie, um, pumpkin pie."

"Pumpkin pie?"

"I know, I didn't like it at first, but once I took a bite of it, it was okay. It was the best dessert I ever had."

"I'm so glad you had fun, Ms. Griffin."

"Oh, I did, Barry. It was wonderful!"

"I'm sure it was."

Barry watched as Amanda made her way to the couch, her body relaxing against the pillows. Amanda turned her eyes to her butler. "Barry?", she said, noticing Barry's nervous look. "Is everything okay?"

You can do this; you can do this. Barry thought, not answering Amanda. "Barry?"

Barry took a deep breath. "Y-yes, madam. I'm fine."

"Are you sure? You seem anxious."

He nods. "I am"

Amanda raises her brow, her body now risen from the pillows. "Why? Is there something wrong?"

"No", he said, rubbing the back of his neck. "No, and yes."

"I don't understand."

Stop fooling around; just tell her.

"Barry, what's going on?"

Biting his nails, Barry clenches his fists, his mouth closed shut before blurting the words: "I TOLD THEM!"

Amanda, shocked, looked at Barry wide-eyed before speaking. "Them? Who's them?"

"Mr. and Mrs. Griffin. I told them that you had a boyfriend!"

"Wait, what? You told Mom and Dad about my boyfriend, and about Dominic. Why would you do that?"

"I didn't mean to; it's just slipped out!"

Amanda grunts. "Barry, you had one job, and that was not to tell Mom and Dad about my love life! You had that one job!"

"I know, and I'm sorry! I really am, madam!"

"*Sorry*, isn't going to cut it. You know how nosey Mom and Dad are about the people I get with! I mean, what did they say anyway?"

Barry lowers his head, his eyes shifting away from Amanda. "Barry, what did they say?"

Hearing this, Barry squints his eyes before turning back to her. "They want to see him; they want to invite him to dinner."

Amanda scoffs, her hand slapped against her forehead. "I should've guessed."

"It's alright, miss", Barry said, approaching her. "I'm sure they'll love him. They may have had issues with the other men, but I'm sure this one is different."

"And how do you know that, Barry. Dominic isn't just some normal boy, he's special, and I don't want classy people like Mom and Dad to throw him away like that! Not like...*her*."

Barry's eyes lowered upon hearing this. "That won't happen, not again. I swear it."

"How do you know?"

"Bring him by the house tomorrow. I'm going to help you."

Chapter 8: The Griffins

It was another beautiful day in St. Mora, and everyone, everywhere, spent it outdoors. Everywhere you looked, there were children playing hopscotch, flying their kites, and bicycling. The day was filled with laughter and joy to go around especially, for the two lovebirds that lay under an oak tree; their eyes gazed at one another as they made out. They had been doing more of these make-out sessions, with many of them being at the school library, the cafeteria, and, of course, the janitor's closet.

Where they, of course, were caught many times.

But that doesn't mean they wouldn't try. And try they did.

Now, they were the best kissers in all of St. Mora; all they had to do now was feedback. "You're getting really good at this", Amanda said with a wide smile.

"Not as good as you, Mandy"

"Oh, I love it when you call me that, Dom Dom."

"Dom Dom?"

"Yeah, it's your nickname. Like it?"

"No, not at all."

Amanda laughed. "I thought you didn't. I'm not the best with nicknames", Amanda's gaze lowers as a certain thought comes up. "Oh, dang"

"What's wrong, Amanda?"

"Nothing, it's just I remembered something. It's about last night."

"Last night?"

Amanda nods. "Yeah, last night when I came home, my butler, Barry, asked me something real important."

"What did he say?"

"My parents just got a hiatus from their business trip and are coming home early to see me."

"Your parents are coming home to see you? That's great, Amanda."

"There's just one problem: they want to see you too."

"Me?", I said, shocked. "What do they want from me? Do they know me?"

"They do now, thanks to Barry. Apparently, he told them about me having a boyfriend and wants to meet you right away. Are you okay with that?"

Hearing this, I put my hand up to my head. "Gosh, I don't know. I mean, we've been dating for, like, what, a week now? I thought meeting your parents would be a little bit further down the line."

"That's not how it was meeting your mom. We were only four days in when you decided to introduce me to her."

"That's different, Amanda. You and I, we-", I stop myself from these words before rubbing the back of my head. "Okay, maybe it's not that different", I let out a quick sigh, my back leaning against the oak tree. "Are you okay, Dominic?"

"Yeah, I'm fine. I just didn't think this would be so soon. I mean, your parents probably expect some prissy, priss gentleman, not some normal guy from the suburbs."

"Don't say that about yourself. Remember how scared you were about Amari finding out about us, and I comforted you. What did I say?"

Hearing this, I let out a quick sigh before answering. "It doesn't matter what anyone said to us; as long as we have our love, there's nothing to worry about."

Amanda nods, smiling. "That's right, you're my boyfriend, *my* boyfriend, and I love you just the way you are."

Dominic sighs, hearing this. "I know, but what if it's not enough. If I'm going to meet your parents, I at least want to make a good first impression on them."

"Don't worry, I can help you with that."

"Really?"

"Of course, what better person to help you than your girlfriend."

I smile happily. "Oh, thanks, babe. How can I ever repay you?"

Hearing this, Amanda grabs me by the collar, her eyes full of hearts before speaking. "How about you teach me a few more of your kissing tricks, hm?"

With these words, I grab Amanda by the waist and speak. "Of course, I will. Come here, you."

With these words, Amanda and I fall back on the picnic blanket, continuing our make-out session.

\#

An airplane flew high in the air, its wings extended out as two sets of wheels stretched their way out from the bottom. The plane descended from the sky to the ground, hopping a bit as it hit the ground, hitting the brakes.

"Alright, passengers. We officially have arrived in St. Mora. Please grab your belongings on the way out. Thank you", said the pilot.

The door to the plane lowers, revealing an elongated staircase that slowly falls from the plane and to the ground, causing a set of wind to fall off. Within minutes, hundreds of people made their way down the stairway, laughing and smiling with each other as they exited the plane.

By the looks of it, that was the last bit of people to come off until two more passengers approached the front door, their backs completely turned as they stood side by side with one another. "Here we are. St. Mora!", said the woman, causing her husband to look at her. "Home sweet home! We should take it all in!"

"Yes", the woman said, taking her husband's hand. "While we still can."

With that, the two figures make their way down the stairway, their hands intertwined as they leave the plane.

\#

My eyes were covered, the feel of cold fingertips covering my sight. "Okay, open your eyes, Dominic."

"Are you sure? You've been covering my eyes for a while."

"Yes, I'm sure. Go on, open them."

With these words, Amanda took her hands from my eyes, which slowly opened wide, revealing a very big mansion that looked to have hundreds of rooms. "Amanda, where are we?" I asked, turning to my girlfriend.

"This is my house."

"Your house?"

"Yep, welcome to Griffin Manor!"

I blinked in confusion. "Griffin Manor? You were raised in this giant house?"

"Of course, where do you think I've been living, under a rock?"

I laughed with a nod. "I guess you're right."

Amanda took my hand in hers. "Come on, let me show you the inside. You'll be really impressed."

"I hope so."

"I AM SO IMPRESSED!", I shout, my voice echoing through the hallway of my girlfriend's house. "This house is amazing! It's like a castle!"

"This is just the first part of the house. Would you like to see the rest?"

I turn to Amanda, my eyes big and wide. "The rest?"

#

A large, wooden door opens wide, revealing Amanda and I, our eyes big and wide as we enter. "This is the living room area. Where we come and talk about our dreams."

"Woah!"

My eyes were full of life as I looked at the large room with the thirty-four-inch screen TV, white sofa, fireplace, and white carpet, which, in fact, had a large, stuffed bear's head popping out. "Holy shit!", I said, making my way toward the ceramic carpet, kneeling as I pointed at it. "Was this a real polar bear?"

Amanda nods. "Uh-huh. My Dad got it from the Alaskan Mountains."

"Woah", I smile, turning back to the bear. "Looks like you won't be terrorizing anyone anymore little guy", I laugh, rising from the carpet before Amanda speaks. "You want to see the cinema?", she said, pointing her thumb back, over her shoulder. "You have a cinema?"

"Mm-hm. It's basically a TV room."

I turn to the ten-inch across from me and speak. "Bigger than that tv?"

Amanda nods, heightening my excitement.

"Here it is, the cinema!"

My eyes were low as I entered the dark, silhouette room, much to my confusion. "Um, babe?"

"Yeah, Dominic?"

"It's dark in here."

"Oh!", Amanda laughed. "Sorry, I forgot!"

I heard two clapping sounds coming from Amanda, but before I could say anything, a fluorescent ray of light flicked on, causing my eyes to widen. Within seconds, the entire dark place suddenly became clear.

To my surprise, I found a large cinema with what looked to be rows of seats, along with a grandiose television set. "Oh my gosh! This is the biggest TV I've ever seen!"

"It sure is! Bigger than other tv's, huh?"

"Yeah, this is great!"

Amanda continued to smile until a shadow behind her approached, which I quickly noticed with a gasp. "Amanda, watch out!"

"Huh?", Amanda turned to find a young man with a mustache staring down at her. "Ms. Griffin, there you ar-ah!", Barry said as I punched him in the nose, causing him to fall on the floor, his hand holding onto his nose. "Ah!"

"Oh my gosh! Barry are you okay?", Amanda said, kneeling before Barry.

"Not really. That boy punched me in the nose!"

My eyes widen in shock upon hearing this. "Amanda, do you know this guy?"

"Yes, he's, my butler. He works here."

"He works here! Why didn't you tell me?"

"I was going to until you kicked him!"

"Amanda, who is this boy?"

Amanda sighs, turning to me. "Barry, this is my boyfriend, Dominic."

"Dominic?", Barry said, rubbing his nose.

"Yeah, this is the one I told you about."

Barry blinks, turning to me, his brow raised. "He certainly isn't as well-mannered as I thought."

I shift my eyes away from embarrassment before speaking. "I'm sorry. I thought you were trying to attack my girlfriend or something?"

"Attack? Why would I attack my Ms. Griffin?"

"*Ms.* Griffin?"

"Yeah, it's a nickname he gives me. Just like the nickname I gave him."

I chuckled. "And what's that?"

"Butler Barry."

I burst out laughing; my head was brought back as I spoke. "Butler Barry? What kind of name is that?", I continued to laugh as Amanda and Barry both folded their arms, their brows raised before I stopped. "I mean, it's a nice name", I smile at them, my teeth showing as Barry and Amanda turn to one another. "I hope we have everything we need to fix Dominic. At this rate, we're going to need everything we got."

"Yes, about that", Barry rubs the back of his head in anxiousness, much to Amanda's confusion. "What?"

Barry sighed. "Mr. and Mrs. Griffin called earlier. They said the plane just landed in St. Mora and are headed to the house now."

Amanda raised her brow. "*Now,* as in what?"

Barry rubbed the back of his head. "An hour."

"An hour?"

"Now, now, miss. Don't panic."

"I have all the reason to panic! One hour isn't enough to fix my boyfriend! I mean, why didn't you tell me this sooner!"

"I just got the call! Besides, maybe if you weren't showing your boyfriend around, I would've been able to find you faster!"

"I only did that because I thought we had more time, but we don't now, do we?"

"Excuse me, guys! Can I get a word here!"

Amanda and Barry turned their heads back to find me staring at them, my arms folded as I waved. "Look, I get you guys are stressed, but fighting isn't going to solve this. If we're going to do this, then we must stick together, okay?"

Amanda and Barry turned to each other and sighed, nodding as they turned back to me. "Okay."

I nod. "Good. Now, let's get dolled up!"

#

Amanda, Butler Barry, and I make our way down the narrow hallway. Amanda and her butler look straight ahead as they make their way down the hall. As for me, I was too busy looking at the shiny white marble floors with a red carpet. I took a moment to get on my knees and touch the shiny, red carpet along with the thick, marble floors, my reflection shining straight through. "This architecture for your floor is stunning."

"I'm glad you like it. It seems like you're enjoying yourself."

"Oh, I am. I've never felt so...so...fortunate!"

Amanda laughed. "When you're born into money, you get nothing but special treatment", she said, lowering her head. "Despite the expectations put upon you."

I looked at Amanda with sad eyes while she turned and smiled at me, making me smile as well. "Tell me about your parents. What are they like?"

With these words, Amanda's smile widens before looking up to the sky. "My parents are what you would call representative. Meaning, they are all about things being fair."

I shake my head in confusion. "I don't understand. What are they again?"

"They're politicians. Well, my father is. He's the kind of man who listens to the issues that are among the people, the being the less fortunate ones."

"So, he's a helper. He helps people. Makes the world better, he makes it good?"

Amanda nods. "As good as he can. That's all we can do, right?"

I nod, "Yeah."

"We're here, children", said Barry, causing Amanda and I to turn our heads to a ruby-encrusted door standing before our very eyes.

"Oh my gosh. Are those rubies?", I said, approaching the door and all its radiant beauty. "They sure are."

"What's behind it?"

"Oh, just my favorite room in the entire house. Barry, show him."

"Gladly, miss."

With these words, Barry grabs the two door handles and clicks them. My eyes widened; my smile wide as a room filled with various clothes was found.

"Clothes? Why would you need a ruby-encrusted door for a few suits and skirts?"

"Not just any suits", Barry said, splitting the doors open wide. To my eyes, I find a room full of various clothes. Tailored suits in various colors are all hung on several hangers, along with another row of suits, suits, and shoes. "Here we are, Master Dominic. All the suits you can wear."

"Wow", I said as I approached the hangers, my hands tracing the clothes. "Are these all tuxedos?"

Amanda nodded. "Yes, every Griffin gentleman wears one. You can't impress Mom and Dad without it."

I smiled, turning back to the clothes. "There are a lot of tuxedos to choose from. I don't know what I should start with first."

"Well, you can start first", she said, holding a blue tuxedo in her arms. "With that said, let's get you dolled up!"

#

Amanda and Barry sat on a couch, with Barry drinking a cup of tea and Amanda with a "Hot Tips Magazine" she flipped through, through with boredom. "Is he done yet?", Amanda said, turning to Barry. "I don't know, ask him."

"Dominic are you done?", Amanda shouts, looking at the wardrobe.

"Almost, I just need to get my belt on."

"Okay, hurry", Amanda said with a sigh.

"Be patient, madam."

"I'm done."

Hearing this, Amanda and Barry looked at the wardrobe, which was now open. I came out with a blue and black latched tuxedo, along with a black top hat sitting atop. "So, what do you think?", I said, flexing my body as Amanda and Barry watched. "Mmm, I don't like it."

"Me neither, take this off of me!"

"Next!"

I soon came out with a second outfit, this time with an orange tuxedo with blue polka dots. I didn't even need Amanda and Barry to answer. By the look of the outfit, it was clear. "Ugly?"

"Very"

"Hideous"

With a quick nod, I closed the drapes to the wardrobe only to open them back up again with a new outfit, one purple sun dress with white gossamer waves, mostly that in the Victorian era.

"Hm, I like this one, but it's...", I said, gazing down at the suit with an odd look.

"Ancient"

"Yeah"

Barry scoffs. "Ancient? That suit belonged to me as a child. I advise you to show some respect."

"Sorry, Barry."

I nod. "Yeah, I want something else."

"Alright, go back in!"

Once again, I close the drapes to the wardrobe, losing all hope. As for Amanda, she was lying back on the couch, her eyes gazing up to the ceiling as she sighed, much to Barry's dislike. "Don't worry, madam. I'm sure we'll find something soon."

"Soon? We don't have it soon; we need it now."

"There's still time. Just be patient."

"There's no patience, Barry. Mom and Dad are going to be here in the next hour. "I don't need time I need a miracle!", with these words, Amanda moves her head back on the couch, letting out a huge sigh of frustration, making Barry feel very much sad.

That is, until a quick thought comes to the surface. "Blimey."

Amanda turned to Barry. "What Cha say, Barry? Barry, where are you going?", Amanda said as Barry rose from the couch, his head turning back to Amanda. "I think I have something that can help master Dom?"

"What?"

"Wait here, I'm going to get it."

With that, Barry made his way down the hall, leaving Amanda in a confused state.

I sat in the closet, my eyes gazing down at the hundreds of clothes looking above me. Frustrated, I let out a heavy sigh, ready to give up, until there was a knock at my door, causing my head to rise. "Master Dominic?"

"Yeah?"

Without another word, a white tuxedo with a red flower. "Put this on right now."

I took the white tuxedo in my hands, my brow raised as I peered down at it. "This?"

"Yes, put it on now! I have something."

With nothing left to lose, I take the tuxedo from Barry's hands into mine, my eyes staring down at the item with a happy smile.

A good hour passed, and the sun slowly set over St. Mora, causing the same light to hit every building in the city. As for Griffin Manor, the evening sunlight hit the bricks of the place. Yet, little did we know, a yellow taxi made its way to the road, stopping dead at the mansion.

On the inside, Amanda and Barry looked at me with happy smiles as I sat in my tuxedo. "So, how does it look?"

"Smashing!"

"Huh?", I said, confused.

"He means he thinks it looks great, and so do I. But we won't approve it until we get your opinion."

"My opinion?", I said, making Amanda nod. "Oh, um, I think it looks good, good. I mean, it's better than those other catastrophes you gave me."

Barry folds his arms again before raising his head in the air. "Oh! Sorry, Barry! I didn't mean it li-"

"It's alright. It's just fashion", Barry said, turning to me. "Now, now that you're in your costume. "Let's fix that hair of yours", Barry said, bringing up a hair dryer and a tooth comb.

But before he could do anything, the doorbell rang, causing the whole three of us to turn our heads. "Who's that", I asked.

"I don't know."

Amanda gulps. "I think I do."

"What do you mean?", I said before Amanda turned to me. "Stay right here, Dominic. I'll go fetch the door!"

"Wouldn't you want me to do it?"

"No, no. I'll do it, Barry! You just go and do Dominic's hair."

With that, Amanda left the wardrobe, making it just Barry, me, and a set of hair products, that he was seconds away from bringing to my head before snatching it away with a swipe. "Don't even think about it!"

\#

A set of knocks were heard throughout the place as Amanda made her way down the hall of the mansion, making Amanda run even faster. "Just a moment! I'm coming!"

After a few more sprints, Amanda finally made it to the door, her posture straight as she looked at the two silhouette figures standing through the glass. Taking a deep breath, Amanda closed her eyes and grabbed hold of the doorknob. "You can do this; you can do this."

With nothing left to lose, Amanda twisted the doorknob and opened the door, letting a beam of light hit her face. She opened her eyes, all smiles. "Mom, Dad?"

Gazing up, Amanda finds two well-dressed Caucasian couples: a broad and very tall, man with patches of grey in his beard and a slim yet tall woman with short brunette hair. They both looked like classy people, but their smiles were big and wide as they gazed down at their daughter. "Hello, sweetheart!", answered Mr. Griffin, extending his hand to her.

Without a second thought, Amanda took her father's hand, shaking it firmly. "So, how was your trip?"

"Oh, it was wonderful, darling", answers Mrs. Griffin, leaning into her daughter's cheeks, giving her air kisses for each one before quickly pulling away. "We saw all kinds of beaches and ate almost every kind of shrimp."

"Don't forget the lobsters, dear."

Mrs. Griffin laughed. "Oh, yes. Those were the best part of the trip!"

Amanda watches as her parents walk straight past her before shutting the door, leaving them back in darkness. "But enough about us, where's that charming boy of yours?"

Amanda raises her brow. "Boy?"

"Your boyfriend, darling. The one that you promised to have us meet here."

"Oh, yes!", Amanda said, her eyes opening wide. "Yes, my boyfriend, he's um-"

"Stop it!", answered a voice echoing down the hall. "Barry, stop it!", said myself as I entered the hallway with a messy hairdo and Barry, with the hair presser and two-comb. "I was just trying to get you a nice silk press!"

"I don't need a silk press! What I need i-"

"Dom?"

Hearing this, Barry and I turned our eyes to the left, where Mr. and Mrs. Griffin stood before the both of us. "Barry?", said Mrs. Griffin, confused. "What are you doing?"

"Me?", Barry hides the presser and two combs behind his back, his posture straightened as he smiled. "I was just giving Master Dominic, a strapping hairdo, you know, for dinner."

"Dinner?", answers Mrs. Griffin, turning to me. "Oh, why you must be the boy dating my daughter?"

"Uhh…"

"Yes, he is!", Amanda said, taking my arm, and pulling me to the classy figures standing over me. "Mom, Dad. I would like to introduce you to my boyfriend, Dominic."

"Dominic? Why, that was the name of my grand-",

"Mr. Griffin's eyes widen as a huge gasp leaves him and his wife. "What's wrong?", I said, touching my hair. "Is it my hair?"

Mr. Griffin, with his eyes still wide, blinks a bit before coming to reality. "Erm, no", said Mrs. Griffin, stepping in. "It's just your tuxedo!", Mr. Griffin said loudly.

"My...my tuxedo?"

"Yes, it belongs to our butler."

"Yes, yes!", answered Barry, stepping in. "Sorry about that, Mr. and Mrs. Griffin; the tuxedo was my idea. I'm so sorry, I'll have it off immediately."

"No, no! It's fine, Barry. It looks great on him."

Don't be shy, Dom. Go on, shake my father's hand."

But I couldn't.

I didn't know why, but for some reason, my whole body was stuck, frozen of some sort. For my eyes were glowing bright green. I didn't know why, but I felt uneasy about something about him. Not to mention Amanda's mother. "Um, Mr. Mitchell?", said Mr. Griffin, making me snap out of my trance. "Are you alright?"

"Yes, he is", Amanda laughed, turning to me. "Dominic, shake daddy's hand. Now", Amanda said, leaning into my ear and whispering. "It's time to make that good impression we talked about"

I face Amanda, causing me to catch my breath once more before taking Mr. Griffin's hand into mine. "NICE TO MEET YOU; I'M DOMINIC MITCHELL!"

Mr. and Mrs. Griffin flinched, their eyes wide with shock at my loud outburst, echoing through the entire house. As for Amanda, she turned straight to me. "Um, Dom? You might want to lower your voice there."

"No, no, dear", Mr. Griffin laughed. "He's quite the jokester."

Amanda blinks, her eyes full of life. "Really?"

"Yes. Also, your hands are sweaty."

"What?", I said, pulling my hands away from Mr. Griffin's and wiping them on my shirt. "Sir, I'm so sorry!"

"It's alright, it happens."

"Um, why don't we go to the living room and talk", Amanda said, turning to her butler. "Um, Barry. Why don't you make dinner."

"Oh, yes. I could use a good meal after that fourteen-hour ride."

"Of course, Mrs. Griffin and you, Mr. Griffin?"

"Oh, I'll just stick with water."

Barry nods. "As you wish."

With that, Barry made his way through the hallway, the presser and two combs still in his hands, before heading out. As for Amanda and I, she turned to her parents and spoke. "Well, I guess we should get going then. Come on, Dominic."

With these words, Amanda and I make our way to the living room, with Mr. and Mrs. Griffin following. "He's quite the charmer", said Mrs. Griffin sarcastically. "I hope this one doesn't turn out like the other nuisances"

"Evelyn, behave yourself", Mr. Griffin said. "This is dinner, after all."

Mrs. Griffin scoffs, before trotting past her husband. "We'll see about that."

#

I sat on the pearly white couch, my smile big and wide as I sat with my girlfriend. My girl and her parents. When I first arrived at the house, I thought they were expecting high-strung, classy snobs, but the more I got to know them, the more I realized they were decent people. Much like Amanda when I first arrived.

The anxiety I felt earlier, was quickly washed away with a drink and a few stories from Mr. and Mrs. Griffin, who, by the look of it, were marvelous people.

"And then Evelyn jumped on the table, knocking off all kinds of items, and then fell right into a pile of lobsters!", Mr. Griffin slaps his leg, letting out a hardy laugh from him to me. "It must've been pretty bad for her to fall that hard!"

Mrs. Griffin shoots Mr. Griffin a look before rolling her eyes.

"Oh, it was! That mouse kept me up all night; I couldn't get any sleep!"

"It sounds like you had one heck of a night!", I said with a smile.

"Oh, I did! A night I would remember for the rest of my life!"

"That's not the only thing you'll remember", Mrs. Griffin muttered.

"Dominic, tell us about yourself", said Mrs. Griffin. "Are you in Amanda's class?"

I face Amanda, her head nodding before speaking. "Uh, I am. I mean, we're in the same math class together."

"Are you? Is that where you and Amanda met?"

I laughed. "Actually, no. Amanda and I met in the school cafeteria."

"Really? Evelyn and I met here. In the Manor."

"Here? Here where?"

Evelyn laughed. "In this house."

"Really, in this house?"

"I know, shocking, isn't it?"

I smile, drinking a tall glass of water, much like Mr. Griffin or in this case, Robert. The four of us continued to laugh until Barry approached us, bringing a tray of what looked to be stuffed seafood with a big smile on his face. "Dinner is ready", Barry said, placing the tray before Mr. and Mrs. Griffin, much to their liking. "Oh, good. Shall we head into the kitchen?"

"Of course. Come on, Dominic."

"Okay, ah!", I said as Amanda pulled me.

Before I knew it, Amanda, her parents, and I were all sitting in the dining room, my eyes big and wide as Butler Barry poured a steamy, hot soup that was poured from a large silver spoon and into a set of silver bowls Mr. and Mrs. Griffin possessed.

The same was soon done to Amanda and me; the creamy, thick white soup poured into our bowls. I stuck my tongue out in disgust at the sight of the carrot peeking up from the grey liquid, but before I could say anything, Barry spoke up. "The next entrée will be served shortly. Until then, enjoy."

"Thank you, Barry."

I didn't realize it at first, but as soon as the meat hit my plate, my mouth began to water.

"Woah", I said, my eyes wide. "What are those?"

"It's chowder."

I raise my brow. "Chowder?"

Amanda nods. "Yeah, it's a special kind of soup. What, never had this before?"

"No, and frankly, I don't think I want to."

"Why not?"

"Because it looks like slop."

Amanda scoffs. "Slop, this is chowder we're talking about, Dom. There's nothing sloppy about it?"

"I don't think it's slop; it just doesn't look appetizing to me."

"How do you know?"

"I don't know, I just don't think it's good."

"Then try it."

"What?"

"Try it, try the soup."

I shake my head. "I don't think I wan-"

"Dominic, open your mouth and eat the soup", Amanda said, holding her spoon up to him.

Here, try some."

"Oh, I don't think I wan-", my words were quickly cut off as my girlfriend shoved the stuffed crab into my mouth. As soon as it was, my tastebuds were enlightened, much to my liking. "Mm!", I said, munching on the finger food. "It's good, right?"

I nod. "Yeah, this is good, really good!"

"You two look so adorable together", said Mrs. Griffin. "You must get along well."

Amanda and I turn to look at each other awkwardly before one of us speaks. "Um, we weren't always like this."

"What do you mean?", Mrs. Griffin asked.

Amanda scratched her head. "Well, Dominic and I had some issues in the past."

"Issues?", said Mr. Griffin. "Like what?"

"Oh, nothing serious, just-"

"Fights!", Amanda said. "A lot of fights. If anything, we didn't really like each other in the beginning. It was bad."

Mr. Griffin scoffs. "Bad? Do you have any idea how many fights your mother and I had when we were married?", she said, eyeing his wife.

Amanda shrugs. "I don't remember you guys having any fights?"

"That's because you were nosey, dear. Then again, you always had a knack for being in other people's business."

"Evelyn", Mr. Griffin said, making his wife scoff, putting her eyes back at her bowl of chowder.

She scoffs. "What? I'm only being honest."

"Perhaps, too honest."

"Oh, don't be so sensitive, Robert. I had enough of that the ride home."

"I'm sensitive!", Mr. Griffin snaps, causing the whole table to get quiet.

Amanda and I look to Mr. and Mrs. Griffin in concern. "Father, is everything alright?"

"Quiet, Amanda!", Mrs. Griffin hissed. "This is between me and your father!"

"This is between all of us, Evelyn!"

"Oh, you're the one to talk!"

My breathing increased, along with my now racing heart, as my eyes glowed green once more. "Um, maybe you guys should take this somewhere else?"

"Oh, hush boy! Like you know anything!"

"That's enough, Evelyn!", Mr. Griffin roars, his fist slamming against the table, making the whole table go silent once again. "Of all days to act like this, you choose today!"

Amanda looked at her parents, her eyes full of concern. "Mom, Dad. What's going on?"

Mr. Griffin does nothing but rise from his seat and say the words that Amanda would not enjoy hearing. "Amanda, could you please take Mr. Mitchell outside for a moment? Your mother and I need to talk."

"But what about dinner?"

"Dinner is over."

#

Amanda and I sat outside on the steps, our heads hung low as we sat out in the cold night. "Well, that was a disaster", I said, making Amanda scoff. "It was shocking than anything."

"I'm sorry, I shouldn't have said it like that."

"It's fine. This isn't the first time I've seen my parents' fight. The only difference between this one is that this one was face-to-face."

"Was it hard seeing them like that?"

She nodded. "It was scary. I've never seen Dad so upset."

"Your mother didn't seem so."

"My mother is complicated. Then again, I've been dealing with her for years now."

"Why do you let her treat you that way?"

"It's not like I want her to, but I can't just disrespect her like that", she sighs. "In your family, your love is given, but for mine, it has to be earned."

"Well, that's bullshit."

She nodded. "It is."

I take Amanda's hand, my fingers intertwining with hers. "Amanda?", I said, making Amanda face me. "Your love will never have to be earned with me. You already have it. I love you, Amanda."

Amanda's eyes lit up, her smile warm and bright. "You love me?"

"I do"

With these words, Amanda and I lean in for a passionate kiss lasting a few minutes. A beam of light hit both our faces, causing Amanda and me to turn our heads in confusion. Standing before us, was a blue SUV van, its windows sliding down.

It was Mom waving. "Hey, baby! You ready to go!? It's late, and I need my beauty sleep!"

I laughed. "Okay, Mom! I'm coming!"

I turned to Amanda, our hands still intertwined. "I guess I'll see you tomorrow."

Amanda nodded. "Yeah, see you tomorrow, babe."

With that, I lean in to give Amanda a kiss, not on the lips but on the cheek, causing her face to glow bright red.

I let go of my girlfriend's hand, my back turned as I walked toward my mom's car and hopped right in. "So, how was it?", Mom asked as the door shut.

"It was good. I had a really good time."

"I'm sure you did", Mom said with a raunchy laugh.

This made me sigh with annoyance. "Yeah, okay, Mom."

"Oh, don't be so sensitive, Dominic. I'm just kidding."

"I know."

"Did you use protection?"

My face turned as red as an apple. "MOM, JUST DRIVE! PLEASE, JUST DRIVE!"

Laughing, Mom stepped on the brakes, letting the car leave the driveway and go down the road, leaving Amanda to wave as we disappeared into the night. "Bye, babe. See you in my dreams."

Amanda continued to wave as the car drove down the road. Yet, little did she know, a pair of silhouette figures stood two stories up from Griffin Manor. Their eyes sinister as they watched a black SUV van enter the house.

#

While Amanda was having a decent night, Mr. and Mrs. Griffin's night was going from bad to worse. Bursting through the bedroom door, Mrs. Griffin walked straight through the door, her eyes looking to the floor. That is until Mr. Griffin enters from behind, his eyes full of fire.

"What the hell is wrong with you?!", he shouts. "Of all days to be a bitch, you choose today!"

"It was pretty hard to pretend by your fakeness."

"What?"

"You, laughing it up like nothing bad is going on between us!"

"Keep your voice down!"

"No, I'm not! Sooner or later, Amanda will know you and I were never on vacation!"

"It's a much better coverup than signing divorce papers!", Robert brings his hands to his mouth, his eyes looking straight to the door. "Dammit! I can't believe I said that out loud."

"I hope it was hard enough for Amanda to hear. You coddle her too much anyway."

"I protect her from the truth! That's what a good parent does. Unlike some people!"

"Just because I'm harder on her doesn't mean I'm a bad parent!"

"You're definitely not a good one."

"And yet, you still married me. Doesn't matter anyway since we both sleep in separate beds now."

"We wouldn't have to if you weren't so difficult."

"Not so difficult as your last wife!"

Robert, with his eyes now full of shock, raises his hand and slaps his wife across the face, making her handkerchief fall to the floor. "Don't you dare mention my wife, ever!"

Evelyn, full of shock. "That wouldn't be the last time I have."

"As long as you live under my roof, you will not bring up the past, including this divorce. You got it?"

Evelyn nodded. "Crystal."

She slaps him back, giving him a painful red mark on the side of his face. "But hit me again, and I'll call the police. Got it?", she said, staring dead at him.

He nods, rubbing the side of his face. "Note taken."

Chapter 9: The Teacher

"Okay, hold on. You said what?", Amari said sitting across the lunch table from me as I fiddled with my fingers. "I told Amanda I loved her."

Amari's eyes widened. "Really? You said that?"

I nodded. "Yeah. I said it."

"And what did she say? Did she say it back?"

"Yeah, she did. I said it, and she said it. It was good. Scary but good."

Amari nodded popping a fry in his mouth. "So, I guess you guys are officially boyfriend and girlfriend now."

"I guess we are. Amanda and I are officially a couple."

Amari pops a fry in his mouth. "Speaking of which, where is Amanda?"

"Oh, she skipped lunch to study for her Spanish exam."

"Really? She skipped lunch?"

"Oh, don't worry. Barry packed her a lunchbox."

"Who's Barry?"

"Amanda's butler."

"Butler?", Amari said, shocked.

"Yeah, he makes her everything."

Amari scoffs, folding his arms. "Lucky."

"So, what have you been up to, Mar? Anything new happening with you?"

Amari shakes his head. "No, not really. Twins are still dick. Moms still absent. Same old, same old. So, yeah, nothing new."

"What about school? You still passing a class?"

"Yeah, grades are alright."

"Alright?", I said.

"Good. My grades are good; that's what I mean by alright."

"Uh-huh."

Amari scoffs. "They're good, Dom! I'm telling you, they're good!"

"I know, I know. I'm just kidding! Stop taking it so seriously, man. Geez."

Amari grunted a bit before popping another fry in his mouth, but before he could even swallow it, the bell rang, causing the two boys to grunt in annoyance. "Curse that damn bell!"

"I know. I swear we never get enough time to finish eating."

"Sixteen minutes isn't enough for everyone!", a heavy sigh escaped me as I shook my head. "Well, see you later, man."

"See ya, man!"

With that, the two boys turn their backs away from each other, leaving the cafeteria.

\#

Amari sat in his classroom, his eyes staring down at his journal, drawing all kinds of doodles. By the looks of it, he wasn't paying any attention to the lesson or to his teacher, Ms. Wilkins. He didn't care to listen, not after what she did. "So, from reading Macbeth, what have we learned from this story?"

Suddenly, the bell rang, causing Ms. Wilkins's students to gather their things and leave their seats. "I guess we're out of time. Remember to read up on Gandalf for next week's quiz. Chapters 4-8."

With these words, all the students made their way out of the classroom door, including Amari, who was seconds from leaving the door. Fiddling with her fingers, Ms. Wilkins raised her hand and spoke. "Amari!", she cried, making Amari stop a few inches from the door before facing her. "Yes?"

Ms. Wilkins approaches Amari, her eyes full of desperation. It was as if she was yearning for something, and the only way to ease it was from Amari Jenkins, A.J., himself. "Um, how are you?"

He raises his brow. "Fine."

She nodded, grinning. "That's great, and how about your friend, um, Dominic, was it?"

He nodded. "Um, yeah. He's doing good."

"He is?"

"Yeah, that whole eviction notice thing was settled."

"It was? By whom?"

"His girlfriend, his *rich* girlfriend. Paid for the whole eviction notice, even got him and his mom a new place to stay at."

"Really? Oh, that's fantastic! I'm so glad things worked out."

"Yeah, me too."

Amari and Ms. Wilkins stand in silence for a good minute, preventing their unsaid feelings from wandering and boiling within them. It wasn't until the silence overtook them both that their words shot open like an erupted volcano! "I'm sorry!", they shout at the same time, causing each other to bust out laughing. "I'm sorry, Amari, I didn't mean to—"

"No, it's fine, Ms. Wilkins. Really."

Their laughs slowly die down, giving Ms. Wilkins the chance to kneel before her student and rest her hands on his shoulders. "Amari", Ms. Wilkins spoke. "I just wanted to say that I'm truly sorry for putting your friend through all that hell. I never wished any harm to come to him. I'm not asking you to forgive me, I just want you to understand."

With those sweet and honest words, Amari pulls his teacher in for a loving embrace, his arms wrapped tightly around her. "There is nothing to forgive, Ms. Wilkins. I know you didn't mean any harm, I just wanted to be mad about something. I should've never put that on you. I'm sorry."

Ms. Wilkins grins before answering. "You are forgiven."

After a few more moments of embrace, Amari and Ms. Wilkins pull away from one another, their smiles bright and full of life. "So, what are you going to do now?"

"Well, I was going to head home, but before I do. How about I take you to see a good friend of mine?"

"Friend? Who?"

Amari said nothing and instead gave Ms. Wilkins a nonchalant look, making her eyes go big and wide. "Oh!"

#

The Summit High library stood proud and tall in the hallway, with hundreds of students sitting down. On the inside, several bookshelves with several genres found:

Fantasy.

On the right.

Horror.

On the left.

And History.

Right under Amanda Griffin.

Who happily had her nose in a book, a *history* book, one with sirens and knights, and a hero who would stop at nothing just to get his family back.

That's right; it's Homer's The Odyssey.

For two hours, Amanda stood in this very spot, reading the epic story of Odysseus, the crowned King of Ithaca, venturing through the seven seas, meeting all kinds of Gods and Goddesses, all just to meet the one he loved.

And Amanda loved every bit of it, for her eyes were glued to that book.

That is, without warning, a pair of hands cuff Amanda's eyes, blinding her from the printed words. "Guess who?", said the mysterious voice, making Amanda laugh. "Dominic, I know it's you."

"Is it?"

"Yes, I know these hands."

"Oh, do you?"

"Yes, I do", Amanda said, reaching her hands up to Dominic's, her fingers touching his. Dominic busts out laughing, his hands now falling from his girlfriend's eyes. "You are so bad at this!"

"I know, I know!"

"Shhhhhh!", answers a student sitting a few feet across from Amanda. "Oh, sorry!"

The boy looked at the couple in anger before going back down into his book. As soon as he did, Amanda and I went right back to each other. "What Cha reading'?", Dominic said, gazing down at her book. "Is it Macbeth?"

Amanda laughs, shaking her head. "No, it's The Odyssey. Have you read it?"

I nod. "Yeah, my English teacher, Mr. Gilbert, gave us a pop quiz on that next week. It was so boring."

I scoff. "BORING!?"

"Hey!", said the boy, causing Amanda and I to turn heads. "If you guys want to talk, could you do it outside!?"

Amanda and I nodded. "He's right. We should go."

"Yeah, we should. Amari's waiting for us", Amanda said. Then, leaning toward my ear, she said. "Do you want to take a trip to the janitor's closet before we do?"

A big, happy grin formed across Amanda's lips. Without a second thought, Amanda took me by the hand, and the both of us rose from the seat, leaving the boy in glasses full of disgust. "Couples, always in each other's faces. Good thing I'm gay."

\#

Amari and Ms. Wilkins sat on the steps of the school, sitting next to each other. "Are you sure this is going to work?"

Denise turned to him and nodded. "Of course, it will."

"But what if he doesn't like me? I mean, I sabotaged your relationship with him, remember? I'm basically bad news."

"Were. You *were* bad news. Today, you're not, and you're going to show it."

"How?"

"By talking, by negotiating", Amari turned his eyes to the hall, where the faint yet loud sounds of laughter were heard.

Hearing this, Amari turns his eyes back to Denise, his eyes big and wide. "They're here."

"They?"

"Dominic and his girlfriend, they're coming, stand up!"

Confused and a bit scared, Ms. Wilkins rises from her chair, his back straight as he dusted his ripped jeans off. "Just stand still. You look great."

"I do?"

"Yeah."

"Hey, Mar!", Dominic called out, his arm raised as he held his girlfriend's hand.

Amari smiles as Amanda and I approach him. "Hey, Dom!"

"Hey, man. So, what is it? Who did you want us to meet?"

"More so *you*"

I raised my brow. "Me?", I said, turning to the young woman standing beside Amari. "Wait, who's this?"

"Um, yeah, that's what I want to talk to you about. Dom, this is Ms. Wilkins", Amari moves to me, his head leaning up to my ears. "This is the one I was telling you about."

"It's lovely to meet you", Mrs. Wilkins said. "Amari's told me so much about you."

I raised my brow as the sudden realization came to the surface, making me frown. "Wait, a minute. Ms. Wilkins, as in *Mrs. Wilkins*?"

"Yes, look I-"

"You're the one who gave Amari that fake money! The one that got my mom, and I kicked out of our apartment!"

"I know, and I'm really sorry about that."

"Sorry!? Are your serious right now?"

"Dom!", Amari said, joining in. "She's just trying to apologize. She's sorry."

"Sorry? She doesn't know what sorry is! My Mom and I almost ended up on the streets because of you. Thankfully, Amanda was able to fix it with her father's money!"

Ms. Wilkins lowers his head in shame. "What can I do to make this better?"

"The only thing I want is for you to leave!"

"Dominic!"

"No, it's alright, A.J."

"No, it's not! Dominic, apologize to her right now!"

"No, I'm leaving now!"

"Dominic!"

"Are you coming with me or not?"

Amari, with these words ringing in his ears, turns his attention back to Mrs. Wilkins and frowns. "No"

"What?"

He faces me, his eyes full of fire. "No, I'm not coming with you. Not after the way you disrespected my teacher."

"I'm disrespectful?", I said, pointing to myself.

Amari scoffs, rolling his eyes before taking Mrs. Wilkins by the arm. "Come on, Mrs. Wilkins. Let's go", he said, leading her down the hallway.

I grunt, my fists clenched. "Fine, leave! I'll just go talk to my girlfriend. She's the only person who listens to me!"

With these words, I head down the school steps, not once watching Amari leave with his English instructor.

#

I was in my bedroom, my feet pacing the floor as I cursed almost every word in the dictionary. All to Amanda, who sat patiently on my bed, propped up on a Pikachu-stitched pillow. "I can't believe this!", I said, enraged. "This is so unfair!"

"Dominic, calm down."

"Why should I? I have just as much right to be angry right now! Amari has the nerve to bring Denise, a jerk who single-handedly ruined my life, but the moment I call him out for it, he accuses me of being disrespectful!", I scoff. "Like it's my fault I got kicked out of my house!"

"Okay, okay!", Amanda said, putting her arms on my shoulders. "Babe, take a deep breath, okay? I need you to calm down!"

With these words, I closed my eyes and took a breath, the air entered my nostrils, lungs, and every other part of my body that was now soothed by the immense taste of air. Within minutes, I release a huge amount of air from my body, letting all my senses return to me.

"See?", Amanda said with a smile. "Feel better?"

I take another breath before nodding. "Yeah, a little."

"Good", Amanda said as I fell onto my bed, my head lowered as I sighed. "I just don't understand why Amari thinks I'm disrespectful. It's like he forgot all about what happened."

"Happened?", Amanda said, sitting down on the bed with me. "What happened?"

I turn to Amanda, my eyes full of sadness, before answering. "You wouldn't want to hear it?"

"I'm your girlfriend, Dom. Your thoughts are my thoughts", she took my hand in hers before speaking. "Just look into my eyes and tell me the truth."

With these words of encouragement, I look into my girlfriend's eyes and speak. "Ms. Wilkins was Amari's old English teacher from back in the day. That is, until he moved."

"He moved away?"

I nod. "Yes, but suddenly, out of the blue, she showed up back in his life. It wasn't long before Amari told Ms. Wilkins about me and my financial situation."

She raises her brow. "You mean the eviction notice?"

"Yeah", I nod. "The eviction notice. As soon as Amari gave me the money, he went right to me. At first, I was happy because I thought things would get better", I lowered my head, and my smile was gone. "Or so I thought when I found out the money was fake."

"Fake!?", Amanda gasps, shocked. "Wait, Amari gave you fake money!?"

"He didn't realize it was fake at first, but once the money was given to me, it was. Before I knew it, my mom and I were kicked out of our apartment. The one place that I called home. The only home I ever knew, and it was all thanks to that damn woman!", saying this, I brought my hand to my face and sighed. "Things were never the same again."

Amanda nodded, marinating all my words. "Well, I can see why you hate her. I would, too, if she got me kicked out of Griffin Manor. But why are you just now telling me this? When you told me you were moving, I had no idea it had something to do with Amari."

I sigh in disappointment. "It's not like I didn't want to tell you I just never thought to do so. Mostly because of you. If you hadn't gotten your dad to buy that vacation home, Mom and I would be on the streets now."

Amanda smiles. "I did help, didn't I?"

I nod. "Yes, you did."

Amanda blushes before shifting her head. "I think you should talk to Amari, Dominic. I know you're angry at him, but you guys are friends, and I don't want your friendship to be ruined."

"Oh, and you would love that, wouldn't you?"

"Love what?"

"Love me and Amari separating as friends. As much as you hate each other, seeing him leave would be heaven."

"Heaven?", Amanda scoffs. "Look, Dom. I may not like Amari, but I don't hate him. If I hated him, I wouldn't have decided to make the agreement of sharing you with each other."

I roll my eyes in an awkward manner before shaking my head. "Yeah, could you not say the word "share" when it comes to me?"

Amanda sighs. "My point, Dominic, is that you and Amari have history; if you let something as meaningless as another guy, get in the way, then things are going to get bad for the both of you", she nodded. "Okay?"

I sigh, shaking my head. "Okay, I'll go talk to Amari."

Amanda smiles. "Good, and while you do that, I'll be at Griffin Manor, helping my father with a few things."

I raise my brow in confusion. "Things? What things?"

"Oh, just things. Boring, not at all important things", Amanda grabbed her purse, whipping it around her shoulder before making her way up to me.

"What's that supposed to mean?"

"Don't worry about it", she gives me a small peck on the lips before turning away from me and heading out, the door closing shut.

I gazed up at my dresser, where a photo of Amari and I were found smiling. I quickly reach my hand to it, bringing my eyes straight to it. As soon as I do, my eyes go straight to the squash yellow telephone sat.

\#

The evening sun burned bright, causing various colors of red, orange, and pink to swirl in the sky. I sat alone on a bench, near an abandoned park. Even though it was spring, I still decided to wear a jacket and my sweatpants. It was weird for some people, but it was fine for me.

I waited a few more minutes until suddenly, my eyes started to glow bright green. I brought my hand to the back of my neck and knew. I turned my head back, and that's where I found her. Without a second thought, Amari took a deep breath and approached Dominic, stopping dead on the bench. As soon as he did, Amari brought his hand up to his hand. "Um, hey, Dom."

I raise my head when I hear this, my eyes looking up at him. "Hey. Looks like you got my text."

"Yeah, I did. Heard you wanted to talk to me about something."

"Yeah", I rose from the bench, my hands in my pockets, looking at him. "For starters, I wanted to say I'm sorry. I was being an ass; I shouldn't have done that to you."

"To me?", Amari said with a raised brow. "What about Ms. Wilkins?"

I shrugged my shoulders. "What about her?"

"What about her?", he scoffs. "Have you forgotten what you said to her?"

"Of course, I remember. Did you think I came here to apologize to her?"

"I assumed you would."

"Well, I didn't."

"Wow, you are unbelievable."

"Says the most gullible guy I've ever met."

"I'm gullible!?"

"Yes! This woman got me kicked out of my and my mom's apartment, and you're just sitting here like she did nothing wrong!"

"She was just trying to help you! She didn't mean to get you kicked out!"

"I don't believe that one bit!"

Amari grunts. "You know what, forget this. I should've known you'd act like this!"

"And what's that supposed to mean!? Where are you going?"

"None of your business! You know, for someone who seems so sincere, you really come off as a dick, the same dick I've been enduring for years but not anymore! I'm done with you, Dom."

"Done? What do you mean done?"

Amari said nothing and just walked away from me. "Oh, so you're giving me the silent treatment now!"

"Amari!", I said as Amari continued to walk away. "Amari!"

Amari continued to walk away, leaving me in sadness. "Wait, it go, Dominic."

"*I* started this. No, *you* started this! The moment he gave you that bag, the moment he pulled that prank on me, was the moment my life changed forever, and it's all because you were too gullible to see past that!"

"Gullible!?"

"Yes, you're gullible! In fact, you're too nice, and that is what got you into this situation you're in now! You were fooled again, and you're going to continue getting it until you learn to open your eyes and see that!"

Amari lowers these words before speaking. "All I wanted was for you to say sorry, not bring up the past. Just shows just how much of an asshole you can be."

"I'm not being an asshole; I'm trying to protect you. You know how Denise is, the situation he put me through. You know it, but you're sitting here and acting like he didn't! If anyone's an asshole, it's you Amari!"

"If I'm an asshole, then you're a bigger one."

"At least this asshole knows when to not make the same mistake twice!"

Amari froze at these words, his eyes full of fire. "You know what, I don't know why I came here."

"I don't know why I'm friends with you, especially with someone like you."

"Wha-what are you saying?"

"What do you think I'm saying? I'm saying I'm sick of you. I want you out of my life!"

Amari blinked, his eyes full of horror which quickly became fire. "Hold on, you can't be serious about this—"

"No, I am! I'm not kidding, but this time, I want you to go! Yes, like you said, there are other fish in the sea!"

"Yeah, and I know just the one", Amari flips his hood over his forehead and speaks. "See you never!"

With these words, Amari turns his head and walks away, leaving me in utter regret, giving him no choice but to touch his neck. "Wait, it go, Dominic."

\#

Amari sat on the steps of Summit High beside Ms. Wilkins—, his eyes held low and sad. "And then I just walked away. I didn't say anything else."

"I'm so sorry, Amari."

Amari faces Ms. Wilkins. "No, I'm sorry. You were just trying to help him and Dominic just spat in your face."

"I agree. That boy is very disrespectful."

"Yeah, he is."

Suddenly, Ms. Wilkins took Amari's hand, her fingers intertwining with his as she looked at him. "But I know who isn't, and that's you."

Amari grins, nodding. "Thank you, Ms. Wilkins."

"You're welcome, Amari."

\#

"You broke up?", said Amanda, staring at me with wide eyes.

"Yeah, we did."

"But how? I thought you guys were friends?"

"We were until we started fighting", I sighed, my fingers combing through my hair as I sat down on the steps. Amanda soon sits beside me, her eyes facing mine. "It wasn't bad. We just said some things to each other that…I wished I could take it back", I sighed, facepalming myself. "I really messed up, Amanda, and now, Amari hates me"

Amanda's head lowered. "Don't beat yourself up. You're not the first one to ruin a friendship."

I turn to Amanda, my brow raised. "What do you mean?"

"That's for another time. Right now, it's time to prepare."

"Prepare for what?"

Amanda gives me a happy grin before speaking. "The auction."

Chapter 11: The Auction

While Amari was rekindling his friendship with Ms. Wilkins, I had to break all of it to my girlfriend. She didn't like listening to me then, but this time she would.

She *really* would.

Now, up the Griffin Manor steps, I raised my hand and knocked on the door. Within minutes, the door opened, but it wasn't who I had thought.

It wasn't Barry.

It was: "Amanda?", I said with a raised brow.

My dizzy, red-headed girlfriend smiled at me. "Hi, Dominic. I saw you coming up the steps. I stopped Barry before he could come."

"She's not lying; she really did that", answers Barry, peeking his head from the door.

I laugh. "I'm sure she did", I said, lowering my eyes in sadness, much to Amanda's dislike. "Is everything okay, Dominic?"

I shake my head. "Not really."

"Why? How'd it goes with Amari?"

I look at Amanda, my eyes low and sad. "Amari and I broke up."

"Broke up?", Barry said with a raised brow.

"Barry, could you leave us alone for a moment?", Amanda said, making Barry nod. "Yes, sorry."

Saying this, Barry turned from the door, walking away. As soon as he does, Amanda closes the front door, leaving me and Amanda alone. "What do you mean broke up? You did talk with him, right?"

"I did but Amari thought otherwise."

"What do you mean? What happened?"

"Nothing, we just argued. Said things really hurt each other. It all happened so fast and before I knew it, he was gone", I grunted, falling onto my knees. "I'm such an idiot! If I hadn't been so angry, none of this would've ever happened. Amari was the only friend I had and now, he's gone. Now, I'm all alone."

Amanda watches as my head held low before shaking her head. "You're not alone, Dominic."

"What?", I said, lifting my head.

"You may not have Amari, but you have something even better: me."

"But Amari, he-"

"Made his choice. You had as much right to be mad at him for what that guy did to you. If Amari doesn't understand that, then that's his problem, not yours."

I nod, thinking about this. "I guess you're right."

"Of course, I am. I can't remember a time when I was wrong."

I lower my head and speak. "That's what Amari used to say."

Amanda's sad look was quickly seen before grabbing my hand and gazing up at me. "Hey, I know what'll make you feel better."

"What?", I said, my head raised.

Amanda smiles. "My Dad is hosting a party tonight with several of the most. How does that sound?"

I smile at these words, my mood changing. "It sounds great!"

#

"This sucks!", I said, standing in my white tuxedo, the same one I wore when meeting Amanda for the first time.

Only I was happy at that time, nervous but happy, and now I was as mad and confused as I looked at my reflection. "Oh, come on, Dom. This is a party."

"An auction doesn't count as a party."

"It does for rich millionaires and businessmen. Those being my father."

I rolled my eyes in annoyance, my spoon dipped back into my bowl of tomato soup. "I don't see how this is going to help me with anything. If anything, it's going to be boring."

"It might be, but it could also be a good distraction from you know who and any distraction is a good distraction. Besides, you don't have anything else to do."

I blinked, looked down at my soup, and nodded. "Yeah, I guess so."

"The party starts tonight at seven-thirty. So, we gotta look sharp."

I laugh. "I always look sharp."

"You sure do."

The two of us lean in for a quick peck on the lips before pulling away. As soon as we did, Amanda brought her lunch box to me and spoke. "Wanna bite off my sandwich?"

I nod, happily taking a bite out of it. "Mmm."

#

The moment the school bell rang, I was in my fourth-period class, reading a soliloquy on "I Am Legend", It was boring, as usual, but this was all we had for this lesson, which was good as time passed. Before I knew it, the bell rang, and I was out of the class and into Amanda's arms, her smile big and bright as she held me.

As soon as she does, we're brought in for a long-awaited kiss, our lips brushing against each other before pulling away. "I missed you."

"I missed you too, baby."

"Ready?"

I nod. "Ready"

"Alright, let's go!"

With these words, Amanda and I headed out the doors of Summit High, our hands intertwined as we ran down the steps.

#

Butler Barry stood on a ladder, his arms raised high, holding a large, sparkly, golden flag over his head, stretched to the side of a door. In his mouth, a silver metal nail stuck from his bottom lip. Within minutes, the nail was taken from his mouth and pricked into the golden fabric before a large, wooden hammer beat it inside with just two knocks.

The door opened wide, revealing two silhouette figures entering the room without Barry noticing. "Hey, Barry!", as soon as he hears this, Barry's hammer hits the front of his thumbnail, tearing the skin there. "Ah-shit! Mmmm!!!", Barry said, bringing his nail in his mouth, sucking the pain "away".

"Barry, you home!?"

"Y-yes! I'm in the living room! Come on in!"

With these words, Amanda and I walk past the corridor and into the living room, laughing and giggling with each other before spotting Barry standing atop a ladder, his back straightened as he sucked his thumb, like that of an infant.

Amanda and I turned to each other in utter confusion at Barry's awkwardness before speaking. "Um, Barry? What are you doing?"

"Hm?", Barry said through his mouth before looking down at his thumb. "Oh!"

Barry took his thumb from his mouth. "I was trying to set the flag up until the channel hit my thumb."

Amanda and I raised our brows, much to Barry's dislike, as his face fell flat. "Don't ask."

"Ah, Amanda, dear!"

Turning her head, Amanda's eyes lit up to find her father, his smile big and bright as he approached her with open arms. "There you are!"

"Daddy!"

I watched as Amanda ran toward her father, her arms wrapped as she was lifted in the air, much to Amanda's surprise and mine, before bringing her down. "Woah! You're in a cheery mood!"

"I sure am! Tonight is a special night for me!"

"What do you mean? Isn't this an auction? Also, hi, Mr. Griffin."

Mr. Griffin gives me a quick nod. "Mr. Mitchell, it seems you've heard about our event."

I nod. "Yes, Amanda told me all about it on the way here. But from your perspective, it seems like a lot more."

"Yes."

"What is it?"

Mr. Griffin smiles. "How 'bout I show you?", Mr. Griffin tilts his head a bit before turning his head back.

Only, I wasn't moving. "Show me?", I said, turning to Amanda. "What does he want to show me?"

"Go on, Dom. Dad's already told me about her."

"Her?", I said, causing Amanda to tilt her head. "Go."

With these words, I turned away from my girlfriend and to Mr. Griffin, who was now a few feet away from me.

#

I walked greatly behind Mr. Griffin, my eyes glued to his broad, toned shape, his height immaculate. I didn't know why, but there was something about him. When I looked at him, it was like I was looking at a king, a great king who, without reason, would proudly bow down to.

He was a man, a man that Dominic would surely like to be.

Someday.

It wasn't long before we made our way to a door; his arms extended as the door opened. We entered a dusty room crowded with all kinds of junk and various ceramics. I looked all around the dusty basement, amazed by the size as I looked. "Mr. Griffin, what is this place?"

"This is where I keep my most priceless treasures."

"Treasures?", I said, turning my eyes to him. "Yes, these "treasures" will be used for the auction."

"Really? Which one?"

Mr. Griffin chuckles. "You're standing right behind it."

My eyes lit up in shock. "What?"

"Turn around."

With these words, I turn my body around, where I find a rectangular-shaped object covered with a white cloak.

I raise my brow. "Um, a dirty, old cloak?"

Mr. Griffin laughs. "It's what's behind the cloak, that matters."

Moving aside, Mr. Griffin makes his way up to the hidden object, taking hold of the cloak before snatching it right off.

My eyes were closed shut at the accumulation of dust that came from the cloak. Soon, the dust settles, my eyes open, and the light comes in. To my surprise, I found a portrait, a painting with golden-framed edges. It isn't long before I find a painting, a portrait of a young, lovely, freckled-faced black woman smiling from the frame.

Seeing this, I turn to Mr. Griffin and speak. "Mr. Griffin, who is that?"

"That is my wife, Mia."

"Your wife?"

"Yes, although she used to be"

"What happened to her? Was she sick?"

Mr. Griffin frowns, his eyes full of sadness. "She was murdered."

I gasp, my eyes widening. "Murdered?"

Hearing this, I turn to the portrait of Mia Griffin, along with the infant cradled in her arms. "Oh", I blinked, turning to Mr. Griffin. "How old was she?"

"Twenty-eight, young."

"I'm so sorry, Mr. Griffin."

"Don't be, it's not your fault."

"It must be painful seeing this painting of her."

"Not as painful as the man that killed her."

"The man?"

"Octavius"

I blink, my brow raised. "Who's Octavius?"

Mr. Griffin clenches his fist, causing both his eyes to squint. "I-I'm sorry. It's too painful to speak."

I placed my hand on him before speaking. "It's okay; I know what it's like to lose a loved one. You don't have to talk about it if you're not ready."

Mr. Griffin sighs, his eyes settling before nodding. "Thank you, Dominic."

"You're welcome, sir."

"What are you two doing in here?"

Hearing this, Robert and I turn our eyes back to find Mrs. Griffin's silk, red dress standing before the door, her brows arched. "Robert, I've been looking all over for you", Mrs. Griffin's eyes widened at the portrait sitting behind Mr. Griffin and me, much to Mrs. Griffin's shock. "Oh, you found it?"

Mr. Griffin nodded. "Yes, it was hiding here in this dusty, old attic with all the rest of this junk."

"Junk? I thought you said it was treasure?"

"It is", Mr. Griffin turned to the portrait, his hand placed on it. "This is but the rest, yeah, it's junk."

"And we should get out of it. It's not good to be around all this dust."

"Not to mention, creepy. It's too dark to be in here."

"I most certainly agree", My eyes widened as I turned my eyes to Mrs. Griffin. Her gaze was bright as she peered down at me. "My daughter is waiting for you upstairs. She wants you to try on the new tuxedo, Barry made for you."

"Really?", I said with my eyes bright. "What does it look like?"

"I don't know. Barry says it's real special."

I smile, making my way past Mrs. Griffin and towards the door, opening it wide before it closes behind me. As soon as it does, Mr. Griffin turns his eyes back to the portrait, much to Mrs. Griffin's delight. "I can't believe I'm getting rid of this and after seventeen years."

"A lot can change in just seventeen years", Mrs. Griffin said, approaching her husband. "Besides, don't you think it's time?"

"Yes. I can't hold onto Mia forever. Getting rid of this portrait will help me finally move on."

Evelyn nodded. "Hey, let's get out of here. It's getting a bit too creepy in here."

"Yeah, you're right."

With these words, Mr. and Mrs. Griffin made their way out of the attic, with Robert heading out first before Evelyn turned her eyes back to the portrait. She looked at it for a few more minutes before closing the door behind her, leaving the portrait once again in utter darkness.

#

The sun sat over the hilltops of St. Mora before slowly setting down on the horizon, disappearing from view. As soon as it did, the orange-red hue quickly turned dark indigo-blue with nothing but a big, white moon that was found.

The day was gone, and night roamed.

I stare at myself in the mirror, my eyes looking down at my tuxedo, my new, more authentic, black and white tuxedo that Amanda picked out for me. As nice as it was, I became conflicted about something, only it wasn't what I was wearing. "I don't get it."

"Don't get what, Dom?", Amanda said, looking in the mirror, her hair tied in a knot.

"It's the portrait, you know, the one in the attic?"

"Yeah, what about it?"

I scratch my head. "Well, it's a picture of Mr. Griffin's, your dad's, wife and daughter. It's kind of weird for him to just get rid of it."

"Weird? Why would getting rid of it be weird?"

"No, I mean, why would he sell it to a group of people? I mean, if he wanted to get rid of it, why didn't he just, you know, throw it away."

"Throw it away?", Amanda said, turning from her reflection, her brow raised. "Why would he do that?"

"I don't know. It just seems like the best thing to do. I mean, I just think it's better than selling it for money. If not, healthier."

Amanda scoffs. "I understand what you're saying, Dominic, but that's something that only normal people would do, and my father isn't normal."

"What do you mean?"

Amanda giggles, knotting my tie to my tux before smiling. "You'll see."

Before I could say anything else, there was a knock, causing me and Amanda's eyes to turn. "Who is it?", Amanda said at the door.

"It's your mother, Amanda. Open the door"

With these words, Amanda makes her way to the door, twisting the doorknob. Within seconds, Mrs. Griffin walks in, her posture tall. "Yes, mother?"

With her posture tall, Mrs. Griffin looked down at us. "I was just coming to see if you were dressed. I also wanted to tell you that the buyers have arrived."

"The buyers?"

"The consumers, babe, the people who'll be bidding on Dad's portrait."

"Oh."

"They'll be paying high amounts of money for it. So, I suggest you get down there."

"Of course, Mrs. Griffin."

Mrs. Griffin shouts at me a wry look before turning her back from me and exiting the room.

I sigh heavily, my head turning to Amanda before speaking. "Give it time, right?"

Amanda brought her arm around my collarbone. "She'll come around. Soon."

#

Amanda and I walked downstairs, together, as we descended the steps to a group of people dressed in tailored tuxedos and dresses, all letting out hardy laughs. "Woah, a lot of people showed up for this auction."

"They sure did. I knew there would be a lot of people coming, but not this many. That portrait must be really special to them."

"Must be."

"You made it!", said a voice before Amanda and me, with Amanda's smile growing big and bright. "Dad!"

I watch as Amanda runs to Mr. Griffin, embracing him in a quick hug before speaking. "I'm so happy you're here with me, Amanda."

"Me too, Dad", Amanda raises her brow, her head turning left and right before speaking. "Where's Mom?"

"Oh, she's in the attic with the workers. She'll be directing the portrait into the place."

Amanda blinks. "Oh, okay."

"In the meantime, I have some very important people for you to meet", Mr. Griffin waves his hand to me, causing me to hop right off the steps and to Amanda and him.

Within seconds, Amanda, Mr. Griffin, and I all made our way down the group of people in their tailored-white suits and dresses, all as lavish as I. It was quite too much for me, but that's when Amanda and I approached three young men. "Ah, Mr. Yorkshire!"

The grey-haired man with the tailored black and white tuxedo turns his eyes to the young man and smiles. "Mr. Griffin!"

The two men let out a hardy laugh before embracing in a quick hug. "It's been years!"

"I know. How have you been?"

"Great. I'll be even greater when I see that portrait tonight. I can't wait to see it."

Mr. Griffin laughs. "I'm sure you can't, but before that, I'd like you to meet someone very special", Mr. Griffin said, bringing Amanda and me to approach a peppered-bearded man. "Amanda, Dominic, I'd like you to meet my dear friend, Henry Yorkshire."

"Pleased to meet you both", Mr. Yorkshire spoke.

"Hi."

"Hello"

"Griffin?", Yorkshire said, looking at me. "Robert, you never told me you had a daughter?"

Mr. Griffin nodded. "Yes, my firstborn."

"And this must be your son."

My eyes widened. "Oh, I'm no-"

"This is my boyfriend!", Amanda said, turning to me. "Dominic, Dominic Mitchell?"

"Mitchell?", he questioned. "That's a strapping name."

"It's Scottish."

"So, Dad, how do you know Mr. Yorkshire?"

"Yorkshire is a famous artist of mine from college. He paints many of the portraits you see hung up on the wall."

"Really?", I said.

"Well, not all of them, but most of the work you see is done by me. We artists can't take all the credit, am I right, pal?", he said, giving Mr. Griffin a quick nudge on the shoulder.

Mr. Griffin nodded.

"Robert?", said a voice, causing Mr. Griffin to turn his head.

Mrs. Griffin stood in her casual red gala dress, much to Mr. Griffin's delight. "Evelyn, my dear. I was starting to worry. Did you get the portrait?"

"Of course, I did", she said, moving to the side, revealing two men in suits, holding a portrait across from each other.

"Wow, that is one magnificent painting", said Yorkshire. "I don't think I painted that one."

"That's because you didn't, Yorkshire."

"Really? Who did?"

Mr. Griffin doesn't speak but stares dead at the portrait of his wife. Yorkshire looked at him as if he was stuck in some kind of trance. "Mr. Griffin?", he said, but Mr. Griffin didn't respond. "Robert!"

Robert sucks in some air, snapping out of his trance before facing Mr. Yorkshire. "I'm sorry, Yorkshire. What did you say?"

Yorkshire looked to his friend quite concerned. "Nothing important. Are you alright?"

He nodded, grinning. "Yes, I'm fine."

The sound of glass clinking is heard throughout the room, causing everyone in the room to spin their heads.

Once everything is settled down, Mrs. Griffin clears her throat and speaks. "I would like to start off by saying thank you for coming out tonight on this momentous occasion. We will now begin our auction, which my daughter will gladly be presenting", Mrs. Griffin faces her daughter. "Amanda?"

"I'm coming, Mother!", she said. Amanda gives me a quick peck on the cheek, smiling. "Wish me luck, babe."

I raise my hand to my cheek before a happy grin form across my friend. "That girlfriend of yours must be something special, isn't she?"

"She sure is", I nod, my face turning red.

Amanda tapped a fork on a champagne glass, causing her to clear her throat and her back to be poised. "Um, excuse me, everyone! Can I have everyone's attention, please?!"

The group of people all turned their heads, including me, Yorkshire, and Mr. and Mrs. Griffin. They all look at her with big eyes as if she were a snack that they could devour in one single bite, triggering Amanda's stage fright. "Um, thank you all for coming out tonight. Um…", Amanda's voice cracked up a bit, causing her palms to sweat as she looked out at the crowd.

Luckily, I was there to support her. In her moment of distress, I took a step from the crowd, which Amanda quickly noticed. I brought my hands up to the creases of my mouth and let out a deep breath. "Breathe, Mandy."

Hearing this, Amanda does so and speaks. "Tonight, I will be presenting this portrait of Mrs. Griffin", I smiled at my girlfriend's achievement. "Now, without further ado, let's start the bidding. Who would like to go first?"

"Two hundred!", said a young woman with her hand raised.

Amanda smiled. "Two hundred? Can anyone go higher?"

"Five hundred!", said a young, bearded man in the corner.

"Ooh, *five hundred*! Anyone else wanna beat that?"

"A million dollars!", said a high-pitched voice, causing the entire room to gasp.

"Wow, a million?! Who-"

"Sorry about that!", said a young woman cradling what looked to be a five-year-old in her arms. "Sorry, that was my daughter! Don't believe a word she just said; she doesn't have a million dollars with us."

Amanda blinks. "Oh, well then, I guess that leaves us back to a thousand."

The mother bops her daughter on the forehead, causing her to let out a small whine before disappearing back into the crowd. "Twenty-thousand!"

What was that?"

"Twenty thousand, right here!", Amanda saw a young black man with a tailored suit, his smile big and wide as he turned his eyes back to Mr. Griffin, much to his shock.

Mr. Yorkshire. "Alright, we have twenty-thousand! Does anyone want to go higher!"

"Fifty thousand!", Mr. Yorkshire shouts with pride.

"Hm, looks like we have fifty thousand, again from Mr. Yorkshire."

Mr. Yorkshire nodded, shooting Mr. Griffin a quick wink, making Mr. Griffin's eyes widen. "Anyone want to go higher?"

"A hundred thousand!"

"A hundred thousand! Who was tha—", Amanda's eyes widen in shock at the sight of her father standing up from his seat. "Dad?"

Amanda turned her eyes to the crowd, turned to me, and shrugged, as I had absolutely no idea what was going on. "Robert, what are you doing?", said Mrs. Griffin, taking Mr. Griffin's arm. "I'm doing what needs to be done."

Seeing this, Amanda moves her hair to the side and speaks. "Okay, we have a hundred thousand. Does anyone want to go higher?"

"Five hundred thousand!", said Mr. Yorkshire, eyeing Mr. Griffin, who obviously was not having it. "Eight hundred thousand!", Mr. Griffin shouts to Amanda.

"No, nine-hundred thousand!", Yorkshire turned to Amanda as well.

Amanda's head went back and forth as her father and rival fought.

"A MILLION!"

"Five million!"

"TEN-MILLION-DOLLARS!", Mr. Griffin makes his way up the stage, both his hands extended out. "IN-CASH!"

Surprised, the whole room applauds the bickering of the two men, with Yorkshire bringing his hat down to the ground and stomping it in rage. As for Amanda, she looked confused, but that didn't stop her from speaking.

"Okay, looks like the portrait goes to…my father!", Amanda said with a half, awkward smile. "Congrats?"

As for Mr. Griffin, he makes his way across the crowd of people—, his back turned as he enters the door, exiting the room. Mrs. Griffin and I quickly noticed this our eyes completely confused before one of us spoke. "Did Mr. Griffin just buy the portrait back?"

Mrs. Griffin nodded. "Yes."

I raised my brow. "Why?"

She frowned. "I think I know."

With that, Mrs. Griffin moved past me, walking toward the door and leaving me in confusion. That is, until my dizzy, red-headed girlfriend approached me. "Hey, did you see what Dad did?"

"Yeah, it was weird."

"Do you know what it was?"

I shook my head. "No."

Amanda turned her eyes from me and to the closed door.

#

Mr. Griffin poured himself a glass of scotch, swallowing it whole in a single gulp. Yet, little did he know, the sound of footsteps trailed behind him, revealing a luminous figure from behind. "What the hell is wrong with you?", she said with her arms crossed.

Treating himself to another intake of alcohol, Robert lets out a hard sigh and speaks. "I'm sorry, Evelyn. I couldn't do it."

"What do you mean? Everything was going just fine until you and Yorkshire were competing!"

"Yorkshire may be my friend, but he is not my friend. There was no way, I was going to let him have that portrait!"

Evelyn crosses both her arms, "Sounds to me like Yorkshire isn't the only problem here?"

Robert turns her head around in shock. "What?"

"Oh, don't play stupid, Robert. Admit it: you won't get rid of the portrait because you're still holding onto Mia!"

Mr. Griffin turns back to her, his eyes full of fire. "What did I say about mentioning Mia?"

"After the way you've been, someone must. You're still holding onto Mia because you refuse to let go of her as well! You're attached!"

"I am not attached!"

"Then let her go."

Robert's lips quivered, his eyes closing shut before lowering his head. "I can't."

"Why not?"

Robert turns his head, his reflection staring back at him through his glass cup. "Because I'm scared. I'm scared that, if I let her go, she'd-"

"She'd what, laugh at you from hell?", she scoffs. "Mia is dead, Robert. There's nothing she can do to us. "Not anymore."

Hearing these words, Mr. Griffin lets out a quick sigh. "Alright, I'm sorry."

"Good", she slaps her husband, her frown visible. "Now, get your shit together! The last thing we need right now is your weakness! You got that!?"

"Got it."

"Um, Mr. and Mrs. Griffin. I don't mean to interrupt, but the picture's stolen!"

"What?!", Mr. and Mrs. Griffin say as I enter the room. "Mr. Yorkshire stole the portrait! If you run, you can catch-ah!", I shouted as Mr. and Mrs. Griffin move past me, walking out the door.

"Be careful, he's fast!"

Mr. and Mrs. Griffin did not listen, for they were too out of the door and into the room of lavish people. Mr. and Mrs. Griffin flipped their heads back and forth in confusion. "Where is he?"

"There!"

Mr. Griffin turns his head to find his wife pointing, causing him to turn back to the crowd. In the far distance, the portrait of Robert's late wife, zooming past several of the lavish guests. "Yorkshire!"

"Ha-ha-ha! Those idiot Griffins, did they really think they could get this photo without me taking it!"

"Yorkshire!"

Henry flips his head back to find Mr. Griffin moving through the crowd, his face angry. "Stop this instant!"

"Try it, Grandpa! Ha-ha-ha! Wah!", Henry's words were stopped as he tripped on the floor, along with the portrait. "Ugh!", Henry said, hitting the ground and facing down. "I never watch where I'm going."

"It's good you did, York."

"Yorky?", Henry turns his eyes back to find the dizzy redhead standing over him, her arms crossed. "You're not going anywhere."

"Is that so, and what are you going to do about it?"

"Not me, *him*"

Saying this, Amanda moves to the side, revealing a man standing before him, making Henry realize. "Oh, him", Henry said with much disappointment.

"Yes, *me*."

"Robert!", Mr. Griffin and Amanda both turned their heads to find Mrs. Griffin and my curly-haired self through the crowd, our eyes wide at the sight of the men. "You got him?"

"We sure did! I tripped him, if you want to know!"

Henry was minutes from rising from the floor, but before he could, Mr. Griffin grabbed hold of him by the collar, his eyes full of fear.

I knelt on the floor, the portrait lying face down on the ground. Without a second thought, I lift the portrait from the floor and turn it to my eyes.

That's when the hard gasp escapes me. "What is it, Dom?", Amanda said, kneeling to me.

Turning to her, I brought the photo to her view. She let out a huge gasp, surprised to see a portrait of Mia Griffin with a large crack in it. "Oh no!", Amanda turned her head back. "Dad!"

"What?", Robert gasped as he saw the crack in the portrait.

He turned to Mr. Yorkshire, his eyes cold and hard, much to Mr. Yorkshire's fear.

#

Mr. Yorkshire was thrown into the police car, his hands behind his back as he raised his head. "You can't do this to me! I have my rights! I hav—" Mr. Yorkshire's words were quickly cut off as the door was slammed by the police officer. "You have the right to shut your mouth!"

"You tell 'em, Marge!"

The black policewoman gave the man with the mustache a quick pound of his fist. Mr. and Mrs. Griffin are standing between them, Mr. Griffin's arms crossed as he speaks. "Make sure he doesn't escape. He has a knack for doing that."

"Don't worry, sir. Well, make sure he's locked up good and tight."

"Good."

Within minutes, the policeman was in their cars, hit the brakes, and drove down the road, the red and blue siren lights blinking in the night. Mr. Griffin watched as the car drove down the road, a big smile forming across his face before nodding. "That's the last man I put behind bars."

"Um, Mr. Griffin?"

Robert turns his eyes back to me, my hazel brown eyes looking up to him before speaking. "Um, everyone's outside."

Hearing this, Robert looked up from me and to the large crowd of people standing before him with worried eyes. "Alright, move along, everyone! There's nothing to see here. I suggest you all go home and leave now!"

With these words, the lavish people make their way past Mr. Griffin, heading to their vehicles. Soon, a trail of cars heads from the parking lot and out of the banks of Griffin Manor.

As soon as he did, Mrs. Griffin, Amanda, and I were left alone, our eyes turning to Mr. Griffin. "Um, Mr. Griffin?", I ask, causing him to turn back to me. "Are you okay?"

Mr. Griffin doesn't speak except to turn his eyes back to the window. "Not really, but my feelings are none of your business. Go home."

"Go home, but what about the portrait? Don't you want someone to help fix it"

"There is nothing to fix! Now go!", Mr. Griffin snaps before walking past me and out the living room door, leaving me, Amanda, and Mrs. Griffin alone. "Dom, this has nothing to do with you. Father's ju-"

"No, it's okay, Mandy. He's right, I should go."

"But—", Amanda's words are quickly cut off as my lips press against hers before pulling away. "I'll see you tomorrow, okay?"

With these words, I turn my head and walk to the door, with Amanda watching. That is, until Mrs. Griffin approaches from behind. "Amanda, you should go to bed. It's almost ten."

"What, but it's only eight."

"I said: **go to bed**!", Mrs. Griffin said with a long, hard stare.

"Alright, alright, Geez."

With that, Amanda walks past her mother and heads upstairs, her feet stomping from behind. Mrs. Griffin rolled her eyes before turning back to the door, where the door was now open to me, but before I could step out, Mrs. Griffin called my name. "Dominic?"

My head quickly shot back. "Yes?"

"What time does your mother need you home?"

I scratch my head. "Um, around nine. About an hour."

"Then we still have time."

"Time? For what?"

"To talk. You want to talk with *me*?"

"Of course. That is, unless you have somewhere else to be?"

Mrs. Griffin doesn't speak, instead, she turns her head and exits the living room, much to my confusion.

#

I sat across the kitchen table, where Mrs. Griffin poured me a cup of tea and soon herself. "Do you always do this?"

"Do what?", Mrs. Griffin said, placing her teapot back on her fine China plate. "Drink tea before bed?"

"Oh, on occasions. Much like today. Only today is special."

I raise my brow, my eyes narrowing. "What do you mean?"

"Do you know why Robert keeps that portrait?"

I raise my brow. "Oh, you mean the day of the auction?"

She shakes her head. "No, for Mia. Today's the day Mia Griffin was murdered."

I gasped, my eyes going big and wide, before bringing the cup of tea to my lips and sipping. "Um, this tea is pretty good. Did you put honey in this?"

"Stop trying to change the subject."

"Change the subject? I'm not doing any of that. I just don't like to talk about death, especially in the middle of the night."

"It's ten, and you need to hear this. Besides, if you're going to be a part of this family, you must know the story."

"You mean the one about Mr. Griffin's late wife? Where she was murdered by some guy, what was his name again?"

"Octavius."

I snapped my fingers. "That's it, Octavius! The guy who killed Mia Griffin", I pause, staring down at my half-empty teacup as I try to retrace my thoughts. "Wait, why did he kill her?"

Mrs. Griffin shook her head, her eyes full of strictness. "He didn't do it on purpose: Robert found Octavius on the Griffin manor doorstep one morning. He said he was looking for a job, one that required paintings. At first, Robert wasn't entirely sure of the scrappy, young man who stepped foot on his doorstep. That is until he recalled the newest member of the family and knew. Without a second thought, Robert welcomed Octavius into their home. Soon, Octavius got the right to work, creating various kinds of paintings for Robert. They were so beautiful that Robert's wife, Mia, ordered him to make a painting for him. Do you know what it was?"

I gasp, my eyes widening. "The portrait, the one we had for the auction?"

"Bingo."

I bring my hand to my head and speak. "Oh, wow. I had no idea. The painting looks so real."

"Yes, Octavius was a brilliant artist. So brilliant that those who saw them would fall in love with those like Mia."

I raised my brow. "What do you mean by that?"

Mrs. Griffin doesn't speak, except to give me a "what do you think?" stare, causing both my eyes to widen. "Hold on, are you saying that Mia…and Octavius…they…?", I said, causing Mrs. Griffin to nod. "Woah!"

Mrs. Griffin continues to nod before swirling her spoon in her teacup. "Yes, I was just as shocked as you. Mia and Octavius were in love; you could say they were lovers. The two were enchanted with each other and wished to share each other's worlds. So, they began meeting in secret, mostly when Robert was away for his usual business trips. They were happy, they were a happy pair, but as time went on, their love for each other grew strong. They were so strong that they decided that they could no longer be apart. That's when they devised a plan, one that would keep them together, so they'd never be apart again."

"What was it?"

Mrs. Griffin raises a brow. "What do you think?"

"I don't know; I was hoping you'd tell me!"

Mrs. Griffin laughs at this before speaking. "Just guess, Dominic."

I sigh before shrugging both my shoulders. "They ran off somewhere. That's what I hear in the fairytale books I've read."

Mrs. Griffin nodded, her smile present. "Yes."

Both my brows lift in surprise. "Really? They ran off together?"

"Yes…and no", Mrs. Griffin said, shaking her head.

I raise my brow, confused. "What do you mean?"

"Mia and Octavius's plan didn't go as planned. For they were caught."

"Caught, by who?"

Once again, Mrs. Griffin didn't say anything, but this time, I knew why. "Oh, no, don't tell me."

She nodded. "Robert returned home from one of his business trips one afternoon, and that's when he found Mia and Octavius in bed together."

"Oh shit", I said, shocked. "Robert must've been heartbroken."

He was, he was devastated. Never in a million years would Robert think that Mia, a woman he loved for years, would choose a penniless artist over him. But she did, and Robert…well, he wasn't so happy about it. Full of rage, Robert attacked Octavius, tossing him straight out of the bed, and hitting the bedroom floor as he threw the first punch. Mia was terrified by the sight of her husband and lover beating on each other. So, she decided to take matters into her own hands and stepped in between the two men, but as soon as she did, the dagger went in between her ribs, causing her to fall right into Robert's arms. In a moment of shock, Robert looked down to find Octavius holding a dagger in his hands meant for Robert."

"Oh no. So, it really was by accident. Mr. Griffin must've been heartbroken."

She nodded. "Yes. A terrible one at that, but don't worry, Robert made sure Octavius paid for it."

"What did he do?"

"For killing his beloved wife, Octavius, was sentenced to eighteen years in federal state prison."

"Eighteen years? It should've been life!"

"Yes, it should have."

I sighed, lowering my head in sadness. "Man, Mr. Griffin must've been devasted."

"It was. Robert was never the same afterward. Robert loved Mia more than anything else in this world."

"Even if she was unfaithful to him? Even when he was betrayed?"

"Love makes us do crazy things", she said.

I looked down at my teacup, which was now empty and sighed. "I guess it does."

Mrs. Griffin and I spent the moment staring at each other, enjoying each other's company. Yet, little did we know, Mr. Griffin was listening from behind the walls.

Soon after, Mrs. Griffin and I were outside, the rain pouring hard. "You might want to put on a jacket while you're at it. It's pouring hard out there."

"Don't worry. I'll be fine!"

"I hope that story of yours won't give you nightmares. I wouldn't want you to be shocked by it."

"Don't worry, Mrs. Griffin. I'm too old for nightmares."

"Are you sure? You seemed scared back there."

"Trust me, Mrs. Griffin, if there's anyone who gets scared, it's my mother. After what happened to my father, she was never the same."

"Your father?", she said with a raised brow. "Yeah, he got into a bad car accident. They said the car flipped over ten times. Soon, the cops came to our house and told my mom. She was devastated, but not as for me when she found out I would go through life without a father. Then again, I was just a baby at the time."

Mrs. Griffin's eyes were wide with shock before speaking. "Wait, your father died in a car crash?"

"Yeah", I said in a sad tone. "It was a few years back."

"I'm so sorry."

"Don't be. It's not your fault."

Mrs. Griffin gulped, her head slowly nodding. "R-right."

"Well, see ya, Mrs. Griffin."

"Dominic, wait!"

I stop my bike dead hard on the grass before whipping my head back, the water droplets hitting my face. "Yeah!"

Mrs. Griffin stands from the house before speaking. "What did you say your name was again?"

"Dominic!", I answer. "Dominic Mitchell!"

A great streak of lightning strikes over Evelyn's head, her eyes big and wide. "Mrs. Griffin, are you okay?"

Mrs. Griffin blinks. "Oh, what? Um, yes, I'm alright."

I give her a quick raise of my brow before speaking. "Um, okay. Well, I'm going to go now! See you tomorrow!", I said, raising my kickstand with my foot before racing down the road and into my mom's car. As for Mrs. Griffin, she was left frozen for a moment before heading back into the house, the door shutting behind her.

#

A large prison, with several barbed wires attached to the gates, was found. Down below, there was a group of guards standing out before the gates, their closed dry from the rain. But it was the inside that was much more dangerous.

"Let me go! "Ugh, I said let me go!", said Yorkshire, kicking as he was dragged in by the two police guards. "Unhand me this instance, or there will be dire consequences!"

The police guard laughs. "Yeah, right. Unless you've got a good lawyer, you show me the consequences!"

"I'm serious; I can do things! I have all the power in the world! Wah!", Yorkshire said, being flung into a cell and hitting the floor hard. "Argh!"

Yorkshire was minutes from turning his head back, but as soon as he did, the bars closed in on him. "No, wait!", he said, grabbing the metal bars. "You can't do this to me! I'm innocent, do you hear me? I'm innocent!"

"Yeah, that's what I thought too."

A gasp leaves Yorkshire, causing his head to turn in shock. "Who said that?"

"You're looking the wrong way."

"What? Where are you?"

"Turn around."

With these words, Yorkshire whips his eyes to the left, where he finds a lonely, silhouette figure standing in the corner. "Hello, Yorkshire."

Yorkshire's eyes lit up in confusion. "What did you just call me?"

"Yorkshire. That is your name, right: Henry Yorkshire?"

Yorkshire nodded. "Yeah, how do you know that?"

"You told me yourself, in my vision."

"Your vision?"

"Yes, I've had many. More than once."

"What the hell are you talking about? Who are you?"

With these words, the silhouette figure emerges from the shadows and into the moonlit floor. To Henry's surprise, he finds a bearded, middle-aged man with a scar on his left eye. "You said you were thrown in here by accident, that your innocent. Well, so am I. Well, *was*."

"Was, what do you me—", Henry quickly stops himself, noticing the nasty scar on his left eye. "Jesus, man. Where did you get that scar?"

The man brings his hand up to his eye and smirks. "This scar?"

"Yeah, did you do that to yourself?"

He shakes his head. "No, but I could tell you who. That is, if you want to know?"

"Yeah, can I get your name first?"

The bearded man grinned. "Octavius."

#

Mr. Griffin sat in his office, gazing out at the starry night before him. "It's a beautiful night, Mia. If only you were here to see it."

Through the reflection of the window, Mr. Griffin saw a portrait with several cracks in it and smiled. He approached the portrait with utmost confidence. "I miss you so much."

Saying this, Mr. Griffin pours himself a glass of scotch and raises it to the portrait. "Salue, my love."

With these words, Mr. Griffin brought the scotch to his lips, but before he could even swallow, a trail of red liquid dispersed into the yellow liquid that was the scotch.

Shocked, Mr. Griffin took his glass of scotch from his mouth, gazing up at the portrait of the smiling woman. Scared, Mr. Griffin raises his hand to his lips and speaks. "What the hell?"

Mr. Griffin gazes back up to the portrait of his wife, gazing down at him with knowing eyes.

Without a second thought, Robert took the pieces of the portrait into his hand and threw it in the garbage. Robert looked at the pieces before lifting a match in his hands and flicking a set of fires. Without a second thought, set it on fire.

"Goodbye, Mia."

Chapter 11: The Virus

"Gah!", Evelyn said, waking from her bed, her hair messy and frizzy. She looked left and right as she found herself in her bedroom.

With a heavy sigh, Evelyn turned her eyes to the clock, sitting on her nightstand. It was seven minutes before eight.

Time to get up.

With her eyes baggy, Evelyn turned her body to the side, hoping to see her husband. To her surprise, there was no one, nothing but an empty bed. She looked down to find a large dent in the bed. She placed her hand there, concluding that Robert had just gotten out of bed.

Seeing this, Evelyn took the sheets from her body and hopped out of bed, slipping on her robe before leaving her bedroom.

A hot, steamy liquid was being poured into Robert Griffin's coffee cup by butler Barry. "I hope this coffee suits your fatigue."

"Thank you, Barry. This fatigue really took a toll on me. I just hope I get over it soon."

"You will, sir. Just be patient."

"Be patient", he repeated before whipping out the daily newspaper, which his eyes looked through. "Good morning, Robert."

Robert lowers his newspaper, his brows raised as he finds his beloved wife standing in a pink dress robe. "Good morning, dear. How did you sleep?"

"Pretty good. Had a nightmare."

"You did?"

"Yeah, but it was nothing. What about you?"

Robert rubs the set of his forehead. "Not well. I was tossing and turning for most of the night. Woke up fatigued."

"Really?", Evelyn said, holding a bowl of fruit. "Do you think it's because of last night?"

"Last night?"

"The auction?"

"Oh! Maybe."

"I feel it is stress, Mr. Griffin."

"Stress?", Mr. Griffin said, folding his newspaper.

"Yes, you're always working, without the slightest break. It is affecting your health."

Robert scoffed. "My health is no concern, Barry. Believe me, I am as healthy as a horse."

With these words, Robert made his way from the kitchen table, passing Evelyn. "Robert, where are you going?"

"To my of-ah!", Robert said, stopping in the middle of the kitchen, and grabbing onto his heart.

Without a second thought, Evelyn hops out of her chair, her feet hitting the carpet floor before trembling towards the bathroom door, the gags now louder. "Robert, are you okay!?"

Robert whips his head back, his eyes wide with shock as he gags. "Mr. Griffin!"

Without a second thought, Robert's eyes go to the back of his head, falling straight to his knees before collapsing to the floor with a thud. "ROBERT!", Evelyn shouts, making her way towards him. "Oh god! Robert!", Evelyn turns her eyes back, facing her butler. "Barry, call the hospital! Now!"

With these words, Barry was out of the bathroom and downstairs, dialing the three digits.

#

I sit at the school lunch table, my eyes looking down at my bowl of spaghetti and meatballs. Only I didn't eat a bite, I *couldn't* eat anything, for my stomach was filled with confusion, and that ate me up more than anything else.

"I heard you and Mom had one interesting conversation last night, Dom."
"What?"

"The conversation, the one you had with Mother."

I raise my brow. "Yeah, how did you know that?"

"Barry, told me. He tells me everything."

"So, did you like it?"

"Like what?"

"The story, you know, of Mia?"

"Oh, that story. Yeah, I enjoyed it."

Amanda looked at me, confused. "You...*enjoyed* it?"

"Yeah, I thought it was an interesting story."

"Dominic, that wasn't just some story; it was real."

"I know."

"Then why would you say it's enjoyable? It's not meant to be enjoyed; it's meant to feel sympathy for Dad."

"What do you mean? I do feel sympathy for Mr. Griffin. Did you think I didn't?"

"No, it's just", Amanda sighs, looking down in silence.

"What is it, Amanda?"

She shook her head. "It's nothing."

"Yes, it is. Tell me."

I watched as my girlfriend poked at her spaghetti and meatballs before looking up at me. "That story my mom told you, it's not something that was just told to you, Dominic. It was told every year to me."

"Every year? Why would he do that?"

"Because my father has issues", she sighed, her fingers combing through her hair. "His wife's death impacted him so much that he just...got stuck. He spent everyday dwelling on it, and he never stopped. And then the auction happened, and well... It's just after all these years, I thought he was finally going to move on, but then he bought the painting back and...", she sighed one final time. "I just think Dad is so stuck in the past that he can't see what's right in front of him, you know?"

With these words, I brought my hand over to Amanda's, gripping it tight before nodding. "I understand completely, Amanda."

"Really?"

"Of course. When I was a little boy, my father died in a car crash."

Amanda gasped. "Oh my god. Dominic, I'm so sorry."

"No, it's okay. I was just a baby when it happened, so I didn't really know much about it. As for my mom, she knew everything. There were these cops at the door, telling her what happened. She was never the same after that, but I can't blame her for that. I mean, that was her husband, a man she loved. That's something that can't be forgotten. Maybe that's the reason why your father is so stuck. He's probably just suffering from heartbreak."

Amanda nodded as her eyes drooped to the floor. "Yeah, he is. I should cut my father some slack", she took my hand, gripping it tighter. "Still, I wish he'd spend more time with us. If he has time to work, I'm sure he has at least an ounce to just…be there."

"Then tell him that."

She sighed. "I don't think I can."

"Yes, you can. You just have to have confidence in yourself."

"I don't think I do."

"And why is that?", I said, folding my arms.

Amanda rubbed the back of her neck. "I don't know, maybe because of…my mother."

"Mrs. Griffin? What does she have to do with your confidence?"

"She has a lot to do with it. Mom wasn't the nurturing type growing up. She was distant and a bit neglectful. Almost as neglectful as my father. Only, he had an excuse: he was busy, but Mom, she had all the time in the world, and she wasted it, thinking only of herself."

"So, she's selfish?"

"In a way. When I was alone, when I needed someone to talk to, she was nowhere to be found. It made it harder for me to talk to people, make friends, all of it. I was alone."

I nodded, marinating every word Amanda said before speaking. "Well, you're not alone now."

Amanda looked up at me, a small yet happy smile forming on her face. "Yeah, I'm not", she reached her hand to mine, holding it tight. "I know you think you're alone, Amanda, but you're not. You have me, and I'm going to be here for you."

"No matter what?"

"No matter what."

With these words, Amanda pulls me in for a quick kiss on the lips before hugging me tight. "Thank god for you, Dominic. If you hadn't come into my life, I don't know what my life would've been like."

"Probably boring, especially with me not being able to give you a good laugh."

She laughs. "You're probably right."

"I know you can do this, Amanda. You're stronger than you think."

"I know."

#

A tall and elongated red door stood in a narrow hallway where a loud knocking sound was heard. Robert Griffin, in a black suit and tie, slowly walks towards it. "I'm coming, Evelyn!", he said with a happy smile.

With a few more steps, Robert stops dead in front of the door. Without a second thought, Robert twists the doorknob and opens the door, his smile big and wide. "Welcome home, beautifu—", Robert's words are quickly cut off by a creepy figure in a black mask standing before him.

His five seconds of joy quickly became a nightmare, one he didn't like. "You're not, Evelyn. Who are you?"

The masked man does nothing except point a gun at Robert, shocking him. "Hey, wait a minute! What are you doing?!"

The masked man took a step closer, frightening Robert. "I'm serious. What are you doing? What do you want?"

"I want my son", said the figure.

"Your son?"

Without any other words, the masked figure nodded and pulled the trigger.

#

"Gah!", Robert shouted, his face beading with sweat.

"Robert?"

Mr. Griffin's eyes cracked open to, surprisingly, his wife. "Evelyn?"

Evelyn grinned, bringing him into a hug. "Oh, thank goodness! I thought you'd never wake up!"

"Wake up?", Robert said, pulling away from her. "Where am I?"

"In the hospital. You were sick."

"Sick? What happened?"

"You mean you don't remember?"

"Remember what?"

Evelyn blinks. "Robert, I found you with your head over the toilet seat, coughing up blood. Before I knew it, you passed out in my arms. You don't remember any of that?"

Robert brings his hand up to his forehead. "I do remember something like that. The blood, the one in my drink."

Evelyn's eyes lit up with confusion. "Your drink?"

Robert grunts. "It's a bit fuzzy, but I'm sure it was real."

"Of course, it was. It was all real."

Robert and Evelyn both turn their eyes to a man in a white lab coat and brown shirt. "Hi, there, I'm Nurse Windle. Are you Mrs. Griffin?"

"Yes", Evelyn said. "Yes, and this is my husband, Robert."

"Robert, Mr. Griffin. How are you feeling?"

"If anything, it's better than I did before. However, I can't remember what happened."

"Why is that?"

"Well, he passed out through most of it."

"Wait, Evelyn. I remember something."

"What's that?"

"Before I blacked out, I had these chest pains."

"Chest pains?"

"Yes, these chest pains have been happening since yesterday."

"Yesterday?"

"Uh-huh", Nurse Windle wrote the information down on her clipboard before closing it shut. "Alright, that's all I needed to hear."

"That's it?"

"Yes, I'll inform Dr. Vincent about your problems."

"Dr. Vincent? But isn't that your job?"

"No, I'm just the nurse, remember. He'll give you the results shortly. Until then, bye."

With that, Nurse Windle left the room, leaving Robert and Evelyn alone together. Evelyn turned to her husband, who was indeed wearing a worried expression. Noticing this, Evelyn took Robert's hand. "Chest pains?", she asked.

"What?"

"Chest pains. You said you had it since yesterday."

"Yeah."

"Okay, so why are you just now telling me this?"

Robert raised his brow. "What do you mean?"

"You know exactly what I mean! You knew about these chest pains, and you never told me? I could've figured it out sooner, could've caught it!"

"I didn't think it was all that serious at first, that it wasn't a big deal."

"Well, it was, and now we have to wait until the doctor comes in with the results", Evelyn sighed, bringing her hand to her face. "I'm going through enough today, and now I have to deal with this."

Robert, sad, tried to bring his hand up to touch his wife's shoulder but quickly took it away as by the looks of it, she was already too upset for an apology.

\#

"Hey, Paula", said a man as he made his way down the hospital hall, greeting the nurses.

"Hey, Vince. Got any big plans for today?"

"Yeah, I just need to see this patient of mine. Yeah, says he's right next door."

"Oh, really? Well, hope he does fine."

"Yeah, well, see you soon."

"See ya, Paula."

The bearded doctor left the nurse Paula to go back to her work while he entered the brown door on his left. He twisted the doorknob and entered the room, where Mr. Griffin was lying in a hospital bed and his wife sitting next to him.

"Ah, it looks like I'm in the right place!", answered the doctor, holding his brown clipboard. "Um, Mr. Griffin?"

"Yes"

"Right!", he said, raising his fist up. "And this must be your wife, right?"

"Yes."

"Good", Dr. Vincent flipped through his brown clipboard. "So, Mr. Griffin, according to my studies, it seems that you had a fainting episode. Is that correct?"

"Yes."

"He also had chest pains", Evelyn added.

"Yes, Nurse Windle told me of that."

Robert cleared his throat. "Um, do you know what was causing it?"

Dr. Vincent nodded. "Yes, I do. It's a heart attack."

Robert's face fell flat. "What?"

"A heart attack. You had a heart attack."

"This can't be. How did this happen?"

"Well, there are many things that can trigger heart attacks: stress, unhealthy diets, even smoking. Do you smoke?"

"No, but I do have a lot of stress."

Dr. Vincent nodded. "What kind of stress?"

"You know, stress. Distress."

"And what do you think causes that stress?"

Robert rubbed the back of his head. "A lot of things: people, my job, and sometimes, secrets."

"Secrets?"

"Yes, secrets. Things that I keep from people, things that I like to keep to myself. Embarrassing things."

"Well, this must be why your heart attack was triggered. You have a lot of emotional baggage. Baggage that must be dumped out."

"What are you saying?"

"I'm saying that whatever it is you need to say, now is the time. That is, if you don't want a second heart attack."

Robert and Evelyn both let out a soft gasp, causing the pair to turn to each other in shock. As for Dr. Vincent, he took his clipboard to his chest. "I'll leave you two alone while I go and get medication."

With these words, Dr. Vincent walked toward the door, leaving Mr. and Mrs. Griffin alone.

Evelyn turned to her husband; her eyes sharp. "Well, isn't this just perfect. A perfect way to start my Friday."

"You say that like you don't want to be here."

"I didn't. I mean, of all the illnesses you could've gotten, you just had to have a heart attack."

"I think this was more than just a heart attack."

Evelyn raised her brow. "And what's that supposed to mean?"

Robert lowered his eyes. "The moment I blacked out, I had this dream."

"What kind of dream?"

"I remember seeing a man."

"What did he look like?"

"He had a scar over his eye."

Evelyn gasped, her eyes big and wide. "A-a scar? Robert, you don't think?"

"I do."

"Octavius!", they cried.

"But he's in prison. Why would you have a dream about him?"

"I didn't know at first, but after last night, I think I know why. In my dream, he held a gun at my head. He shot me in cold blood, which is exactly what he wants to do now! That and something else."

"What, what else does he want?"

"A son, Evelyn. He wanted his son."

She raised her brow, confused. "Wait, his son? Octavius has a son?"

"I'm afraid he does. At least, I think he does."

"What do you mean? Don't you know?"

"No, I never even recalled he did have a son."

"So, how do you know if he has a son or not?"

"Because I did something to him, Evelyn! I put him behind bars. Something like that would make someone vengeful! So, whatever that dream was telling me, I think I should take it seriously!"

Evelyn brings her hands up to her eyes before speaking. "I guess you're right. Besides, you did put him behind bars."

"It's also his last year. He has what, four months?"

"Three and then he's out."

Robert brought his hands up to his forehead. "I'm scared Evelyn."

"Don't worry, we're going to be okay."

"Are we?"

She nodded. "We will. We just need to find the son, whoever that may be?"

#

A sea of students rushed from the school doors of Summit High, with many of them in groups as they descended the steps. It wasn't long before Amanda and I descended them as well, our hands held tight as we made our way down.

"I hope Mom isn't late again. I hate having to wait for her."

Amanda laughed. "I know how you feel."

"You do?"

"Yeah, Barry takes forever to get me to the school especially when he must stop at the jewelry store or when he stops to get me ice cream. So, yeah, I feel yuh."

I scoffed hard. "Yeah, okay."

Amanda and I were now down the steps when suddenly, a great, big limo approached us, and without warning, the car window slid down, revealing Butler Barry's worried expression. "Ms. Griffin, get in the car, now!"

"What, why?"

"Now, Amanda! Your father's in the hospital!"

"What!? What happened?!"

"I'll explain along the way. Just get in!"

With these words, Amanda turns to me, giving me a quick peck on the lips before hopping in the limousine, the door shutting behind me. As soon as he did, a loud beep was heard from behind me. "Dominic!"

Hearing this, I turned my eyes to the back, and to my surprise, I found my mom's van. "Dominic, come on!", said Mom, peeking her head out of the van.

I turn my eyes back to the black limousine, my heart racing as the engine roars. That's when the horn beeped again. "Dominic?", Mom said, this time with more malice.

Without a second thought, I ran towards my mom's car, my hands hitting the glass before speaking. "Mom, I want to go with Amanda!"

"What? What are you talking about?"

"I want to go with Amanda; I want to go to the hospital with her!"

"The hospital? W-why do you want to go there for?"

"Her father's sick. I want to be there for her!"

The sound of the limousine's engine is heard, causing my head to turn back. "Mom, please!"

With a deep sigh, Mom gives me a quick nod. "Okay, but you had better be home before eight."

"I promise! Thanks Mom!"

With these words, I take my hands from the glass and head straight for the limousine, leaving my mom in distress. "This could be a sign."

"Put on your seatbelt, Amanda", said Barry looking through the rearview mirror. "Is it on?"

"Yes, it's on! Come on, let's get to the hospital already!"

"Ok, just let me press on the ga-ahh!"

"What? What is it?"

"It's master Mitchell!"

"Mitchell, wait, do you mean Dominic!?"

"Yes, he's right at the door!"

Amanda turns her eyes to find her curly-haired boyfriend banging his hands on the glass. "Barry, let me in!", he spoke through the glass. "Let me in!"

"Let him in, Barry!"

"Alright, alright!"

Barry pops the lock of the car, much to my joy, as I run from the glass and to the window, where I make my way inside the car. "Dominic, what are you doing here?"

"What does it look like? I'm going to the hospital with you!"

"What, no! Dominic, your Mom's waiting for you-"

"My Mom already gave me permission!"

"But-"

"Amanda! Your father's sick. There's no way I'm letting you go alone! Take it or leave it!"

With these words, my dizzy, red-headed girlfriend brings me in for a kiss, this time more passionately, before pulling away. "I love you."

"I love you too. Now, let's get to the hospital. Barry!"

"On it!"

With these words, Barry hits the brakes, causing the limousine to go down the road.

\#

Robert lay in bed, dead asleep, as his wife, Evelyn, sat next to him. "Robert", she whispered.

Robert doesn't move an inch. "Robert!"

With that, Robert opens both his eyes wide, finding Evelyn looking at him with a happy smile. "Hey, babe."

"Hey."

"Are you okay?"

"Yeah. Where's Amanda? Is she here yet?"

"No, not yet."

"Good."

"I think it is. After seventeen years of being married to you, I've learned that you're not the one to face things. If you recall?"

"It's not going to be like that this time. I *will* tell Amanda."

"I hope so."

Robert was seconds to open her mouth when suddenly, the door opened. As soon as it does, Dr. Vincent's head pokes through. "Hey there, Mr. and Mrs. Griffin. Um, do you have two kids?"

Robert and Evelyn turn their heads to each other in confusion. "Two kids?"

Without speaking, the door bursts wide open, causing a young man and woman to barge in. "Mom, Dad!"

"Amanda, slow down, we're already here!"

"Amanda!?", said both Evelyn and Robert.

"Mom, Dad!"

Amanda took her hand away from me and jumped right in bed, embracing her father with a loving hug. "Oh, Daddy!", Amanda said with tears. "I was so worried about you! I thought you were gone."

"Gone? What do you mean?"

"Barry told me everything."

"He did?", Robert said in shock. "What exactly was that?"

"Don't worry, Mr. Griffin. I only told her what she needed to hear", said the young, mustache man entering the room. "Barry?"

Barry smiles. "Hello, Mr. Griffin."

Robert looked at Barry and then at his daughter, her eyes full of pleading. "Daddy, Barry said you were sick? What are you sick with?"

Robert faced his wife, his eyes full of fear as she nodded. "Um, I think we should leave my daughter and him alone for a moment."

"We should. Come now, master Mitchell."

Evelyn lets out a quick yet silent gasp as the thought comes back to haunt her. But that had to be put aside, for this moment was more significant. "Come on, guys, let's leave my daughter and husband alone."

With these words, Evelyn, Barry, and I made our way out the door, closing it shut as Amanda and her mother were now alone.

#

I stood in the corner, my eyes gazing up at the lights that sat on the hospital ceiling. It wasn't long until the sound of a door closing was heard, causing my head to lower. Standing at the door was Evelyn Griffin, her back turned as Barry was found comforting her.

"It's alright, Mrs. Griffin."

"I know. It's just so hard seeing him like this. Besides, how will Amanda take this."

"It will be difficult for her to process, but in time, she will accept it."

Evelyn sighs, nodding slowly before spotting the curly-haired boy looking at her. Without thinking, Barry turns to me. "Um, Barry, could you go get me some coffee from the office downstairs?"

"Of course."

"Thank you, Barry."

With that, Barry turns away from Evelyn, making his way down the hall, leaving her and the curly-haired boy alone. Seeing this, Evelyn brings her hand to the back of her neck and speaks. "I see you came along."

I nod. "Yeah, I heard about what happened to Mr. Griffin. I wanted to keep Amanda company."

Mrs. Griffin nodded. "That's nice of you, Dominic", she shifts her eyes to the left before speaking. "Um, Mrs. Griffin. Can I talk to you about something?", Griffin turns back to me, confused. "Of course. What is it?"

"Do you hate me?"

Evelyn raises her brow, confused. "What do you mean? Of course, I like you."

"Are you sure? Because it seems like you give me the cold shoulder. Like when I try speaking to you, you just turn your head or look at me like I did something wrong. I'm not trying to be rude or anything; I just want to know why you do this?"

Mrs. Griffin gives me a long and hard look before turning her eyes to the sunlit window and sighs. "It's not you that I hate, it's myself."

"Yourself?"

She nodded, still looking out. "As a child, I didn't have much. My mother and father were poor, so poor that one day, they decided they couldn't take care of me anymore. So, they decided to run off and leave me behind."

I blink, my eyes filled with shock. "But they did leave you with someone, right?"

Mrs. Griffin shakes her head. "They didn't."

I raised my brow, confused. "Then who took care of you?"

Mrs. Griffin looked to the floor, sad. "I had to take care of myself."

I blinked, shocked by Mrs. Griffin's words. "I'm so sorry, Mrs. Griffin. I had no idea."

"Don't be", she said, now turned to me.

Without a second thought, I pulled Mrs. Griffin in for a hug, shocking her a lot. "Mr. Mitchell!?", she exclaims.

"Forgive me, Mrs. Griffin. It's just that I know what it's like to lose a parent. Not the way you lost them, but I know. See, I lost my father when I was young. My mom said he was in a terrible car accident that really broke her."

"I'm sorry."

"It's okay. Things are much better now. My mom's got a great job as a nurse, and I've got these paintbrushes from my dad"

Mrs. Griffin's eyes widened upon hearing this. "Wait, what?"

I pause, facing Mrs. Griffin. "I said I got these paintbrushes from my dad"

Mrs. Griffin raises her brow. "Why would he leave you paintbrushes?"

"Because he was an artist. My Mom told me about all the paintings he made. Though, I never got to see any of them."

Mrs. Griffin's eyes were full of suspicion. "What did you say your name was again?"

"Dominic", I said with a smile. "Dominic Mitchell."

Mrs. Griffin's eyes widened in shock, but before she could react, the sound of footsteps slid against the bleached hospital floors. "I'm back!", said Butler Barry, walking towards us with a handful of snacks.

Mrs. Griffin and I turned to Barry, who had a plastic coffee cup in one hand and some snacks in the other. "I got you that coffee you wanted, Mrs. Griffin."

Mrs. Griffin smiles while taking the coffee. "Thank you, Barry", Evelyn turned to me, her eyes full of suspicion before speaking. "You okay, Mrs. Griffin?"

Barry smiles before turning to me. "Oh!", Barry brings out the bag of chips, one resembling a curly, orange shape. "Che-ttos. As they call them, right?"

I laugh. "Yeah, thanks, Barry."

Barry turns his eyes to them before speaking. "Where is Amanda? Is she still in the room?"

"Yeah, looks like it. I'm worried about her."

"Don't worry, I'm sure she's doing fine. Right, Mrs. Griffin?"

Mrs. Griffin nodded. "Right."

"Oh, by the way, what was it you wanted to tell me, Mrs. Griffin?"

Mrs. Griffin's eyes lit up hearing this before speaking. "Um…"

"No!", said a voice, causing Mrs. Griffin, Barry, and I to turn our heads back to a dizzy, redhead, her eyes full of tears. "Amanda, wait!"

"No!"

"Amanda?", I speak.

"Mrs. Griffin?"

Before we knew it, Amanda fell to her knees, her hands covering her face as she sobbed. "Amanda!"

I was the first to comfort her, my arms wrapping around her feeble body as she cried. "Amanda, what happened!?"

Amanda shook her head, not wanting to speak. "Amanda, please!"

"He had a heart attack!", Amanda said under her breath. "Dad had a heart attack!"

"A heart attack?", I said, gazing up from Amanda to Barry and Mrs. Griffin.

"How did that happen?", said Barry.

Saying this, Amanda takes her hands from her eyes and speaks.

Barry and I all gasp, leaving Mrs. Griffin to turn away from us. "He said there was a blood clot"

"A blood clot!"

"Oh my god. Mrs. Griffin, did you know about this?", answered Barry, turning to her.

Mrs. Griffin turns to Barry. "Of course, I did."

Amanda raises her head in shock. "Wait, you did?"

Mrs. Griffin turns her eyes to her daughter. "Yes, and for the record, your father is not dying; he's just sick."

"Yes, but not *this* sick!"

"Amanda, calm down."

"No! Don't tell me to calm down, Dominic!"

"Amanda, liste—"

"Amanda! Stop it!", Mrs. Griffin snaps. "You're embarrassing yourself!"

"I'll embarrass myself all I want, Mother!"

"Amanda Griffin!", Mrs. Griffin said, stomping her foot. "Watch your tone when you talk to me! There are worse things happening than this!"

"What do you mean?", I said, much to Amanda's confusion. "What worse things are you talking about?"

With a quick sigh, Evelyn looked her daughter in the eyes. "I was going to tell you this the day we got home, but your father insisted we keep it under the rug. Amanda, your father and I are getting a divorce."

Amanda's eyes widened upon hearing this. "A-a what? W-why would you do that?"

"The same reason why all parents do it: they stop loving each other."

Amanda gasps, tears welling up in her eyes. "Don't start with those tears, Amanda. I've already got enough to deal with as it is."

"She has a right to be sad, Mrs. Griffin", I speak, wrapping my arms around Amanda.

Mrs. Griffin scoffed, her back turned as she walked away from us and back into the room. I turned my attention back to Amanda, tears now falling from her eyes. "Amanda, everything's going to be okay."

"Everything will not be okay, Dominic! *I'll* never be okay! Never again!"

"Amanda!", I shout as my girlfriend rises from the floor and runs down the hall. "Amanda, wait!"

I rose from the floor, my hand reached out as I turned back to Mrs. Griffin and Barry, giving me quick nods. With that, I turned away from them and headed down the hall, leaving Barry the only one left. "I guess I'll just wait here."

Meanwhile, Mrs. Griffin made her way back into the room with machines beeping. That is, until they were replaced by the sound of sniffles.

Facing upwards, Mrs. Griffin finds her husband lying in bed crying. Confused, Mrs. Griffin shuts the door behind her and speaks. "What is it?"

He sniffs again, answering. "You were right, Evelyn. When you said I coddle Amanda too much, you were right. I spent my whole life sheltering her from painful things that the moment they came around, she broke."

She nodded, her eyes intensifying. "You won't have to worry about that any longer. We have bigger fish to fry right now."

He raises his brow. "What do you mean?"

"I found him, Robert. I found the son."

#

"Amanda!", I said, turning a corner of the hospital. "Amanda, where are you!?"

I make my way through the hallway, my eyes searching through the place as I walk. "Amanda!", I call out one final time before turning another corner. That's where I found her.

Amanda, her head buried between her knees as she sobbed. I let out a sigh of relief before approaching her. "Amanda?"

"Go away", she speaks.

"No, I'm not leaving you here."

"I said go away!", she said, her eyes now up.

I near her, falling straight to my knees. "No"

Amanda, wanting to say more, lets out a sad sigh before leaning in to hug me, sobbing silently as I shush her. "It's okay", I said, holding her tight. "It's going to be alright. I'm here."

"Ms. Griffin!", echoed a voice, causing Amanda and I to turn our heads.

Butler Barry turned a corner and, to his surprise, found Amanda and I embracing each other. Seeing this, a happy smile formed on his face. "Oh, thank goodness. I thought you'd scurried off!", Barry said, spotting Amanda, causing his smile to transition into a sad frown. "Oh, deary."

These were the words that caused Amanda to burst into tears, causing me to hold her even tighter. Before they know it, it's just Barry, Amanda, and I all hug each other.

I was Amanda's boyfriend. At that moment, I wouldn't leave her side.

#

"No", said Robert in shock. "No!"

Evelyn looked at Robert. "Evelyn, you can't be serious. Please, tell me you're joking."

She shakes her head. "I'm not, Robert. It's his, it's Dominic's. He's the son of Octavius. I mean, I think so."

Robert raises a brow. "You think so?"

"I know I just-"

"Just what, Evelyn?"

Evelyn sighs, making her way over to her husband's side. "His name is Dominic, Dominic *Mitchell*."

Robert's eyes widen to this. "Mitchell?"

Evelyn nodded, causing Robert to shake his head in denial. "No, no. There are thousands of Mitchells out there. Whoever this kid is could be another Mitchell, right?"

Evelyn shakes her head, triggering Robert's emotions. "Come on, Evelyn. You can't tell me that this kid is the son of the man that killed my wife! I mean, what proof do you have to say that?"

She sighs. "Um, remember that newspaper, the one we kept in that box?"

Robert raised his brow. "You mean the one in the attic?"

"I saw the name, Robert, the last name. They're the same."

"No, that's not enough evidence."

"His mother's single!"

Robert's eyes lower. "What?"

"His mother's single; he has a single mother", Evelyn sighs. "He told me just how hurt his mother was when he found out about his father. That sounds an awfully lot like the woman that we met."

"That woman, do you really think?"

She shakes her head. "No, I just assume."

"Then how do you know it's him? How do you know any of this is real?"

Evelyn looked at her husband quite seriously before leaning into his face. "Have you forgotten what you did? You threw a man in prison for the murder of your wife. Now, you're having these nightmares of a man who wants to not only kill you but find his son! If that doesn't say something, then nothing does."

Robert lowers his eyes in sadness before sighing. "Where's the newspaper?"

"In the attic, the same place I kept that box?"

"That box? You kept the newspaper in a box?"

"Of course, I keep everything in a box."

Robert sighs, lowering his head. "We have to figure this out."

"We?"

"Yes! If this boy really is who we think he is, then-"

"*We* aren't doing anything. It is you who will."

"What?"

"I am no longer your wife. That means I don't have to deal with any of your problems, including this one. Goodbye, Robert."

"YOU STOP RIGHT WHERE YOU ARE, EVELYN!"

Evelyn, shocked, stops a few inches from the door, not once facing her husband. "Don't even think for a second that you can just walk out of here and leave me! Not after all we've been through, after all I've done for you! That is, if you forgot?"

Evelyn grunted, hearing this, her fists clenched as she let out a small exhale. She turned her eyes back to her husband. "Alright, fine. What do we need to do?"

#

Griffin Manor stood proud and tall in the evening light. That is, until a black SUV made its way up the road and into the parking lot. It wasn't long before the car opened wide. Without a second thought, Evelyn zooms her way out and up the staircase of the house.

The door busted wide open, her heels clinking against the marble floor as she made her way through the kitchen, the living room, and finally up the staircase. Her heart raced as she ran up the steps, not hearing anything but the name that rang in her mind.

Mitchell.

Mitchell.

MITCHELL!

"No!", she speaks, entering the hallway before turning her head to the small, purple doorway. Without a second thought, Evelyn bursts through it, finding herself in a room full of cobwebs.

This place seemed familiar, almost to a certain night. As it was, Evelyn made it possible. She turned to her left and found a small purple box, the same box Dominic had been curious to see before.

Only, he never got to see what was in that box. But Evelyn would.

With the box now in her hands, Evelyn grabs the sides of the chest and lifts the lid. Before her very eyes, she finds a dusty, old brown newspaper sitting below.

Evelyn blew it off, taking off all the cobwebs from it. She saw a paper with a headline that read: **Homicide Kills Spouse of Rich Millionaire! Sentenced to Seventeen years! Family devastated!**

she then looked down at the second initial, revealing a photo of a young man with curly hair, hazel eyes, and a goatee: Octavius Mitchell.

Mitchell.

"No", Evelyn gasped, throwing the newspaper onto the floor. "No, it can't be!"

Evelyn held onto her heart tight, her eyes gazing down at the newspaper. "It is."

Chapter 12: The Ballad of Prom

Prom.

A day in which every couple celebrates being with their beloved. As for me, I hate it. The chocolates, the roses, and, worst of all, the corny ass remarks couples give each other. It's like Valentine's Day, but worse. It's all so blah!

Or so I thought when I met Little Miss Perfect, a.k.a. my girlfriend, Amanda Griffin. I love Amanda; she's the one that made me like Valentine's Day. Without her, I would be in my bed, going off on heart-shaped candy alone.

That was me during the past sixteenth Valentine's Day, but not this Valentine's! This time, I was going to give my girlfriend the best Valentine's Day ever, and what better way to do that than to the Valentine's Day ball!

That's right, Summit High will be having a Valentine's Day party on, of course, Valentine's Day! I first heard about it from my English instructor. I didn't really hear him at first, but once he said these words, I was all ears: "Make sure you treat your partner with all the love he or she deserves."

I leaped for joy at this! Once the bell rang, I closed my journal and stormed out of the class, ready to get all the items my girlfriend so rightfully deserved.

All I had to do was start.

And start I did.

#

Amanda sat in her Geometry class, bored out of her mind. Her instructor, Ms. Fu, was describing the importance of semi-circles and their degrees. "Now, this is important. When drawing a semi-circle, you need to make sure that the degree is approximately 180. If it's not, then it's not a semi-circle along with several other shapes that deal with it…"

Ms. Fu's words quickly faded as Amanda's mind quickly went somewhere else, and it had nothing to do with math. What she thought of as much viler.

Her father, lying in a hospital bed, with nothing but tubes up his nose.

Tubes.

That's all Amanda remembers entering that room. Tubes that were hooked up to an oxygen container. It was the most horrifying thing she ever saw. But none as horrifying as the result that was found out.

Heart attack?

That's impossible, her father, who was as healthy as a horse, somehow had a heart attack and he was only 54! He was also a good man; he never did anything to hurt anyone, so why would he, a good man, have a heart attack. It was unfair.

Then again, life was unfair.

Amanda spent the last few moments staring out the window, while Ms. Fu was still giving her students the lecture of a lifetime. It wasn't until Amanda started chewing on her pencil that her name was called. "Ms. Griffin!"

Amanda's eyes widened in shock, causing her to stop and gaze up at Ms. Fu, who had her hands on her hips. "Didn't you hear me?"

"What?"

"I told you to solve for the degree. That is if you were listening?"

Amanda blinked, turning to her along with the rest of the students, their eyes all staring up at her. Feeling anxious, Amanda takes her pencil from her mouth and speaks. "Um, 42?"

With these words, the whole class burst out laughing, pointing directly at her as they laughed. As for Ms. Fu, she still had her hands on her hips, her brow raised up at Amanda, causing her to shrink in embarrassment.

\#

Soon, the bell rang, and Amanda made her way out of the doors of Geometry class. Thanks to the little incident in class, Amanda was forced to get detention on Saturday.

Great, first her father had a heart attack, and now this. Could this day get any worse?

With a sad sigh, Amanda makes her way to her locker, twisting the combination. As soon as it opened, Amanda's eyes widened. To her surprise, Amanda finds a pair of pink balloons jumping from her locker. Amanda was shocked at first until she found the words that were written on them: "I Love You" and Be Mine"

Confused, Amanda then looked back in her locker and found a folded pink piece of paper. Without a second thought, Amanda takes the paper and brings it to her eyes, but not before unfolding it. As soon as she does, she finds a set of words written in bold red letters: Meet me in the gym XOXO-Dominic.

Amanda looked down to find a set of poorly drawn hearts written below, making Amanda giggle. "Aw", she said before putting the notecard in her pocket. "Okay, Dom. I'll play along with your game."

With this in mind, Amanda grabs the balloons before closing her locker shut and walks down the hallway, with a slight scent of hope.

#

Amanda made her way through the gym, her eyes lowered as she looked through the place. It was quiet and dark, making her very confused. "Hello!", Amanda shouted, her voice echoing as she made her way through.

"Dominic?"

Amanda took one step, and before she knew it, a light flicked in the distance, causing her to turn her head. To her surprise, she finds four mysterious figures standing in the distance.

Confused, Amanda raises her head before speaking. "What the-Dom?"

"Hello, Amanda."

"What is this?"

"*This* is my proposal."

Amanda's eyes widen. "Proposal?"

With these words, I turn my shoulder to a red button, one that I quickly push. Within seconds, a huge beam of light burst through the ceiling, causing Amanda to flinch as she gazed up. "Ah! Dominic!"

"It's okay, Amanda, just look up!"

"I can't! It's too-", Amanda's words were quickly stopped when a group of words was found before the ceiling lights, "Bright."

Wiping her vision clear, Amanda gazed up at the lights where the words were now visible in bold red letters: "AMANDA GRIFFIN, WILL YOU GO TO PROM WITH ME?"

"W-what?"

"So, what do you say?"

Amanda peers down from the ceiling and at me kneeling on the floor with a bouquet of roses. "Be my date?", I said with a wide grin.

Seeing this, Amanda brings her hand to her mouth. "Oh, Dom", Amanda suddenly pauses as the thought surfaces into her brain. "Wait, are those lilies?"

"Yes."

"I'm allergic to lilies?"

"Oh!", I peer down to the white-petaled flowers, before laughing. "Well, if I throw them away, will you go to the dance with me?"

"As long as my face doesn't swell up, then yes!"

"Alright!", I said, flinging the lilies away.

With these words, Amanda and I embrace in a celebratory hug, but not before I lift Amanda in the air and twirl her around, causing us both to laugh.

\#

At a suburban area of St. Mora, a small yet cozy house was found. Inside was Amari sitting on a couch, laughing hysterically with a young, black comedian with an unusual set of gums in his mouth, cracking up all kinds of jokes with his microphone, making his audience laugh.

That, including Amari. "Ha-ha-ha! Oh, Martin Lawrence is a riot!'

"He sure is", said Ms. Wilkins, placing a small plate of cookies on the coffee table. "Ooh, cookies", Amari said, retrieving one.

"Careful Amari, they're hot."

"I know, I know", Amari blew the cookies off before going a bit straight into it. "It's so nice of you to drop by."

"Yeah, thanks for letting me stay here, Mrs. Wilkins."

"Oh, you're welcome, A.J. Anything for my favorite student."

Another laugh leaves Amari, much to Ms. Wilkins's curiosity. "You really like that, Martin, don't you?"

"Oh, yeah. He's one funny dude! I can't get enough of him."

"Neither could I. There were many Friday nights I remember watching him. He truly was hilarious. Still is."

"Yep."

Ms. Wilkins sat on the couch beside Amari, her eyes glued to Amari as he laughed. She smiled at him lovingly as Amari continued to laugh. It isn't until his last laugh that he faces Ms. Wilkins, who is staring down at him. Confused and a little bit awkward, Amari breaks the silence by speaking. "Are you okay, Ms. Wilkins?"

"I'm fine, Amari. I'm more concerned about you."

"Me?", he said, pointing to himself.

"Yes. How are things going with them?"

Amari shifted in his seat, and his demeanor changed. "It's pretty much the same. My brother still treats me like shit, and my mom…", he paused, making Ms. Wilkins confused before he sighs. "She could be better."

"But she's not, isn't she?"

He nods. "No, she's not."

With these words, Ms. Wilkins pulled her student in for a warm embrace, one that Amari did not hesitate to give into. "Thank you"

"You're welcome", she pulled away from Amari, leaving the two of them in silence again until one of them spoke up. "So, are you ready for your very first school prom?", she said with a smile.

"Yeah, it's the first time I get to look fancy for school. I have a whole tuxedo and everything", Amari looked down at his wristwatch and gasped. "Uh-oh!"

"What's wrong?"

"I have to get home", he said, slipping into his jacket. "The delivery man will be here any moment to deliver my suit."

"I thought you said you already, had it?"

"I do, it just didn't get delivered until today. See you at the party, Ms. Wilkins!", he said, running out the front door of her home and outside the front lawn, hopping on his bike down the road.

As for Ms. Wilkins, she stood there in front of the door and sighed. "I have an extra one if you'd want it."

#

The school bell rang for dismissal, causing the sea of students to come out. Yet, this time, they were holding hands; jocks, goths, and even the nerds all had their dates. And so did Amanda and I.

"I can't wait until tonight, Amanda. It's going to be great."

Amanda nods. "Yeah, it will."

I turn my eyes to Amanda, her eyes low with sadness. "Hey, what's wrong?"

"What?"

"You look sad. Is there something wrong?"

"What, no. I was just thinking of something."

"Of what?"

Amanda flips her hair away. "It's nothing."

I frown, crossing my arms. "Amanda?", I said with a serious tone.

Amanda sighed, her eyes on the floor. "It's my father."

My eyes softened. "Oh."

"I'm just worried he'll end up in the hospital again."

"What do you mean? He got out yesterday."

"Yeah, but what if it happens again? What if he…you know…dies"

"You can't think like that, Amanda."

"How do you know? You don't have a sick relative."

"No, but if I did, I'd at least try to be positive about it. If something bad happened to my Mom, the best thing I could do was be there for her, just like she was with me. Besides, your father has medicine that'll help prevent the heart attack from happening."

Amanda looks up at me, nodding slowly. "I guess you're right. It's just my father's such a good man. He didn't deserve that."

"That's what my mom says. It's the good people that suffer the most."

Amanda moves some of her hair from her face before sighing. "I'm sorry for getting upset."

"Hey, you didn't ruin anything. You're allowed to be sad, Amanda. My Mom tells me that all the time."

Amanda shakes her head. "Not mine."

My eyes were lowered in sadness, causing me to bring her in for a loving hug. We did this for a good ten minutes before heading out of the Summit High hallway.

\#

Robert Griffin stared out the window, his eyes gazing out at the mountains sitting out before him. He had a worried look, much like how he was when he found out about the heart attack.

The sweaty palms, the cold sweats.

The darkness.

It was all so terrifying, but none were as bad as the words his wife had told him.

He's the son.

"No"

Seventeen years.

"No!"

Mother of Joana Mitchell.

"No-"

"Robert!"

Robert turns his eyes to the left, where he finds his beloved wife, walking towards him with a silver tray in her hands. "Oh, hello, dear."

"You look distressed. You wouldn't want that in the condition you are in."

"I know, it's just all so stressful."

"You think you're the only one who's stressed? You're not. Believe me, this is hard for me too, Robert", Evelyn places the silver tray in front of Robert, causing him to let out a small sigh. "I'm sorry, Evelyn. I'm just-"

"I know, you're scared. Trust me, I am, too, but if we're going to figure this out. We need to face the truth, okay?"

With these words, Robert took his prescription pills and popped one of them into his mouth, accompanied by a glass of water. As soon as he swallowed, Robert looked at his wife and nodded. "Okay."

With that, Evelyn lifted her arm which held a newspaper so Robert could see. It had a photo of a brown Sudan car and a headline that read: **Homicide kills lover! Family devastated!"**

Evelyn's lips quivered after seeing this, along with her hands shaking as she looked further down. That's when they saw it.

Another photo was of a young black male who resembled the young boy who entered their mansion.

"No", Evelyn said, peering below the photo and finding the name written in black and bold.

Octavius Mitchell.

"NO!", Robert snapped as he held onto his heart, huffing and puffing. "Robert, Robert, calm down! Breathe, breathe!", Evelyn commanded as Robert slowly did so.

"He's, he's the son!"

All through his nose, he breathed through his nostrils, taking in deep, shallow breaths as he exhaled air. He did this a few more times before letting out his final breath. "Better?"

Robert nods. "Yes, yes, I'm fine now."

Evelyn looks to her husband with a worried tone before Robert turns to him. "It's true. I can't believe it. You were right."

She nodded. "He's the son. It all makes sense. The car accident, the mother,

"Seventeen. That's how old he is."

"And how old the case is", Evelyn brings his hand through his hair. "What are we going to do?"

"What we always do is keep it in a box", Robert brings his hand to his wife's shoulder. "I don't have very much time left."

Evelyn nodded. "I know", she took his hand, squeezing it tight. "I know."

\#

Amari bicycles up the street, his eyes squinting hard as he pedaled up the road. It isn't long before he spots a delivery truck heading down the road. Amari's eyes lit up with joy as he saw this. "Oh, yeah!"

With these words, Amari pedaled on his bike harder until he was all the way up the road and to his house. Without a second thought, Amari hopped off his bike, his posture straight as he found a brown cardboard box sitting on the front of his face.

He looks down at the words written on the white sticker, the font written in bold: **From: US Postal Service of America**

To: Amari Jenkins

Without a second thought, Amari grabs the box and brings it into the house, the screen door closing behind him. Amari made his way through the living room, through the kitchen, and down the hallway without much thought that his two brothers were bumped right into them. "Move it or lose it, y'all!", he shouts, heading down the hall and into his room, leaving his brothers in a daze. "What the hell was that about?", asked Zane.

"I don't know, let's find out", said Tony, turning his eyes to the hallway. "Let's find out."

The two brothers make their way down the hallway, their grins wide and sinister.

#

Amari places the cardboard box on his bed, the postal sticker gazing up at him before speaking. "After all this time…", Amari brings his hands up to the tape, stripping it straight down from top to bottom. Before he knew it, the tape was off, and the box opened wide.

Within seconds, the box opens, and Amari brings out a black and white, tailored tuxedo. It was perfect and just his size. "I have my suit."

"What suit?"

Hearing this, Amari turns his head back to the two boys, Amari's twin brothers, Tony and Zane, standing before him. "What Cha got there, Amari?"

Amari hides his suit behind him, hiding it from the view of his brothers. "None of your business. What are you doin' in my room?"

"We'll say once you show us what you're hiding?"

"I ain't hidin' nothin'! How 'bout stop being so nosey and get out!"

Tony and Zane turn to each other, their eyes rolling before they reach their hands out to Amari and yank the suit from his back. "Hey!", Amari said, gripping his suit. "Give it back, give it back!"

Before Amari knew it, his suit was snatched from his grasp and into his brother's hands. Amari watches as his brothers hold the tuxedo up to them, their grins visible before laughing. "What the hell is this?"

"It's my suit, I'm supposed to wear it to the dance!"

Tony snickers. "The dance?"

"Yes, for tonight's prom! Now, give it back!"

Zane and Tony turn to each other, their eyes still on the suit. Until the sound of a door opens from behind, and the voice is heard. "Boys, I'm home!", said a voice, causing them to turn around, their eyes big and wide, much to Amari's shock. "No, no!"

Tony and Zane laugh hysterically. "Let's see how Mom likes your little suit?"

"No, Mother!"

Tony and Zane made their way through the hallway, and Amari chased behind them as they laughed. "Stop, guys, stop!"

The boys didn't listen, for they were too invested in showing their mother their brother's suit. "Mom, mom!", shouted the boys, going past the kitchen and into the living room. As soon as they do, a woman in a lingerie dress is found, putting her purse on the sofa. "What a day."

"Mom!"

The young woman turns her eyes back to the two boys approaching her. "Mom, check out this suit we got from Amari!", Zane said, holding it out to her.

"No!", said Amari, hopping in the back of his brothers. "Mom, that's my suit! I'm supposed to be wearing it at the prom tonight!"

"The prom? Why, that's ridiculous."

"It is?"

"Yes, this suit, it's too small for you."

Amari raises a brow. "It is?"

"Yes", she takes the suit from Zane and Tony and puts it into her arms. "How can you even wear this when it has all these rips and tears in it?"

"Tears? What tears?"

"Boys", Gwen throws Amari's suit to Tony and Zane, their grins large and wide. "Show your brother how it's done."

With that, Tony and Zane take both ends of the suit, stretching it firmly before forming a tear. "No!"

The tear opens more, causing a zig-zag to strip farther down. "No, stop! I need that for the prom!", Amari said, falling to his knees.

"I'm sorry, Amari, but it looks like you won't be attending the prom tonight. You will be staying here and watching the home."

"What?", Amari's ripped tuxedo is thrown back in his hands. "But what about Tony and Zane?"

"They will be going to the prom."

"The prom, but that's what I was going to do."

"Sorry, Amari. Only good boys get good things, and *you* are not that person."

Amari lowered his head, sad, as Tony and Zane laughed at him. Amari rose from the floor and headed down the hallway, sobbing as his "family" members' laughs died out the further he went down through the kitchen, down the hall, and back into his room, his face falling flat down on the bed.

"Those bullies! They ruined my tuxedo; they ruined my prom!", Amari grunts, his fists squeezing the tuxedo tight. "I'm going to get them back one day! I swear it!"

With that, Amari throws his tuxedo across his room and into his trash can, never to be seen again.

\#

"Hold still, Dom."

"I am, Amanda."

I stood in my bedroom, in front of my mirror, where my girlfriend, Amanda Griffin, was helping me with my hair. That is, curl ironing it. "Are you sure you're doing this right, Amanda?"

"Of course, I know how to curl iron hair; just look at me?", Amanda said, showing off her silk-pressed hair. "It looks good."

"It sure is, and so will yours."

I nod. "Yeah, I guess you're right."

Suddenly, a knock on the door is heard, causing me to turn my head. "Come in!"

With these words, the door opens wide, revealing a big-haired white woman to enter. "Hey, hey guys. How's everything going in here?"

"Hey, Aunt Sue! Everything's going okay."

"Okay?", Sue said, entering the room. "That doesn't sound so happy?"

"It's fine, it's just that Amanda's trying to do something with my hair an-"

"It's called a jerry curl, Dom, and it looks good on you! Now, turn your head and let me finish!"

"Alright, alright. Just make sure it's not bad."

"And what's that supposed to mean?", she said with her hands on her hips.

"Nothing, it's just, I've never had anyone do my hair except mom."

"He doesn't", Aunt Sue laughs. "There's no one in this world who can do hair like Joana. At least, that's how Dominic feels?"

"It's not that mom's the best at hair; it's that she's the only person, *woman,* that I know can do hair."

"Well, today she's going to see how good of a hairdresser I am. That is, if you let me finish?"

With these words, I let out a heavy sigh and leaned my head back into my girlfriend's hands. "Alright, get started."

A happy smile forms across Amanda's face. "Good."

#

Mom sat at the kitchen table, her eyes gazing down at a weekly women's magazine, all while drinking a hot cup of black coffee. She wore a pair of blue scrubs, which meant only one thing.

Work.

As much as she hated working, she also hated wearing her Scooby Doo scrubs. She liked the cartoon, but she didn't like to wear it. Then again, it was the only thing left in stock. So, she was stuck with this.

But it wasn't all bad as she still had a job. That was better than anything.

Joana was seconds from bringing her cup of coffee up to her lips until a strange figure caught her eye, causing her to turn. "Octa-Dominic?"

"Hi, Mom!", I said, standing in my white tuxedo, all with my grandiose jerry curl. "So, what do you think?"

Mom squeals. "You look handsome!"

"I know! I was a bit skeptical at first, but I like it!", I said, flipping a bit of my hair. "Now, my hair's curlier than ever!"

She laughs. "It sure is."

I smile as Mom straightens out my tuxedo. "You look good."

"Not as great as she does."

Mom raises her brow. "She?"

I turned my head away from Mom and to the hallway. "Amanda, you can come out now!"

With these words, a silhouette figure makes its way through the darkness of the hallway and into the kitchen light. To my mother's surprise, Amanda enters the room with a sparkly, white dress, white slippers and a pearl necklace wrapped around her neck. "Hi, Mrs. Mitchell."

Mom's eyes light at the beautiful young woman standing before her. "Oh-my-goodness. Don't you look fabulous!"

Amanda laughed, bashfully. "She sure does", I said, taking my girlfriend's hand in mine. "Hold on! Stay just like that! I want to take a photo of you two! Sue, get the camera!", Mom said, heading down the hallway, leaving Amanda and me alone. "Your mom seems pretty excited."

"Of course, she is. Too bad, she must work tonight. I really wanted her to take us to the prom."

"It's okay, Dom. There'll be plenty more things for her to do with you."

I nod, making a half-smile. "Yeah, I guess you're right."

"Besides, at least you got this photo."

"Yeah."

"Dom!"

Amanda and I turn our heads to find Aunt Sue standing beside Mom, with a camera in her hands. "Okay, you two, get together."

Amanda and I laugh before the both of us huddled together, my hand wrapped around her arm. "Perfect."

With these words, the camera flashed, and a photo came out. "Got it!"

With these words, Joana takes the photo from the camera and brings it to her eyes. "Ooh, you two look so cute!", Mom squeals.

"Can we see?"

Mom gave a quick nod to me before turning the photo back to Amanda and me, our hands intertwined as we looked. "It's beautiful."

Amanda smiles. "Yeah, our first prom picture."

Mom nods. "Yes, now let's take another one!"

"No!", I snap. "That's all we get, mom."

"Oh, come on, Dom."

"No, he's right, Joana", said Aunt Sue stepping in. "The dance will be starting soon. Plus, you need to get to work."

Mom rolls her eyes. "Oh, it's only seven-thirty. I still got time."

"Yeah, right. Come on, guys!", Aunt Sue said, turning away from her friend and to Amanda and me.

#

Amanda and I were outside, making our way into the luxury SUV Aunt Sue owned. Amanda was the first to head in, but before I could take even a step inside, Mom called my name out. "Dominic!"

My eyes quickly shifted back, and my mother walked towards me, her arms folded. "You show her a good time, you hear?"

I smile. "I will, Mom."

"I mean it, Dom. I've taught you too well about how to treat a woman."

"And you've done well. I'm sure your teachings will rub off on me."

"I hope so."

Suddenly, the car beeps, causing Mom and I's head to turn. "Come on, Dom!"

"I'm coming, Sue!", I said, turning my eyes back to my mom, who had both her arms out. Without a second thought, I pull Mom in for a warm, loving hug. "I'll take care of her, Mom. I promise."

"I know you will. Go on."

With these words, I turn away from Mom and head straight towards the car, the door closing shut behind me. Before I knew it, the engine started, and the car went down the road. Mom waved me goodbye as I went down the road but as soon as the car disappeared, a sharp pain went through Mom's head.

"Ah!", she said, bringing her hand to her forehead. "Shit!"

Joana rubbed the center of her forehead, her eyes squinted as she did. Within seconds, the pain soon subsides, and Joana's breathing diminishes. "Shit", she breathes. "That was a wild one. Wilder than earlier."

With these words, Joana turns her eyes back to the house, ready for work.

Little did she know, a black SUV was parked at the edge of the road, a few feet from my home. On the inside, a mysterious figure in black was found wearing a pair of binoculars over its eyes, where it watched the young woman walk back into her house, closing the door shut behind her.

Without a second thought, the figure takes her binoculars from her eyes and gasps. "It's her", said Evelyn Griffin. "It's her, Robert."

Robert, sitting across from her, looked at her with desperate eyes. "So, it's true?"

She nodded. "He's the son, and that is his mother. *That* is Octavius's family."

He blinked. "What are we going to do?"

"What do *you* think we should do?"

With these words, Robert clenches both his fists and speaks. "We need to tell him; we need to tell him."

Evelyn shakes her head. "Not tonight. We can't tell him tonight."

"Of course, not tonight. But soon."

Evelyn nodded. "Soon."

With these words, Evelyn switched on her engine and hit the brakes, heading down the road.

#

The Jenkins house stood proud and tall in the night. But as calm as it was on the outside, there was much commotion on the inside.

Good commotion.

"Boys! Come on, it's time to go!", said Gwen, staring at herself in the mirror and applying red makeup to her lips.

She wore a sparkly, red dress, matching the hue of her lipstick along with her mascara. Except her mascara was black, which, to her, suited her lips well. "Boys, hurry up! I don't have all night!"

"We're already here, Mom!"

Turning her head, Gwen's eyes lit up with life as she finds two boys smartly dressed in yellow tuxedos with white shackles. Ms. Jenkins brings her hands up to her face. "Oh, look at my two handsome boys!", She made her way up to them, taking both their faces as she smiled. "You look so handsome."

"Thanks, Mom."

Gwen gives them a quick peck on the cheek before speaking. "Alright, let's go. John will be at the place soon. Can you believe I'm dating the vice principal of Junior High"

"No, we can't believe it, mom."

"Kind of surreal. You must've been extra flirty to get a date with him."

"That's why he calls me the 'Stank Master'."

Tony and Zane laugh, causing Gwen to do the same before grabbing her purse. "Come on, let's get going."

"Wait, Mom. What about Amari?"

"Who?"

"Amari, isn't he supposed to watch the house tonight?"

Gwen nods. "Yes, he is."

"Do you want us to go tell him?"

"No, I'll do it. You two go wait in the car."

"Okay."

With that, the twins make their way out of the living room, leaving their mother alone.

#

Amari was in his room, his eyes peering down at his black and white tuxedo. From the abomination look of what was his "brothers" outfits, it would've been much better to have his suit worn, making him stand out from both his shitty brothers.

And his shitty mo-

There was a knock at the door, causing him to turn his head away. "It's open!"

Saying this, the door opens wide, revealing Mrs. Jenkins, walking slowly into his room, her eyes looking everywhere. "Well, it seems you've fixed the place up a bit."

Amari grunts. "What do you want?"

"Oh, nothing. I just wanted to tell you that the twins and I are leaving. While we are, you will-"

"Take care of the house. I know. Could you just leave now"

Mrs. Jenkins sucks her teeth before turning her head back, eyeing my tuxedo. "Your suit looks better ripped."

Amari whips his eyes back to the door, which was now closed shut by his stepmother. Fired up, Amari threw his tuxedo on the ground and burst out of his room, his stepmother halfway in the hallway. "Why?!", he shouted across the hallway, causing Gwen to turn her head back. "Why what?"

"Why do you and the guys treat me like this!? I've done nothing but treat you guys like family. For ten years, I've done that! But no matter what, it seems like you just treat me like shit!"

"Shit? Just who do you think you're talking to with that tone, boy? You're just like your father: ruthless!"

"I'm not ruthless, and I am not my father!"

"Are you sure about that? If I recall correctly, he blamed *you* for making him leave us. You're lucky he didn't take you with him."

Amari grunts, his fists clenched before letting go. "Yeah, that's what I thought. Now, if you excuse me, I need to go on my date. At least I have one."

Amari's stepmother made her way down the hallway, leaving Amari in sadness. Without a second thought, Amari turns his eyes back to his room, slamming the door shut behind him.

Before he knew it, Amari was back in his bed, face-down first. It wasn't long before he heard a car leave. Amari looked through the window, moving his curtain to see a car, an SUV, leaving the parking lot and down the street.

Sad, Amari closes the curtains shut and plops back on his bed, grabbing his tuxedo tight before bringing it to his face. "Of all the things I can't have, the prom was the only thing I was going to get. But now, it's ruined."

With these words, Amari brought his pillow up to his face, wallowing in his sorrow. That is, until a sudden thought rose from the surface, giving him the notion to bring his pillow from his face, his eyes wide with newfound hope. Hope that he will gladly use.

"I think I know who can help."

#

Amari stood before a house, one that he was happily familiar with. Without a quick inhale, Amari brings his hand up to the door, knocking on it. Within minutes, the door opened wide to reveal Ms. Wilkins in a sparkly, red dress with a diamond-encrusted necklace around her neck. She looked at Amari, shocked and a bit confused. "Amari?"

"Hey, Ms. Wilkins."

"What are you doing here? Aren't you supposed to be at prom?"

Hearing this, Amari raises his tuxedo to Ms. Wilkins's eyes, causing her to gasp. "Oh my gosh", she said, stepping out her doorway, her hands tracing every inch of shreds. "Amari, what happened?"

"My brothers, they ripped it in half. I was wondering if you could stitch it up for me?"

With a heavy sigh, Ms. Wilkins takes Amari's suit and opens the door. "Come inside."

#

Amari sat in a chair, his eyes looking to the floor as he waited for Ms. Wilkins, who was sitting in front of a sewing machine, where Amari's tuxedo was being fixed. "Almost finished, A.J. Just a few more sew-ins, and you'll tuxedo will be as good as new."

"Thanks, Ms. Wilkins."

Ms. Wilkins continued sewing in silence until a deep sigh left her. "Why do you let those boys treat you that way?", she said, facing Amari.

He shrugged, shaking his head a bit. "I don't know."

"Yes, you do. Those boys torture you, and you just sit there and take it."

"Sitting there and taking it is the only thing I'm good at. It just works for me."

"It shouldn't. You need to stand up for yourself; you need to fight."

"I don't know how. Even if I could, I wouldn't want to."

"You must. No one is coming to save you but you, Amari."

Amari's eyes lower in sadness as Ms. Wilkins returns to her sewing machine, taking the tuxedo from the electric needle and to her eyes. "Finished."

She brings the tuxedo up to Amari's eyes, grinning. "So, what do you think?"

Amari's eyes widen with joy as he holds the tuxedo up to his eyes and smiles. "It's perfect. I love it."

"I knew you would. Go on, put it on. We don't want to be late."

"We?"

"Of course, you didn't think you were going alone, did you?"

#

Summit High stood proud and tall in the evening light. Speaking of lights, there were thousands of them shining from the glass windows. Huge beams of red, blue, green, and purple with several silhouette figures dancing about them.

But that was just the inside, for the outside was much more perilous. On the outside steps of the school, there were cars huddled behind each other, their horns honking loudly. By each car came various teenage children hopping right out of them, waving their caregivers goodbye.

The same was soon done to the sharply dressed, curly-haired boy and his girlfriend, who he gladly helped step out of the car in her sparkly red dress and shoes. As soon as we got out, I closed the door and waved. "Thanks for driving us, Aunt Sue!", I said, waving.

"Anytime, Dominic! I'll be out here when you get done! You two have fun!"

"We will!"

"Not too much fun, though!"

"Okay, Sue! Bye!", I said in embarrassment.

Aunt Sue made one final wave before heading out of the road, leaving me and Amanda alone. I turn to her, her smile big and wide before her hand is brought out to me. "Ready to have the best night of our lives?"

"I nod, taking her hand in mine. "Of course, I am."

With these words, Amanda and I made our way up the steps of Junior High, hand in hand with the rest of the students and their dates.

The moment we headed in, everything was dark.

Dark but light.

Except those lights were flashy and colorful. Red. Blue, Green, and Purple; all these colors shining down at us. It blinded me at first, but the sooner we headed in, the better our vision became.

Speaking of vision, there were many people there. Nothing but bodies hitting each other's hips and thighs together in the lights. It reminded me of those clubs, mainly the ones I saw on TV, except their clothing was less revealing.

Basically, a PG version of the club.

"Well, here we are", said Amanda, turning to me. "At prom."

I nod. "Yeah, so what do you want to do first?"

Amanda scoffed. "What do you think?", she took her hand in mine, holding it tight as she pulled me to the dance floor. Our hands were still held tight as we were jumping up and down the place. Seeing this, Amanda turns her head back to me and nods. "Let's do what they're doing."

"Really?"

"Yeah, I mean, they're jumping up and down."

"Exactly."

I rub the back of my neck. "Um, okay."

With these words, Amanda and I bent our knees and jumped down in the air, our arms pumping up and down as the disco music played from above.

By the looks of it, this prom was starting off to be pretty good. As for some, their day was just getting started.

\#

Joana sat in her office, her eyes peering down at the paperwork she was filling out. It was eight o'clock, a few minutes before nine, and there was nothing interesting going on. It was a slow night, and with slow nights comes staying in your office and catching up on filling out patient forms.

At least, she didn't have to worry about any more pain-staking headaches. If there was anything she hated more, it was headaches at work, and the worst part was that she couldn't call out. Luckily, she took an Advil before leaving so she wouldn't have to suffer.

At least for tonight.

Sighing, Joana moved her patient's book away from her before leaning back in her chair. She turned her eyes to the left but there was no one. "I wish Sue was here."

She looked at the white telephone sitting on the table. "We would prank phone call each other nonstop. "It was a great time", she sighs, staring up at the ceiling. "I also wish I could take Dominic to the prom-, *his* prom. Instead, I'm stuck here at work, alone. Can this night get any worse?"

Suddenly, there was a knock at the door, which caused Joana's eyes to light up. "Yes?"

Within seconds, the door opens wide, revealing a blonde-haired woman to step in, her face full of distress. "Are you Joana Mitchell?"

Joana nods. "Yes."

"We need you, now!"

"Now, for what?"

"Come quick, it's an emergency!"

Hearing this, Joana rises from her seat and exits her office. Before she knew it, she was following the blonde-haired woman. The two of them turn a corner, causing them both to find a young man in a hospital bed, his body wrapped in bandages, screaming in pain."

Joana's eyes widened in shock at seeing this. "Oh my god! Is he okay!? What happened!?"

"We'll talk about that after you get this man to the urgent care! Out of the way, everyone, a patient coming through!"

Joana gave a quick nod to the nurse before slipping on her mask. With that, the two nurses made their way down the hallway, and into urgent care.

Even on a boring night, her job still needed to be done, and it would.

\#

Amanda and Dominic spent the last half-hour dancing, their hair messy from the jumping. It wasn't until they were sweating that one of them finally spoke up. "Okay, that's enough dancing", Amanda said, causing me to nod in agreement. "Yeah...we should...stop", I said, sweaty and out of breath.

"You're sweating, Dom"

"Yeah", I wipe some of the sweat from my brow, nodding. "Yeah, I am. I need a cold drink."

"Me too", Amanda looks over my shoulder, her brow raised. "There's one over there in the corner."

I turned my head back, finding a table of plastic cups and a container containing what looked to be pink liquid. "Oh, didn't see that there", I turned my eyes back to Amanda. "I'll be back."

"I'll be here, waiting."

With these words, I make my way over to the drink stand, my eyes right on the red plastic cups that stood on the table. Without a second thought, I reach over to the cups with another hand reaching towards mine, triggering the feeling I had in the back of my head. "Oh, sorry!", said a voice.

"Oh, no. It's fine, I-", my words were quickly cut off as I found a freckled-faced girl standing before me, her smile big and wide. "Nomi!?"

Nomi's hazel brown eyes widen to her name. "Oh, I remember you. You're Dominic, right?"

"Uh", my plastic cup slips from my hand a bit before nodding. "Y-yes", I clear my throat. "Um, were you trying to get something to drink?"

"Uh-huh. Um, my boyfriend was thirsty."

I nod. "So, is my girlfriend."

Her eyes lit up hearing this. "Oh, you have a girlfriend."

"Yeah, she's-"

"Right here!"

Nomi and I turn our heads back to find my girlfriend, Amanda, standing before us, with her arms folded and her brows raised. "Dominic, what are you doing?"

"Oh, I was just talking to Nomi."

"Oh, were you now?", she said, turning to Nomi. "What were you talking about?"

"None of your business, boogie."

"Boogie!?'

"Hey, what's going on here?", said a buff guy coming up towards Nomi, his arm wrapped around her. "Babe, you were supposed to get us drinks. What happened?"

"Nothing, I just met up with an old friend."

"Friend?"

"Yeah, me", said Amanda. "Don't worry, I was just leaving."

"Oh, were you?"

"Yes, and so is my *boyfriend*. Come on, Dom."

"But don't you still want drinks?"

"No, I'm not so thirsty anymore. Now, come on!"

With that, Amanda and I leave the drink stand, but not before I whip my head back to eye Nomi and her boyfriend still standing there. "What are you looking at, Dom!?", Amanda snaps, causing me to turn back in shock. "Um, nothing!"

"You were staring at Nomi, weren't you!?"

"What, no. I was ju-"

"I don't want you staring at her or any other girl, do you hear me!?"

"Okay, okay. I'm sorry."

With these words, Amanda and I stood in silence, causing me to speak. "Do you want to go back and dance?"

Amanda shakes her head. "No"

I shrug. "Okay, then what do you want to do?"

"I want to piss. I'm going to the bathroom."

"Amanda!", I called out, but she was already too far away.

With that, I turn my eyes away from the place and leave. But as soon as I did, a young man in a tuxedo was making his way into the ballroom, where many of his fellow classmates danced.

Amari looks around him before speaking. "This looks fun. Too bad I didn't bring a date", he snickers.

"Would you like to dance with me?"

Amari faces Ms. Wilkins, giving her a look. "I'm your student, Ms. Wilkins. That wouldn't look right, trust me."

She scoffs, her hands on her hips. "You say that like I'm some old lady."

"I don't; it's just that I want someone close to my age, is all. I'm not trying to be mean, okay?"

With these words lingering in the back of her head, Ms. Wilkins let off a quick sigh. "Oh, alright. I understand."

"Goof. Maybe I'll steal one of these lovely ladies while their boyfriends ain't lookin'", he laughs to himself.

Ms. Wilkins laughs. "I don't think that'll be necessary, Amari."

"It could work. Until then, I guess I'll just have to wait and- SEEEEEEEEEE!!!", Amari's words are interrupted at the sight of two poorly dressed twin boys standing at the drink stand along with their mother, who was grooming with someone who looked to be a man in his mid-40s.

"Amari, what is it?"

With his hands trembling, Amari brings the walkie-talkie up to his lips and speaks. "Oh, just a dragon and her two minions."

"What?"

"It's my mom, my stepmom, and my brothers. They're here, right over there!"

Ms. Wilkins watched where my hand was pointed and found a middle-aged woman, her two sons, and some very young man.

"Gwendolyn", she said.

Amari nods. "Yeah, it's her. Of all the places she could have her dates, she chooses my prom!", he turns to Ms. Wilkins, his eyes full of worry. "I can't have them see me! I can't!"

"They won't. I'll make sure of that besides it's dark."

He nods. "Yeah, guess you're right."

"Go, find somewhere to hide!"

"Got it!"

Amari ran through the ballroom, his feet moving fast as he made his way through the ballroom. "Got to get away from here!", he said out of breath. "I've got to get away!"

In the small corner, Amari finds a set of chairs sitting in the distance. "Perfect! Okay, I just need to get out of th-argh!", Amari's falls right to the floor and onto his butt. "Hey!", answered the mysterious, curly-haired boy Amari gazed up at. "Watch where you're go-", the mysterious figure looks down at his raised brow. "Amari?"

Amari raises his brow, shocked. "Dom?"

#

Joana and the blonde-haired woman stood in a room, their eyes gazing down at the young man lying in bed, his left arm and right leg wrapped in bandages. The only thing that wasn't covered was his face, which had but a few bruises on it.

"He's lucky to be alive", answered the blonde-haired woman, turning to Joana. "Good thing you put those bandages on. If it weren't for that, he'd be toast."

"Yeah. What happened to him? Did he get in a fire?"

"More like an explosion."

"Huh?"

"He was just on his way home when suddenly, this car came in and hit him. He tried to get out but before he could: "BOOM!" his car exploded. It wasn't long until the doctors came in and brought him here."

Joana had her hands to her mouth before speaking. "Damn. I hope he doesn't have any family."

"Actually, he doesn't. He's never been married nor had kids."

"Oh, really?"

She nodded. "Yeah, he's pretty much single", she raised her brow, her grin making her feel confused. "Hold on now. What are you thinking about?"

"Nothing, it's just he's not the only one that's single. Give you any ideas?"

Joana scoffs. "Ideas? Whatever *ideas* you're thinking of, it's not what you think."

The blonde-haired nurse nods. "Okay, if you say so."

"What's that supposed to mean?"

"I think you already know."

The nurse leaves Joana alone in the room, leaving her with a confused look. That is until a slight slurring noise comes from behind. "Hello?"

Joana's eyes lit up, causing her to turn her eyes back to the young man in bandages, who now was sitting slightly upright in bed, his eyes looking straight at the woman in blue scrubs. "Um, excuse me, miss. Where am I?"

Joana smiled, her eyes looking at him. "Don't worry, you're safe", she made her way toward the young man, her smile warm and comforting. "I'm Nurse Mitchell."

#

I stood before Amari, my eyes full of anger.

He scoffs. "What are you doing here?"

"Um, not hiding from my family, that is."

I raise my brow. "What?"

"Nothing", he said, rising from the floor and dusting himself off. "Where's your cranky girlfriend?"

"Don't you dare!", I snap. "You're not going to say anything bad about Amanda, not tonight!"

"Why not? You had loads to say, Ms. Wilkins. That is, if you recall?"

"This isn't the time nor the place to bring up old baggage."

"Hm. Where have I heard that before?"

I grunt, my hands clenched. "Don't you have somewhere to be? A date?"

"I don't have one. I came alone tonight."

I scoff. "Of course you did. You're always by yourself."

Amari sucks his teeth and rolls his eyes. "Whatever man, I have somewhere to be."

"Amari?", said a voice, causing Amari and me to turn our eyes and face my red-headed girlfriend standing before us both. "Amanda?"

"Yeah. What are you doing here?"

"Nothing, babe", I said, walking toward Amanda, my arm around her waist. Amari was just leaving."

Amari raises his brow, his head slowly nodding. "Yeah, I was."

With these words, Amari sucks his teeth, rolls his eyes before turning back to the ballroom, leaving Amanda and I alone. "You, okay?", I nodded, turning to Amanda. "Yeah."

"I didn't mean Amari."

"What?"

"I mean *her*. Are you okay with Nomi?"

Without speaking, Amanda looks up from my gaze and to the young, freckled-faced girl slowly dancing along with her boyfriend. Only, she wasn't looking at him at all; it was Amanda. "Not really."

"Why? Did something happen between you two?"

"I don't want to talk about it."

"Are you sure? Because it seems to bother you."

"I said I don't want to talk about it!"

I frown, my face angry. "No, you will talk about it. Something's been bothering you all night, and I'm not leaving here until you tell me!"

Hearing this, Amanda lets out a deep sigh. "Fine. You want to know why Nomi and I don't like each other? It's because we used to be friends."

"What?", I said, confused. "You and Nomi?"

"Yes", Amanda crossed her arms, her eyes still gazing up to Nomi, who was now looking at her boyfriend, the two of them gliding across the floor. "We met last summer, not too far from school ending. For most of it, things were good, but a few weeks later, things changed."

"What do you mean?"

Amanda holds herself. "We had a fight, a real, nasty one. Before I knew it, we stopped talking to each other. That is, until tonight."

I frown, my eyes low. "From what Nomi said to you, earlier. It looks like she's still holding some resentment."

"Of course, she is. That's what Nomi does: holds grudges."

I looked up at Nomi, who turned to look not at Amanda but me. I gasp, quickly turning away as I look at Amanda with a sigh. "Look, whatever happened to you guys, let's not let it ruin our night, okay?"

Amanda sighed, turning away from Nomi and her boyfriend, who were now walking away, hand in hand. Seeing this, Amanda turns her eyes back to me and nods. "Okay"

I smiled, taking Amanda's hand in mine before dragging both of us off to the ballroom floor.

#

As good as things were going for Amanda and me, things were getting much better with Mom. Inside the hospital room, Joana was standing over a sink, washing her hands with the soap that sat on the kitchen counter next to her.

Yet, little did she know, her patient, Isaac Newman, stood behind her, his back now right-side up, looking at Joana from behind. He smiled at her through the bandages. It isn't long before his eyes gaze down at her figure, head to toe.

He had been staring at her like this since the moment she said her own name. She was gorgeous, especially from the front. He just hoped she wasn't seeing someone.

There wasn't a ring on her finger, so she wasn't married. But that didn't stop her from getting with a few lucky guys. He just hoped that lucky guy would be him.

"I'll be right there with you, Isaac."

Isaac blinked, snapping out of his thoughts before speaking. "What did you say?"

Joana turns back to him and smiles. "I said I'd be right there with you. Getting these bandages out of my hands is difficult", he laughs. "You know how it is?"

Isaac smiled, his eyes following Joana as she made her way past the sink and to the set of paper towels she ripped from the rack, drying her hands before dumping it in the trash can. "Alright, that's done. Sorry for taking so long."

Isaac shakes his head. "No, it's fine. I don't mind waiting, especially for a great nurse like you."

Joana goes red a bit hearing this. "Why, thank you", she cleared her throat as she turned away from him. "Alright, let's lie you back down."

"No!", Isaac snaps, much to Joana's concern. "Mr. Newman."

"Sorry, I didn't mean to snap at you. It's just I can't go to bed until I tell you this."

"Tell me what?"

Isaac smiles, taking Joana's hand in his. Joana's whole face goes red. "Isaac?"

Isaac smiles, his posture becoming straightened. "Miss Mitchell, is that right?"

Joana nods. "Yes."

"I noticed the shoes you are wearing. They seem like good shoes, good enough for dancing."

"Dancing?"

He nods. "I'm a pretty good dancer. I was hoping you are, too."

Joana raises a brow. I'm sorry, are you asking me out?"

Isaac jerks his head. "If I said 'yes' will you agree?"

She blinked. "Are you sure this isn't the morphine talking?"

Isaac laughs, shaking his head. "Trust me, ma'am. I'm as sane as you are."

Joana smiles. "Well, I hope that sanity will help you stay light on your feet. That is if you healed before then."

A happy smile forms across Isaac's face as he speaks. "Oh, don't worry, miss. I'll be healed before then."

"Good. Now, let's get you to bed, shall we?"

"Yes, ma'am"

#

Amanda and I had finally started to have fun again. We fed each other chocolate hearts and drank some of the punch. Nomi and her boyfriend left son; Amanda and I were back on the dancefloor, only we were slow dancing, holding each other close as we glided to Whitney Houston's "I Have Nothing"

I peered down at her, a smile found on her face, much to my happiness. "Feeling better?"

Amanda nods. "Yes, I'm glad she's gone."

I nod. "Yeah", I shift my eyes back in sadness. "This night has never been more peaceful. Especially without him around."

Amanda raises her eyes up to me. "Oh yeah, I forgot about Amari. You two were fighting, weren't you?"

"Fighting? No, more like a friendly argument."

"It didn't seem friendly to me."

I sigh. "I just don't see why Amari would choose some schoolteacher over me. I mean, this guy got my mom, and I kicked out of our home. Why would he even remotely consider getting back with him?"

"He probably didn't want to lose him as a friend."

"Lose him?", I scoff. "If there's anyone who needs to worry about losing, it's me, the good friend! Amari should've known that. He should have known that!"

"Some friends can't really decipher who's a good friend and who's a bad friend. Sometimes, they need to explore both sides. I think that's what Amari is doing."

"Exploring?", I shake my head. "Yeah, I don't think so. He made his decision on who he wanted to be with. There's no exploring that had to be done there, and that's all I have to say about that."

"Is that so, Dom?"

Amanda and I whipped our heads back to find Amari and Ms. Wilkins standing before us both. "Amari, were you listening to that?"

"Of course, I was listening! I have ears, dumbass!"

I roll my eyes, shifting them straight to Ms. Wilkins. "And why are you here?"

"I'm one of the teachers at this school. If you forgot?"

"Look, whatever you two heard, it was the truth. Something you wouldn't be able to handle."

"Hey, I can handle the truth. You're the one who can't!", said Amari.

"I was talking about Ms. Wilkins!"

Amari grunts, about to charge at me until Ms. Wilkins stops him. "Amari, stop! Just let it go!"

"Yeah, just let it go, Mar! But wait, you can't do that either, can you? Come on, Amanda", I said, taking my girlfriend's arm and walking away.

"I don't give a damn how you feel about Ms. Wilkins! She may have made some mistakes in the past, but she's proven himself to be a much better friend than you ever were!", I stop dead in the center of the dance floor, my head whipping back. "What's that supposed to mean?"

"You know exactly what I mean! That is if you had a brain!"

"That's it! Ahhhhhhhh!!!", I shouted, running towards Amari and tackling him down to the floor.

"Amari!"

"No, kid!", said Amanda, stopping Ms. Wilkins. "Let 'em fight. Whatever it is they need to get out, they'll do it here."

As soon as we do, I immediately start punching him. "You selfish son of a bitch! I was only trying to help you!"

"Help me?!", Amari takes hold of my shoulders before flipping me on my back, with him atop. "You were guilt-tripping me! Trying to make me feel bad about choosing Ms. Wilkins."

"You *should* feel bad! After everything this boy has done to me, you thought that it was a good idea for me to forgive him. Are you serious?"

"I just thought we could be friends!"

"No!", I flip Amari over, with me now on top. "You thought it was good for *you* to be his friend! This was all out of selfishness!"

"Selfishness!"

Amari flipped me back over again, but before he could give me a taste of my own medicine, his name was called. "Amari!?"

Amari looks up from me, his head raised to Ms. Wilkins, who had his hand pointed to the left. Seeing this, Amari whipped his eyes to the left to see two twin boys standing here, along with their mother, whose hands were on her hips. "Amari Lanchester Jenkins!"

Amari's eyes widened in shock; his body was completely frozen, and the only things mobile were the words that came from his mouth. "M-mom?!"

"What in God's name are you doing here!?"

"I-I was just-"

"No!", shouted Ms. Wilkins, stepping in. "Please, don't be mad at Amari, he-"

"Be quiet!", Gwendolyn snapped, her hand raised. "Don't defend him! I know exactly what he did! Amari, get up!"

"But Mom!"

"We're going home, now!"

Sighing, Amari rises from me, his eyebrows frowning at me. "Thanks a lot", he said before stepping off. Before I knew it, I was back on my legs, with Amanda coming up to me. "Dominic, are you okay?"

I shake my head, my eyes wide with fire. "No"

I watched Amari leave with his mother and twin brothers, all of them disappearing in the crowd, but not before Ms. Wilkins turned her eyes back to me, his gaze looking straight to me before disappearing into the crowd.

#

Soon, the prom ended, and everyone was outside, along with Amanda and me. We made our way down the steps of Summit High; Aunt Sue's car was parked right before it. Within seconds, the glass window went down, and Aunt Sue's head poked out with a smile. "Hey, guys! So, how was Dominic? Oh my god, what happened to you!?"

Angry, Amanda turns away from me and speaks. "Don't ask."

Griffin Manor stood big and tall in the evening light. But as beautiful as things looked on the outside, bad things were stirring on the inside.

"No", said Robert, his hands in his face. "I can't believe this."

"Believe it, Robert. It's true."

Robert sighs. "I always knew Octavius had a son. I just didn't know it was him. Does he know who his father is, who he really is?"

"Of course, he doesn't, Robert! According to his mother, his father died in a mysterious car crash."

"A car crash, she said that?"

"Yes."

Robert raised a brow. "So, she lied to him?"

"She probably didn't want him to know. Lying was the best option for him anyway."

"She can't protect him forever. Octavius will be released from prison soon. One way or another, he'll find out."

"He's not going to find out. Not yet. We just need to wait until things boil down. Until then, we prepare for him while we still can."

Mr. Griffin's eyes lower in sadness. "But what about Amanda? What do we tell her?"

"Nothing, not until the time is right."

Robert's eyes widen in shock before the sound of the door opens wide. "Mom, Dad I'm home!"

Mr. and Mrs. Griffin whip their heads back to find their daughter and her wavy-haired boyfriend. Seeing this, a happy smile forms across their faces. "Hello, darling. How was the dance?"

"It was good. At first."

Mr. and Mrs. Griffin's face falls flat. "What do you mean? What happened?"

Amanda turns her eyes from them to me. "Dominic, do you want to tell them?"

Pissed, I look up to Amanda's parents and speak. "I got into a fight."

"A fight?"

"I got into it with a guy. It's no big deal", I sigh, turning to Amanda. "Well, for me anyway. I'm sorry for ruining your night, Amanda."

Amanda shakes her head. "It's alright, Dom. You didn't ruin my night. In fact, you made it better."

"What?"

"You, beating up your friend, made me forget all about the incident with Nomi."

"Really?"

"Yeah, I never had a more fun night than tonight. So, if I'm being honest, it was a pretty good night. Thanks babe", Amanda leaned in to kiss me on the cheek, causing me to blush. "You're welcome, Amanda", I look back at Mr. and Mrs. Griffin.

"Hey, Mr. and Mrs. Griffin, can we keep this to ourselves. I don't want anyone else to know about this."

Robert and Evelyn look at each other before nodding. "Of course, we won't."

I let out a sigh of relief. "Thank you. I'm glad I have people who can keep my secrets, too."

Robert and Evelyn turn to each other, their eyes full of confusion. "Thank you."

"You're welcome."

With that, my hand is grabbed hold of, causing me to raise my head up. "Come on, Dom. Let's take you to the car. I want to kiss you in front of your aunt."

I laugh. "Oh, then we don't want to keep her waiting."

With these words, Amanda and I walk out of the living room, leaving Mr. and Mrs. Griffin alone together. "So, when do you think we should tell them?", he said, facing his wife.

Evelyn watched as Amanda and I walked out the door, hand in hand. "We'll tell them when we're ready."

#

Amari was in his bedroom, his eyes gazing up at his mother and twin brothers. "I told you to stay in the house", said Gwendolyn. "I told you to stay here while your brothers and I were away. Instead, you chose the prom. You *chose* to disobey me! Why?"

Amari frowns, his fists clenched before speaking. "You know exactly why I did what I did."

"What?"

"You guys treat me like shit! For years, you've done nothing but mock me, and it's all because Dad left you!"

Gwendolyn scoffs. "Your father had nothing to do with this!"

"Oh, really? Then what was with you dating the vice principal!"

She gasps. "Yeah, I saw everything!"

Gwendolyn clenches her fists. "So, what if you saw it didn't mean anything!"

"Yes, it did! Just like the last man you got with! They're nothing but replacements for Dad, and you know it!"

"Don't you talk with that tone of voice, young man!"

"I can talk to you however I want!"

Gwen grunts. "You sound just like your father! It's no wonder he left!"

"Yeah, because he hates you!"

"Well, he obviously hated you too! Leaving you here was probably the best option for him, leaving you here with *my* family!"

"You know what, maybe I don't want to be a part of *your* family anymore!"

Gwen pauses, her face narrowing. "And what's that supposed to mean?"

"It means I'm moving out!"

Amari rose from his bed and headed for his closet, where he grabbed a few of his clothes and stuffed them into a suitcase. As for his "mother", she crosses both her arms. "So, that's it. You're just leaving?", she said.

"Are you going to stop me?", Amari said, glancing back to Gwen, who hadn't answered. "Yeah, that's what I thought."

With these words, Amari zips his suitcase shut and heads straight out the door, much to Gwen's rage. "Fine then, go! We don't need you!"

Amari makes his way through the hallway, but not before bumping into two twin boys. "Just where do you think you're going?"

"Fuck off, Zane!"

"What was that, freak!?"

Amari punches Zane in the face, along with Tony, before heading out of the house. Before he knew it, he was outside, with nothing but the sound of crickets chirping.

It was cold, but none was as cold as his family. For years, he's experienced nothing but the worst of them, but that is all behind him now. Now, he was free.

Amari was about to leave when suddenly, he found a white Honda Civic standing before him, the headlights hitting him. Amari brings his hands up to his eyes, the light blinding him. It isn't long before the lights go off, and the door to the car opens wide, revealing a young woman standing in a sparkly, red dress, her eyes full of concern. "Amari?"

Amari's eyes widen seeing this. "Ms. Wilkins?"

She smiles, approaching him. "Ms. Wilkins, what are you doing here?"

"I followed your mother's car. I was worried about you. I saw how furious she was with you at the dance, and I couldn't go home without knowing you were alright", she raised her brow, noticing the suitcase in his hands. "Amari, did something happen?"

Hearing this, Amari let out a few sniffles before falling straight to the ground, crying. "Amari!", Ms. Wilkins cried. "Shh, shh", she said, holding him. "Amari, what's wrong?"

"You were right, Ms. Wilkins. I needed to stand up for myself, and I did."

"What are you talking about?"

"I told them. I told them that I was done with their harassment towards me and that I didn't want to stay with them anymore. So, I left, but I don't know where to go?"

With these words, Ms. Wilkins gives Amari a warm and sympathetic smile. "You can stay with me."

Amari sniffs, looking up at Ms. Wilkins. "Really?"

"Of course, there's more than enough room. That is if you want to stay in a motel?"

"No! Definitely not!"

She grins, standing on her two legs. "Well then, let's get going", she said, extending her hand out to him. Without any hesitation whatsoever, Amari takes Ms. Wilkins's hand and rises from his feet. Before he knew it, Amari was in Ms. Wilkins's car, and the two of them were driving down the road. As for his stepmother, she was peeking through the curtains. "Good riddance", she said, closing the curtains.

Chapter 13: The Headline

I lay peacefully in bed, my arms and legs spread out under the sheets as I slept. The sun peeked through the curtains, hitting the edge of my face, but before it could grow, two shadow figures approached me. My eyes were still closed as they grew nearer.

It isn't long before I hear giggles, making my eyes slowly open. "Ooh, he's waking up."

"Shh! Be quiet", said a familiar voice, quickly catching my attention. "Hm?", I said in confusion.

"Wake up, Dominic"

"Wha-what?"

Within minutes, my eyes opened wide, but as soon as they were, colorful confetti popped into my face. "Ah! What the world!?"

Wiping my eyes, I find two women, my mom and Aunt Joana, with big and bright smiles, and they wore red pointy hats. "Happy birthday, Dominic!"

"Woah!", I said, rising from the bed. "What's this?"

"What do you mean? It's your eighteenth birthday", Mom said, laughing. "You didn't forget, did you?"

"I guess I did", Aunt Sue slipped my birthday hat on my head. "There you go. For our birthday boy."

"Thanks, Aunt Sue."

Mom pulls me in for a tight hug before kissing me on the cheek. "Happy eighteenth birthday, baby. I love you so much!"

I giggle. "Thanks, Mom. So, what are we going to do for today?"

"Well, we have a special birthday breakfast prepared for you."

I gasp, my eyes big and wide. "Pancakes!"

"Chocolate-chip pancakes!"

"Awesome!"

"Yeah, come on, birthday boy!"

With these words, I hope right out of bed with Mom and Aunt Sue, ready to have the best birthday ever!

\#

I watch with wide eyes as Mom and Aunt Sue bring a four-stacked, chocolate-chip pancake cake with what looks to be eighteen waxed candles sitting above it. "Happy birthday to you", they sung. "Happy birthday to you, happy birthday, dear Do-mi-nic. Happy birthday to you!", I clap joyfully as the cake is brought straight to me.

"Make a wish, baby."

A wish? What did I need a wish for? I had a loving mother, a great aunt, and the best girlfriend I could ask for. I had everything I needed right here. I didn't need anything else in the world. Well, except for one thing.

With a deep breath, I lean into the candles and blow them right out, causing Mom and Sue to clap. "Yay!", Mom cheered as Aunt Sue clapped happily for me.

"What did you wish for pumpkin?"

I shake my head. "Can't tell."

Mom and Sue turned to each other, confused, before turning back. "Why?"

"It's a secret. Therefore, you have to respect that."

With these words of encouragement, Mom and Aunt Sue shake their heads. "Okay"

"Good", I smile back before holding out my silver fork. "Now, let's dig in!"

Mom and Sue cheer happily as we raise our forks and dig into the pancakes, biting into every single cake before eating.

We do this for a good few minutes before a knock is heard on the door.

Within seconds, our heads raised from each other, our brows raised. "Who's that?", I said, turning to Mom, her eyes turning to me. "I don't know?"

I watch as Mom rises from her seat and heads out of the kitchen and into the den. Before she knew it, she was walking towards the front door of the house, where a strange silhouette figure stood in the distance.

This is where Joana starts to get a huge sense of déjà vu as if she's been here before. With her mouth dry, Joana takes a deep breath and grabs the doorknob, twisting it open.

As soon as she did, a young man, stood in a flashy red suit with a bouquet of roses in his hands, his smile present. "Hi, Joana."

Joana looked at the man, confused, before speaking. "I'm sorry. Do I know you?"

The man laughs hysterically. "Oh, come on. Have you forgotten me already?"

Joana recognizes the smile the man had, causing her to gasp in shock. "Isaac!?"

He nods. "Yes."

Joana puts her hand through her hair. "Oh my gosh! Isaac, I'm so sorry! I totally forgot about today!"

"Forgot about what?", said a voice, causing Joana to turn to her curly-haired son. "Dominic, have you been standing there the whole time."

I raise my brow. "Yeah", I turn my eyes to the odd-looking man with the flowers in his hands. "Who's this?"

Mom turns away from me and to the nice man. "Um, Dominic, this is Isaac", she said with a toothy grin.

I approached Isaac with the utmost confidence; only my hands were completely folded, showing nothing but intimidation to the tall man smiling before me. "You must be Dominic. Joana has told me all about you. Put a there", he said, holding his hand out to me.

I shake my head, much to Mom's surprise. "Dominic, be nice now."

"No, I don't want to shake his hand."

"Dominic-"

"I don't want to shake his hand", I turned my head back to Mom, my expression blank before a happy smile formed. "I want to hug him."

"W-what?", Joana said, confused.

Without a second thought, I ran straight toward Isaac, my arms extended wide as I embraced him in a warm, loving hug. "Dominic! What are you doing?"

"I should be asking you the same thing, Mom. It's obvious, isn't it?"

"What do you mean?"

I turned to Mom, letting go of Isaac. "Now, I know why you haven't been around lately. It's because you didn't want me to know about your friend, your *boyfriend*."

"Dominic!", she snapped.

"It's alright, Joana. He can call me what he likes."

"Not boyfriend, this is our first date!"

"First date or not, you've definitely been spending a lot of time with him."

Mom rolled her eyes. "I was going to tell you after our date. I just didn't realize it would be this early", she said, looking at Isaac. "Oh, it's okay, Joana. We don't have to go right now. I just wanted to surprise you with these roses. I know they're your favorite."

Mom smiled, taking the roses from him. "They're beautiful, Isaac."

He smiled. "Not as beautiful as you."

Mom laughed. "I don't think you can call me that when I'm standing here in my house robe."

"That's why you should go and change."

"What?"

"Go on, mom! Go and slip into something nice while I chat with Isaac!", I said, pushing Mom out of the room. "Dominic, why are you rushing me all of a sudden?"

"I'm not rushing you. I just want you to freshen up, you know, for Isaac", Mom raised her brow at me. "You better not be planning anything, Dominic. I know how sneaky you can be."

"There's no plotting, Mom. Just a friendly man-to-man conversation."

"Mm-hm", Mom looks up from me and to the man in the living room. "I won't be long, Isaac!"

"Please, take all the time you need, Joana. We have all the time in the world!"

"Okay, thanks", Mom peered back down at me, scolding. "I mean it, Dom. No plots, no schemes, got it!"

"I got it, mom. Now, go."

With that, Mom made her way down the hallway, her back completely turned as she headed out. As soon as mom turned a corner, my eyes were right on Isaac, my eyes full of fire, and my smile was gone. "Looks like it's just you and me, mister."

\#

Water poured down from the shower head and onto Joana's body. A small bar of soap was washed all over her, scrubbing every inch of dirt that she had. Before she knew it, a whole set of stuff was scrubbed onto her, from her arms all the way down her legs and private areas.

Before she knew it, she was covered in soap suds, causing her to come up to the shower head and let the warm water wash all of it down the drain. Within seconds, she shuts off the shower head and opens the curtains, stepping out of the shower with nothing but a towel wrapped around her.

Soon, Joana was in her bedroom, a set of dresses lying on her bed. She brings it up to her, showing it off in the mirror as she smiles. Without a second thought, Joana puts the dress back on her bed and takes the towel from her body and down to her feet.

As soon as she did, Joana grabbed her dress and slipped it all the way from her feet to her torso.

Then, she stopped.

The dress stops right at her chest, where she notices the small bump located on the side of her left breast. "Huh?", she said, her brows narrowing.

Within minutes, Joana lifts her arm high and moves her right arm to it, pressing against her breast. She does this a few more times before finding the hard, non-mobile lump just sitting there.

Confused, Joana lowers her arm, her eyes full of concern, before slipping back on her dress. "Probably just a cyst."

#

I sat across from Isaac, my arms folded as I looked at him. "So, where did you meet my mom?"

Isaac scratches his head. "Um, we met in the hospital."

I raise my brow. "The hospital? You don't mean the hospital my mother works at?"

He nods. "Mm-hm. I was in a serious car accident. Luckily, I got out with a broken leg and bruised arm. But I wouldn't have recovered if it weren't for your mother."

"Oh, wow. She must've been a great nurse. Oh, who am I kidding? Of course, she is!"

He smiles. "Yes, she is."

"I'm ready."

Hearing this, Isaac and I turn our heads back to Mom, standing in a sunshine yellow dress with white floral patterns, all with her hair in a bun and a green purse sitting at her side. "Mom, you look beautiful."

"Thank you, baby."

"Wow, Joana, you look absolutely stunning", Isaac said, taking both her hands. "Really, you do."

"We should get going now."

"Yeah, we should", Mom turned her eyes back to me. "Um, excuse me for a moment."

Isaac looked confused as Mom grabbed my arm and headed up the steps. Before I knew it, we were back inside the kitchen. "Mom, what's going on? Is everything okay?"

She nodded. "Yeah, it's just I feel guilty."

"Guilty, about what?"

"Well, it's just, it's your birthday, and I don't feel right leaving you all alone. Especially on a day like today."

"It's okay, mom."

Mom raises her brow. "It is?"

"Yeah, I mean, I already spent most of the morning with you, and it was a good morning, especially since you were here to share it with me. If that's not a great birthday, then I don't know what is."

"Really? So, you're okay with this?"

"Of course, go on your date, Mom. You deserve to spend a day with someone you like. Besides, Dad would love to see you happy."

Joana's eyes widen before rubbing the back of her neck. "Y-yes, he would."

Aunt Sue raised her brow in confusion as Joana headed out. "Alright, I should get going now. I'll see you later today, baby, okay?"

"Okay, mom! Bye!"

Aunt Sue watched with sad eyes as Mom took Isaac's hand in hers, leaving the house. "Dominic are you sure you're okay with your mother not spending her birthday with you?", she asked.

"Yeah, I'm fine! Now, the real party can begin! Woohoo!"

"This party? What are you talking about?"

"Amanda's planning a special party for my birthday today!"

Aunt Sue's eyes widened. "Sh-she is?"

"Yeah, she said it's a surprise."

Aunt Sue raises her brow. "How is it a surprise when she told you?"

"I don't really care if she tells me or not; I just want to know what she's got planned! Come on, let's go!"

"Let's go?"

"Yeah, I need you to drive me to her place. What do you expect me to do, walk?"

Aunt Sue rolled her eyes before taking both her keys from the kitchen table and into her hands. "Alright, let's go."

#

Griffin Manor stood proud and tall in the afternoon light. But as great as it was on the outside, things were getting festive in the house.

"Okay, people! That's it!", said Amanda, gazing all around all the people, placing a set of presents on the kitchen table. "That's it, set them right on the table, that's perfect!", Amanda gave the men a quick thumbs up before turning to the left, where there was a set of caterers holding a display of what looked to be chocolate-covered balls, much to Amanda's joy.

"Ooh! Can I have one of those?", she asks, coming towards the caterers, taking the chocolate ball from the silver tray and into her mouth, chewing slowly. "Mmm!", Amanda said with much delight. "So good! Keep it up!", she said with another raised thumb.

Within seconds, Amanda headed out of the kitchen and into the living room, where her butler, Barry, was standing atop a ladder, straightening a "Happy Birthday" flyer. "Make sure that flyer is as straight as possible, Barry!", Amanda shouts, causing Barry's head to turn back. "We need things perfect when Dominic arrives!"

"Do not worry, Ms. Griffin! I've never missed things up before, and I won't start now!"

"I know you won't, Barry!"

"By the way, how are those presents holding up! There should be thirty of them, right?"

"Thirty-*eight*! I want nothing but the best for my boyfriend, and that includes giving him all the presents he wants! No matter how many there are! Besides, none of these presents will ever compare once he sees my present. Speaking of which, where is it?"

"Where's what, madam?"

Amanda looks around herself. "My present. It's, there it is!", Amanda looked to the left, where there was a purple box sitting on a small coffee table. Within seconds, the box is in her hands, her smile big and wide. "There you are! I was starting to worry!"

Amanda investigated the box, which made her squeal. Her smile was big and bright as she closed the box. "Yep, just like I hoped. All I need now is a bow, and the only place I can find that is...", Amanda gazes up from the box and up the steps. "In Mom and Dad's room!"

Barry was nailing in the flyer when Amanda walked by. "I'm going to find a bow for my present, Barry!"

"Ah!", Barry said, hitting his thumb. "Make sure to get that flyer fixed before then, okay!"

Barry grunts, grasping his thumb. "O-kay!", he winces before speaking. "I hate this job."

#

"I didn't say anything!", Barry shouts aloud before going back to the flyer, hitting the nail in before hitting his thumb. "Shit!", Barry gasps, holding onto his mouth in shock.

A newspaper stood in the hands of Mr. Griffin, his eyes right on the headline written in bold: **Homicide kills baby! Father devastated!"**

Mr. Griffin sighs but not as much as he did with the name he found below:

Octavius Mitchell.

"I don't think I'm ready for this, Evelyn."

"Don't worry, Robert. Everything's going to be alright."

"How, Evelyn? I mean, how will he even take this?"

"We can't control that, Robert. All we can do is to try and explain."

Robert lowers his eyes in sadness, which Evelyn quickly notices. "Look, Robert, I know things aren't the best, but I want you to know that things will get better with time. For now, let's try and enjoy what's left of today, okay?"

With a deep sigh, Robert looks back to the newspaper, the headline present, before nodding. "You're right", he turned back to his wife, taking her hands in his. "You're right."

With these words, a loud knock was heard at the door, causing them to speak. "Yes!?"

"Mom, Dad, it's me! I need a bow for my present. Do you have one?"

With these words, Mr. and Mrs. Griffin turn their eyes back to the newspaper, Mrs. Griffin shoving it back in the box. "Come in, Amanda!"

With these words, Mr. and Mrs. Griffin's biracial daughter enters the room, her purple box in her arms. "Hey, mom, dad. I don't mean to bother you at such notice, bu-"

"What do you want?", Mrs. Griffin snaps, causing Amanda to stop. "I need a bow for my present."

"What kind of bow?"

"Red, a red bo-", Amanda was seconds from saying something else before finding a purple box, similar to hers sitting on the bed. "Hey, what's that?", she said, heading to the bed and placing her box on it. "It looks just like my prese-"

"No!", said Mr. Griffin, taking the purple box in his hands. "Um, you can't touch this!"

Amanda raised her brow. "Why? What's wrong with it?"

"Nothing, it's just, Evelyn, help me out."

"Files!", Evelyn shouts. "Yes, there are files of old politics your father picked up."

Amanda raised her brow. "Um, okay. Well, I still need a bow for my present."

"Of course, Robert gets the bow!"

"Yes, dear!", Robert said, turning his head back to the dresser, opening it wide, revealing various colorful bows.

But before he could reach and grab one, the door knocked, causing Robert and Evelyn to turn. "Who is it!?", Evelyn said with rage.

"Mrs. Griffin!", said Barry, his head peeking through. "What is it, Barry?", Amanda asks, much to Barry's happiness. "It's Dominic, Ms. Griffin! He's here!"

She gasps, hearing this. "Really? He's here!?"

"Yes, he just pulled up in the driveway! Come on, let's go!"

"Okay!", Amanda turned back to the bed where the two purple boxes were, only she took one of them. "I'll be taking that!", she then snatches the red bow from her father's grip. "Thanks, Dad! I'm coming, Dominic!"

Mr. and Mrs. Griffin watch as their daughter leaves the room, shutting the door behind her as she does. As soon as she does, Mr. and Mrs. Griffin both let out a sigh of relief. "That was a close one", answers Robert.

"Yeah. Come on, we should get down there."

"Right", Evelyn makes her way to the bed, taking the purple box in her hands. "In the meantime…", Evelyn takes the box to the dresser and places it in the colorful set of bows. "Let's try to keep thing under wraps."

With these words, Evelyn closes the dresser, leaving the box in utter darkness.

#

"Okay, open your eyes, Joana."

"Open them, are you sure?", Joana said with two hands cuffed over her eyelids. "Yeah, go on. In three, two, one."

With these words, Joana opens her eyes and, to her surprise, finds a giant Ferris wheel before her. But not just that, there were also rides, game sets, and all types of games in the center.

"Isaac, is this-"

"Yep, it's an amusement park!", he said with utmost excitement. "I thought it would be a good place for a first date. That is if you like it?"

Joana shakes her head. "No, no. I like it, Isaac. It's cute."

"Really? Oh, thank goodness. I was worried you wouldn't an-"

"Isaac!", Joana said, placing her arm on Isaac's shoulder. "I love it."

With these words of reassurance, Isaac's worried expression turns into a happy expression. "Good", Isaac holds his arm out before speaking. "Well then, if that's settled, let's see what's out here, shall we?"

Joana takes Isaac by the arm and smiles. "Gladly"

With that, the two look in the distance and head into the park.

#

"Everyone, ready positions!", Amanda said to everyone in the room, kneeling on the floor.

Aunt Sue's SUV stopped in front of Griffin Manor, and the engine shut off. As soon as Aunt Sue takes out the key, she turns back to her "nephew" sitting in the back and speaks. "Alright, little guy, are you ready to have the best birthday of your life!?"

"I sure am, Aunt Sue!"

"Alright, then, let's get in there! Unless you want me to stay here."

"What? Aunt Sue, this is my birthday; if I'm going to celebrate it, I'd want it to be with the people I love."

Aunt Sue's eyes lowered in sadness. "Too bad your mother can't be here with you."

I rub the back of my neck. "Yeah, I'm kind of bummed about it too, but I think it's nice that Mom's finally meeting new people, especially since dad", I laugh to myself. "Now that I think about it, if he were here right now, he'd probably be going all out today."

Aunt Sue smiles. "I'm sure he would."

I wipe a tear from my eye before speaking. "Alright, that's enough sadness. Come on, we should get in there."

"Right, come on."

With that, Aunt Sue unlocked the door, and both of us hopped out of the car, our eyes gazing up at Griffin Manor. Before we knew it, we were up the steps and in front of the mansion door. Excited, I turned to Aunt Sue and spoke. "You ready?"

She nodded. "Are you?"

I nod back. "Sure am!"

"Then let's do this."

With these words, I bring my hand to the door and twist the doorknob. Before I knew it, the door opened wide. At first, it was plain dark, increasing my confusion. "Um, hello?"

Saying this, the lights flipped on, and a whole village of people came shouting: "SURPPPPRRRRRIIISSSSSEEEEE!!!"

My whole face lit up as a whole parade of people cheered and applauded me with exuberance. "For me!?", I said, my hand placed on my heart. "Aw, guys, I had no idea!", I said sarcastically.

"It's great, isn't it?", said a voice, causing me to turn my head back to my red-headed girlfriend, her smile big and bright as she eagerly greeted me. "Amanda, hey, babe!"

"Hey, you!", Amanda pulls me in for a quick peck on the lips. "Happy birthday. How old are you now, twelve or eleven?"

I laughed, giving Amanda a quick nudge on the shoulder. "I'm eighteen, Amanda."

Amanda snapped her fingers. "Eighteen, right", She looked up from me and to the young woman smiling down at her. "Oh, who's this?"

I turn my eyes back. "Oh, this is-"

"Sue Anne", Aunt Sue speaks, reaching her hand out. "I met you at that dinner party, if you recall?"

Amanda blinked, taking Aunt Sue's hand. "Oh, you're the lady who offered me that dessert, pumpkin pie, was it?"

Aunt Sue nods. "Mm-hm."

"Oh, well, it's nice to meet you again."

"You, too."

Amanda finally let go of Aunt Sue's hand. "Well, with that settled, let's get this party started! Yeah!", I said, causing Amanda and I to cheer before pulling us off into the crowd.

Throughout that evening, Amanda, Aunt Sue, and I spent the hour partying, eating all kinds of finger food from the caterers. Amanda and I fed each other crab puffs, along with those chocolate balls, many of them with various flavors: strawberry, peach, and cherries.

Aunt Sue spat the cherry one out in disgust, throwing it straight into the trash can.

As for mom, she was enjoying a thick wrap of cotton candy with Isaac, but not before eating corndogs. Some of the ketchup fell on the side of Joana's mouth, which Isaac quickly took notice of. Within seconds, Isaac grabs a napkin and brings it to Joana's face.

But before he could wipe it off, Joana took the napkin from his hands and into hers, wiping the ketchup from her face, much to Isaac's confusion.

Soon after, I was outside, my eyes blindfolded as I swung a bat back and forth at a great, big donkey pinata with thousands cheering me on, including Mr. and Mrs. Griffin, who managed to enter the festivities. It isn't long before I make a big swing at the pinata, and a big load of candy guts fall out of the donkey.

The crowd cheers me on, with a few men lifting me up as they did. It was fun, but I wasn't the only one.

As for mom, she and Isaac were on a Ferris Wheel, with many couples holding each other as they descended. Isaac, feeling bold, noticed the couple and tried to do the same with Joana, but before he could even touch Joana, she took his arm and brought it back down from her grasp. Isaac, confused, wanted to say something but just turned away, feeling embarrassed.

#

After a glorious day of fun, Aunt Sue, Amanda, and I were in the living room, where what looked to be hundreds of blue, purple, yellow, and green wrappers and ribbons were scattered across the hardwood floor.

For about an hour. I was unwrapping all my thirty-eight birthday presents, and I was exhausted but none from what was inside the presents, which were mostly a few new clothes, water guns, and He-Man action figures. "Man, those were a lot of birthday presents. I swear I couldn't keep count."

Amanda laughs. "Well, they were thirty-eight of them?"

"Thirty-eight?! Jesus!"

"Yeah, yeah. I know it was a lot, but I wanted to make sure you had everything you wanted, since it's such a special day."

I smile, giving Amanda a small kiss on the cheek. "And I loved every single one."

Amanda smiles, peering down at the purple box sitting under the table. "Well, then, you're going to love the present I have for you", Amanda winked at one of the caterers, who quickly made their way out of the living room and into the kitchen.

"What do you mean?"

Amanda smiles. "Turn around."

With these words, I turn my head back to find two women holding a tray of a triple-stacked chocolate fudge cake with a set of sparklers on the top of 18. Within seconds, my eyes lit up in happiness as the people started to sing. "Happy birthday to yo-"

"Um, no! No, guys, it's okay. I already heard that song today; I don't need to hear it again."

The caterers both turn to each other, their shoulders shrugging before making their way towards the table and placing it down on the table before me, the sparklers still going off. "Okay, make a wish, Dominic."

I close my eyes, leaning into the sparklers before stopping. "Wait, where's Aunt Sue?"

"Aunt Sue, oh, she's still in the bathroom?"

"She is?", I laugh. "Those crab puffs must've really gotten to her. Well, I'll just wait for her."

"Wait, are you sure, Dom?"

"Yeah, I don't want to do this without her."

Amanda nods. "Okay", she then looks around. "Speaking of which, where's Dad?"

"You're father's upstairs, Amanda. He forgot to take one of his pills", said Evelyn, raising her brow. 'Speaking of which, he's been up there for a minute now. I should go check on him. Don't go anywhere, Amanda", Amanda's mom said, heading upstairs, her red pumps clinking with each other.

"Okay, mom. Hurry back!", Amanda then peers down at the purple box sitting under the coffee table. Seeing this, she turns back to Dominic and speaks. "Well, while you wait. Do you want to open your last present?"

I turned back to her. "My what?"

Amanda didn't speak, instead, she reached for the box from under the table and held it out to me. "Wha-what is this, Amanda?"

"Oh, just something put together."

"Really? What's inside?"

Amanda hands the box to me with a smile. "See for yourself."

With these words, I took the purple box in my hands, my curiosity heightened.

#

Joana and Isaac walked on the dock, the evening sun hitting their faces as they walked. "It's a nice sunset", said Isaac, bringing out a quick nod from Joana. "Yeah, it is."

"Almost as lovely as you"

Joana turned her eyes back to Isaac, who quickly tried to lean in for a kiss. Joana, as expected, pulls away. "Isaac, no."

Isaac raises a brow. "No?", he scoffs. "No, what?"

"You know what."

"No, I don't. Why can't I kiss you?"

Joana shifts her eyes away from Isaac, hugging herself as she looks out at the sunset over the diamond-encrusted sea horizon. "Why can't I, Joana?", Isaac said from behind. "Why can't I wipe spilled ketchup from your face? Why can't I wrap my arms around you when we're going down the Ferris Wheel? Why, why can't I do that? What am I doing wrong?!"

"Nothing!", Joana snaps, her eyes now turned back to him. "Nothing is wrong with you, Isaac! It's me, I'm what's wrong!?"

Isaac raises his brow. "What do you mean?"

Joana sighs, turning back to the docks. "Joana, what's wrong?"

Joana proceeds to look out at the docks, her hazel brown eyes peering down at the sea before speaking. "I haven't told you about my husband, have I?"

Isaac shook his head. "No"

"My husband, he...left."

"Left?", Isaac blinked. "Like abandoned you?"

"Something like that", she turned her eyes back to Isaac. "He, uh, he left me, me and my son. He left and never came back. I guess being with you, I just fear you...that you might..."

"Hey!", Isaac said, coming towards Joana. "I wouldn't do that to you. I would never leave you."

Joana, with tears in her eyes, shifts her eyes away from Isaac. "I'm sorry."

"Don't be sorry, it's alright."

With these words, Joana looks into Isaac's eyes and, without hesitation, leans in and kisses him. Isaac takes Joana by the waist, returning the favor. The two spend the next few minutes like this before pulling away. "Woah", said Isaac. "I feel light as a feather."

Joana giggles before nodding. "Me too."

Isaac jerks his head a bit, his narrowing. "Well, should we go then?"

Joana nods. "Yeah, I think I'd like that."

With these words, Isaac and Joana walks down the docks, their hands now touching as they head home.

\#

Meanwhile, Evelyn made her way up the steps and to her bedroom door. As soon as she did, Mrs. Griffin took a deep breath and knocked on the door. "Robert, it's me. Are you in here?"

There was no answer, making Evelyn worried.

She knocks again. "Robert, are you okay?"

Without a second thought, Evelyn twists the doorknob and opens the door, entering her bedroom. "Robert."

Evelyn looks left and right of her room when she finds her husband standing before the dresser, his head hanging low. Nervous, Evelyn opens her mouth and speaks. "R-Robert?", she said shakily. "Are you okay?"

Robert, without hesitation, turns his eyes back to Evelyn, his eyes full of fear, before holding the purple box in his hands. "What are you doing with the box?", she asks.

Robert shook his head and pulled out what looked to be a picture frame of their daughter and his curly-haired boyfriend kissing him on the cheek with brightly colored flowers on the sides.

Evelyn's eyes widen in shock at the sight of the picture. "That's not our box?"

"But if that's Amanda's present, then where's-", Evelyn gasps, her eyes whipping to the steps below. "Oh my god!"

Without a second thought, Mr. and Mrs. Griffin ran out of the room and down the steps, the box in her hands.

\#

"Amanda!", shouted Evelyn as she went downstairs. "Amanda!"

Evelyn and Robert soon made their way to the last step, their heads turning as they turned a corner, entering the living room. "Amanda, where's Domin-", Evelyn's words are quickly cut off as Amanda sits on the couch, her eyes full of fear as she gazes up at her parents.

Seeing this, Mr. and Mrs. Griffin looked down at the curly-haired boy sitting on the couch, his head low.

He was quiet, and so was everyone else. The only way to cut it out was to speak up.

"Dominic?", she said, walking slowly towards him. "Are you alright?"

Hearing this, I raise my eyes from the newspaper and look at them. "Is this him?", I hold the newspaper out to them.

"What do you mean?", said Mrs. Griffin.

"This man, the one with the beard. Is this him?", I said, pointing to the young man in the photo.

Mr. and Mrs. Griffin turn to each other, their eyes brooding with fear, much to my confusion. "Yes, it's him. That's the man that killed my wife."

Saying this, my head lowers back to the newspaper, much to Mr. and Mrs. Griffin's confusion. "Dominic?", said Mr. Griffin. "Are you alright?"

Hearing this, Dominic raises his eyes to them and speaks. "Then why does he have my last name?"

Their eyes widen hearing this, making my eyes glow bright green. "You're both hiding something from me, aren't you?"

Mr. and Mrs. Griffin both face each other before looking at me. "Dominic, there's something you should know."

The front door of Griffin Manor opens wide, with Dominic heading out. "You're lying! You're both lying!"

"Dominic, wait!", said Amanda, running out the door, but before she could catch up with him, her parents grabbed her by the shoulder. "No, Amanda!", said Mrs. Griffin, gazing down at her. "Let him go!"

"But I can't just let Dominic go! What if he gets hurt!"

"Leave that to me!", said Aunt Sue, heading out to her car, the engine turning right on as she headed down the road, leaving the Griffins behind.

As soon as she does, Amanda breaks down and cries.

#

Isaac opened the door for Joana, happily serving her. "Here you go, m'lady."

Joana grins. "Such a gentleman."

Isaac and Joana both giggle as they enter the house, but as soon as the door is closed, Joana spots a shadowy figure sitting on the couch. "Who is that?", said Isaac in shock.

"I don't know, Dominic?"

The shadow figure raises his head before speaking. "Hi, mom."

Mom lets out a sigh of relief before speaking. "Oh, thank goodness. Dominic, what are you sitting in the dark for?"

"You tell me. You seem to keep a lot in the dark these days? Unless that's what they say?"

Mom raises her brow. "They?", she said as I rose from my chair, walking towards Mom. "Dominic, what's going on?"

I finally made it up to mom, my eyes looking right at her. "Does Octavius Mitchell sound familiar to you?"

She blinked. "O-Octavius?"

"Not enough information, eh? Well how about now?", I said, holding the newspaper out to her, the headline visible. "Look familiar now!?"

My eyes widened in shock before taking the newspaper in her hands. "Dominic, where did you get this?"

"Oh, just from a little place I like to call the Griffins!"

"The Griffins!?"

"They told me, mom. They told me about how you lied to me. Is that true?"

Mom blinked, her mouth becoming dry. "Answer me, Mom! Is my father alive or not!"

Mom looks at me with horror in her eyes before slowly nodding. "It's true. Your father is alive."

My eyes widened in shock, much to my mom's disappointment. "Dominic, please understand. I was only doing it to protect you. I couldn't let you know."

"Know what, the truth? The truth that I'm the son of a murderer and that my father is a cold, sadistic man!?"

"Murderer?", said Isaac. "You told me your husband died in a car crash?"

"So did I! Apparently, my mom's not as honest as I thought!"

"What else could I have done? I find out my husband ends up murdering someone he had an affair with, and I'm just supposed to be okay with that!? You're my son, Dominic; I wasn't just going to let you live with that!"

"But you can live with this: lying, keeping secrets from me. You know, I always knew you had issues, but now I see what you really are: a coward!"

Joana's eyes widen in shock, hearing this, but not before hearing the woman enter the steps. "Dominic!"

Dominic turned his head back to find Aunt Sue standing at the door. But Joana didn't realize her, all she could hear was the one word beaming through her head. "I am not a coward, Dominic! You know I was trying to do the best I could for you! I may be a liar, but I'm *not*. I'm a mother, *your* mother!"

My eyes drop to the floor in sadness, that is, until all the past thoughts come to the surface of my mind. "Are you?"

Mom blinked. "What?"

"What mother makes her son pay for her own eviction notice, hm? What mother makes up these stories about her son's father being this angel from heaven, and what mother chooses to go on a date on her son's birthday!"

"What?! You said it was okay for me to do that!"

"Yeah, but you know, deep down, I wished I never said it because this is the worst birthday I have ever had!"

"You think you have bad days! Do you have any idea how hard it was when I heard what happened to your father? The pain I went through! Believe me, Dominic, *I* have had worse days!"

"That's no excuse for how you've behaved these past eighteen years!"

"Well, excuse me for not being a great mother!"

"You definitely could've been a better one!"

"YOU SHUT YOUR GOD DAMN MOUTH!"

"Joana!", shouts Aunt Sue as I fall straight to the floor, my hand on my face.

Mom watches in shock before peering down at her hands, realizing what she's done. "Joana!", said Aunt Sue, snapping Joana back to reality as she held me. "What the hell did you do that for!?"

Mom blinked, her lips quivering. "Sue, Dominic, I'm sorry. I didn't mean to-ah!", Joana said as she felt this unbearable pain in her forehead.

"Joana?", said Isaac as Joana's eyes began to roll in the back of her head.

"Mom!"

With these words, Mom collapsed to the floor, her arms and legs spread out as the world went dark.

#

I looked up at the heart meter, the beeping sound going on and off as mother lay in the bed, her eyes closed shut.

Aunt Sue sat next to me, comforting me as she slept. As for Isaac, he stayed in the room for a few seconds before leaving to get coffee. But that was two hours ago.

He never came back with that coffee.

That jerk.

That quitter.

That *coward.*

I sigh, gripping my mother's hands tight.

They were cold to the touch, almost as if she was...

No, not yet.

Her lungs were still flowing, and her heart was still beating. Besides, she was too strong of a woman to let whatever knocked her out cause her to sleep so long.

Too strong of a black woman.

Within minutes, a man in a white coat and brown clipboard enters the room, causing me and Aunt Sue's head to rise. "Doctor Benjamin?", said Aunt Sue.

"Hi, you must be a friend of Mrs. Mitchell?"

Aunt Sue nods. "Yes, she passed out in her home. She's been sleeping like this all night."

"Yes, I know about that. The results came in."

"What is it? What's wrong with her?"

Dr. Ben looked at the curly-haired boy sitting before the mother and spoke. "Are you her son?"

I nod. "Yes."

He gives me a frightened look. "Um, I don't think you want to hear this."

I shake my head. "No, I can handle it. I've heard scarier things today; whatever it is, I can take this too."

He nods. "We found a lump in your mother's right breast, and it's malignant."

I raise my brow. "Malignant?"

"It means it spread. Your mother has breast cancer, son."

My eyes widened in shock upon hearing this. "No!", Aunt Sue said. "No!"

Without a second thought, I ran out of the hospital room, with Aunt Sue, calling out my name. But I didn't hear her; all I could hear was the sound of my own heartbeat.

At that moment, there was only one place to go, and that was where it all started.

\#

Amanda walked on her hardwood floor, biting her nails as she paced the floor. Mr. and Mrs. Griffin stood before the chimney; the fire roaring as they sat in chairs. "Amanda, please stop biting your nails like that. It's not lady-like."

"I'm worried, mother."

"Well, find some other way to stop because biting your nails isn't one of them."

She scoffs. "You're filing your nails!"

"As a stress-reliever, if you'd realize I am very stressed out."

"Oh, you're stressed out. My boyfriend literally stormed out of this house after learning the worst secrets of his life, and you guys are sitting here like it's nothing! Like you don't care!"

"We do care, Amanda."

"Oh, do you? You sit here and keep a secret that you knew like it never happened."

"We were going to tell him sooner, Amanda, but we just couldn't find the time. That is, until today."

"Maybe if you had been paying better attention to the boxes, we could've done it privately, little miss nosey."

"The boxes looked similar; I didn't know."

"It's not your fault, Amanda. We are the ones who should've kept better care of the boxes."

Evelyn scoffs, her eyes rolling as she filed her nails.

Amanda sighs, her fingers combed through her hair before speaking. "How long did you guys know about this?"

"Not too long before we looked in the newspaper. We saw Dominic's last name in the paper. That's when we put the pieces together, and well, here we are."

Amanda shakes her head. "I just hope he's alright. Hearing a secret like that must be bad."

"Don't worry, dear. Whatever happens, we'll be right there to help him, okay?"

Amanda sighs before nodding. "Okay. I just hope there aren't any more secrets you need to keep from me."

Robert glanced up at Evelyn, who was shaking her head. "No", he said. "Not at all."

Amanda, not really convinced, nods anyway. "Okay."

With these words, the front door of Griffin Manor opens wide, revealing a silhouette figure standing in the doorway. "Amanda!", the figure called out,

"Dominic!"

Amanda rushes towards her curly-haired boyfriend, hugging him tightly. "Oh, thank goodness you're okay, Dominic! I was so worried about you!", she pulls back. "Why are you all wet?"

"I ran all the way here in the rain."

"By yourself? Why?"

Hearing this, I break out in tears and fell onto the floor, with Amanda kneeling before me. "Dominic, what is it?"

"It's my mother", I sob, peering up to her. "She has cancer."

Amanda's eyes widened in shock before pulling me in for a loving hug. As for Mr. and Mrs. Griffin, they watched with utter shock.

At that very moment, all they could do was stand there and pray for me.

My mother and me.

Part III

Chapter 14: The Artist and the Singer

I sat in a wooden chair, about ten centimeters from the dining table that stood before me. Not to mention my half glass of margarita sitting on the polished, wooden surface of the table. I quickly took a sip, my eyes looking at the jazz band playing on the stage, gladly entertaining those who came.

I watched as several people danced around the room, without a care in the world. In jazz clubs, no one cared who you were. Here, everyone just kept to themselves, making it the perfect place to come to. Especially, for someone like me.

I took one long sip of my margarita and leaned back in my chair, my eyes closed shut as I listened to the sweet silence of jazz music.

But before I could move from my seat, another margarita glass was placed on the table. Much to my confusion, I gazed up at the mustache waiter standing over me. "You're margarita, ma'am"

I blink, my eyes narrowing with confusion. "I'm sorry. I think you're mistaken, sir. I didn't order another margarita."

"It was from the gentleman."

"Gentleman?", the waiter points to the left, my eyes following in his direction.

Far in the distance, a young, chiseled-faced man sits at the bar, his smile warm and welcoming as he waves back at me. Confused, I slowly raised my hand, waving back solemnly before glancing back at my margarita glass, pointing right at it.

He nods, smirking visibly.

"I will leave you two alone now. Enjoy your drink."

With that, the waiter turned his head and walked away from the dinner table. I was alone again or so I thought, once I noticed the mysterious young man walking towards me. I look away, pulling my hat over my eyes.

Unfortunately, that didn't stop him from pulling up a seat and speaking to me. "Hi, there", he said, standing before me, my hat still shielding my eyes. "Why are you hiding your face?"

"No reason at all", I say, shaking my head. "Why did you buy me a margarita?"

"I can't buy a cute girl a drink?"

I scoff. "Yeah, like I haven't heard that before? You're going to have to do better than that."

He smirks at me. "Okay", he pulls out a seat, much to my confusion. "What are you doing?"

He smiled, sitting across the table. "I'm sitting with you."

"More like invading my privacy."

He chuckled. "What privacy? We're in a nightclub."

"You know what I mean! Who are you, anyway?"

"That's just what I was about to ask you."

I scoff. "Oh, really?"

"Yes."

With these words, I sit back in my seat, looking straight at the handsome young man and smirk. "I'm guessing you're one of those guys who "just don't know when to quit", are you?"

He nods with a smile. "No, I don't."

I smile before bringing my hand across the table, his eyes meeting mine. "Joana Smith."

Without hesitation, the man takes my hand and shakes it firmly. "Octavius", he smiled. "Octavius Mitchell."

#

The image dies out, forming a submissive, white void.

Soon, the white void fades, entering us into a faint beeping noise. That beeping noise was heard from the heart meter sitting above.

"Joana", said a familiar voice, causing two hazel-brown eyes to slowly crack open. "Joana, wake up."

Now more awake, I looked to find her friend, Sue Anne. With all my strength, she muttered. "Sue?"

Sue smiles, tears through her eyes. "Hey, girl. How ya' feelin'?"

I bring my hands up to my head. "Ugh, I'm a little dizzy. Where am I?"

"In the hospital. You fainted, remember?"

I blink, my eyes narrowing in confusion before nodding. "Yes, I was at the house. I just came home from the date with-", I gasp, looking at Sue. "Isaac! Where's Isaac!"

"Isaac left."

"Where?"

Sue lowers her head in sadness. "He's gone, Joana. He never came back."

Hearing this, my eyes lower in sadness. "He said he would never leave me. I guess I was wrong."

Sue brought her hands to mine, gripping my hands tight. "Joana, there's something you should know. It's about your illness."

I raise my head in confusion. "What did you say? Illness?"

"Yes, Joana, you're sick."

"Sick? What do you mean?"

"The doctor, Joana, he found this lump inside one of your breasts and...", Sue grips the sheets of the bed, the tears in her eyes. "You have cancer, Joana."

My eyes widen in shock. "What?"

"I know it's hard to take in."

"There's nothing to take in because I don't have cancer!"

"Yes, you do, Joana."

"I felt a little dizzy, so what? I'm still alive."

"Yes, but what you don't understand is-"

"I'm fine, Sue! I'm fine and completely healthy!"

"No, you're not!", Sue snaps. "The tumor they found in you is malignant. It's spreading through your body as we speak. You're not fine, you're dying!"

My eyes widen in shock, much to Sue's concern. "Joana, I'm sorry, I didn't mean-"

"No", I sniff. "Don't be sorry. I know about the bump."

Sue raises her brow. "You do?"

"I noticed it on Dominic's birthday. The day I went on that date with Isaac. I looked in the mirror, and that's where I found it, just sitting there. At first, I thought it was just some kind of cyst, but now I know what it really is."

"What?"

"Karma. This cancer's my karma, Sue."

"Joana, what are you talking about?"

"Think about it, Sue. I spent the past eighteen years of my life, lying to my son about a man who he thought was six feet under. Not only that, I pretended like he never even existed when he did."

"Joana don't beat yourself up for that. You were just doing what any sane mother would do to protect her kid."

"Yeah, bu-wait. Where is he?"

"Where's who?"

"Dominic? Where's Dominic?"

Sue shifts her eyes away from me. "I don't know."

"What do you mean, you don't know? Where is he?"

"With our daughter."

Shocked, Joana turned her head back to find a young white man and his wife standing before the door. My eyes widen in shock seeing this. "Mr. Griffin?"

"Hello, Mrs. Mitchell", he said happily. "It's been a long time."

\#

It was a good half hour the moment Dominic called, and he hadn't called since. I lay in my bed, my body turned to the open window before me. It was morning, and the sun peeked into my room, through the virgin white curtains.

It was a beautiful sight, gladly reminding me of another moment in my life.

\#

"Are we there yet?", I say, walking beside Octavius.

"Almost, just wait a few more minutes."

"I can't wait that long."

"Yes, you can."

Taking a few more steps, Octavius and my feet stopped dead at a large apartment complex. "Here we are."

I look at the set of steps before me before facing him. "This is where you live?"

"Yep. What, did you think I lived in a hut?"

"No, maybe a hut."

He chuckles before taking my hand. "Come on"

With that, I was walking the steps of what was Octavius's home, stopping dead at the door.

Otto faces me, his smile warm, and his eyes intensified. "Get ready."

I roll my eyes. "Just open the door."

With a quick shrug, Octavius twisted the lock and opened the door.

It was dark, dark and cold. Two things I don't enjoy. "Where's the lights?", I say, facing the silhouette figure standing beside me. "Otto?"

Saying this, the dark room became bright, where, to my surprise, a mannequin stood beside me. "What the hell?", I said confused. "Otto?"

"Right in front of you."

I turn my eyes to the front of the room, where I find Octavius standing before me behind several, about five virgin white sheets.

I raise my brows, quite confused. "Otto, what is all this?"

He glances back at the canvases before eyeing back to me. "This is my gallery, my art gallery."

"Art? You're an artist?"

He nods. "Yes."

"Wait, is that why you brought me here? To see some paintings?"

"Not just some paintings", Octavius walks towards the first picture and yanks the sheets from it, revealing a painting of a young woman in a red dress and black hat sipping mindlessly on a margarita.

My eyes widened when I saw this, full of shock. "Oh my god. Is that—"

"You?", he speaks, nodding. "Yeah."

I blink, my stomach queasy. "Where the hell did you get this?"

"Jo-Jo, it's okay."

"Have you been following me?"

"I haven't."

"I'm getting the hell out of here, now!"

"Jo-Jo, wait!"

I ran my way towards the door, my hand twisting the door wide open. But before I could leap out, the door shuts right before my eyes.

"What the—", I said, noticing the green hue surrounding the door. "What the hell?"

"I know this may come as a shock to you", I heard Octavius say, before facing him, with his eyes glowing bright green and with his hands raised. "But I can't let you leave."

I blink, noticing Octavius's eyes lit up with green. "Are you magic or something?"

He says his head a bit, his eyes still glowing bright green. "You could say that?"

#

A white door stood before the curly-haired boy standing before it, his eyes wide with fear. Feeling defeated, Dominic lowered his head and sighed. "Everything okay, Dominic?", Amanda asked

"No. I'm scared."

"About what?"

"My Mom. The last time I saw her, we were fighting. I called her a bad mom. How can she look at me when I said that."

"Dominic, that doesn't matter anymore. I'm sure your mother forgives you. Besides, she has—"

"Don't say it!", he snapped. "Please, I've already had enough surprises for one day."

"That's not the only surprise."

He turned to his girlfriend. "What do you mean?"

Amanda sighed. "Dominic, there's something my parents didn't tell you about your father."

"My fa…what are you talking about?"

"This is his last year, his year of prison. In a few months, he'll be released."

"Released?", Dominic said, shocked.

#

"I know this may come as a shock to you."

"A shock? This is more than a shock! This is fear! How many months until he's released?"

Amanda gave him a long, hard look before speaking. "Five."

"F-five?"

"Yes."

He gasped, my hands going through my curly brown hair as my back hit the wall. "Oh, man. What am I going to do?"

"Don't worry, Dominic."

"Don't worry, my father's getting released in five months! How can I not be worried scared if anything!"

"I know you're scared, but trust me, things are going to be alright. Mother and Father have a plan."

"Does it involve sending him back to prison?"

"No, but it involves you not getting hurt. But that's not important right now. Now, you've got bigger things to worry about", she said, pointing to the door. "But first, I need you to calm down."

With these words, he shut his eyes. "Okay."

"Put the past aside and go meet your mom."

I smiled happily at this blissful memory as I lay in bed. My eyes were closed shut as I reminisced. But that's when I heard footsteps enter my room. "Mom?"

My eyes opened wide in shock, causing my head to turn back. To my surprise, I found *him* standing before the door.

There he was.

My son, my beautiful, curly-haired son. The son I gave life to, the son I loved, and the son. I lied to.

I lied to my son, for eighteen years. I did that.

I did that, and he still came here. He came for his mother, his sick, twisted mother.

How could a son like him love a mother as evil as me? I shut both my eyes, not to reminisce but to break down in tears. "I'm sorry", I say, sobbing. "I'm sorry, Dominic."

Without a second thought, Dominic ran straight to me, the flowers falling straight to the floor as my son held me in his arms. "It's okay, Mom. It's okay."

Dominic shushed me as I sobbed. Yet, little did I know, Dominic's girlfriend, Amanda Griffin, stood before the door, her eyes on me.

But not as much as her parents standing over her.

I smiled happily before she left.

#

About an hour later, the doctor came in and told me about the lump in my breast. He told me that I would start chemotherapy a few days in the week. Until then, I would just go home and rest.

Sue Anne drove us home, the moment I was discharged. Amanda offered to take us, but Dominic called it off, saying he just wanted to go alone. He held my hand the entire ride home. As soon as we entered the house, I went straight up the stairs and into the bedroom.

Dominic was right beside me the moment I made it to my bed. He pulled the covers up to my body, his eyes full of tears as I laid my head against the pillow. As soon as I do, he kneels beside me and speaks. "Are you comfortable, Mom?"

I nod. "Yes."

I take Dominic's hand, gripping it tight. "I'm alright, baby. What about you? Are you okay?"

He scoffs. "Me? I'm okay."

I raise my brow in concern. "Are you sure?"

Dominic lowers his head in sadness before slowly shaking it. "That's what I thought", I say, much to Dominic's sadness. "It's just that you're sick, and I'm worried that you, that you might…"

"Baby", I say, bringing my hand to his face. "You're not going to lose me. I swear that's not going to happen."

"How do you know?"

"I'm going to get chemotherapy soon. Once I do, the cancer will be dead, I swear."

He sniffed one final time. "I just don't want anyone else to go. I mean, I already lost father."

Hearing this, I pulled Dominic into a warm, loving hug. The two of us spent the next few moments holding each other until they were asleep, snuggled up against each other.

Soon, I was dreaming, dreaming of him. Him and me, him and that wonderful night. Only, this time, it was the day.

#

I sat in a chair, my eyes big and my mouth gaped with shock as several canvases flew above me, one of them being the painting of me in the red sun dress.

"This isn't real."

"Oh, it's real, all right", Otto said with a smile. "And so are these paintings."

"So, these paintings, you have visions?"

"Yes. Of you and of them?", he said about the young man smoking a pipe, the old woman sipping coffee, a black cat standing over a ladder, and a great, big oak tree standing in the sunlight. "Every painting I've made was all conjured from dreams, though many of them aren't when I'm awake."

"And these visions, when do they happen?"

He shrugs. "There's not much of a when than a just. My visions come and go like the wind, but when they do, I must paint them out. Like, I must just get it out of me before it, you know, fades away."

"Did that include me?"

"But I thought you said you didn't know me?"

Octavius faces Joana, his eyes sad and low. "I didn't. I just saw you in my dreams."

I raised my brow. "That's a bit creepy."

He shrugs. *"In a way. But it's not my fault. My visions, they just come to me. I can't control it, but that's what makes it fun."*

Joana shakes her head in disbelief. *"I think I need to sit down."*

#

The sun peeked through the virgin white curtains. Below, was me lying in bed, my bare skin sowing as I lay on the pillow. Everything around me was quiet, as I slept. That was until a large shadow approached me. "Jo-Jo", *said a voice, causing me to grunt.* "Jo-Jo, wake up."

Shifting my body, my eyes slowly peek open. In doing so, I find Octavius kneeling before me, his smile warm and welcoming. "Wakey, wakey."

I raised my brow, confused. "Octavius?"

"Hey there."

I said, rising from the sofa, bringing my head to my forehead as I looked around the room. "Where am I?"

"In the studio. You slept the night, remember?"

I shake my head. "No, I don't remember. Now that I think about it, I don't remember anything from last night."

"Probably was that tequila."

"Tequila? You mean those shots we took together?"

Octavius nods. "Woah, that must've been some huge shots."

"They were we drank nine of them! Well, you did, I only drank like three", *Octavius joked.*

Still, in my pink dance cress, I grabbed my purse and rise from the sofa, much to Octavius's confusion. "Joana, where are you going?"

"School."

"School?"

"Yes, you know that place where you go to learn?"

"But wait, what about your painting?"

"I'll come back for it tomorrow, okay?"

"Not that painting, the other painting."

I stopped dead in the distance, causing myself to turn back to Octavius, who was, in fact, standing beside another one of his hidden canvases, one that confused Joana greatly. "Octavius, what is that?"

"Do you sing?", he asks.

"What?"

"Do you sing?", the portrait lowers from Octavius's eyes, revealing a young, black woman standing on a stage in a sparkly white dress and a crowd cheering her on.

"Who the hell is that?"

"Who do you think? It's you."

I laugh. "No, it's not."

He nods. "Yes, it is."

"No, it's not, Otto."

"Yes, it is! I saw it in my vision, Joana. It's you."

"Look, I already paid you money for one portrait, but I'm not going to pay for another one, okay"

Octavius stood there, eyeing me and walking to the door before folding both his arms and nodding. "I see what this is; you've got stage fright, don't you?"

"What?", I say, turning my head back. "Yeah, that's it. You've got stage fright, and you don't want to admit it

"Uh, it is."

"It's the future, your future, and whatever it is, it's in singing."

"No, it's not!", I snap. "My singing career died a long time ago. The moment I was on that stage, I froze. There is no way I'm going through that again!"

"Okay, so you froze one time."

"Not one time, several times! I froze constantly!"

"Well, you're not freezing here, now, are you?"

Joana turns her eyes back to Octavius and to the portrait, causing Joana to turn her eyes back and sigh. "I know this may sound strange, Joana, but I think I know now why you and I met. I think you and I are supposed to help each other.

My back was still turned as Octavius spoke. "Look, you're afraid to sing on stage, and I'm too scared of failure. Together, I think we can make something out of this. That is, if you're willing to try?"

I stand back before sighing. "My whole life, I've dreamt of being on stage singing, but I don't even know if I can do it."

"That's why you've got me", he said, bringing his hand out to me. "I'll help you with your stage fright and you with my paintings. What do you say?"

I turned my head back, a small grin forming on my face, before reaching my hand out to him. "I say let's do it."

Octavius smiles. "Well, then, it looks like we are in an agreement."

I nod. "We sure are. Now, can I please go now? My college roommate is probably worried sick about me."

#

"Mom, mom!", called a voice, causing both my eyes to shoot open. To my surprise, I find my son, Dominic, staring down at me. "Mom, are you okay?"

I blinked, looking at him. "Wha-what? What do you mean?"

"You were talking in your sleep. You were saying things."

I raise my brow in confusion. "What was I saying?"

Dominic was seconds from answering before a knock was heard at the door, causing our heads to turn back. "Come in."

With these words, the doorknob opens wide, causing Sue Anne's head to pop in. "Oh, there you are, Dominic. I was looking for you."

"You were?"

"Yeah, I just wanted you to help get your mom's plate from downstairs."

He blinks, thinking to himself. "Um, yeah. Sure", Dominic turns back to me. "We'll talk later, Mom."

With that, Dominic left the room, passing Sue Anne, who quickly turned back to me, her best friend sitting patiently on the bed. With these words, I turn to her and smile. "Hi, Sue."

"Hey, Jo-Jo."

I laugh. "You haven't called me that since college."

"Yeah, well, I just thought it was necessary for this moment", Sue Anne sits next to me, her legs tangled up to her. "So, how have you been?"

"I've been better."

"Good. I'm glad to see you at your best."

"What about you? How've you been since all this?"

Sue sighed. "I've been worried and scared for you", she takes her hand in mine, gripping it tight.

"I know, Sue."

She wipes her eyes a bit. "It's just that we've been friends for a long time. Seeing you like this makes me scared."

"This isn't the last time you've feared me. Remember that time you thought I went missing?"

Sue blinks before speaking. "Oh, yeah. I do."

Sue's white curls quickly turn to a blonde girl, her eyes bright with youth but none of courage.

"Oh my gosh, oh my gosh!", said Sue, looking through her dorm. "Where's Jo-Jo? Her bed is still straight. It's been straight since last night! Where is she?"

Sue, scared, looked across her room before turning back to a red telephone sitting on her bed. "The phone, of course!", Sue said, running toward the phone and dialing numbers. "I just need to call the police."

Sue raised the phone to her ear, waiting for someone to pick her up. She taps her fingers on the bed, waiting patiently until suddenly, static peaks through. "Police department?"

"Hello, is this the police!?"

"Um, yes. I just told you."

"Okay, listen, sir! I need to report a missing case! My college roommate, she's missing!"

"What is this person's name?"

"Joana Smith."

"Eye color?"

"Hazel brown."

"Race?"

"Black and sh—", the phone line suddenly cut off, much to Sue's confusion. "Hello, sir, are you still there?", Sue grunted, slamming the phone back on the rack, her fists clenched. "Racist ass cops!"

Feeling hopeless, Sue brings her hands up to her face and sighs. "If a white girl goes missing, the police are on the case, but when it's a black girl, you're all alone!", Sue grunts before falling onto her knees, her head gazing up at the window. "I guess the only thing I can count on now is God himself", Sue shuts both her eyes and begins to pray. "God, I don't know if you're real or not, but if you are, please bring my friend back safe and unharmed. Just send me a sign, any sign."

With these words, the door knocks, causing Sue to turn her head back in shock. "Dang, God. You're good."

With that, Sue rose from the floor and headed straight to the doorknob, but before she could twist it, she took a deep breath and sighed. "If she's standing behind this door, she's real. If she's not, then-"

"Sue?", said a voice behind the door. "Are you in there? It's me, Joana?"

Sue gasps loudly before twisting the doorknob and opening the door wide. To her surprise, she finds her curly-haired best friend standing before her, her smile big and bright. "Hey, Sue."

"There is a God!", Sue said before pulling her friend in for a warm, embracive hug. "Thank goodness, you're alright, Joana! I woke up this morning and found your bed still neat. I thought you were kidnapped or worse!"

"Hey, hey, it's okay, Sue. I was just out with someone."

"Someone?"

"A friend of mine. I think you'd like him."

"Him?"

"Me!", said the curly-haired man, walking towards the two women. "She means me."

Sue raises her brow as she peers down at the young black man in the brown coat with paintbrushes sticking out of his pocket. "Joana", she said, turning back to her. "Who is this?"

"This is Octavius, Octavius Mitchell."

"Hi, nice to meet you", he said, holding his hand out to her.

With these words, Sue takes Octavius's hand and snaps his fingers into two. "Ahhhh!", he screamed in pain, but before he could do anything else, Octavius was flipped on his back, with Sue's foot squishing his face. "Sue, what are you doing!?"

"What's it looks like?! I'm protecting you!"

"Sue, what I said wasn't a lie!"

"That's what he wants me to think!"

"What the hell is wrong with you! I did nothing wrong to her!"

"Shut up, pervert!"

"Sue!", Sue is taken by the arm and brought to Joana's eye level. "He did not take advantage of me, okay! I did!"

Sue pauses, thinking. "Wait, what?"

"That's why I stayed out so late. I was out at a bar when I met him. Before I knew it, we were back at his place, and well, things had gone from there."

She blinks. "So, he didn't kidnap you? He's not a pervert?"

"No, he's just an ordinary guy I stayed over with."

"Ordinary?"

"Shh!", Joana snaps. "Do you want your arm fixed or not!?"

Octavius sighs. "I would if someone gets their foot off of my face!"

Joana looked up at me. "Sue, please, let him go. I need him."

With a quick sigh, Sue let her foot off Octavius's cheek, along with his arm, which he quickly let go of. "Thank you!"

I helped Octavius up, and our smiles met until Sue Anne stepped in between them. "He's not staying with us, is he?"

#

A group of prisoners stood in their cages, their voices echoing through their cells. As for one prisoner, he was spending his evening looking out his window, breathing in the sulky, sweet air before exhaling. "What a beautiful day it is. Soon, I, too, will be apart from that world. Until then, I'm in solitary confinement", he sighs. "No big deal. At least I still have this"

Octavius peers down at the crystal-diamond ring he held in the palm of his hand. He smiled, looking at it, but as soon as he did, he heard his cell door opening. "Hey, Otto. I'm back!", Otto turns his head back to find his mustache white man walking up to him with an orange jumpsuit.

Yorkshire.

"Did you miss me?"

"What do you mean? It's been two minutes."

He shrugs. "Yeah, but still."

Octavius raised his brow. "You got the stuff?"

"The stuff?"

I slap my hand against my head. "Oh, yeah, you're white. The candle, do you have the candle?"

"Oh, yeah!", he said before digging into his pocket. "Yeah, here it is."

Yorkshire holds out a waxed blue candle with white swirls. "Here you go."

"Thank you, Yorkshire. I owe you a million."

"A million dollars?"

I scoff. "Do you see any million dollars on me?", he said, walking to the window. "Besides, letting you stay here is enough."

Octavius places the waxed candle on the front of his window, the evening sunlight hitting it. Otto looked out at the sun setting on the mountainous horizon of St. Mora. "Hey, Otto, what's that candle for?"

He sits there in silence before peering down at his ring. "Have I ever told you about my wife?"

He blinks. "Your wife? Wait, you married?"

Otto slips his ring on his finger. "*Was*. That is until I leave."

"What do you mean? What happened to your wife?"

Octavius glances back at Henry. "Why do you think I'm in prison?"

He blinks. "Oh, dude. I'm sorry."

"Don't be. It's not good to dwell in the past", Octavius twists his ring in his hands. "But for today, we will."

Octavius, with his grey beard now turned black, is found peering down his broken arm, which was now wrapped in a bandage.

I was a young man, in my prime when I found a young, pristine, woman who, without trying, stole my heart. I also met another woman, only I didn't like her.

And she didn't like me either.

"How's that arm doing?", said Sue Anne, looking at me.

That white bitch broke my hand, and she asked me how I was doing!

"I don't know, how's your leg doing?"

"What? My leg? Why would you ask that?"

"Oh, I just want to make sure it's still straight before I split it in half!"

Sue scoffs, rolling both her eyes. "Oh, relax, it wasn't that bad."

"Not that bad? You broke my arm!"

"You screwed my best friend!"

"I did not and if I did, I'm sure she's screwed plenty other guys before me!"

"Yeah, but you're one guy who I don't like!"

"Well, neither do I. There, you happy!?"

"Alright, alright, you two, that's enough bickering!", Joana said, making her way to them.

"What do you mean? I'm just getting started with my insults!"

"So am I!"

"Nobody is insulting anyone. We have a big night tonight. So, I suggest you two get your act together and learn to get along."

Sue and I suck both our teeth before shifting our eyes away from each other. "What's that in your hand?", I say, noticing the white piece of paper cradled in her hands. "Oh, this? This is just something special I made."

"Something special?"

"And what's that?"

Joana let out a sigh. "Okay, okay. It's my song. I thought I'd sing this tonight for the club."

"Really? That's great, what's the song called."

Joana rubs the back of her head, her smile present. "My Angel, that's the name."

I smile through my goatee. "I like it. Sounds like a love song."

Joana laughs, blushing a bit. "Uh, yeah. You can say that. I think it'll be a great song for the show."

"Well, we won't know unless we hear it."

"Hear it?"

"Yeah, if you're going to sing, you'll need to sing it."

I blink. "Um, I'm a little nervous."

"It's okay to be nervous, Joana", I said to her. "How do you think I feel when I speak my work out to other people. However, this isn't other people; this is just me and Sue."

Joana smiles. "You're right. Okay"

With these words, Joana peers down at her paper and sings.

#

Three bowls sat on the bed, completely empty, as Mom, Sue, and I all sat together. "Mm, that was good, Chow Mein, Aunt Sue. The cilantro really made the flavors pop."

"I'm glad you liked it, Dominic. What about you, Joana? Did you like the chow mein?"

"Yes, really appetizing and healthy."

"Thank you, I'll make sure to keep making more healthy meals for you", she took Joana's hand in hers. "Until you get better."

Joana smiles. "I'm so lucky to have two loving people in my life."

"Neither could we, Mom. There's no better mother, a better friend than you."

With these loving words, Joana brought Sue and me into her arms. "I love you guys."

"We love you too, Mom", I say. "We will get through this together."

"Yes, together."

With that, the three held each other in silence until it was bedtime. As soon as it was, Joana was asleep in bed, her body lying on the bed. "She looks so peaceful", I say, looking up to Aunt Sue. "Doesn't she, Aunt Sue?"

Sue nods. "Yeah, she does. That's a strong woman you got there, Dom?"

I nod. "Yeah, I'm really lucky to have her in my life", my smile quickly turns to a heavy frown, causing me to turn my head back to her. "Did you know?", I ask.

Aunt Sue turns her eyes to me. "Know what, sweetie?"

"About…him, my father. Did you know he was a murderer?"

Aunt Sue gives me a long, hard look before sighing. "I did."

With that, my head lowers in sadness. "I thought you did."

"I'm sorry, Dom. Your mother and I didn't want you to find out this way."

"Neither did I, especially on my birthday."

Aunt Sue lowers her head in shame. "Is there anything I can do for you?"

I shook my head. "No. I just want to be left alone."

Aunt Sue tries reaching her hand to Dominic but quickly stops and sighs. "Alright."

With that, Aunt Sue turns her head and leaves me alone. She remembered the last time she felt alone and that was when she was with a certain someone. Someone she would rather not remember.

#

Sue Anne peeks through the curtains, looking through the crowd. "It's a big crowd out there. Are you ready, Joana?"

Sue turned her head back to Joana, patting out her sparkly, red dress and shoes. "Uh, not really. I think my dress is too tight."

"What do you mean? It looks great on you."

"Mm, I don't know. I think this makes me look fat."

"Joana, you look perfect."

"I don't feel perfect. What if I can't do this? What if I freeze up?"

"You're not going to freeze up. I promise you."

Joana lowers her head in sadness, not so full of confidence. "No, Sue, I can't."

"What do you mean you can't?", said Octavius, walking in with a tuxedo before the two women. "Joana, what's going on here?"

Sue sighs. "Joana's nervous. She doesn't want to perform."

"What? Joana?"

"I'm sorry, Otto. I just can't do this; I can't freeze up again."

Hearing this, Octavius clenches his fist in anger and stomps his feet, much to Joana and Sue's shock. "No!"

"What?"

"No, I did not come to this show in this sharp-ass suit just to see you call it quits! Get up."

Joana does so, her posture straightened as Octavius walks up to her. Once he did, he put both his hands on her shoulders and looked her dead in the eye. "These are some words that help me whenever I feel doubtful. Repeat after me: "I am strong."

"I am strong', she repeated.

"I am confident."

"I am confident.'

"I can do all things through God."

"I can do all things through God."

Octavius nods, his smile present. "There, now you should feel much better."

Joana nods. "Yeah, yeah. I do. Thank you, Ott-I mean Octavius."

"Otto's fine, Joana. Just like tonight will be, right?"

Joana nods happily. "Right."

Sue folds both her arms, impressed by Octavius's encouraging words. With that, Octavius gives Joana a quick peck on the cheek. "Now, go out there and make those people cheer their hearts out, beautiful."

Joana nods before heading out but not before squealing to Sue. "Wish me luck!"

"Always!"

With these words, Joana made her way out of the curtain and walked out to the stage, with Sue and Octavius walking behind her. "That was good encouraging words you gave her, Otto. Really helped her come alive."

"Thank you, Sue. I really appreciate th-ah!"

"Otto?", Sue asked, turning to him. "You, okay?"

"Paper."

"What?"

"Paper! I need paper!", Otto said, his eyes glowing green.

"Okay, okay. Just hold on!"

"Hurry, I'm about to lose it!"

"Okay, here!", she said, holding a small piece of paper along with a pen from her purse. "Here", she said, holding it out to him.

Without a second thought, Otto takes the paper on a wooden barrel and starts scribbling, much to Sue Anne's confusion. "Otto, what are you doing?"

"Be quiet. I'm almost done."

"Done with what? Otto, what are you drawing?"

Otto spends the next few minutes scribbling until suddenly, his eyes turn back to their original hue, and his hands stop moving. With that, he drops the pen in his hands and brings it up to his eyes.

His and Sue Anne's. "Wait, is that...?", Sue turns back to Otto, his eyes big and wide. "Yeah"

#

Joana stood up on the stage, a microphone standing before her. Joana took the microphone in her hands; as soon as she looked up, there were thousands of eyes staring up at her.

Joana, with her hands trembling and her mouth dry, takes a deep breath and speaks. "Um, hi, everyone", she said through the microphone, quieting the audience. "Um, my name is Joana Smith, and I'm here to sing you a special song of mine."

Joana hears a set of laughter come from the crowd, followed by countless whispers from them, much to Joana's worry. That is, until she recalls the words:

You are strong, you are confident, and you can do all things by God.

With these words, Joana closes her eyes and takes a deep breath, ready to sing:

Who are you?

What do you see?

What are you?

Someone I can't be.

A beam of light.

Seen from hindsight.

A speck,

Unseen from-

I paused, my words quickly cutting off as the hundreds of eyes stared right at me.

Unseen from...

I pause again, causing me to turn my eyes back to the two figures standing behind the curtain. "What's going on? What's she doing?"

I stand before the stage, my mouth opening and closing. "Oh, no. She's freezing up", Otto said.

"Oh, man. What do we do?"

Hearing this, Otto looked down at the hand drawing, his brows lowering. "What are you doing?"

Otto looked up from his drawing and at Sue. "What I need to do."

"What? What are you talking about?"

"Hold this", Otto said, exiting the curtain and onto the stage.

A force bound to cross the tides!

"Get off the stage!"

You are my angel!

My shining star.

I am your angel,

So near, yet so far!

"I just remember the crowd booing her", Aunt Sue said, reminiscing. "They just kept booing, but Joana...she just kept singing. Until..."

You're out of reach,

Your hands and feet.

I wish I could touch you!

'Cause without you, I'll fall from the sky,

Without you, I'll wither and dieeeeee!!!!

A second tomato is thrown onto Joana, but this time, it's her face.

This time, she falls straight to her knees.

"Go home, loser! We don't want you here!"

Joana, having taken as much as she could, droops her head and sobs.

As for the crowd, their boos quickly turned to laughs, laughing the poor woman off in her misery.

That is, until another voice was heard.

No, you won't, dear.

Joana raised his head in confusion, her eyes bleary from the tomato as she looked up at the man holding his hand out to him. *"He* came"

For I, your angel, is here.

Joana peers up at Octavius's hand and, without hesitation, grabs it in her hand. Before she knew it, she was brought to her, their eyes meeting. "You came for me."

"Of course, I did", Otto said, wiping the bits of tomato from my face. As soon as he did, Joana turned her eyes back to the audience, who was still whispering. "But what about them?"

"Don't worry about them. It's just you and me now."

With these words, Joana looked right into Octavius's eyes. *Don't you worry, dear. For I, your angel, is here.*

Joana smiles, taking the microphone in his hands. *And as long as I am. I vow to never leave your side.*

Here, to save you. Otto smirks.

Joana smiles. *To cherish you.*

Now both: *But most of all: to love you.*

The room spun around Otto and Joana, with the audience completely disappearing, leaving as if it was, in Otto's words, just them.

And then it was.

Joana, happier than ever, looked into Otto's eyes and said, *I love you.*

Otto repeated. *I love you.*

With these loving words, Otto and Joana pressed their heads into each other.

I am your angel.

With these words, a burst of cheers is heard, snapping Joana and Otto out of their little fantasy world and back to reality.

A reality that was good.

Happy, Joana and Otto took each other by the hand and bowed before the white crowd, who was now cheering even more.

As for Sue Anne, she held a piece of paper in her hands. But not just any piece of paper, Otto's paper.

Raising the paper to her face, Sue finds a picture of Joana and Otto bowing proudly to the crowd of white people. With that, she brings it to her heart and smiles, cherishing this memory.

It was a great night, the happiest night of my life.

Aunt Sue smiles, thinking to herself. "I've never heard a livelier cheer than I did that night."

Dominic, Joana's son, smiles proudly. "You must've been proud of her."

Sue nods. "Very. I was also proud of Otto. If it hadn't been for his help, Joana would never have been able to conquer her stage fright. Soon, we became the best of friends", she lowers her head in sadness. "Or so I thought when he did what he did."

Dominic lowers his head. "It makes me want to cry. After everything she did for him, that he would just break her heart like that. Aunt Sue, do you think I'll become like him."

"What? Why would you think that?"

"It's just, I've been curious about who my father was my whole life, and now that I know the truth, I'm afraid that I'll be just as bad as him."

"Dominic, you are nothing like your father. You may have his appearance, but you are not him. Octavius didn't just leave your mother, but you as well. If anyone's a monster, it's him."

I lower my head, making a small nod. "Yeah, I guess you're right", I shift my eyes back to Mom, lying peacefully in bed, before sighing. "Still, it's not fair."

Sue sighs, nodding. "I know, Dom", she turns back to mom. "I know."

Sniffing, I turn to Aunt Sue. "Um, I should get to bed now. We got a big day ahead of us tomorrow."

"Okay. Goodnight, Dominic."

"Goodnight, Aunt Sue."

Sue took a deep breath as she watched me walk down the dark corridor hallway before entering my bedroom and closing it behind me. Sighing, Sue turns back to the door. "You don't deserve this, kid", she looked at Joana lying in bed. "You don't."

\#

Octavius, Sue Anne, and I headed out the front door, laughing joyfully as they headed out the front door of the club. "I can't believe it, I did it! I conquered my stage fright!", said Joana, happily.

"You sure did, Joana! How do you feel?"

"I feel amazing! Like I can do anything!"

"Does this mean you're going to continue singing?"

Joana rubs the back of her neck. "Um, no."

"What?", Sue and Otto say in shock.

"I mean, singing was nice, but now that I did it, I realized that what I really wanted was to get over my stage fright, and I did. Now, I feel satisfied."

"But I thought singing was your dream, right?"

"It is and I did it. Now, my dream's complete, and it was even better when I got to do it with my best friends."

"Best friends?", said Otto. "Is that what we are?"

"Yes", I said, grabbing him by the collar and leaning in for a kiss before pulling away. "My boyfriend. Unless you're okay with that?"

Otto laughs, taking Joana by the waist. "I think I can handle that."

Otto and I were seconds from pulling in until Sue Anne popped in between them. "Alright, you two. Do that in your own time. Right now, what do you say we get ourselves some victory dinner at my parent's house!"

"Yeah!", said both Otto and Joana.

"Don't worry, they're not racist."

"Hope so", Otto replied.

With that, the three best friends make their way down the road, heading out for a great victory dinner.

Joana lies happily in her hospital bed, a warm smile on her face as she slept the night away. Well, for her, that was.

\#

A set of eyes was closed, a streak of darkness forged to it. From that standpoint, you'd think these eyes belonged to Joana, but they weren't.

For it was none other than Octavius Mitchell.

"Psst, Otto?", said a voice, causing Otto's eyes to shoot right open. "Hey, Otto, are you okay?"

Confused, Octavius turns his eyes back to his cellmate, Henry Yorkshire. Otto looked at him, quite perplexed. "What?"

Henry sways his head with a smile. "Sorry, it's just I saw you staring out the window again and got a little concerned."

Otto raises his brow before turning his body back to the window, the city lights gleaming through them. "I was just lost in thought, is all."

Henry sways his head a bit in protest. "Mm, you seemed to be lost in thought for quite a while now. Anything you want to talk about?"

Otto looked down at his left hand, where a diamond-encrusted ring was found. Without a second thought, Otto takes the ring out of his hand and into his palm, the moonlight hitting it. "What's that?", Henry asked. "Is that a ring?"

Otto nods. "Yes."

Henry raises his brow. "Is that your ring?"

Otto clutched his hand before bringing it to the center of his chest, where his heart was. "It's my wife's."

"Who's your wife?"

"Someone I once knew."

Henry lowers his eyes in sadness. "I'm sorry, man."

"It's alright."

Henry rubs the back of his neck. "Well, I guess I'll be going to bed."

"Not so fast, Henry."

Henry stops dead at his cell door before glancing back. "What is it, Otto?"

Still at his window, Otto straightens his posture, his head raised before turning back to him. "Do you know what I look like?"

He blinks, his brow raised in confusion. "What?"

"My face, Henry. Do you know what I look like?"

"No", Henry said, shaking his head. "No, I've never seen your face. You always had that hoodie over it."

"Would you like to see?"

Henry gulps, his fists clenched. "Um, sure."

With a cocky grin, Otto takes the helm of his hoodie and raises it over his forehead. To Henry's surprise, he finds a black and grey-bearded man with small patches of grey hair sticking out, a small set of wrinkles under his eyes, and a huge scar slashed on his left eye.

Henry stands there, completely in awe of the young man. At that very moment, there were a million things he could say to his fellow prisoner, but the only thing that came out was this: "Woah"

Otto smirks, nodding. "Woah, indeed."

Chapter 15: The March of Time

Women.

They're amazing! They can do several things all at once, without fail—, cleaning, cooking, and even raising kids like me. They manage to get through the most "unbearable" pains of childbirth and periods. They're basically superheroes!

But even superheroes get knocked down.

Bruised.

Even sick.

There was just one woman I never thought could get knocked down, and that was my mother: Joana Mitchell.

She was sick, with the worst illness anyone could have cancer.

Damned cancer!

The day she was emitted from the hospital, I knew this was going to be the hardest day of my life, and in fact, it was.

January

"Almost there, Mom. Almost there!", I said, taking Mom to the bathroom with Aunt Sue beside me. Mom was covering her mouth, as if she was going to hurl. "Just hold on, Joana", said Sue, opening the bathroom door wide. As soon as we entered the room, Mom lifted the toilet's handle and puked.

It was disgusting, but none as disgusting as the bit of vomit that ended up at the end of my hair. I watched as Aunt Sue pulled some of Mom's hair from her face, holding and shushing her as she did her business. "Just let it out, Joana. Get that bad stuff out of you."

I stood there as mom slowly lifted her head from the toilet, her eyes low and dim as she turned to Sue. "I'm done", she said with a nod. "I'm done."

With that, Aunt Sue turned to me and turned back to the toilet. Getting the hint, I made my way toward the toilet and pressed the lever, flushing Mom's vomit down. Before long, Mom was back in bed, her body lying under the sheets. Sue sat next to her bed, her hand placed on her forehead, soothing her. I watched with worry as Mom lay in bed. This was the third night in a row she had vomited, and it really took a toll on my sleep. Night after night, I recall being shaken awake by Aunt Sue in the middle of the night, her eyes bloodshot red, telling me to help her with Mom. There were times when I would have to bring a bucket and washcloth to the hallway, where Mom would be found lying there in her own filth. If only she'd made it to the bathroom fast enough but didn't. Those were the worst nights of all for me, especially when I had to clean Mom's face with the washcloth. That is until she'd turn away, not wanting to look at me. I know why she did it, not to be mean but because she was mad. Mad that I had to see her like this, that she was sick, that she was weak. But…when the going gets tough, sleep is something that's earned. At this moment, there was no sleep; there was only being awake. "Dominic", said a voice. "Dominic"

My eyes shot open, causing me to find Sue looking at me, her eyes dark and baggy. "She's okay. Go back to sleep."

With these words, I turned my head and made my way out of the bedroom. I didn't really notice at first, but the moment I left, I could've sworn I heard a faint "I love you", It was sad and low, but I knew who it was.

Mom.

As soon as I left Mom's room, I entered my own, the door shutting behind me. As soon as I did, my back was against the door, my body sliding down the door, my face cupped in my face as I sobbed. "Why her?", I say. "Why her?"

That was the first month of Mom's chemotherapy, and the next one *wasn't* any better.

#

February.

Little snippets of hair fell on the white marble floor of the bathroom. The hair was black and curly, much like my hair, but it wasn't mine. "Are you sure you don't want my help, Mom?", I say, watching my mother snip pieces of her hair from the top of her head. "It's alright, baby. I can do it."

"Are you sure?"

"Mm-hm."

I watched with fear as the scissors snipped a bit more of Mom's hair. That is, within seconds, they stop. They stop and start to shake. "Mom?", I say, the scissors still shaking. "Mom?"

Mom's hands continued to shake, her eyes squinting with frustration as she did. "I-I got it, baby. I-ah!"

A quick gasp escapes me as the pair of scissors slip from Mom's hands, hitting the floor with a thud. "Oh no!", said Mom in shock.

"It's okay, Mom", I said, kneeling on the floor and retrieving the scissors. Mom sighs, her head held low in shame. "I'm sorry, baby. The scissors…they just slipped."

"It's okay, Mom", I said, comforting her.

Mom's cancer was really getting the best of her. She could hardly do anything anymore. No cooking or cleaning; she couldn't even walk to the bathroom without falling. Soon, she would have no choice but to be completely bedridden. That's what scared me the most: seeing my mom in bed, hooked up to life support with little to no breath left in her lungs.

But that's not going to happen. That I knew. As long as I kept my head up to the sky, things would soon look up, and this hellish nightmare would be over. All I had to do was wait.

Until then, I would be there for Mom. No matter what.

With a sad yet small smile, I rose from the floor, the scissors now clenched in my hands. "Here, let me do it."

Mom was about to say something in protest but quickly brushed it off. Within seconds, she turns her head back, waiting for me to do my business. Snip after snip, Mom's hair fell onto the floor, some big, some small.

Soon, a whole pile of it was on the floor, which I had to sweep up. As soon as it was all in the trash, Mom had a whole yellow scarf with red flowers.

I looked at her, my smile widening. "You look beautiful, Mom."

Mom smiled. It's the first I'd seen in two months. "Thank you, baby."

Without a second thought, I pulled Mom in for a hug, which shocked her before finally giving in. "Oh, baby', Mom said softly, my thick, curly hair coiling through her fingers.

#

April.

The morning sun peeked from my bedroom curtains and onto my bed, which, in fact, was already made up. I stood in front of the mirror, already in my school uniform, as I brushed my hair. Before I knew it, I hopped right into my sneakers and headed out the door.

I headed downstairs, my backpack trotting behind me before making the last step. But the moment I turned the corner, I found Mom sitting at the kitchen table with a cup of chamomile tea in her hands. I stepped a few inches back, not wanting to be noticed.

But that was stupid.

She was my mother, and I was her son. No matter how ill she was. With a heavy sigh, I make my way into the kitchen, causing Mom to turn her head. "Oh, hey baby", she said, smiling at me.

I smile back. "Hey, mom. Can I sit here?"

Mom nods, weakly. "Of course."

With that, I pulled up one of the wooden chairs from the table, and my backpack plopped down on the tile floor before gazing up at Mom. The two of us spent a good minute in silence before one of us spoke up. "Where's Aunt Sue, mom?"

"Sue's in the bathroom, doing her hair. She'll be down shortly."

I mouth a quick "oh" before nodding. "I see you wearing your school uniform."

"Yeah", I say with a happy smile. "It's red and blue, the same colors as our school."

"It looks great on you."

"Not as great as your scarf."

"What?", Mom said, bringing up the pink all-over scarf from her head. "Oh, yes. This is just something I put together."

"Put together?"

Mom laughs. "I, um, I made it."

I smile, nodding happily. "It looks good on you."

"Really? I thought it was a bit too much."

"What, why would you say that?"

"Oh, you know, because…", Mom's eyes lower in sadness before sighing. "You know?"

I lower my head, before eyeing Mom's frail, veiny hand, one that I quickly grab hold of. "Mom, it's okay."

Mom sniffs, nodding to me. "I know, baby. I just wish things were different."

With these words, I pulled Mom in for a warm, loving hug. Unfortunately, it didn't last long, as the sound of a car beeping was heard, causing my eyes to crack open. In doing so, I found a black limousine parked outside. "Oh", I said, pulling away. "Mom, my ride's here."

"What?", Mom said, turning back to the window where a tall, lean man stood. "Oh! Yeah, you should go. Wouldn't want to be late for school."

I grab my backpack from under the seat before pulling up my chair and heading out the door. As soon as I was outside, I noticed Barry wasn't the only one standing outside the limousine, Amanda was as well, her red hair blowing in the wind as she waited for me.

Without hesitation, I walked right from my door and to the limousine, but the moment my foot hit the pavement of the road, I turned my eyes back to the house, and my body language changed.

I was scared, scared to leave mom behind. This was the fourth time I would leave mom home by herself. Well, not entirely by herself, as she had Aunt Sue, but even with her, I still felt the same amount of dread. What if something bad happened to Mom, and I wouldn't be there to help her?

What would I do then?

Either way, I didn't like leaving her.

I didn't like leaving at all!

But as tough as it was, I had to go.

I had to leave.

It's what mom would want.

With a sad sigh, I turn my eyes away from the house and head straight to the limousine, Amanda and Barry waiting patiently. "Sorry for taking so long, guys. I was ju-", my words quickly stopped as I was pulled in for a hug from my loving, nurturing girlfriend.

I quickly returned the favor, by planting both my arms around her waist, hugging her firmly. "Thank you, Amanda."

"Anytime, babe."

With that, Amanda, Barry, and I entered the limousine, the door shutting behind us as we entered. But before we could take off, I found Mom standing inside the window, watching me from inside, her eyes full of sadness.

I looked at her, placing my hand on the glass window before mouthing the three subtle words: *I love you.*

With that, the limousine leaves the parking lot of my house before driving down the road, disappearing in the distance.

\#

I couldn't focus on school, throughout the whole day; I was sad. Whenever the teacher was talking about an important assignment, I just spent it staring out the window in a daze. I was depressed, and when you're like that, nothing else matters.

Not even people. People like my girlfriend.

I recall taking out a few textbooks from my lockers, but as soon as I turned my eyes, Amanda stood before me, waving happily as she spotted me. Unfortunately, I didn't wave back. Instead, I just closed my locker and walked off, leaving Amanda in confusion.

Soon, lunch arrived, and everyone was stuffing their faces with hotdogs and cheeseburgers. As for me, I didn't eat a nibble. I just didn't have the stomach for it.

I was sick, and when I was sick, I couldn't do anything.

Not even eating.

"Dominic", said Amanda, sitting across from me. "Please, eat something."

I sigh, scooting my yellow lunch tray away from me, much to Amanda's worry. "You need to eat, Dom."

"I can't."

"You *can*. Just try."

"How can I, Amanda? How can I do anything when my mom's at home, going through hell?"

"Just because she's suffering, doesn't mean you have to."

"And what's that supposed to mean? Are you saying I should just give up on her?"

"I'm saying you should stop beating yourself up for something that's not your fault. You're going through enough right now, but the last thing you need is to hate yourself."

I slam my fists on the table, shocking Amanda and several other students, who spun their heads. "Dominic", Amanda said under her breath, much to my shock. "Amanda, I…"

I turn my eyes back to the various eyes staring at me. Embarrassed, I lower my eyes in sadness. "I-I'm sorry. I'm not trying to project anything on you, Amanda."

"I know", Amanda reached her hand across the table, taking mine. "Just talk to me."

With these words, I raised my head up to Amanda, her eyes staring back at me, and sighed. "I've been having these…nightmares."

Amanda blinks, confused. "Nightmares? About what? Your mother?"

"No", I look into Amanda's eyes. "It was him, my father."

Amanda's eyes were wide open. "Your-your father?"

I nod. "Yeah, it started the night Mom came home from the hospital. I remember waking up in bed in cold sweats, my mind spiraling out of control. They were so bad that I'd lose sleep."

"I can see that", Amanda said. "Your eyes are pretty dark."

I sniffed a bit, my hands raised to my dark eye sockets. "Yeah, they are", I sigh heavily.

"Dominic, there's nothing to be afraid of. Your fathers still locked up."

"But for how long? It's already April. How do I know he won't come and look for me!? What if…", I sigh, my head lowering in silence.

"What if what?"

I blink, looking back up at her. "What if he comes for your father?"

"What? What do you mean?"

"Well, he did put my father behind bars. You don't think he probably held some kind of… I don't know, a grudge toward him. I mean, it's been seventeen years."

"Who holds a grudge that long?"

"I don't know, but if he did, then your father's life could be in danger. *Your* life could be in danger."

"Dominic, my father has connections everywhere. If he knew something was going to happen to him, he'd tell us."

I raise my brow. "Would he?"

"Yes, what you don't think he can?"

"No, it's just he's sick. I don't think he'd have the energy to-"

"Is that what you think?! That my father's just some weak, old man who can't handle himself!? He's not as ill as you think, Dom!"

"I didn't say that! I just-"

"Just what?"

I grunt, rising from my seat. "I JUST WANT EVERYONE TO BE SAFE! YOUR FATHER PUT MY FATHER BEHIND BARS ALL BECAUSE A WOMAN THAT THEY BOTH LOVED DIED! IT'S ONLY A MATTER OF TIME BEFORE HE, I DON'T KNOW KILLS AGAIN! ONLY THIS TIME, IT'LL BE FOR VENGANCE! DO YOU WANT THAT, AMANDA! DO YOU WANT YOUR FATHER TO DIE!"

Every student in the cafeteria had their heads spun back to me and Amanda, their eyes wide as they stared at me. Shocked, I turned back to Amanda, who now had tears falling down her cheeks. "What?", I said, shocked. "Amanda, I-"

Amanda cuffed both her hands on her face, now sobbing. "Amanda, please, don't cry. I'm sorry."

Amanda didn't listen, instead she rose from her chair and ran out of the cafeteria. "Amanda, wait!", I called out.

But Amanda was already down the hallway, bursting through the doors, disappearing. Frustrated, I knocked my lunch tray on the floor in anger, my spaghetti and meatballs hitting the cafeteria floor with a thud. With nothing but shame in my heart, I put my hand on my face and sighed.

#

I walked the entire way home, my hoodie over my head as I did. I didn't want to go with Amanda as I was too embarrassed to talk to her since lunch. So, I avoided her.

She wouldn't like that. But, at that moment, I didn't care. I just wanted to be alone.

And alone I was.

Before I knew it, I was back at the house, the screen door shutting behind me. As soon as it did, I made my way through the living room before turning a sharp left and entering the kitchen. The kitchen was quiet, almost as if no one was in there.

Or so I thought when I turned my head to the left. To my surprise, I find Aunt Sue sitting at the kitchen table, with a pile of bills sitting before her. Confused, I walked right up to her. "Um, hey, Aunt Sue."

Aunt Sue turned to me and spoke. "Oh, hey, Dom."

"What are you doing?"

Sue sighs. "I'm just looking through these bills."

Bills.

Piles of it.

I looked at them, each of them reading a certain word I've seen before:

PAST DUE.

I looked at the others, each of them saying the same thing:

PAST DUE.

PAST DUE.

PAST DUE.

Ever since Mom got sick, the bills started piling up left and right. Yet, this house was a vacation home that belonged to my girlfriend, who, in this case, was fabulously wealthy. So, we shouldn't be seeing any bills show up in the mail. But we did because, in the words of my mother: *"When it comes to bills, I can do it all by myself."*

I sighed, thinking about this. She may be my mother, but she was prideful. Perhaps, *too* prideful.

But that was before she was sick. Back when she could move around, when she was fit. But she's not now; she's terribly ill. She needed help, *we* needed help.

The sooner Mom realized that the better.

But that was in the past, and I needed to stay in the present. "You look tired, Dom."

"What?"

"I said you look tired."

"Oh", I rub my dark eyes. "Yeah, I was just about to go upstairs. Speaking of which, is mom up there?"

"Yeah, she's in her room."

With these words, I turned my head away from Aunt Sue and headed up the steps. "Make sure to knock, Dom!"

"I will!"

With these words, Sue went right back to the pile of bills sitting next to her and sighed. "What am I going to do?"

#

I stood before Mom's bedroom door, my eyes full of fear. With a deep breath, I knocked on mom's door. "Mom?"

There was no answer, so I knocked again. "Mom, are you in here?"

Without a second thought, I opened the door wide, the bedroom standing before me. To my surprise, I found Mom in bed, asleep. I let out a quick sigh of relief and quickly shut the door. She needed her rest, and so did I.

Mother turned her eyes back to me. "Oh, hey, baby. I didn't realize you made it home."

"I did. Are you okay?"

She nodded. "Yeah, I am. I was just thinking."

"About what?", I said, sitting next to her.

"About you, Sue, about us"

I sit next to her, taking her hand in mine. She takes my hand as well, holding it tight. "You seem tired, baby."

I nod. "I just haven't been getting as much sleep lately, is all."

"I understand. These past few months have been hard on you, hasn't it?"

"Yeah, they have."

Mom smiled, only it wasn't a happy one. "I'm sorry for putting you and Sue through this."

"It's okay."

"No, it's not okay", she sighs. "This cancer has not only taken a toll on my body but you guys as well. It just isn't fair."

"Life isn't fair."

"Yeah."

Mom gripped my hand tighter, our eyes meeting each other as I smiled before turning back to Mom and nodding. "Well, I'm going to my bedroom."

With nothing else to say, I made my way out of the bedroom, the door closing behind me. As for Mom, her smile was gone.

Before I knew it, I was back in my bedroom, plopping back on my bed, staring back up at the ceiling. I rubbed my eyes, which were still dark. According to that, I haven't had real sleep in weeks. This was the only chance I got.

But before I could, I reached into my pocket and pulled out my cellphone. I pulled up my screen, and that's where I found a text bubble:

Amanda, I'm sorry. Please, talk to me.

I looked at the name written above:

Amanda.

I sighed, my head looking up at the ceiling. Amanda hasn't talked to me since our fight. Then again, I don't blame her. I was rude to her. Mom always told me how to treat women with respect, and I didn't do that. No girl like Amanda deserved that.

With a sad sigh, I turned my phone off and shut both my eyes, falling asleep.

As soon as I woke up, it was pitch black.

Real dark. As if it was nighttime.

Turning to my left, I found my clock reading 8:45.

With my eyes wide, I raised my head from my pillow and switched my lamp on, light entering my room. I looked back at my cell phone to see if Amanda had contacted me.

I pulled up the text bubble on the screen, and not to my surprise, she doesn't. The text message was still the same. "She's never going to talk to me again."

With a heavy sigh, I lay on my pillow, my eyes staring up at the ceiling as I sighed in utter silence. Or so I thought once the door was knocked. "Dominic?"

"Go away, mom."

"I'm coming in."

I grunt heavily before raising my body from the bed before Mom enters the door, finding me sitting on the bed, my head turned as I stared out at the night sky from the window. Seeing this, Mom lets out a heavy sigh and speaks. "Dominic, are you in here?"

"Yeah"

"I just wanted to tell you that dinner's ready."

I nod. "Oh, okay."

Mom raised her brows. "Are you okay, baby?"

I look down at my phone and sigh. "Mom, have you ever told someone something that really hurt?"

Mom doesn't hesitate to nod. "Yes, why?"

I look down at my phone in sadness, much to Mom's concern. "What is it, baby?", she said, sitting next to me.

With a heavy sigh, I turn to Mom. "It's Amanda. She's mad at me."

"For what?"

"We got into a fight at school. I said something to her that really upset her, and now she won't answer any of my text messages."

Mom raises her brow. "Okay, well, what do you want to do?"

I shrugged. "I don't know."

"Well, have you tried calling her?"

"No", I shake my head.

"Well, you should."

"I can't. I'm afraid. What if she won't talk to me?"

"I have cancer, Dom. I don't think there's anything you should be afraid of."

I lower my eyes before nodding. "I guess you're right", I sighed. "It's just these past few months have been hard on me."

"You think they haven't been hard on me? For the past four months, I've been completely bed ridden. I can barely walk, let alone stand and…tired, I'm always tired."

I frowned, and my hand was placed on my mother's hands. "I know, mom."

Mom smiles. "Just talk to her, baby. You won't regret it."

"Yeah", I said as Mom rose from my bed before grabbing her wrist. "Mom!"

Mom turns her eyes back to me, very confused. "What is it?"

Without a second thought, I pulled Mom in for a loving embrace. "Thank you."

Mom smiles and hugs me right back. "You're welcome, baby."

With those words, Mom let go of me and headed out of the room, leaving me all alone with me and my thoughts. "Alright", I said, reaching into my pocket and retrieving my phone. "Showtime"

Without a second thought, I dialed a few numbers on my phone and brought it to my ear, waiting in utter desperation to hear my girlfriend's sweet, sweet voice again. *"Dominic?"*, said a voice, causing both my eyes to widen. "Amanda?"

#

Joana heads down the steps, her breathing slow and delicate. She couldn't run down the steps on a full spree like she used to. Thanks to her illness, she had no choice but to take it slow. Yet, that didn't stop her from getting a few breaths from her system. Just one step was enough to get her huffing and puffing. I guess that's what happens when your body deteriorates. Sad but true. As soon as she reached the last step, she turned to the left to find a large wine bottle being poured into a tall glass, a glass that was almost empty. To her surprise, Joana finds Sue, with her head lying flat on the table, her snores heard from the distance.

She must've fallen asleep from all that drinking. Wine would do that to you.

Concerned, Joana walks towards the table and shakes Aunt Sue. "Sue?"

Sue's snoring suddenly stops, causing her head to rise. "J…Joana", she murmured, rubbing her eyes. "Hey, Sue."

"What happened? Did I doze off?"

Joana nods. "By the looks of it, yeah. Is everything okay?"

Sue blinks a moment before speaking. "Oh, um, yeah."

She raises her brow. "Are you sure?"

Sue nods. "Yeah, it's just all these bills are starting to pile up on me. It's been stressful", Sue shook her head, causing a happy smile to form on her face. "But enough about me, how are you doing?"

Joana lowers her head in shame, much to Sue Anne's concern. "Joana, what's wrong?"

Joana fiddles with her hands before speaking. "It's me, isn't it?"

"What?"

"It's me, my cancer. That's why there are so many bills."

"Oh, Joana", Sue extends her arm, bringing Joana to sit next to her. "This has nothing to do with you. Things just haven't been so up lately. Everything will eventually work itself out."

Joana lowers her eyes and sighs. "No, it won't."

"Sure, it will."

"*No*, it won't", Joana turns her eyes back to the pile of bills lying on the table. "These bills are piling up by the minute, and they're not going to get paid by sheer luck. We need help."

"What kind of help?"

With a small sigh, Joana reaches into her pocket and pulls out a black card. Sue Anne sneered at the card in confusion. "Where'd you get that?", she said, noticing the numbers printed on the card.

Joana turns her eyes back to Sue and smiles. "Oh, an old friend gave it to me."

Joana lay in the hospital bed, her eyes staring right at the middle-aged man smiling down at her in the cashmere suit. "Hello, Joana. It's been a while."

Joana turns her eyes away from him. "I don't really feel like talking right now."

Robert nods. "I understand. I just wanted to see how you were doing."

Joana shuts both her eyes. "I'm fine. Please, go away."

"Bu-", Robert stops himself before sighing. "Alright, I'll go."

A tear fell from Joana's eye as Robert turned his back from her, but before he could leave the room, he dug into his pocket and pulled out a black card with a set of numbers found in white writing. "If there's anything you need...", he puts the card on Joana's eating table, "give me a call."

With that, Robert leaves the room, the door shutting behind him. As soon as he does, Joana rises from the bed, her head turning back to the black card that sat on the table, and picks it up in her hands, her eyes full of confusion.

Joana, snapping out of the memory, looked down at the card and sighed. "I've been avoiding him for too long. It's time I made the call."

\#

But she wasn't the only one making the call.

"Amanda don't hang up. Please", Dominic answered.

"I'm not."

A happy smile forms across my face, relieved. "Baby, listen. I'm sorry, okay. What I said was shitty, and I shouldn't have made you feel like crap an-"

"Stop, Dominic! It's okay, I don't care about that anymore."

I blink in confusion. "You're-you're not?"

"No, it's all water under the bridge now."

I sigh, my heart no longer beating out of my chest. "Oh, what a relief. I'm so glad you're not mad."

"Me too. Hey, could you do something for me?"

I nod. "Yeah, what is it?"

"Come to the window."

I raise my brow. "The window?"

"Yes, now. Please."

Confused, I rose from my bed, walking all the way across the room before stopping dead at my window, my eyes searching through the blinds. And that's where I see her.

My red-headed girlfriend was standing in a white fur coat, all matching her pants and boots. She waved back.

I waved back, putting my phone back to my ear. "You look pretty."

Amanda doesn't reply and brings her phone to her ear. *"Um, can you come meet me, like now?"*

I nod happily. "Um, yeah, sure."

"Thanks"

"Give me five minutes, okay."

"Okay"

With these words, I ended the phone call between Amanda and me, the blinds shutting as I left my bedroom.

#

I ran all the way down the steps, my feet full of happiness. For four months, I've felt alone, alone and scared. But now, for the first time, I was walking on air.

Making it to the last step, I make a sharp turn into the kitchen, where my mom and Aunt Sue sat at the kitchen table, their eyes looking right at me. "Dominic?", said Mom. "Where are you going, baby?"

"It's Amanda. She's waiting for me outside."

"Outside?", Aunt Sue said as I passed her. "What's she doing there for?"

"I don't know. She wants to talk to me about something. I gotta go."

"Wait, Dominic-"

"Let him go, Sue", Mom said, stopping her. "Amanda's obviously here to talk with him. He needs to face her. Just like I need to face him", Mom said, holding the card out to Sue.

Sue nods with a smile. "Do it."

With these words, Mom dials a few numbers on her cellphone and reaches it to her ear. Within seconds, some static was heard, and a voice came through. *"Hello?"*

Joana smiles happily. "Hello…Mr. Griffin?"

"I know that voice? Mrs. Mitchell, is that you?"

"Yes, it's me. Mrs. Mitchell: Joana Mitchell."

"Mrs. Mitchell, yes. It's so nice to finally hear from you. I've been expecting your call."

\#

The screen door shut behind me, as I walked down the little steps of the front porch. It was cold outside, quite chilly. Good thing I brought my jacket, or I'd freeze to death. Turning to the left, I found my girlfriend in her white fur coat, her hands in her pocket as she stared out into space.

Smiling, I open my mouth and speak. "Amanda?"

Turning her head, Amanda turns her eyes back to me and nods. "Hey, babe", she said, moving some of her hair back.

I notice this strange behavior. "Is everything okay?"

With these words, Amanda grabs me right by the shoulders and speaks. "Dominic, there's something I need to tell you."

"Tell me what?", I said, making Amanda's eyes shift to the left. "Amanda, what is it?"

With a sigh, Amanda looked at me. "Remember, when you told me that your father could come back for my father, that he may hold a grudge?"

I nod. "Yeah"

She nodded. "You were right. He's coming for him."

\#

"You're calling awfully late. Is there something wrong?"

Joana nods. "Yes."

"What's it about?"

Joana sucked in some air before exhaling. "I need you to help me pay these bills, these medical bills."

"Medical bills?"

"Yes, they've been piling up for months now, and look, I know I said I didn't need your help before, but I really need it now."

#

"What do you mean he's coming?"

"I mean, your father's coming for him. I heard him and Mom talking about it."

"Talking about what?"

"Just listen! A few hours after I got home from school."

Amanda opened the door to Griffin Manor, her eyes full of tears as she ran upstairs and accidentally knocked into Butler Barry, confusing him. "Ms. Griffin, are you alright?"

Amanda doesn't reply and instead keeps running down the hallway. Turning a sharp left, she found a large door, leading to a small office. Without anything else holding her back, Amanda twists the doorknob open. "Dad, I need to talk to yo-", Amanda's eyes widen as she finds her parents pacing the floor.

"As soon as I entered the house, I found my parents pacing the floor like they feared something. I didn't realize it until I heard them speak."

"Are you sure about this, Robert?", said Mrs. Griffin, puzzled.

"Of course, I am. The dream was real. I'm serious, Evelyn!"

Evelyn sighed, her hand up to her forehead in frustration. "Look, just run it by me one more time."

Robert closes his eyes, letting out a deep sigh. "I was standing before a prison, a big prison with all these barbed wires and fences. Suddenly, I found a gate, a large metal gate standing right before me. Suddenly, I hear this loud noise, like that of a horn. It hurt my ears so much that I had no choice but to close my eyes. But then, suddenly, the loud noise stopped and that's when I saw him, standing right at me."

"He was standing before you?"

"Yes."

"And what was he doing?"

Robert's eyes widen. *"He was...smiling at me and not just a regular smile; it was sinister, almost evil. But that wasn't as bad as what he said to me.'*

"And what did he say?"

"He said: I'm coming for you, you and your family."

I remember gasping as I heard this.

Evelyn raises her brow. "Are you sure this isn't just one of your spiritual dreams, like the one you had with that Dominic boy?"

"No, this is nothing like that. Not when I've had it for three nights now!"

"Three nights?"

"Yes, and I'm sure it'll be a fourth. He's coming, Evelyn."

Evelyn puts her hands through her hair. "What are we going to do?"

"Don't worry, I already have a plan."

"And what is that? What plan do you have to stop him? To protect us!?"

With these words, Robert turns his eyes away from his wife and to his drawers, opening them wide. Evelyn watches in confusion as her husband digs through his drawers. "What are you looking for?", Mrs. Griffin asks, confused.

"The thing that will stop Octavius."

With these words, Robert turns his eyes back to his wife and holds out a Taurus 605 pistol.

Amanda gasps, closing the door behind her before running down the hallway. "A gun?", I say, confused.

Amanda nods. "They're going to kill him. At least, that's what I think."

"You think?"

"I closed the door behind me before I heard any more. All I know is that my father's life is in danger, and I don't think a gun is going to solve it?"

"If it means keeping you safe, then I don't see any other way."

"Oh, Dom, what are we going to do? We only have one, two…three weeks left until March! That's not enough time!"

"Maybe not to us, but for my father, it is. Look, I don't know what's going to happen. All I know is that he has a plan, and as his daughter, I need to have faith that he'll get through this together."

I nod. "Right."

Amanda takes my hand in mine before speaking. "Hey, let's keep this between you and me. I haven't told anyone else about this, and I'd like to keep it that way, okay?"

I nod again. "You're secret's safe with me."

With these words, I pull Amanda in for a warm embrace. "I love you, baby."

"I love you too, babe."

\#

Joana watched her son and girlfriend from the blinds as she was still on the phone. "Your daughter came by the house tonight. Just wanted to let you know."

"I know, my butler told us before she left."

"Good."

"And don't worry about the medical bills; it's all taken care of."

"Thank you, Robert."

"Of course. Is there anything else you need from me?"

With these words, Joana peeked through the blinks, looking at her son, who was now kissing his girlfriend. "Actually, there is one more thing I need."

"What is it?"

"It's my son, Dominic, remember?"

"Yes?"

Joana lets out a quick sigh before speaking. "I need you to promise me something. Promise me you'll keep him safe, safe from *him*. My cancer is really taking a toll on my body. If something happens to me and I'm not here, make sure he's safe, okay?"

The phone goes silent for a few seconds until his voice finally comes through. *"You have my word. No harm shall come to him as long as I live."*

A tear falls from Joana's eye as she watches Dominic wave her red-headed girlfriend goodbye. "Thank you, Robert."

"Anytime. It's nice to hear from you again."

Joana nods. "Yours too. Goodnight, Mr. Griffin."

Goodnight, Ms. Mitchell."

With that, Joana ends the call and puts her phone on the kitchen table, her eyes closing shut as she lets out a sigh of relief.

As for Mr. Griffin, he was not so relieved. He was afraid, more afraid than anything else in his life. His life was in danger, and he didn't have any time left. But he knew just how to fix it. Falling back into his seat, Mr. Griffin took the pistol from the table, analyzing it with his eyes.

He gripped it tightly in his hand, his eyes full of fire. "I don't care what my dreams say. I'm going to get you back, and no one is going to get in my way."

With those words, Robert puts his gun back in his drawer and locks it shut.

\#

St. Mora's police department stood proud and tall in the night, with hundreds of guards guarding the cells where thousands of prisoners stayed. Prisoners, like Octavius Mitchell.

As usual, he would be presiding at the window, staring out into the abyss of the night sky. But not tonight. Tonight, he was doing what all prisoners were doing at this time: sleeping.

Well, somewhat.

With his hands behind his neck, Octavius lay below his bunk bed, gazing up at the ceiling, contemplating in silence. Yorkshire was up, too, his eyes staring out before speaking. "Hey, York."

"Hm?"

"Can I ask you something?"

"Yeah, sure. What is it?"

Otto blinks. "Do you believe in karma?"

Yorkshire raises his head from his pillow. "Karma?"

"Yeah, like, a certain fate or destiny of some sort. Like when someone does something bad, only to be punished for it later."

Yorkshire lets Otto's words marinate within him before nodding. "Yeah. I mean, look at me; I stole someone's portrait without asking, and well, here I am, in prison. Why, what did you do to get in here?"

Otto sucks in some air. "Nothing. Nothing that was bad."

"What do you mean?"

Otto breathes heavily before speaking. "The man who put me in here saw me as a criminal, but I'm not. I'm a hero."

Yorkshire raises his brow. "Are you sure? Because a hero wouldn't be locked up in here."

"Exactly", Otto turns to his side, much to Yorkshire's confusion. "Otto, you're not like angry at his guy, right?"

Otto shuts both his eyes in silence, leaving Yorkshire in confusion. "Otto?"

There was no answer.

With a heavy sigh, Yorkshire rolled to his side, his eyes shut as he fell asleep. As for Otto, his eyes were now wide open, thinking of Yorkshire's question, which was in dire need of an answer.

And he knew exactly what it was.

Yes.

Chapter 16: Aunt Sue's Own

Two doors split wide open, revealing two nurses strolling a pregnant woman lying on her back, screaming in pain.

"We've got to get this woman to the E.R. stat; she's losing a lot of blood!"

"The baby's breached; we'll need to do a C-section!"

"No, no!", answers the woman. "Don't cut me open!"

"I'm sorry, ma'am, but there's no time! Get her on the table now!"

"No, no!"

The blonde-haired woman is lifted by the nurses before being placed on a silver table. As soon as they do, she's injected with morphine. Only, it didn't stop her screaming. "Ow, ow!"

"Doctor, she's hemorrhaging! Get the scissors!"

Soon, a pair of scissors is brought up to the blonde-haired woman. As soon as she saw this, she passed out.

A good hour passes, and the woman awakes in bed, her belly small and clean as a whistle. But the pain was still there.

Gaining consciousness, the woman turns her head back to another blonde-haired woman, who, in fact, looked a lot like her. "Mom?", she said, looking around the room. "Where's my baby?"

The woman begins to cry, much to the woman's shock. "No", she said. "No!"

"I'm so sorry, Sue."

"NOOOOOOOOOOOOOOOOOOOO!!!!!!"

#

"Gah!", said Aunt Sue, rising from her pillow, little trinkets of sweat protruding from her face.

Looking around, she finds herself in her bedroom, letting out a sigh of relief. "Just a bad dream", she breathes, wiping the sweat from her face. "Just a bad dream."

Soon, Aunt Sue was downstairs, pouring herself a hot brew of coffee, the morning sunlight peeking from her window as she raised the cup to her lips.

Sipping, Aunt Sue let out a sigh of relief as she drank her morning beverage. It was almost ten, and the sun dawned hot on St. Mora. The house was silent and empty, much to Aunt Sue's joy.

She liked it silent, as silence was peaceful.

That is until footsteps make their way down the steps and into the room. "Morning, Aunt Sue."

"Good morning, Dominic. Sleep well."

"Yeah, better than the last few nights."

"That's good", Aunt Sue takes another sip of her coffee before pulling away. "Is your mother up yet?"

"Yeah. She's in the bathroom. She said she'll need your help with bathing her."

She nodded. "Yes, I'll be up there soon."

Dominic smiled, nodding. "Okay", my head suddenly lowers before frowning. "Hey, Aunt Sue. I wanted to tell you that I'm going to the movies with Amanda today after school. Mom said it was alright, I just need your permission."

Sue nods. "Of course, go and spend time with your girlfriend. You deserve some time for yourself."

"Sweet! Thanks, Aunt Sue!", Dominic hugs my waist, his smile big and bright.

"Now, get yourself to school. Wouldn't want to miss that, now, would we?", Aunt Sue raises her brow to me, much to my understanding. "Yeah, I wouldn't."

"Good."

A loud beeping noise is heard from the outside, much to my surprise. "That's Amanda. Gotta goes, Aunt Sue!"

"See you later, Dominic!"

With that, I head out of the front door, before shutting it behind him as he heads out the front porch. Aunt Sue was about to get back to her morning cup of brewed coffee, until: "Sue Anne!"

Aunt Sue turns her head back to the stairs and smiles. "Coming, Joana!"

Sue Anne places her coffee on the kitchen table before heading upstairs.

#

Joana lay in the bathtub, the water hitting all the way up her two breasts as she lay her head back in silence. Or so she was when the small footsteps made their way into the bathroom. "Oh, you started without me?"

Joana opens her eyes wide to find Sue Anne standing over her. "Why didn't you tell me you were taking a bath, Joana?"

"I thought I'd give you a little break today."

"A break?"

"Yeah, you've been working hard taking care of me. I thought you deserved some time for yourself."

"Oh", she raises her brow. "Wait, then why did you call me up?"

Joana's eyes widen before reaching over the tub and grabbing the pink shampoo bottle in her hands. "Oh, because I need you to wash my hair", she giggled, smiling at Sue Anne.

Sue Anne scoffs. "I thought you didn't need me."

"Yeah, but this is one thing I do need you for."

Giggling, Sue Anne took the shampoo bottle from Joana's hands and smiled. "Lay your head back."

Joana did so, her eyes closed shut as the sound of the shampoo bottle popped open. Before she knew it, the pink liquid rubbed on her head, quickly turning into bubbles the more she did. "Hm, strawberry", Joana mutters.

"What was that, Joana?"

"The shampoo, it smells like strawberries."

Sue laughs, nodding. "Yeah, it does."

Joana shifts her eyes to the dark marks under Sue Anne's eyes, much to her concern. "You tired?"

"What?"

"You have dark marks under your eyes."

Sue's eyes widen before the realization kicks in. "Oh, these? They must've come from last night. I was tossing and turning through most of it."

"You were? Why?"

"Oh, it was nothing, really. Just a restless night is all."

Joana raises a brow. "Are you sure?"

She nodded. "Yeah."

"Sue, you know you can talk to me, right?"

"Yeah, I know. I'm fine, Joana. Really?"

Joana sighs softly before nodding. "Okay. I just wanted to kn-oh!"

"Joana!", Sue said, holding Joana steady as she gripped the edge of the bathtub with her head lowered as she cupped her mouth.

Without a second thought, Sue grabbed a bucket sitting next to the toilet and brought it right over to Joana. "Go on, let it out."

Joana gripped the bucket tight before vomiting into the bucket, gagging as she did. "Ugh!"

As soon as she was finished, Joana pulled away from the bucket and leaned her head back against the bathtub, breathing heavily. "Better?", Sue asks, making Joana nod. "Yeah. I'm sorry, Sue."

"Don't be sorry. It's not your fault."

"I hate having you see me like this."

"Joana, I don't care what you look like. I love you just the way you are."

Mom sniffs, nodding. "I know. I just wish this was over."

Sue nods. "It will, Joana", she takes his hand in hers, gripping it tight. "It will."

Mom turns back to Sue and smiles. "I guess I need you more than I thought, huh?"

Sue laughs. "Are you kidding? I'm the one who needs you. Who else could change a diaper like you?"

Joana laughs before nodding. "Yeah, I guess you're right."

"I couldn't tie my shoes without you, Joana. Believe me, I need *you* way more than you need me."

Joana smiles happily. "Thank you, Sue."

"You're welcome, Joana."

Joana dug back in her hair, which was still full of soapy suds. "Almost forgot. Can you rinse my hair out for me?"

Sue nods. "Of course. Anything for you, Joana."

\#

As soon as Sue finished with Joana's hair, the two women decided they'd go to the park. Sue slipped Joana into a yellow sundress, all while wearing a scarf that matched her dress. As for Sue, she wore a pair of skinny jeans and a white blouse with red floral patterns.

As soon as she got her purse, Sue and Joana were out the door, into the car, and walking down a trail in St. Mora National Park. "Isn't this a great place"

"It is beautiful. So lively. I wish I could bring Dominic here."

"Dominic's at school, remember?"

"Yeah, I just wished he was here with us. Instead of school. We haven't had much time to spend together lately."

"I know. Don't worry, Joana, I'm sure your two will have your day."

"I hope so."

"Until then", Sue takes Joana's hand in hers, causing her to turn back. "You'll always have me."

She smiles, nodding happily. "Yeah, I do."

I smiled back, happier than I had ever done before. Not because I was smiling but because *she* was smiling. I loved to see her smile; something about it just brightened the room. This was the first time in months since I'd seen her smile, and I didn't want it to end.

"You want to sit down?", I ask.

"Yeah, I'm starting to get tired."

I nod. "Okay"

Joana and I made our way to a small green bench to a nearby streetlight in the distance. It took a few steps, but eventually, we made it, and for someone with cancer, it was victorious. "Here we are", I say as Joana sits down on the bench, her breath heavy.

I put my hand on her shoulder, counting her breaths. "Are you okay?"

She turns to me and nods. "Yeah…", she huffs. "I just…need…to catch my breath."

I nod, letting her breathe. "Just take it slow."

She gives me another nod before gazing up at the sky. "It's so beautiful today."

"Yeah, it is", I said, looking at her. "I couldn't imagine a more beautiful one."

A flash of light was made, capturing a photo of the two women holding hands. Far in the distance, a young boy with glasses looked through a camera lens.

Sue makes one final nod before suddenly pausing. Not too far in the distance, Sue notices a woman, a mother, strolling down the trail with a baby carriage. This causes her to freeze as a shocking memory surge back to her mind.

"Sue?", answers Joana concerned.

Sue starts to hyperventilate, causing her to fall back on a nearby bench. "Sue, what is it?"

Sue was now having a panic attack as traumatic visions started to come up.

Sue sitting in a chair.

Sue crying.

Baby carriage sitting before her.

Only, there was no baby inside.

There was no baby at all.

"No, no, no!", Sue said, shaking her head.

"Sue! Sue, calm down!"

"No, no! It's happening, it's happening again!"

"What's happening!?"

Sue was now sobbing, her head low as she exhaled. "Sue, what's going on?"

"Everything alright here?"

Joana and Sue both turn their heads to find not just a woman but *the* woman standing before both, along with her baby carriage. Sue lets out a shocked gasp, much to Joana's concern. "Sue, what is it?"

Sue stands up from the bench, her eyes looking directly at the young mother before turning back to Joana. "We need to go."

"Wait, what?"

"Now!"

Without a second thought, Sue takes Joana by the hand before dragging her off, leaving the young woman in confusion.

#

The drive home was awkward. Sue didn't speak to Joana the entire way; even when she asked questions, I didn't say a word.

My lips were sealed.

That is, until the both of us walked through the front door, that Joana finally decided to speak up. "Okay, what's going on with you?"

"What?"

"You heard me? What's going on?"

Sue shakes her head. "I don't want to talk about it."

"No, we *are* going to talk about this!"

"Just leave it alone, Joana, okay!?"

"No! You've been acting weird all day. You're not going anywhere until you tell me what's wrong with you."

Hearing this, Sue lets out a huge sigh before speaking. "I had a dream, a nightmare the night before."

Joana raises a brow. "A nightmare? About what?"

Sue lets out a slow, heavy breath before speaking. "It was about a baby", I turned back to her, tears rolling down my face. "My baby"

"I don't understand, Sue."

Sue sighs before turning around to Joana. "Do you remember that night when you and I were in the car? That night when we were looking for a job?"

"You mean that night when you asked me to move in with you?"

"Do you remember what we talked about?"

"About the jobs?"

"No, about the miscarriage."

Joana's eyes widened in shock. "Yes, I remember now. You were sixteen; you were young."

"Yes", she sniffs before turning back to Joana. "I remember it like it was yesterday. Seeing that young woman, that *mother*, with her baby made me feel…helpless."

"Helpless?"

Sue sighed, falling back into the chair next to the kitchen table, her fingers dug into her hair as she did. "I see all these mothers out there, with children warm in their beds, and I…", Sue sighs, shaking her head. "All I had was an empty crib.

Hearing this, Joana lowers her head in sadness. "Oh, Sue. Why didn't you tell me about this?"

"I didn't know how. I was devastated. I guess I'm still trying to recover from my trauma."

Joana nods. "We all are, Sue", Joana rests her hand on Sue's shoulder. "You're not the only one."

Sue nods. "I know. I just didn't want you worried."

Joana scoffs before pulling me in for a loving embrace. "I'm always going to worry about you, girl."

Sue wrapped her arms around Joana, touching the cotton fabric of her dress. "I'm going to head upstairs. Take a nap."

Joana nods quickly. "Okay."

I nodded before rising from the table; my eyes turned away from Joana as I approached the steps. But as soon as my foot touched the front of the steps, her eyes were full of sadness. She was thinking of her, of Joana.

Her Joana.

Or so she thought when her long-time best friend brought some unprecedented news to her:

With that, Dominic took his eyes off Joana and to the staircase, his frown present.

#

I entered my room, my eyes full of tears as I shut my door. I quickly passed my bed, heading right for the curtains, which I quickly closed shut, engulfing my room with darkness. Wiping my tears, I lay back on my bed in sadness, sobbing quietly into my pillow.

I do this for a good minute before sleep takes over me. That's when I began to dream:

Sue Anne ran through the hallway of the hospital, her sneakers sliding against the polished floor as she ran. It isn't long before she turns to the left and finds a brown door with a number written on the front:

221.

With her hair a mess and her posture straightened, Sue Anne sucks in some air and twists the doorknob. As soon as she enters the room, a loud whine is heard, causing Sue's head to rise. To her surprise, she finds her best friend, Joana, lying in a bed with her three-day-old son cradled in her arms as he sobbed.

"No, no, no. Shh. Don't cry, baby."

"Joana?"

Joana looked up from the baby and at me, standing at the window. "Sue!", she said happily. "Come in, come in!"

Sue shuts the door behind her, walking in. "Is that the baby?"

"Mm-hm. My son."

Sue kneels next to Joana, her smile bright as she peers down at the baby. "It's a boy, isn't it?"

"Yeah."

"I could tell he has Otto's eyes. Where is he?"

"Octavius went downstairs to get coffee. He'll be back soon."

Sue smiles happily at the baby, one that Joana quickly takes notice of. "You want to hold him?"

Sue pauses. "What?"

"Don't be scared. Go on, take him."

"Are you sure? I'm scared I might drop him."

"Trust me, Sue. You won't."

With that, Sue lets out a huge sigh before nodding. "Okay."

Joana smiled happily as she brought Joana's baby in her arms, whose cries quickly turned to quiet cooing as she did. "Ha! Did you see that? He stopped."

Joana nods. "He sure did. Looks like you're a natural."

Sue rocks the baby boy, whose hazel-brown eyes smile up at her. "Yeah, guess I am."

#

"Sue? Sue, wake up!"

I rose from my pillow, where a line of drool protruded from it, much to Joana's disgust. "Um, Sue, you got a little…", Joana points to the bottom of his lip, which I quickly notice before wiping my mouth. "Ugh, sorry, Joana. I must've dozed off."

Joana laughs. "You sure did. You were snoring loudly."

"I was snoring?"

"Yeah, I could hear you all the way upstairs."

I scratched the back of my neck. "Guess I woke up the whole house, huh?"

"Yep."

I blink before looking down at the rectangle object in Dominic's hands. "What Cha got there?", I asked, curious.

Joana looked down at his object. "Oh, this? This is something I got from the shelf."

"Oh, really? Can I see?"

Joana came over to my bed, sitting right next to me as she handed the object to me. "It's a photo of us. Mom, me, and you."

"Oh, wow", I chuckle. "Is Dominic wearing bunny slippers?"

"Uh-huh. I thought it looked cute on you, especially when I was born on Easter."

I nod. "Yeah, that sounds like you."

Joana laughs in reply. "Yeah", Dominic lowers his eyes to the floor before speaking. "Um, Sue? Is everything okay with you?"

"What do you mean? Everything's fine; how can everything not be?"

Joana sighs, taking her hand in mine, much to my shock. "Sue, you know you can talk to me about anything, right?"

#

A bowl of salad, mashed potatoes, and roasted chicken were lying on the kitchen table. I was the first to shove a spoonful of potatoes into my mouth. "Mm, these potatoes sure are good, Joana."

"Yeah, no one can make mashed potatoes like you, Mom."

"I'm glad you guys like it."

I smile, looking around at Dominic and Joana, their smiles big and wide as they laugh, enjoying themselves.

Most people would see a son and mother, but to me, it was a family, *my* family.

With that in mind, I held my cup and raised it in the air. "A toast, guys."

Dominic and Joana both turn to me, their smiles present, before raising their cups as well. "A toast to family", I said.

Dominic smiles, nodding his head. "A toast to friends."

"To good health", said Mom proudly. "To life."

"To happiness!"

"To joy!"

"To a long life!"

"To fighters!"

"But more importantly: to love."

Dominic and Joana nod before the three of us raise our glass cups together. "To love!"

With that, the three of us clink our glass cups together in unison before drinking for our happy, healthy family.

#

Chapter 17: A Mother's Love

"And he all lived happily ever after. The End."

A young woman shuts the book of The Hungry Caterpillar, with a young boy lying beside her in bed. "That ends The Hungry Caterpillar for today, Andy"

"Read me another one, Mommy."

"Not tonight, baby. You must leave with Daddy, remember?"

"Why can't I just stay with you? Why can't we all just stay together?"

"Oh, honey", she kisses him on the forehead. "You know why we can't do that."

Within seconds, the sound of footsteps made their way into the bedroom they lived in, and that's where a young black man made his way into the room, a happy smile on his face. "Andy, it's time to leave. You ready to go?"

Andy shook his head. "No"

"Well, you're leaving now. Come on, get your things."

Andy turned his eyes back to his mother, giving off quite a sad look that his mother did not enjoy. "Now, don't give me that look, Andy. You heard your father."

"No, I want to stay with you, Mommy", Andy nuzzles into his mother, his arms wrapping around him.

She hugs him back, kissing his forehead before finally letting go. "I'll see you tomorrow, baby"

"Bye, Mommy"

"Bye, Andy"

#

"Ms. Wilkins, Ms. Wilkins!"

Ms. Wilkins's eyes shot wide open to a young boy with a lightning rod in his head who was looking down at him. "Are you alright?"

Ms. Wilkins blinks, wiping the sweat from her brow. "Yes, what is it? What's wrong?"

"That's what I wanted to ask you. You were talking in your sleep."

"I was?", Amari said with a raised brow. "What was I saying?"

"Not much, just weird murmuring. Something like that. Were you having a nightmare?"

"Yes, but I don't want to talk about it"

"Are you sure?"

Ms. Wilkins shakes her head. "Yes, I'm fine."

#

After three hours, the sun finally rose, and Amari was up and ready for school. He hopped into a shirt and jeans before strapping his backpack on his back and heading out the door. "Alright, Ms. Wilkins. I'm leaving; see you after school!"

"Okay, see ya!"

With that, Amari closes the door, leaving Ms. Wilkins alone with his thoughts. "Have a good day."

Summit High's bell rang loudly as hundreds of students made their way up the steps and into the hallways. Amari was the last to enter the school, his head held high as he walked through. Today was a special day for Amari, as today was none other than his birthday!

That's right, this young boy was now a young man. He was eighteen, officially a grown-up, which meant no longer having people boss him around. From now on, he was going to get the one thing he so rightfully deserved: respect.

With that in mind, Amari made his way to the lockers.

His lockers.

Ha-ha.

Amari twisted the lock, unpinning his combination before the locker opened wide. As soon as it did, Amari retrieved his school textbooks, slipping them into his backpack. Zipping it up, Amari shut his locker, but before he knew it, something hit him from behind. "Hey!", he snapped.

"Oh, sorry, man! I was…Amari?", said the curly-haired boy.

"Dominic?"

The two boys looked at each other in confusion. "Um, hey."

"Hey, haven't seen you in a while."

"Yeah, I've been…busy."

"Busy, with what?"

Dominic scoffs. "None of your business!"

"I was just asking."

"I don't need to tell you, my business! Gosh, I don't even know why I'm talking to you!"

Amari grunts. "Why are you being like this? I didn't say or hurt you in any way!"

"That's not the point; the point is that I have class, and you're in my way! Now, move!"

With a quick nudge, Dominic walks down the hall, leaving me alone with my thoughts.

My angry thoughts.

"No", I say, shaking my head. "No, I'm not going to let this ruin my special day", Amari turned his head back, but before he could leave, he turned, his eyes full of sadness. "You at least could've wished me happy birthday. You always remembered, even on a bad day."

With that, Amari sighed heavily and headed out of the hallway for the first period. Yet, little did he know, a mysterious figure in black walks from behind the lockers, watching Amari walks off in the distance alone.

She took takes her hoodie off her head, presenting a devilish grin. "My plan is setting in motion."

#

School was boring, as usual, but that didn't stop me from having the best birthday ever. During the first period, my class was given a substitute, and she was a fun one because, unlike my moody teacher, Mrs. Tucker, this substitute thought we should watch a movie instead of work.

Score!

But the day only got better as they served my favorite meal at lunch: pizza.

But not just any pizza, *pineapple* pizza!

I stuffed my face right away, the gooey cheese sticking to my fingers. That is until I licked it off.

It was the best meal I ever had. Then again, having some wings with hot sauce would be much better.

And a soda.

A Coke, maybe.

But this works fine, for my birthday that is.

Soon, my last class of the day arrived, and I found myself in Gym class. I was excited to go to this class as today was a special day. We were having a tournament, a volleyball tournament.

One by one, they smacked me in the face, causing me to fall flat on my face. It wasn't long before the coach blew the whistle, the volleyballs stopped hitting me, and I was still on the floor, dead.

"On your feet, Jenkins!"

With this command, I raised my body, but a shadow approached me before I could get back on my feet. "Need a hand there, man?", I turned my head to find a hand reaching out to me.

As soon as I took it, I found the curly-haired boy in a yellow uniform. "Dominic!?"

Dominic blinks. "Wait, Amari!?"

The two of us peered at the same yellow shirts we were wearing. "You're on the yellow side? You're on my team?"

Dominic stretches the fabric of his yellow t-shirt and shorts. "I guess I am", Dominic slaps his hand away from me. "So much for helping you."

I grunt, rising from the floor back on my feet. "Well, looks like we'll be teammates for today."

"Trust me when I say, "We're not teammates.""

Once again, Dominic walks away from me, leaving me by myself.

At that very moment, my birthday went from good to bad.

#

We were surrounded.

Standing before us was a gang of male players in red all lined up before the yellow team, one in which, Dominic and I stood, yet in between male players. They looked down at the set of red dodgeballs standing before us.

"Ready, boys!", said Coach Wilson, making the boys crouch down to the dodgeballs.

"Ready? Now!"

With these words, Coach Wilson blew his whistle, and the boys grabbed their dodgeballs and stepped right back before attacking. Within seconds, several dodgeballs flew past the entire gymnasium. Several of the yellow team were hit, along with the other team, causing them to hit the ground hard with a thud.

As for Dominic and I, we were right on our feet, dodging the balls with every bit of our bodies. We were fast, fast enough for the smart and cunning red players. All we had to do now was keep it up, and we would-

"Shit!", I said as a dodgeball flew past me, inches from my side, before quickly dodging away.

"Ah!", Dominic said, jumping past the dodgeball. "Watch it, man!"

"Sorry, man. Nothing personal!", said the young white boy throwing the dodgeball to Dominic. "Ah!", I said as I accidentally bumped into Dominic, causing the both of us to turn back in shock. "Oh, sorry, Dominic, I-"

"Watch where you're going!"

"Hey, I'm just trying to-"

"Get out of the way!", Dominic said, pushing me past two dodgeballs, instantly hitting him in the jaw. "Dominic!", I say, but as soon as I do, another dodgeball hits my jaw, too, causing drool to fall out of my mouth before collapsing to the floor.

With that, Coach Wilson blows his whistle, ending the fight. "That's Round 1, Red team wins!"

"What?!", shouts the both of us.

The players of the red team come together to high-five each other, much to Amari and Dominic's annoyance. "Look what you did!", Dominic shouted, causing Amari to turn back to him. "What are you talking about?"

Dominic grunts before turning away from Amari, much to his annoyance. "What's your problem!"

"Leave me alone!"

"No! I'm sick of this, Dom! Why do you keep treating me like a piece of shit!"

"You say that like you don't remember, you know, with Ms. Wilkins?"

"Is this what this is about? Ms. Wilkins!"

"It's what it's always been about! From the moment I saw you today, I'm reminded of how much you hurt me!"

Amari grunts, rolling his eyes. "Get over it already, Dom. I swear, for someone so whiney, you're prone to hold a grudge!"

"I have a right to hold one!"

"Look, I don't care how much you hate me; you and I are on the same side now! So, you need to put your differences aside and work with me!"

"Bullshit! I'll never work with you again! Not after the way you treated me!"

Amari scoffs. "You don't have a choice! If you want a good grade, then you must!"

"I'd rather hate you than get a good grade!"

Dominic walked off in silence with these words, leaving Amari alone in anger. "I'm starting to think who's the mature one here."

With his fists clenched, Amari turns his head and walks off.

#

Meanwhile, Ms. Wilkins was at her house, vacuuming the carpet in her bedroom. She had meant to do it earlier, but she got distracted by it this morning.

Before she knew it, it was the afternoon. So, she decided to take manners into her own hands and do it. After all, it was now or later.

Ms. Wilkins had continued to vacuum when, suddenly, she hit the side of her nightstand, causing a photo to fall, hitting the white carpet floor.

"Oh no", Ms. Wilkins said as she retrieved the photo from the floor, facing it with her eyes.

That's when she found a photo of a smiling boy. Ms. Wilkins smiles at this young boy, her fingers tracing through his hair. It wasn't long before Ms. Wilkins found herself sitting on the bed, getting lost in the young boy's eyes.

She was distracted again, but all for the right reasons.

"Oh, Andy", she said. "If only I could hold you one last time."

#

"Denise, I can't do this. Not anymore", said a young, white man sitting across his wife, her eyes full of tears. "Lawrence, please. Don't do this."

"I'm sorry, Denise, but my mind is made up. Andy is moving to New York with me."

"No!"

"Yes!"

"NO!"

"Mommy?"

Denise and Lawrence turn to find a little boy staring up at his parents, his eyes full of concern. "What's going on?"

Wiping her eyes, Denise rose from the table and made her way to her son. "Everything's just fine, Andy."

"No, it's not", said Lawrence, rising from his seat. "Andy, get your things, we're leaving now."

"What? No."

"Now, Andy!"

"Daddy, I don't want to leave, Mommy!"

"It's alright, Andy. You don't have to leave if you don't want t-Andy!"

To Denise's surprise, Andy was taken from her grasp and into Lawrence's arms. "Andy!"

"Mommy!", Andy said as he was carried out of the front door of his house. "Mommy!"

"No, Andy!"

"Mommy! Mommy! Mommy!"

Ms. Wilkins quickly snapped out of her little daydream as she was hurt by her own thoughts taking over her mind, causing her to start sobbing. As for the photo, she hugged it to her chest, as if she was holding her little boy once more.

#

Amari was in the locker room putting on deodorant as he masked the sweaty part of his pits. It wasn't long before he put the deodorant back in his locker, but as soon as he closed it shut, he saw Dominic leaning against the locker, his arms folded as he looked at me.

"I don't suppose you're here to apologize."

Dominic shakes his head. "No, I'm here to say you're right."

Amari blinks. "W-what?"

"I may still be mad at you, but we are still a team, and we need to work together if we want to win this game. So, I guess what I'm asking you is…", Dominic reaches his hand out to me. "Truce, for now?"

Amari looked down at Dominic's hand, his brow raised before grabbing it. With that, the two boys shake hands, furthering their agreement. "Truce."

With that, the boys pull away, leaving them in an awkward silence. "So, what do we do now?", Dominic asks.

Amari smirks, turning away from Dominic. "Now, we win."

Soon, Amari and I headed out of the locker room and into the gym, our players sitting on the bench as they awaited us. As for the red team, they were scolding us with pleasure, ready to take us down one by one. Or so they think.

"What are we going to do, Amari? I mean, do you know the last time we fought these guys?"

I nod. "Of course, I do. Why else are we playing against them? It's because they think we're weak, but we're not."

Dominic lowers his head to the floor. "They're bullies, that's what they are. Always trying to put us down."

"That's what bullies do best. But not this time."

Dominic nods. "Right."

Back in the present, Dominic and I stood out in the gym, our eyes hungry for justice as we knelt before the red team, eight red dodgeballs sitting before us. "Ready, boys!?", said Coach Wilson, making the two teams kneel even further down the balls.

"Ready, now!", Coach Wilson blows his whistle hard, causing the yellow and red team to grab their balls from the floor and into the air.

Within seconds, four of the red players were smacked in the face, causing them to fall right on the floor with a thud. As soon as they were, Coach blew his whistle, and the boys were back on the bench.

"Woo-hoo!", said Dominic and I, our hands close to a high-five before quickly pulling away. "Um, nice throw."

"Yeah, thanks."

With that, a few more dodgeballs came our way, hitting two yellow players and hitting the floor with a thud. This causes Coach Wilson to stand over the two boys.

Coach Wilson blows his whistle. "You're out!"

The blonde-haired boy rubs the edge of his face, as he heads to the bench, along with several other of his red teammates.

"And then there were two", Dominic said, turning back to me, my nod visible. "Yep-ah!", Amari said, falling to the floor as a dodgeball knocked him right in the forehead, causing him to collapse to the floor.

Coach Wilson's whistle was blown, causing Amari's eyes to shoot open.

"You're out, yellow team wins!"

"Huh? Wha-what?!"

"Amari!", said Dominic, peering down at him. "Get up", he said, reaching his hand out.

Without hesitation, Amari takes Dominic's hand in his before pulling him up. Yet, as soon as their eyes met, they pulled away. "Uh, thanks."

Dominic nods. "You should be we just won."

"Wait, what? We did?"

"Yeah."

Amari blinks. "But there was only one person left. Who knocked him out?"

Dominic doesn't say anything, except walk away from Amari, much to his confusion. "Dominic?"

Dominic continues to walk away, not once answering.

#

Ms. Wilkins sat at her coffee table, sipping a cup of chamomile tea. She loved chamomile tea as it eased her nerves, especially after her little "water sprinkles". She sniffed, wiping her eyes as she reminisced about the moment when her whole world was taken from her.

Her son.

Her Andy.

As for her husband, her *ex-husband,* Lawrence, she didn't give two shots about it. He was the reason for their separation, the reason why their son died. There was never a day where she didn't think about him, his smile, his hazel brown eyes, not to mention his smile that lit up the whole room.

He was an angel, and Lawrence was the devil.

One she couldn't escape.

#

"No, no, no!", Denise said, slamming on the brakes.

Denise looked up at the streetlights, one being in red. "Come on, come on!", she beeps her horn, trying her best to signal the red BMW sitting in front of her.

In front of it was the black SUV sitting in the front, the one that Lawrence and her son were in.

She beeps again, this time slipping her forehead out of the window. "Lawrence, give him back now!"

Suddenly, the door to Lawrence's window slips down, revealing his middle finger thrown in the air.

Denise scoffs at this, her blood boiling at the sight of her husband's immature behavior. Before she knew it, the light turned green, and Lawrence rushed right out into the intersection.

Denise was about to do the same, but before she could, a car slammed in with the black SUV, throwing it completely off course before a few more cars slammed into it from the side.

"ANDY!", Denise screamed, getting out of the car.

A small hand reaches out from the car, making Denise's eyes widen.

"Andy!?", she said, kneeling before the vehicle where a little boy, cut and bruised, popped his head from the broken glass window. "M-mommy", he speaks before hitting his head on the ground.

Denise pulls his son from the rubble and into her arms, holding him tightly.

"It's alright, baby", she said. "It's going to be alright."

"Mommy", Andy, with a half-smile from his bleeding forehead, brings his hand to his mother's cheek. She quickly takes it, a tear rolling from her eyes.

Andy smiles one final time before both his eyes slowly close shut, scaring Denise. "Andy?", she said, shaking him. "Andy?"

She shakes him again, but Andy does not respond. In fact, his chest stopped heaving the moment his eyes closed shut. "Andy!", Denise cried. "Andy, wake up!"

Andy didn't, for he was as frozen as a statue. With despair in her heart, Denise pulled her son in for a hug and cried to the sky, rocking him back and forth for the last time.

"NOOOO!!!!!"

Soon, Ms. Wilkins was back in the present, her hands cuffing her eyes as she sobbed once more. Only, this time, she was truly devastated.

Her cup of tea that was once on the table, was now on her hardwood floor, broken into pieces. If this didn't tell you she was upset, nothing did.

Nothing.

#

Dominic was in the gym, sitting on the bench, back in his clothes, as he picked his backpack up. He dug into his backpack, and that's when he found it. Raising his hand up, he finds a metal key chain. "Huh?", he said, holding the key chain out before his hazel-brown eyes. "What's this doing here?"

"You took it."

"What?"

"My keychain! You took my keychain?"

"What? Amari, I didn't take your-", Dominic's words were quickly cut off as the keychain was snatched from his hands and back into Amari's, his fiery eyes peering down at him. "

"Dominic?"

Pausing, Dominic turns his head back to find me, back in my normal school clothes, standing before him, much to Dominic's annoyance. "Go away."

"No, I'm sick of this. I'm sick of you pushing me away."

"Look, I played the game with you, and we won. Now, we can finally go our separate ways."

"You're not going anywhere until I speak my mind."

"There is nothing I need to hear from you."

"Did you beat the red team for me?"

Dominic pauses, turning his head back. "What?"

"You heard me. Did you, or did you not, beat the red team?"

Dominic sighs. "Yes, Amari. I won for you guys, okay? I saw the guy smack you in the face with the dodgeball, and I got him back, but not for you. It was for the team."

"I'm a part of the team."

"Not in my book."

Amari grunts. "Dammit, Dom! Can't even admit you did it for me!"

"I didn't do it for you! Why do you even care about this?"

"Because you've been avoiding me ever since I hooked up with Denise!"

"Exactly, you got with him and left me high and dry all because I didn't like her!"

"I just wanted you to forgive her."

"Just because you forgave him for what he did doesn't mean I have to! You should've been able to understand that, especially when you knew what he did to me. But no, instead, you decided to be selfish and ungrateful. You left me high and dry like I never even existed. That's why I'm angry, that's why I hate Denise, that's why I hate *you*!"

Amari's eyes widen in shock. "You…hate me?"

"Yes", Dominic folds his arms. "Now, can I go home now and be with people who aren't heartless jerks?"

I frown, my fist clenching. "You asshole! I hope I never see you again!"

"I hope I never see you again for the rest of my *life*! I'll be just fine without you! So, if you need someone to be there for you, don't bet your luck because I won't be there!"

With these words, I clenched both my fists and opened my mouth, only there were no words coming from it. With a deep sigh, I watch Dominic leave the gym, disappearing into the evening light.

Yet, far in the distance, Denise watched with anticipation as the two boys parted ways. "

#

Amari walked the whole way home sad. As good as the game went with Dominic, he for some reason, felt, in a way, defeated. He thought all about what he said, his words echoing in my head.

Selfish.

Ungrateful.

Even the most painful words hurt me more than anything.

I hate you.

Sad, Amari opened the front door of Ms. Wilkins's home and entered it without hesitation. "Ms. Wilkins, I'm home!"

Closing the door, Amari walks further into the room, throwing my backpack on the couch. "Ms. Wilkins?"

"I'm in the kitchen, Amari."

Amari made his way through the living room and into the kitchen. To his surprise, he finds Ms. Wilkins standing before a stove, cooking.

Amari approached Ms. Wilkins and found a pot of what looked to be tomato soup bubbling.

"That looks good", he said.

"Yes", Ms. Wilkins gives Amari a small smile before returning to her pot. "It's tomato beef stew."

"Beef stew? I never tried that before?"

"Go sit yourself at the table, I'll make you some."

"Okay."

Without a second thought, Amari went straight to the table and pulled up a chair to sit.

As for Ms. Wilkins, she pours two bowls of beef stew and brings it to the table.

Before they knew it, they were both sitting at the table with bowls of soup in their eyes. Amari looked down at the bits of beef sitting in the sea of tomato cream sauce.

"Don't be shy", said Ms. Wilkins picking up a spoon. "Go ahead, try it."

With these words, Amari picks up his spoon and scoops up the tomato beef stew into his mouth. As soon as he does, his eyes widen. "Oh my god", he said, surprised. "This is really good."

Ms. Wilkins smiles. "I knew you'd like it."

"This has got to be the best thing I've ever eaten, like, in a long time."

"Andy said the same thing."

Amari paused. "Who's Andy?"

Ms. Wilkins stirs her bowl of soup before gazing up at Amari. "He was my son."

"Really?"

"Mm-hm."

"You never told me you had a son before."

"That's because I never talked about it before."

"Before?"

She sighs, dropping her spoon in her bowl. "My son was taken from me a few years ago. My husband and I were divorced, and he got full custody. I haven't seen my son since then. I was heartbroken."

Amari's demeanor changes from fine to shocked. "I'm so sorry. I had no idea."

"It's not your fault."

"Not yours either!", Amari reached his hand across the table, grabbing Ms. Wilkins's hand. "I'm so sorry that happened to you. All mothers deserve a child."

Those words give Ms. Wilkins an instant thought, giving her the notion to shake her head. "Not all mothers."

Amari lowered his head, indicating he knew exactly what she was talking about. "I don't like to talk about that."

"You should. It would make you feel better."

Amari sighed, looking at Ms. Wilkins. "I just never had a mother. One that was, you know, loving, nurturing. All I had was…favoritism. It really sucked."

With these words, Ms. Wilkins rises from the table and brings Amari in for a hug. Amari was shocked at first but quickly wrapped her arms around her.

"What was that for?", he said, pulling away.

Ms. Wilkins smiles. "I just thought you could use one."

"A hug?"

"No, a mother."

Amari's eyes go big and round at those words. "You?"

She nodded, revealing a toothy grin. "I may have lost one son, but I found another. I found you, A.J. So, what do you say?"

With a happy smile, Amari pulled Ms. Wilkins in for a hug, smiling happily as he did. "Of course."

#

As for Dominic, he was in his room, lying in his bed. Sitting on his nightstand, there was a photo, *the* photo of Amari and Dominic making silly faces in the photo.

After all these months, Dominic kept the picture of them. As angry as he was with him, a part of him, still cared for him. Still thought about him.

With a deep sigh, Dominic put the photo back on his nightstand, but before he could go to sleep, he gave the picture one final look before speaking. "Goodnight, Amari", he said with a sad sigh.

With that, Dominic shuts off his lamp, leaving everything in darkness.

Chapter 18: The Checkup

It was a beautiful morning in St. Mora, and the sun was shining bright in the sky. The Mitchell home stood big and tall in the morning light, especially for the family in the house. With my head under a pillow, I was dead asleep until my alarm clock hit seven, causing it to go off. My head popped up from the pillow in shock, my eyes full of sleep crust. "Wha-what!?"

Turning my head, I found my alarm clock still going off, ringing horrendously loud through my eardrums. Irritated, I raised my fist and slammed the snooze button. Then, I fell back on my pillow, letting out a sigh of relief. But just as I go back to sleep, I hear a loud scream, causing my eyes to widen in shock. "What the hell?", I said hopping out of bed.

Opening my door, I stopped dead in the hallway, and that's when I heard a familiar voice again. "Mom?"

I raced down the hallway, my heart pounding, before making my way into the kitchen. To my surprise, I found Mom and Sue Anne, her eyes lit with joy as she peered down at a pancake with three lit candles.

"What's going on here?"

Joana and Sue Anne turned their heads back to find Aunt Sue standing before the table. "Dominic, you're just in time", Joana said with a smile.

I rubbed my eyes in confusion. "Time for what?"

"For Sue Anne's birthday", said Joana.

She blinked. "It's Sue Anne's birthday, again?"

"Yeah", Joana giggles. "What? Did you forget?"

She blinked. "I guess I did."

"I already lit the candles, Dominic. But now that you're awake, we can get started."

"With what?", Sue asked.

"The song, Sue."

"Oh, yeah! Sorry, I'm still not all the way awake", I say, walking over to them. "Wait, how old are you, now?"

"Forty-two."

"Forty-two? Wow."

Sue's face fell flat. "What is it?"

"You just look so beautiful; you look at such a young age."

Joana smiles, her face turned away as she blushes. "Aw, thank you, Sue."

Joana wrapped both her arms around Sue, much to my joy as I watched. That is, before looking at the cake. "Make a wish, Aunt Sue."

With these words, Sue turned back to the three lit candles before sucking up some air and blowing them right out. Within seconds, Mom and I clap cheerfully for Joana before hugging her. "We love you, Aunt Sue."

"I love you too, Dominic."

I kissed Mom on the cheek before pulling away. "Alright, let me get the candles out of here. Um, Sue, can you get the forks."

"Yeah, sure."

Joana watches with happiness as she watches Sue Anne leave her at the table before turning back to the cake. She was happy, happier than she'd been several months ago. As bad as this cancer had been, she was lucky enough to have her son and best friend by her side. Not a lot of people could say that, but for Joana, she could. She was thankful, and she would continue to do so until the very end.

"Hey, Aunt Sue. I know this might come as a shock, but Dominic and I were wondering if you wanted a birthday party?", I say, placing three forks back on the table.

"A party?"

"Yeah, Dominic thought it would be nice."

"He did?"

"I did", I say, standing behind Joana with plates. "We thought you would want one, you know, since the…cancer. Have something to look to."

Sue smiles, taking my and Mom's hands. "Guys, you know how I feel about parties, especially when they're about me. For today, I don't really want one. I have everything I need right here."

I nod, my head lowering. "Okay, Aunt Sue."

"Hey, don't be upset. I just think celebrating should wait, you know, until the time is right, okay?", she said, turning back to Mom, who nodded quickly. "We understand, Mom."

I nod. "Yeah, we understand."

"Good", she said, nodding. "I'm glad we're in agreement."

With these words, the telephone rang, causing Dominic and Sue to stop their business. As for Joana, she stared right at the telephone. "Who could that be?", said Dominic.

"I don't know", Sue Anne said, walking towards the telephone, taking it from the handle and to her ear. "Hello?"

Sue and Joana watched as my head lowered as she listened to the strange voice coming from the phone. "Oh, really? Today?", I turn back to Joana, her eyes full of fear, before turning back to the phone, nodding. "Okay, she'll be there. Thank you. Goodbye."

With these words, Sue put the phone back on the handle before turning back to Dominic and Joana. "Who was that, Sue?"

Sue rubs her hands together. "That was Dr. Vincent. They wanted to know if you could come in for your P.E.T. scan."

Joana blinks. "P.E.T. scan?"

Sue nods. "Yeah, you know, with your cancer?"

Joana's eyes widened a bit before she lowered her head a bit. "It's okay, Mom", Dominic said, placing a hand on her shoulder and making Joana nod. "I know, baby. It's just I haven't had a checkup since…the day I found out I had cancer."

"We know", Sue said, walking towards Joana and Dominic. "They just want to see if everything's ticking."

She nodded. "Yeah, I know."

Sue smiles before speaking. "I'll go run your bath water."

With that, Dominic nods to Sue before heading out of the kitchen and down the hallway, leaving Dominic and Joana to themselves.

\#

Amari lay in bed, his eyes closed shut as he did. That is, until his head jerks, causing both his eyes to slowly slip open. His eyes were blurry, so he couldn't see what was going on around him. That is, until he rubbed his eyes.

With his blurriness gone, he saw Ms. Wilkins, his newly found mother, sitting on the edge of the bed with a set of balloons, her smile bright and lively. Rubbing his eyes, Amari sat up from his bed. "Ms. Wilkins?"

"Happy Birthday, Amari."

Amari smiles, looking up at the helium-filled airbags floating above him. "You got me balloons?"

"Of course, I did. It's your birthday, after all."

"Wow", Amari takes the balloons, his smile happy. "This is the best thing that's ever happened to me."

"Wait until you see what I have for breakfast."

He gasps. "No, you didn't!"

"Yes, I did! Chocolate chip pancakes!"

"That's right! Your favorite."

"Awesome! This is the best birthday ever. Thanks, Ms. Wilkins."

"Please, Amari", she puts a hand on his shoulder, smiling. "Call me, mom."

He smiles, holding onto Ms. Wilkins, his hands still holding onto the balloons. "Got it, Mom."

\#

"Kendrick!", called a nurse in blue scrubs as she peeked her head from the door.

The elderly, white male, in a cowboy hat turned his eyes to the young nurse in scrubs. "Come this way, sir!"

Seeing this, the young man grabbed his cane and headed to the nurse, the door shutting behind the both from view.

Sitting far in the distance, Joana poked her head out in fear before slumping back in her chair, letting out a sigh of relief. "Don't be scared, Mom", I said, taking Mom's hand.

"Yeah, just breathe."

Mom nods. "I know. I just hate checkups."

I nod. "We know. Don't worry; I'm sure this'll be a quick one."

"Yeah."

Joana nods. "Yeah, you're right. Thanks, guys."

The nurse soon reappears from the door, holding a clipboard up to her eyes. "Joana Mitchell!"

Joana jerks a bit in her seat before Sue takes her hands. "Calm down, Joana."

"It's okay, mom. Do you want us to come with you?"

Joana sighs before shaking her head. "No. I need to do this alone."

Sue and I nod in understanding before Mom rises from her chair. In doing so, we watch her make her way to the young nurse, her smile warm and welcoming, before leading her down the hallway, the door closing shut behind them both.

As soon as it did, Sue and I let out huge sighs before answering. "You think she's going to be, okay?", said Aunt Sue, causing me to turn back. "Yeah, of course she is. It's mom, she's strong. Always has, always will."

#

Dominic and Aunt Sue sat in the waiting room; their eyes full of anxiousness as they did. "How much longer?"

"Don't worry, I'm sure mom's going to walk out of the door any minute now."

Aunt Sue lowers her eyes in sadness. "I just hope it's not something bad. This cancer has been hard enough, knowing something worse could happen."

I nod, my eyes shifting away. "I know. This hasn't been an easy time, especially for Mom. I just hope there are no surprises."

Aunt Sue nods. "Yes."

"Sue? Dominic?"

Sue Anne and Dominic both raise their heads to find Joana standing before them, her smile present. "Mom?", Dominic said, rising from his seat. "You're back."

Joana nods, wiping a tear from her eye, which Dominic quickly notices. "Joana, what's wrong?", answers Sue.

Sniffling, Joana's smile grows wider before both her arms are extended wide. "I'm free. I'm free from my cancer."

A surprised gasp escapes from Dominic and Aunt Sue. "Really, Mom? You're free from cancer!?"

"Yes! The chemotherapy killed every cell in my body, I'm cured!"

"Oh, Joana. This is great news", they say, pulling Joana in for a warm, loving embrace.

"Yeah, we should totally celebrate!"

"I already have an idea."

Dominic pulls away in confusion. "Really, what?"

Joana smiles. "Remember that party you wanted to throw me? Well, I want to have one."

"Really, you want a party?"

"A 'I Beat Cancer', party! But before we do that, I'd like to do something else first."

"Really? What's that, Joana?"

"I want us to spend the rest of the day together. Just a day to do whatever we want with each other, as a family. Is that alright?"

Dominic and Sue nod. "That's just fine, Mom."

"Yes, just fine. After all, there's no better time than now, right?"

Joana nods. "Yeah, it is."

With that, Aunt Sue, Joana, and Dominic all embrace in a happy hug as one big happy family.

\#

Amari sat at the dining table, eating the last few bits of chocolate chips left on the plate that he cleaned up with his fork. Not to mention the syrup he licked from the fork before plopping it down on the plate, letting a content sigh. "That was the best breakfast I've ever had, like in forever."

"I'm glad you liked it. There will be much more to do today."

Amari raises his brow. "Today?"

"Yep, we're going to have a full day of birthday", Ms. Wilkins said, wiping her hands with a napkin. "That is if you want to."

"Want to? Of course, I do. What's this full day of birthday?"

"Whatever you want it to be."

"Really?", Amari gasps, his eyes widening with joy. "Well, in that case, I want to have a day."

\#

Aunt Sue was in the mirror, putting on a set of green, emerald earrings, along with the white suit dress she wore. Her hair was up in a neat bun, which she found very sophisticated. It wasn't long before the sound of footsteps was heard that made Aunt Sue's head rise. "How do I look?"

With these words, Aunt Sue turns her head back to find Joana and Dominic standing in a yellow sun dress with golden hoops hanging from her ears. As for her head, she wore a hat, which matched her sundress well.

Seeing this, Sue Anne brings her hands up to her face and smiles. "Oh, Joana. You look beautiful."

"What about me?", said Dominic, wearing his white tuxedo, which is mainly the same one he wore for prom and his first meeting with Amanda Griffin's parents.

"You look good too, Dominic. Both of you."

"You look great, too, Sue."

"Thank you, Joana", Sue looked around the room for each other before speaking. "Well, we're all here. Should we get going?"

"Yes, but before we do", Joana takes Sue and Dominic's hands with hers, her smile big and bright. "I just wanted to say how thankful I am to have you guys in my life. I never would've gotten through this without you guys. So, thank you."

"Oh, Joana", Sue said before leaning in for a hug.

"We love you, mom", said Dominic.

"I love you too, baby. Both of you."

Pulling away from each other, Aunt Sue, Dominic, and Joana turn to the door and leave the house with their hands still intertwined, ready to seize the day.

Their day.

Chapter 19: The Outing

I lay in bed, the covers under my body. It wasn't long before both my eyes opened wide. She finds herself in bed, in her room. Well, not just any room, but her boyfriend's art studio. She'd been staying there for quite some nights now.

And they were wonderful.

She recalled many mornings watching Octavius stand on his canvas painting. She loved to do this as it was the best part of her day, especially when. Unfortunately, he wasn't here today.

Confused, Joana rises from the covers, looking around the room. "Otto?"

She sits there for some time before hopping out of bed and into her pink robe and slippers. She walked through the room before finding a canvas sitting in the corner. "Huh?", she said, making her way toward the canvas covered in a white sheet.

If there's anything she knew about this, it is that Octavius would only do this if there was a future vision in it. Could this be it?

With no thought in mind, Joana reached her hand up to the sheet, but before she could rip it off, a shadow approached her. "I thought I'd find you here."

Turning her head, Joana finds her beloved artistic boyfriend standing before her. "Octavius?"

He smiles. "Good morning, angel."

Joana laughs. "Angel?"

"Yes, that's how I see you", Otto looked at the hidden painting. "I see you've seen my painting."

Joana pauses before turning back. "Oh, you mean the one with the cloak under it?"

Otto nods. "I made it last night. It's for you."

Joana turns back to Octavius, her brows raised. "Me?"

"Yes. It's extra special. Go on, look."

With these words, Joana turned back to the canvas and took the sheet off. To her surprise, she found a ring, a diamond ring that Octavius held out to Joana.

Who, in fact, was in her pink robe.

Shocked, Joana brings her hands to her mouth and speaks. "Otto, is this-"

"Yes, it is", Octavius said, knelt on the floor, a large diamond ring held out before Joana.

Joana gasps, smiling happily. "So, what do you say? Will you be my wife, Joana?"

With tears filling her eyes, Joana wraps both her arms around Octavius and speaks. "Of course, I will."

#

"Mom? Mom!"

My eyes shot wide open, my mind slowly slipping back into reality. My son, Dominic, sat before me, with a face of confusion. "Mom, are you okay?"

I blink, before rubbing my eyes. "Um, yes."

"Are you sure?", said Sue Anne.

"Yeah, I'm okay. I was just reminiscing."

He blinks. "Reminiscing? About what?"

"Oh, just things. Old things."

"Old things? Like the past?"

I nod with a smile. "Is it about the cancer?"

I shake my head. "No, it's about you."

Dominic puts his hand to his chest. "Me?"

"Mm, hm. I'm always thinking of you. Speaking of which, how are you feeling?"

"How am I feeling?"

"Yeah, we haven't talked that much since all of this. So, I just want to check in."

Dominic fiddles with his fingers. "I'm good, I'm *better* than before."

"Before?"

"Well, I've been having some trouble with Amari."

"Amari? You mean your friend?"

"Not anymore. We had a fight, and it was bad. Now, we don't talk anymore. Sometimes, when I pass the hall, I don't even talk to him. I just leave."

"So, you avoid him?"

He nods. "Yeah."

"Why?"

"I don't know. I guess I'm still mad at him. I mean, he did leave with that woman."

"What, girl?"

"Ms. Wilkins, a woman that I really don't like because, well, she got us kicked out of our home, Mom."

Mom's eyes widen. "What?"

"Yeah, she's the one that gave Amari the fake money. Because of her, we were kicked out of our apartment. One day, I met her, telling me how sorry she was."

"And what did you say?"

I lower my eyes. "I didn't say anything, just yelled at her."

"Why would you do that?"

"I was mad. She ruined my whole life, I mean, *our* life. As bad as things already were, she just made it worse. I've been angry ever since."

Mom raises a brow. "So, are you mad at Amari or at the woman?"

"I'm mad at both. I don't know."

Mom brings her hands across the table

I nod. "Dominic, I don't know what Amari did to you, but I do know what it's like to hold resentment towards someone. The last thing I want is for you to not hold onto it. The best thing you can do is forgive them, even if they don't feel the same way."

Dominic looked down at his hands and sighed. "I guess you're right, mom. Being angry is kind of exhausting."

"So, you'll do it? You'll forgive Amari?"

He nods. "If you can, then so can I."

I smile happily before patting my son's curly head, causing him to laugh.

#

Octavius stood looking out at the prison window. Once again, he was looking out of the window, lost in his thoughts. Only he wasn't frowning but smiling. "My sentence is almost up. Soon, I will have my revenge."

It wasn't long until the sound of his cell door opened wide, causing Octavius's head to rise in suspicion. "I hope you're here to send me off."

"Oh, I definitely will until you join me for lunch."

Otto grunts, much to Henry's annoyance. "Oh, come on, Otto! You never have lunch with me."

"I like to be alone, Henry. I'd rather stare out at the empty void."

"A *void* doesn't give you nutrition. Come on, man, you need to get out of this cell. What do you get to lose?"

Thinking to himself, Octavius peers down at the ring in his hand, the diamond shining bright. With that, Otto sucks in some air and speaks. "Well, since it is my last day. I guess it wouldn't hurt."

"Really?"

"Yes."

"Alright, let's go!"

#

While Henry and Otto's lunch was just beginning, I just finished mine with my son and friend. Soon afterward, we walked out of the burger joint and took a nice walk in the park, the same park Sue and I walked in a few weeks ago.

I have always wanted to take Dominic to this park, and now, I have finally had the chance to do so. We walked through many trails, eyeing all kinds of trees and thorn bushes. Dominic held my hand the whole way. He never usually liked holding my hand as he thought he was 'too old' for it. But today, he did, and I loved every minute of it.

Soon, we walked to a nearby pond where several white-feathered ducks swam, floating atop the watery surface. Dominic asked if we could feed them. I said yes.

Sue gave him money to pay for the duck food. As soon as he got it, the food was thrown right into the water, causing several of the ducks to squirm their way toward it, their little orange beaks pecking and nipping at one another as they fought for their meal.

Dominic laughed at the sight of the ducks, his smile big and bright as he laughed. I loved his laugh more than anything in this world. Ever since she got cancer, all mom did was cry, but now, cancer-free, she was, and I loved every minute of it.

Soon after, we went to the aquarium, where we saw various types of underwater fish. I watched as Dominic pointed at the stingray fish. Of all the fish out there, the stingray was my favorite. The last time I was at the aquarium, I was with Aunt Sue. She usually was the one who took me places as mom would be at work.

I always wished for Mom to be at the aquarium with me at the time, but now that she was, everything was perfect, especially with Aunt Sue here to watch us.

"Are you enjoying yourself, baby?", Mom said, turning to me.

"Yeah, mom. Are you?"

Mom nods. "Yes. I'm enjoying myself."

"Good", I say, my smile big and bright.

Mom smiles at me, causing me to speak. "You have such a pretty smile, Dominic."

"Really, mom. You think my smile is pretty."

"Of course, I do. What, you don't think it is?"

"No, it's just, I never realized it before."

"Well, you should. You have a beautiful smile, Dominic."

"Thanks, mom. That means a lot to me. I couldn't ask for a better mom than you."

Mom smiles, her hand raised to my cheek. "And I couldn't ask for a better son. I have no regrets about having you, Dominic. That, I know."

With these words, Dominic wraps his arms around Mom, embracing her in a warm, loving hug. "I love you, mama."

I smile, bringing Dominic in. "I love you too, baby."

One that Aunt Sue noticed from behind, causing her to raise her camera up to her eyes before flashing the light. Within seconds, a camera slides out of the slit before being pulled out.

Aunt Sue's smile grew as she found the photo of Dominic and Joana hugging. "Yep", she said, waving the photo to her eyes. "This is one for the books."

With that, I pull away from Dominic and speak. "Dominic?"

"Yeah, mama?"

She coughed. "Um, before the party, there's one last place I'd like to go."

"What is it, Mom?"

I smile softly before speaking. "Home."

#

A group of prisoners in orange jumpsuits were lined up, their hands carrying trays as they approached the old lunch ladies slabbing hot bowls of chicken soup, all with a slice of bread, fruit, and some milk.

Otto was one of those prisoners, slurping up all kinds of pre-packaged herbs and spices. Which, he didn't mind. Food was food, no matter where it came from. If he went to bed with a full belly, he was good.

"Hey, man!", Otto raises his head to find Henry placing his tray on the table before pulling up his seat. "I see you're slurping down that soup. Must be good."

"Yeah", Otto nods, biting into his slice of bread.

As he eats, Henry notices the scar on Otto's left eye. He stands there, completely transfixed, as if it carried several answers, answers that needed to be answered. Otto was still peering down at his slice of bread when Henry spoke. "Hey, Otto."

Otto looked up from his tray. "Yeah?"

"Um, not to be rude, but I was wondering where you got that scar?"

Otto blinks, his brow raised. "What?"

"Your scar, the one on your eye, your left eye", Henry said, raising his hand on his eye.

Otto's eyes widened in shock, causing him to bring his hand up to his left eye. "Oh. I don't like to talk about it."

"Why? What happened?"

"I said I don't want to talk about it."

"Come on, just tell m—"

"I SAID NO, HENRY!", Otto shouts, his fists slamming on the table.

"Why do you care so much?"

Otto didn't say anything except turn his back on Henry and walk out of the cafeteria, leaving him sitting alone at the table.

\#

A young, black woman in a white, poofy dress is found covering her eyes, all the while walking beside her devoted husband. "Keep those eyes closed, Joana."

"I am, Otto. How much longer do I have to do it?"

"We're almost there. Just a few more steps."

Joana takes a few more steps on the concrete ground before suddenly stopping. "Okay, open them."

"Now?"

"Now."

With these words, Joana takes her hands from her face, causing both her eyes to open. As soon as they do, a bright and joyous smile forms across her face. "Oh my gosh!", she said, turning to her husband. "Otto!"

Octavius' smile widens before turning back to the apartment building. "You like it?"

"Like it? I love it!", Joana brings her lips up to Octavius's face, kissing his cheek. "Thank you, baby."

"Wait 'till you see the inside."

"The inside?"

Before she could do anything else, Joana was lifted by Octavius, bridal style, before the two of them walked down the paved parking lot.

\#

"Mom?", said a voice, causing me to open my eyes to my son, who was sitting across from me in the car. "Mom, we're here."

"Hm?", I say in confusion.

"We're here, we're at the house."

Hearing this, I turn my eyes to the window, and that's when I see it. Without a second thought, I unlocked the car, opening the door wide. I took a step out onto the concrete driveway, like it was the first time.

"Are you sure you want to do this, Mom?", said Dominic, standing beside Sue Anne, who had made her way up to me.

I turn to him and nod. "Yes, baby, I'm sure.

Sue Anne smiles happily before Dominic takes his hand in mine and smiles. "Alright, let's go."

With a quick nod, Aunt Sue, Dominic, and I walked into the apartment building. Before I knew it, we were walking down the hallway with a young, middle-aged man guiding the way.

Mr. Thompson, the new landlord.

"Alright, here we are", Mr. Thompson said, stopping in front of the door. "You might want to be quick, as there'll be other people coming soon to rent out the place, okay?'

"Of, course", I said.

Dominic nods. "Don't worry, we'll be in and out."

With a quick nod, Mr. Thompson twists the lock to his door, opening it a few inches wide. "Here you go."

With these words, Dominic, Sue, and I make our way through the door, entering the apartment. I was the first to enter, and as soon as I did, an entire wave of nostalgia hit me like never before. "Oh", I say, my hand on my heart.

"Mom?", said Dominic, staring up at me, concerned. "Are you okay?"

I smile, nodding. "Yes, I'm alright. I just got a little bit nostalgic. It's been so long since I've been in the apartment."

"We understand, Joana", answers Sue. "If you want to be alone, that is."

"No, Aunt Sue, we should stay with Mom-"

"No, Dominic", I said. "It's alright. I would like to be left alone."

Dominic raises a brow in confusion. "Are you sure?"

I nod. "Yes."

With these words, Dominic and Sue Anne made their way out of the apartment. "We'll be waiting for you out here, Mom."

"Ok, baby."

With a quick nod, Dominic shuts the door behind him, leaving me all alone in the empty apartment.

Perfect.

My eyes were glued to the door, not once taking my eyes off it for a minute. This door wasn't just a door, it was the start of a new beginning, *our* beginning.

\#

The door opened wide to find the young bride and groom, laughing happily as they entered the apartment. "Here we are", said Octavius, putting Joana down. "Home sweet home."

As soon as Joana was put down, her eyes trailed every inch of the empty building. "Otto, it's beautiful."

"You like it, don't you?"

"Like it?", Joana pulls her husband in for a kiss on the lips before pulling away. "I love it."

"Alright, lovebirds. Stop fooling around", said the large middle-aged man. "You've still got rent to pay."

"We know, Mr. Winslow."

With that, Mr. Winslow throws a set of keys into Octavius's hands. "Thanks, Mr. Winslow."

"Thank you for giving me rent money. Also, rent's due next month."

With that, Mr. Winslow exits the apartment, leaving Joana and Octavius alone. "So, the apartment's ours. What do you want to do now?"

With these words, Joana took the keys from her husband's hands and jingled them in her hands, grinning seducingly. "I think I might have an idea."

With that, Octavius picked up his wife, causing her to laugh before the two of them made their way to a door leading to the bedroom.

My eyes were closed shut as I reminisced before suddenly shooting back open. Standing before me, I found the bedroom door staring back at me.

Just like the front door, I stared at it for a while, but not too long, as my hand was already on the doorknob.

A lot of things happened behind this door, some good, some bad, but mostly good. Especially the birth of my newborn son.

Without a second thought, I opened the door. In doing so, I find two lone figures, a man and a woman, standing over a crib where a tiny hand reached its way up to them both.

"Oh, look, Otto", I speak, taking the curly-haired baby's hand into his mouth. "He's teething."

"He sure is."

"Oh, he's perfect. Our very own baby boy."

"What do you think we should call him?"

"I already picked a name. Let's call him Dominic."

"Dominic?"

"Yeah, it means 'Lordly', 'Belonging to God', "It's perfect for him."

Otto nods, smiling. "Yes, it is."

The memory soon fades, bringing me back to reality. In doing so, I turned back to a large, empty space, a space in the distance with a window sitting above. I stared at this window for a good minute, my eyes widening as another memory rose to the surface.

Within minutes, the sunlit room quickly turned dark and grey as rain poured from the window, hitting the glass. I was standing out that window, anxious and scared.

Scared for Octavius, who wasn't back from his local "visit" from the Manor, Griffin Manor.

He said he would call me when he arrived, but he never did. Or so I thought when I heard the knock at the door, only it wasn't who I expected.

Knock, knock, knock!

My head quickly turns back from the window, making my way towards the door. Without a second thought, I exit the living room and make my way towards the door, opening it wide. "Octavius?"

I was so happy to hear that door knock that a big smile held on my face. Only until I found the person standing before me. One that wasn't Octavius but Robert Griffin himself. "Mr.-Mr. Griffin?"

He nods, his smile sad and low. "Hello, Mrs. Mitchell."

"What are you doing here?"

"It's Octavius."

My eyes widen in shock. "What about him?"

Without saying another word, Octavius brings his hand up to me and speaks. "Just come with me. Please. I'll explain on the way to prison."

"Prison?", I say, shocked.

I stood before myself, watching myself cry as if I was standing outside my own body. In this case, I was. At this moment, the memory would have faded by now and brought me back to reality.

But no, not this time.

I wasn't going to run. I was going to watch it play out.

All of it.

I closed my eyes and took a deep breath. Before I knew it, my eyes shot back open, only I wasn't in my apartment; I was instead in a room, a dark, misty room where two, lone figures sat across each other.

A young woman cradling her young in her arms and her young man with a white bandage over his eye. It was a big bandage, so big that whatever happened to him must've really hurt, but none as hurt as the wife was.

"Joana, I swear, whatever he told you, it isn't true."

"Oh, it's not?"

"Yes, I swear!"

I lowered my head in shame, my eyes closing. "He told me, Octavius. He told me you kissed Mia."

"What?"

"The Griffins, they told me you kissed Mia? You kissed her, and you never told me."

The man's eyes widened before speaking. "Joana, that...that was nothing."

"Nothing?"

"The kiss, it meant nothing to me. I swear, it didn't."

"Save your breath, Otto. I get it."

"No, Joana, please just listen!"

"I've heard enough, and honestly, I don't want to hear anymore, ever again."

"What are you saying?"

With these words, I take the ring, the ring that was a symbol of my love for Octavius, slipped from my finger and into his hand. "What are you doing, Joana?"

"Goodbye, Octavius", I say, walking out of the room, leaving Octavius in shame. "JOANA, PLEASE COME BACK! JOANA, JOOOOAAAANNNAAAA!!!!!"

My eyes welled up as I watched myself leave that prison cell that day, with the painful indication that it would be the last time I'd ever see his face.

And it was.

For eighteen years, that memory played in my head. For years, I hated him for what he did, but as awful as it was, holding onto it just made things worse. As much as I hated him, a part of me still loved him. Yes, he betrayed me and hurt me, but after all that, I loved him. I still, in a way, forgave him. I guess that's why I lied to him, to Dominic. I wanted him to remember him as if he was this great man, a nobleman. But that wasn't the truth, was it?

I guess I was also lying to myself. No matter how much I tried to deny it.

But it didn't matter now. None of that mattered anymore. The past was gone, long dead. At that moment, the only thing that mattered was now.

Was *them*.

Speaking of which, they were waiting for me, just behind that door. I just had to wake up first to see it. With these words, I closed my eyes, clicked my heels three times, and said the magic words:

"I forgive you, Octavius."

Within minutes, my eyes shot wide open, and I found myself back in the empty apartment. No dark jail cell, no stormy weather, just me and the sunlit room. In doing so, I turned to my left, finding the door standing before me.

Without a second thought, I twisted the doorknob and opened it wide. In doing so, I find my beloved son and friend standing outside, their eyes peering up at me. "Hey, Mom", said Dominic. "You finished?"

I nod, my smile widening. "Yes, I am", I turn my head back to the room. "I think I made peace with some things."

Sue Anne nods, happily. "That's good, Joana."

"Yeah, it is", I say, leaving the three of us in silence before I speak up. "Well, what are you guys standing around for? We got a party to celebrate!"

Dominic and Sue's silence quickly turns to cheerfulness as the three of us leave the premises, ready to end the day right.

\#

"Hats, balloons, chips, dip, soda...", I recited, looking at the kitchen table where those items were sitting. I nod before peering down at my brown clipboard. "Yep, everything's here."

"You forgot one thing, baby", said Mom from behind, causing me to turn my head back to her. "What's that, mom?"

Mom smiled before reaching into her pocket and bringing out a spray bottle. "String!"

"Wha-ah!", I shouted as a line of green string hit my face, surprising me. "Mom, stop!"

Mom laughs as I raise my hands up, blocking the string. I turned my head to the kitchen table, where another set of spray strings was found. Without a second thought, I take the spray from the table, grip the handle, and a red line of string exits from the bottle and onto Mom's face. "Ah!", she screams happily before spraying more green string on me.

Soon, the two of us were now covered in string, our laughs filling the air until Aunt Sue entered the room. "Is that string, I see?!"

Mom and I turned our heads back to Aunt Sue, who, without a second thought, extended her arms out. "Go on, let me have it!"

Without hesitation, Mom and I raise our spray cans and press the levers. To her surprise, Aunt Sue is covered in red and green string, stretching every inch of her arms and down to her legs. Soon, our cans ran out, leaving Aunt Sue smothered in string, much to our shock.

"Oh my god. Sue, we're so sorry."

"Sorry, for what?", Sue said, looking down at herself. "Looks like Christmas came early this year."

A laugh escaped from Mom and me before Aunt Sue took the red and green string from her body and peered up at us, looking dumbfounded. "What are you guys staring at? Let's get this party started!"

"Yeah!"

#

The walls of the one-bedroom apartment were wide and narrow. The whole place was dark and quiet, much like something in a horror movie. Only, the horror was yet to occur, and it all started with the front door that opened wide.

Suddenly, the entire room was full of laughter as two people entered the house, hand in hand. "I can't believe he said that to you", said Ms. Wilkins.

"Yeah, but he tried to."

"He must've had a knack for fun."

"He sure did."

Denise smiles before wrapping both her arms around her boyfriend's neck. "Did you enjoy your birthday?"

"I sure did. Thanks for giving me the best day ever."

"The day's not over yet."

He raises his brow. "It's not?"

"Nope, we still have one more thing to do."

"What's that?"

"Movies. I thought we could end the night by watching a little movie. *Your* favorite movie."

"*My* favorite movie?"

"Yes. What would you like to watch?"

Amari brings his hand to his chin, thinking what to think. "How about Crocodile Man!"

"Sounds great! You got set up the TV, I'll go make the popcorn."

"Ok."

With those words, Amari and Ms. Wilkins part away from each other

#

Joana sat on the toilet, his eyes peering down at the pink pregnancy stick in her hands. It was turned around, completely hindering the symbol. With her knees shaking, Joana takes a deep breath and turns the pregnancy test over.

To her surprise, she found a plus sign on the glass screen. Joana lets out a quick gasp, causing her to cover her mouth. "Oh my god."

Suddenly, there was a knock on the bathroom door, "Joana? Are you in here?", said a familiar voice.

Without hesitation, Joana rises from the toilet, her eyes bright, before heading to the door. "Joana?", the voice said again before the door

opened, revealing her beloved fiancé, now husband, staring before her.
"It's a plus, Otto!"

"What?", said Octavius confused.

"It's a plus!", Joana held up the pregnancy test to Octavius's eyes, and Octavius quickly smiled. "No way, really?"

"Yes! We're pregnant, Otto; we're going to have a baby!"

"Oh my god!", Otto said, surprised.

Without a second thought, Otto lifts Joana in his arms, twirling her around in happiness.

"Mom?", I say as Mom holds me in her arms.

Mom's eyes open wide, finding me staring up at me. "Are you alright?"

Back in reality, Mom looked down at me and smiled. "Yes, I'm fine."

"Are you sure? You seemed like you were drifting off again."

"Yes. I was just…just…"

"Reminiscing?"

She nodded. "Yes, reminiscing."

Mom and I spent the next few minutes gliding back and forth as we danced, leaving us in silence. Until the thought comes back. "Oh, yeah! Mom, I forgot to tell you!"

"Tell me what?"

"I got my acceptance letter in the mail, I got accepted!"

Mom gasps in surprise before pulling me in for a hug. "Oh, Dominic, I'm so happy! We must tell Sue."

"Sue already knows."

"She does?"

"Yeah, I told her when you were with the doctor?"

Mom's eyes widen in shock before lowering her face. "Um, of course, you did."

I smile happily before hugging Mom tight. "Things are finally looking up, after several months of hell, I'm glad that we can finally be at peace. I love you, Mom."

Mom smiles, bringing me to the place. "I love you too, baby. I always…will…"

"Mom?", I say, pulling away from her. "Are you o-Mom!"

Within seconds, Mom collapses to the floor, shocking Aunt Sue in the making. "Joana!"

I watch in tears as Mom's eyes roll in the back of her head. "Mom!", I cry. "Mom, Mom, wake up! Open your eyes, please!"

"I'm calling 9-1-1!"

"Hurry!", I shouted as Aunt Sue grabbed the phone handle, dialing the three digits, while I tried my best to "comfort", Mom.

"Mom! Mom!", the tears were now flowing from my eyes. "Mom, please don't leave me! Mom, MOMMMM!!!"

#Amari walked into the house, looking around the room, his eyes full of confusion. He spends the next few minutes looking under the place. He was looking for something, he just couldn't find it. "Hey, mom. Do you know where the remote is?"

"Check my bedroom!"

"Okay, thanks!"

With that, Amari exited the living room and went down the hallway into Ms. Wilkins's bedroom. Amari looked around the room, looking at every inch of the room, under pillows, in the closet, and even under the bed. Amari huffs, feeling annoyed by his lack of discovery. "Where the hell is the remote?"

Amari looked around the room when, at the corner of his eye, finds a nightstand. Without a second thought, Amari approaches the nightstand, grabbing the handle before opening it wide. To his surprise, he finds a black remote sitting inside. "There you are!", Amari said with a wide smile.

Without hesitation, Amari grabs the remote, not once noticing the photos sitting under the place.

Happy, Amari opened the nightstand's drawer and placed his keychain in. But before he could, he found a set of photos sitting on the bottom. Confused, Amari reached in and grabbed the photos into his hands. In doing so, he saw various photos all wrapped up in a bow. But not just any photos; there was a boy in it, a young boy with a warm and happy smile.

Amari looked at the photo and noticed the name written below it: **ANDY.**

"Andy?", Amari raises his brow, quite confused. "Who the heck is Andy?"

Amari flipped through the second photo where another person, a little black girl, was found: **MADISON.**

The third photo where an Asian boy was found: **RYAN.**

Amari's eyes widened at the sight of the children that were presented in the photos. Who were these children, and why did Ms. Wilkins have photos of them? As scared as Amari was, he truly became afraid when he found the last photo. A boy, a young, light-skinned boy with dreads. It didn't take much for Amari to learn the young boy's name and words, which are written below: **AMARI JENKINS. MY ONE AND A MILLIONTH CHILD."**

"What-the-hell!?"

With his heart in his stomach, the photos fall out of his hands, scattering across the carpet floor. Amari sits back on the bed, his hand on his chest as it raced.

Little did he know, small footsteps were heard. "Amari?"

Amari raised his eyes, finding his "mother" standing over him with a bowl of popcorn and her eyes full of concern. "Are you alright?"

Amari looked down at the photos scattered on the floor, photos that Ms. Wilkins quickly noticed. "Amari?" Ms. Wilkins drops her bowl of popcorn on the floor before kneeling to the floor and gathering the photos. "What are you doing with these photos?"

Amari raises his brow. "You tell me"

Ms. Wilkins stands there, puzzled. "What do you mean?"

"Those kids, who are they, and why am I on it?"

Ms. Wilkins looked at Amari completely wide-eyed before her expression went flat. "Amari, those children are all mine."

"But I thought you only had one child?"

"I do", she raised the picture of the young, light-skinned boy. "Andy was an excellent student."

"Student?"

"So was Missy and Ryan."

Amari's eyes widened as Ms. Wilkins walked towards him, meeting his eye level. "And so are you, Amari."

Amari's heart began to race again, but only this time, his eyes were involved. He was looking straight at the door that was wide open for him. "Um, I think I need to go to the bathroom."

With that, Amari hopped right off the bed, running past Ms. Wilkins before heading to the door. But before he could make his escape, the door shut before him. "I'm afraid there's no escape for you, A.J."

Amari faces Ms. Wilkins, who was holding the remote. Amari frowns at this, his eyes full of concern. "Let me out!"

"I don't appreciate your tone"

"Let me out, now!", Amari shouts before facing the door, frantically twisting the doorknob. "Help! Help!", he cried. "Someone, please help!"

Amari continued to bang on the door, yet little did he realize, Ms. Wilkins's shadow approached him from behind. "Help, please, someone he-", Amari's voice quickly cuts off as a syringe is injected into his neck.

Before he knew it, Amari collapsed, falling headfirst on the floor, with Ms. Wilkins standing over him with the most sinister grin. "Did you really think you could get away from me that easily? If you did, you were dead wrong."

With these words, Amari's eyes close shut as the world goes completely dark before him.

#

Octavius Mitchell stood out at his caged window, his eyes low and sad. For he was pissed, really pissed at his friend. How can he say such things to him and not feel the need to answer.

Suddenly, the sound of his cell opening was heard, causing his head to rise. "You know that was really uncalled for."

"I don't care, get out!"

"I'm not going anywhere."

"GET-OU—" Otto's words are suddenly put to a halt when a shiny, diamond ring is held out to him by Henry. "Where...give me that that!", Otto said, snatching the ring from Henry's hands. Otto brings the ring to his heart, before turning back to Henry. "Where did you find this?"

"In the cafeteria. Next time you storm off, make sure you clean up behind yourself."

Otto grunts before placing the ring back on his finger. In doing so, he rises back to his feet and sneers at his cellmate. "What do you want from me?"

"What I've wanted the day I met you: to know you, and by the looks of that scar on your eye, it-ah!", Henry's words are quickly stopped as Otto grabs ahold of his neck, his back now against the bricked walls of the prison cell. "Stop mentioning my scar", he said, staring Henry dead in the eye. "It's not just a scar; it's a reminder of all the pain, all the loss, and all the suffering I have endured for the past years. If you as so much think you can just get shit out of me, think again"

Henry grabs hold of Otto's hand, his grip incredibly strong. "I know about the girl...I know about Mia."

Otto's eyes widen in shock. "What?", Otto loosened his grip, causing Henry to fall straight to his knees, coughing hard. "How do you know about Mia?"

"You talk in your sleep", Henry coughs a bit before rising off the cold, prison floor. "You talk a lot about her."

Otto flinched before returning to his window, his eyes low and sad once more. Henry sighs at this before speaking. "Otto, I'm not saying any of this to hurt you. I just want to know why you're so upset. But I can't help you, if you don't let me."

With these words, Otto peered down at his ring, twisted it with his finger, and finally, raised his head. "Remember that story I told you about? The one about my wife?"

Henry nods. "Yeah."

Otto peers down at the ring and sighs. "I don't like to talk about this much, but the day I was put behind bars, was the same day my wife left me."

Henry raises his brow. "She left? Like left you or *left you*?"

"She left me, took the ring off, and placed it right in my hand. All because of *her*."

"Her as in Mia?"

"Yes", Otto turns to face Henry. "But that's not important. Not now, anyway. What's important is that the Griffin line falls, and Mia is avenged once and for all."

"Avenged? What do you mean? Are you going to kill them?"

"Kill, murder, doesn't matter. If I get my revenge, Mia will finally be put to rest, and my heart will finally be whole again."

"Whole? How will taking someone's life make you whole? If anything, it'll just make you dead inside."

"I'm already dead inside. I've been for seventeen years. If anything, the Griffin's end will bring me back to life."

"Think of what you're saying, man."

"I know exactly what I'm saying? I'm getting my revenge, one way or another."

"No, this isn't right. What you're plotting is insane!"

"Not as insane as the life that was taken from me. I won't rest until justice is served."

"Your idea of justice is wrong! Justice is something you earn, not take!"

Otto shakes his head. "You don't understand, Henry."

"No, you don't! You're doing all of this because of some woman."

"She wasn't just some *woman; she* was a person with a life—a life that was taken from her!"

"And killing them would do what, bring her back? 'Cause it won't!"

Henry's words quickly make Otto go silent, his eyes slowly drooping to the floor. "See?", Henry speaks, noticing Otto's change. "You're starting to believe it, aren't you?", Henry lets out a quick sigh. "Look, I've met the Griffin, and frankly, they're not the friendliest people, but that doesn't mean they deserve to die. This is your last night in prison. If I were you, I'd just be living my life to the fullest, not retaliating on some folks who, in all honesty, probably aren't even thinking about you, let alone remember you. Doesn't that sound like a better option?"

With his eyes still drooped to the floor, Otto raises his head, his eyes looking dead at Henry. "It does."

A warm and happy smile forms on Henry's face. As for Otto, his smile was not present. "Which is why I'm doing it."

Henry's face falls flat in disappointment. "Are you serious?"

"Yes, did you really think your silly speech was going to stop me? Make me change my ways? It wasn't."

"Otto, please don't do this."

"I'm sorry, Henry, but I'm going with my plan."

"Otto, please, they have a daughter!"

"What?"

"Mr. and Mrs. Griffin, they have a daughter. Her name is Amanda Griffin. If you kill her parents, think of the pain you'll cause her. Do you want that on your conscience? *Do you!?*"

Otto blinks, his eyes wide with shock as he thinks to himself. "I...I don't know."

Henry makes a quick nod. "Well, when you do know. I'll be in the Healthcare unit, putting ice on my neck. At least there, I'll be treated with care. Something you obviously don't have."

With these words, Henry turns away from Otto, leaving his cell and Otto to his submissive, timid thoughts.

Chapter 20: The Last Stand

Octavius Mitchell.

The mysterious man, the man with no face, stood in his prison cell alone, his smile big and bright as he stared out at the place. He peers down at the ring in his hand, the diamond raising it up to his eyes. "Hey, Otto", said Yorkshire walking up to him. "I see you're staring out your window of yours again."

Otto nods, smiling. "Yes, I see you have your neck brace on?"

Henry nodded; his hand brought up to his neck. "Yeah, no thanks to you."

Hearing this, Octavius brings his ring up to his eyes and sighs. "I'd like to apologize to you, Henry. About choking you. It was wrong of me."

"Look, I really don't care about that right now. I just want to lie down and go to sleep", Henry walks straight to his bed and sits right down, letting out a quick sigh of relief, much to Octavius's happiness. "You may not want to sleep just yet."

"And why is that?", Henry said, his eyes now closed.

Otto turns his eyes from the window and back to Henry. "I've thought about our conversation, and I've come to a decision."

Henry turned his head back to his cellmate, his brow raised. "A decision?"

"Yes, ever since you left me alone, I had a lot of time to think about what you said."

"You have? Well, what is it?"

Otto stood there in silence, his eyes closed shut as he thought of what to say. Once they opened, he knew. "You asked me if I could really kill a man, that if I could look at myself in the mirror again if I did. Well, you were right; I wouldn't be able to see myself the same. Which is why I've decided not to kill them."

A small sigh of relief escapes from Henry, causing a big grin to forge on his face. "Why, Octavius, that's great!", he said joyfully. "Oh, I knew my words would knock some sense into you. I'm so glad you changed your mind."

"Who said I changed my mind?"

Henry's happy smile quickly lowers, much to his surprise. "I'm sorry?"

"I didn't change my mind on anything, Henry. I said I wouldn't kill them; that doesn't mean I wouldn't get them back."

"Wait, what? But you said-"

"Octavius Mitchell!?"

Octavius and Henry both turn their heads to a tall, broad guard standing before their cell, the cell that was wide open. "Congratulations, your seventeen-year sentence is officially over. Get your things, you're going home."

"Finally", Octavius turns his eyes back to Henry and smirks. "See you, Henry."

"Octavius, stop!", Henry said, taking Octavius's arm. "What are you going to do to them?"

"What?", he said, turning back.

"If you're not going to hurt them, then what are you going to do? Just tell me something, please!"

With his eyes still on him, Octavius takes his arm away from Henry and speaks. "Do you remember the night we met? The night you found me staring out that window?"

Henry turns his eyes back to the window and nods. "Yeah."

He grins. "Let's just say, you're going to see two more doing the exact same thing."

Henry's eyes widen in shock as Octavius pulls away from Henry and speaks. "Nice knowing you, Mr. Yorkshire."

With that said, Octavius walks right out of the prison cell, the door closing shut behind him. Henry stands there quite dumbfounded as Octavius turns his eyes back to him for the last time and smirks.

#

I sat in the hospital room, the heart monitor beeping. Mom, her hair short as ever, lay in bed. This time, she wasn't asleep but wide awake. "I'm sorry, baby", she said, holding my hand.

I take her hand, grasping it tight. "Don't apologize, mom. You're going to be okay."

Mom coughs, much to Aunt Sue's concern, as she brings a rag to her mouth. "No", she said through coughing. "It's not that, Sue."

Sue nods and removes the rag from her lips. "Sorry, I just thought you-"

"It's alright, Sue."

Sue was about to say something else before shutting her mouth, nodding solemnly before I let out a sigh. "I don't understand", I say, cutting into the conversation. "You beat the cancer. What could have made you fall out like that?"

Mom breathed heavily, as if it was the longest sigh she had ever made before answering me. "I didn't beat the cancer, Dominic."

"What!?", I say, shocked.

"I didn't beat the cancer. I-I lied."

"You lied?", I blink in confusion.

"When I went to the checkup this morning. The doctor said that I wouldn't last the day."

"No", said Aunt Sue.

"He said I was going to die before sundown."

"No!", I cry. "Mom, why didn't you tell us the truth before?"

"I'm sorry, baby", Mom said, a tear falling down her cheek. "I just wanted you to have one last day with me to be special."

Aunt Sue and I cried, holding Mom as she, too, began to weep. "I'm sorry, guys. I'm so sorry."

#

"Amari…", said a whispering voice.

"Amari…", said it again.

Hearing this, Amari's eyes opened wide, gasping in shock as a young woman stood over him, grinning sinisterly. "Wakey, wakey."

"Ms. Wilkins, what are-ah!", he turned to the left to find his arms and legs tied up with rope. "What?", he said, jerking his body. "What is this!?"

"Don't bother trying to move. You won't break free."

He grunts. "What have you done to me!?"

"What I do to all children who disrespect me."

"What are you talking about!?"

"Shh", she said, placing her hand on Amari's lips. "Be quiet, or else you want to sleep again", she said, waving the syringe at him, making Amari's lips go sealed. "Good boy."

Ms. Wilkins made sure she was laughing. "Look how feeble you are. I should've used this kind of treatment on you before. You listen more when pain is involved. No wonder you left your family."

"My family was horrible to me. I had no choice."

"So, was Madison's. And Ryan's and, of course, my little Andy."

"What are you talking about? I thought Andy was your son."

"He was until my husband wanted to take him away from me. As a mother, the last thing you want is to have a child ripped from your arms. It's the most painful experience of all. I tried to get him back, but fate had other plans. Not only did I lose my son, I lost my heart. I was nothing but an empty void, one that I could fill. So, I did just that: a home, a warm bed to sleep in, all the things they could ask for. But when they chose defiance, they were punished! At first, I thought you would be different. I thought you wouldn't leave. But you did. And now you will suffer greatly."

Amari gasped, his eyes big and wide before slowly lowering his head in shame as he knew exactly what she was talking about. "Ms. Wilkins, no! Please! I'll make it better, I'll-"

"It's too late! You made your choice, and now you must deal with the consequences!"

"Ms. Wilkins, please! I'll do anything!"

Ms. Wilkins didn't say anything; instead, she turned her eyes away from Amari and to her cell phone, which sat on her nightstand. "What are you doing?", Amari asked as Ms. Wilkins dialed a few numbers on the phone. "Who are you calling?"

Ms. Wilkins grins as she raises the phone to her ear. "No one important."

\#

I lay in my mother's arms, a tear falling from my face as I cried. Mom, the nurturing type, combed through my curly brown hair as she hummed to me.

A tune.

A tune that, for some reason, was familiar to me.

"My angel", she said. "My angel."

Aunt Sue sat in her chair, wiping a few tears from her eyes as she listened to Mom's voice fill the room's silence.

Her sweet, calm, angelic voice.

Unfortunately, Mom's singing was soon interrupted once my phone rang. Only, we didn't listen, for we were all too upset to do anything.

Too sad to care.

Within a few minutes, the phone rang again, causing all our heads to rise. "Who's that?", I say, confused.

"I don't know."

"It's probably no one, baby", said Mom. "Probably just a telemarketer."

I turned my eyes from Mom and straight to the telephone, which, in fact, was still ringing, much to my suspicion. "No, I-I feel like I need to check."

"Dominic, it's probably no one."

"No", I say, walking towards the telephone. "I don't think so."

With that, I take the telephone from the rack and bring it to my ear. "Hello?"

"Dominic Mitchell?", said a strange voice.

"Yeah, who's this?"

"That information is classified. Just listen to what I have to say."

I scoff. "I'm not hearing anything until you give me your name."

I hear a loud, long sigh go through the phone. *"Fine. Does the name Amari Jenkins come to mind?"*

My eyes widen. "Amari? What do you know about him?"

"He's your best friend. Well, it was, until I took control. Ring any bells?"

My eyes frown into an angry snarl. "Ms. Wilkins."

"Ding, ding, ding!"

"Where is he?"

"Oh, don't worry. He's fine, for now, that is", Ms. Wilkins laughs through the phone, much to my annoyance. "Listen to me, if you put one finger on him—"

"Listen, if you hurt him, I swear you'll regret it."

"Yes, *you'll* regret it."

I grunt, gripping the phone tight. "You have one hour. Don't keep *him* waiting."

With that, the phone cuts off to static, leaving me in a daze.

Ms. Wilkins puts the phone back on the handle, an evil smirk present on her face, before turning back to Amari, staring up at her from the bed. "What are you smiling for? Who was on the phone?"

"Who do you think it was?"

Shocked, Amari's eyes widened in shock. "No, you didn't."

She nodded. "I did."

Amari raises his head, his eyes wide with fear. "Ms. Wilkins, I beg you. Whatever you told him-"

"Shh!", Ms. Wilkins silences him. "I don't want to hear any more out of you. Are you here? Nothing!"

Amari flinches at the sound of Ms. Wilkins's words, causing him to stop, his head slowly falling back on the bed board. Ms. Wilkins nods in response. "That's right, Amari. Obey your master. You have no choice now."

"What do you mean?"

"Do you know why I drugged you, tied you up to the bed, beat you like a Hebrew slave?"

"To punish me? Make me your pet?"

"Pet? No, that's not what you are. Well, not anymore. You're better than a pet", Ms. Wilkins brings her hand to Amari's chin, her eyes locking dead with hers. "You're my bait."

#

I put the phone back on the handle, my head lowered in sadness. "Dominic?", answers Mom as I turn my head back to her and Aunt Sue. "Is there something wrong?"

I blink, turning back to the telephone and them both. "It's Amari."

With these words, I turn my head back and speak. "It's Amari; he's in trouble."

"What?", said Aunt Sue.

"Amari's in trouble, he's in trouble, and he needs my help."

"Okay, well, what do you want to do?"

I put my hands in my fist, struggling to think. "I-I don't know."

"I think you do, baby", said Mom.

"What?"

"Go get him, Dom", said Aunt Sue.

I gasped. "Really? You'd let me go."

Mom sighs. "I never really liked Amari. Mostly because I thought he was a bad influence on you, but now I see he's just a scared kid in need of guidance. You're the only one who can give him that guidance."

"But I already did. I told him what he needed to do, but he didn't listen."

"Everyone deserves a second chance, Dominic. No matter what they did", Mom moves her eyes to the left in shame. "You may not be able to save me, but at least you can save him. A life for a life."

My eyes well up with tears. "Mama", I say under my breath. "I can't leave you."

"Don't worry, baby. I'll be here when you get back, okay?"

I sniff, before nodding. "Okay"

I kissed Mom on the forehead. "I love you, mom."

Mom presses her forehead on mine. "I love you too, baby. Always."

"I'll take care of her, Dominic", said Aunt Sue. "Go, go save your friend."

I nod. "Right."

With that, I make my way to the door, but not before turning my head back. "I'll be right back."

Mom smiled, nodding happily as I exited the room, but before I could, I turned my eyes back to the phone, confusing Mom and Aunt Sue. "Dominic, what are you doing?"

I dial a few digits before bringing the phone to my ear. "I'm getting a ride."

\#

A limousine parks in front of a small apartment home, stopping dead in front. I gaze out the window, my eyes full of fear. "You sure this is the place?", I turn my eyes back to Amanda, her hazel brown eyes gazing back at me. "3285 Burlington Road, yeah, it's the place."

Amanda gives me a quick nod before turning her head to the driver's seat. "Barry, pop the lock."

"Yes, Ms. Griffin."

Without the press of a button, the doors of the elongated vehicle unlock, causing me to pop the door wide open. As soon as it does, I head out of the car, with Amanda coming out from behind. Soon, the two of us stood side by side each other, staring out at the apartment home. In doing so, Amanda turns back to me, her eyes full of fear. "You sure you don't want me to come with you?"

I shake my head. "No, this is my fight. Besides, I can't have my girlfriend banged up."

Amanda laughs, her smile present, before taking her hand in mine. "I'll be careful."

"I know you will."

Amanda and I lean in for a quick kiss before pulling away. "I love you, Dominic."

"I love you too, Amanda. Go on, get out of here."

With a quick nod, Amanda turns back from me before heading back into the car, her door shut behind her. As soon as it does, the limousine drives off, leaving me all alone. Turning back to the house, I find myself staring directly at it.

My eyes glowed bright green at the sight of it, indicating just what was waiting for me on the other side. This was it, the final showdown with this woman. There was no turning back, for I was in the endgame now. With both my fists clenched and eyes stoned, I walk straight up the steps, before stepping up to the front door.

\#

Meanwhile, back at the hospital, Joana lay in bed next to Sue Anne, who was stroking what was left of the hair on her head as she hummed. Joana smiled happily; her eyes half-way open as she listened to her best friend's soft humming. "My angel", she sang. "My beautiful angel."

Joana's eyes slowly start to crack open at the sound of her friend's sniffs. "Sue?"

Sue Anne was found wiping away a few tears from her eyes. "Sue, don't cry."

She sniffs. "I can't help it. You're dying, and there's nothing I can do to help you."

"What do you mean? You've already helped me."

"How?"

Joana takes Sue Anne's hand, gripping it tight. "If it weren't for you, I would've never been able to raise such a young and noble son. You were always there for me, Sue. Through the good and the bad times. You're my best friend."

Sue nods. "Best friends."

Joana smiles as Sue pulls her in for a loving embrace. "I love you, Joana."

"I love you too, Sue Anne."

#

As soon as I entered the house, the front door was already open. It wasn't locked, and I didn't even have to knock. It was just open for me. As strange as it was, I knew what it meant. I was expected by *her*. Of course, she would. For someone so possessive, I wouldn't be so surprised if she wanted to hurt me. At that very moment, I had no idea what to expect. All I knew, was that my best friend was in danger, and I wasn't leaving here until I found him.

"Amari?", I said quietly, stepping further into the room. "You here?"

As soon as these words are said, a strange sound of something falling is heard. My head shifts to this, my eyes wide with fear. "Amari?"

I walked slower, my feet creeping on the carpet floor as I made my way to the white door, that was quite oddly open. My eyes glowed green again, only this time, the feeling was way more intense.

Found you.

With my fists clenched, I made my way up to the door, my heart pounding out of my chest.

This is it. Don't get scared now.

With these words in mind, I twist the doorknob and burst open the door. "No more hiding! Show yourself, Ms. Wilkins!"

"Mm-um!", said a voice, confusing me. "Ms. Wilkins?"

"Mm-mum!"

Walking further into the room, I make my way around the bed, and that's where I find him, tied up in rope. "AMARI!"

"Mm-mm!", he cries, his mouth covered in tape.

"It's okay, Amari! It's okay!", I say, making my way towards him, his head shaking as I break his hands-free from the rope, his cries heightening. "It's okay, Amari. You're going to be okay."

But Amari continues to shake his head, much to my confusion. "What, what is it? What are you saying?", I snatch the tape from his mouth, giving him the chance to speak. "It's a trap!"

"What?"

Within seconds, the sound of something slamming shut is heard, causing Amari and I to whip our heads back in shock. To my surprise, I find Ms. Wilkins standing there in a sparkly, red dress, her smile quite sinister. "Hello, Dominic. Long time no see, I presume."

I rose from the floor with a frown as I stood before her. "Let him go, Ms. Wilkins. Now!"

"I don't think that will be necessary. You see, Amari is very special to me."

"Is torturing him to death, defined as "special" because it's not!?"

"Why would you care what I do to him? You're not even his friend anymore, Amari means nothing to you now."

I shake my head. "Amari's always meant something to me. He's, my family."

I hadn't noticed before, but Amari was smiling from behind. "Aw, that's so sweet. You make me sick."

"Not as much as you. You think you can just go through life, dismantling other people's lives without any consequences. Well, you thought wrong! I'm ending this right now!"

"Oh, yeah!", reaching into her pocket, Ms. Wilkins pulls out a knife, aiming it directly at Dominic. "Dom, watch out!"

Quick as a flash, I jumped right off the floor and onto the bed, dodging the bullet that went straight for the lamp, shattering it into a million pieces. Ms. Wilkins fires again, this time into the mattress of the bed. The bullet was two seconds from hitting me, but I managed to hop off the bed in time before it did.

As for Amari, he was busy trying to untie himself. He managed to get the first knot out by the time I made my way to bed. Now, he needed to do the same for the second. A third bullet is fired, hitting me right in my arm. "Ah!"

"DOM!", Amari cries as I hit the floor with a thud.

Ms. Wilkins's eyes widened in shock, before a small grin formed on her face. "I…I did it?", she said as a tear fell from Amari's eye, mouthing a small "no".

"I did it! Ha-ha! I got him!", Ms. Wilkins screamed in victory of her defeat before walking up towards me. "Well, well, well. Looks like you lost, Dominic. Too bad, I was really looking forward to having a second member."

Amari lowered his head in shame, causing Ms. Wilkins to laugh. "I guess what they say is true": you never know what you have, until it's gone."

Amari, filled with despair, starts to cry at the death of his best friend. That is, so he thought when he noticed Dominic's eyes open wide, giving him a quick nod and wink.

Shocked, Amari quickly turned away from me and to Ms. Wilkins, who was now walking towards him, the gun still in her hand as she laughed. "Your friend lost the deal, which means you belong to me now."

"Think again, bitch!"

Turning her head back, Ms. Wilkins finds Dominic up on his feet and running straight towards her. Before she knew it, she was tackled, hitting the floor with a thud. "Ah!", she said, struggling from my grip. "Impossible! I thought I killed you!"

"Not quite. Looks like you need to work on your aim!"

With these words, I snatch the pistol from Ms. Wilkins's hands and turn back to Amari. "Amari, catch!", I say, throwing the pistol across the room.

Amari caught it without fail, as his hands were now free. "No!", Ms. Wilkins shouts, kicking me in the groin before falling to my knees.

As soon as I do, she goes straight across the bed, straight for Amari. "GIVE ME THAT GUN!"

"Amari!", I shout.

With his heart racing, Amari raises the pistol up to Ms. Wilkins and pulls the trigger.

Bang!

That is what I heard; the moment Amari raised that gun. My eyes were closed shut as I was afraid to see what happened. That is, until Amari spoke. "Dom?", he said, causing me to raise my head. To my surprise, I found Amari standing before me, the pistol fired, and Ms. Wilkins spread out on the bed, holding her wound. "You-you shot me!", she screamed in pain. "You shot your mother!"

Amari, with his hands trembling, dropped and looked at his mother, shocked. "I-I'm sorry, mother. I didn't mean to. I—"

Before Amari could finish his sentence, a loud knock was banged on the door, startling him. "THIS IS THE POLICE! COME OUT WITH YOUR HANDS UP!"

Amari gasps, looking at the door. "Oh, no!", he said as I rose from the floor, much to Amari's shock. "Dominic!"

"It's okay, Amari. I'm alright."

"What?", looking at me with horror. "But how?"

I opened my jacket wide, revealing a black set of armor under it. "It's a vest. Amanda gave it to me for protection. Don't worry, I'm fine."

With these words, I bring Amari in for a warm, loving embrace. "I'm sorry, Dominic. You were right about Ms. Wilkins. You were right about everything."

I wrap my arms around him, holding him tightly. "Everything's gonna be okay. I promise."

Within seconds, the door burst wide open, revealing Amanda and several police officers. Their eyes widened at the sight of the young woman bleeding out on the bed, along with the two young boys looking in horror.

Before we knew it, Amari and I soon made our way back outside, my arm around his shoulder as we walked out. As for Ms. Wilkins, she was handcuffed and put in a police car. They managed to patch up her wound before leaving, which was good for her as she was lucky to be alive. Amari, who was wrapped in a blanket, watched as Ms. Wilkins, the only woman who loved him, was taken inside the police car. But before she drove off, she gave him one last look, and mouthed three words that would shake him forever: *"I'll kill you."*

"Amanda, help me get Amari to the car", I say, causing Amanda to nod as the two of us grabbed Amari by his arms. At that moment, all he wanted was to be somewhere quiet, somewhere safe. And what better place was that than the limousine that we all rode in.

Tired and exhausted, Amari fell asleep on my shoulder, his eyes closed shut as he slept. I noticed the keychain hanging over his neck, where the name "Abigail" was found. Whomever that was, it must've been someone very special to him.

As for me, I stared out at the limousine, the streetlights hitting the edge of my face as we rode by. I never really liked the streetlights before, but after everything I'd been through, it was the most beautiful thing I'd ever seen.

"Are you okay, Dominic?", said Amanda, her eyes full of concern.

I give her a half-smile and nod. "Yeah, I just want to get back to mom."

Amanda takes my hand, gripping it tightly with hers before nodding. "We will, just sit tight. For now."

I nod to her before turning back to the lights, hitting my face. "Okay."

\#

Sue Anne was in the hospital room, face-down on the covers as she slept. Mom's beeping monitor was still going off, indicating that her heartbeat was steady, much to Sue's joy as she started to wake from her nap. "Oh, boy", she said, yawning. "I fell asleep. I must've dozed off, Joana."

Sue shifts her eyes to the left. "Joana?"

Joana, with her eyes closed, lay in bed, asleep, her smile present. "Joana?"

Sue takes Joana's hand before quickly pulling away, letting out a small gasp.

Her hands were as cold as ice. Perhaps it's, too cold.

"Joana?", Sue said, shaking her. "Joana!"

Sue proceeds to shake her, but she doesn't budge.

She didn't wake.

"Joana, Joana!", Sue said in tears.

Before she could cry, the heart suddenly made a different sound. One Sue couldn't believe she was hearing.

Beeeeeeeeeeeeeeeeeeeeeeeeeeeeeeeeeeeepppppppppppppppppppppppppppppppppppp ppppp!!!!

Now she was crying.

With nothing else to do, Sue Anne brings Joana's lifeless body into her arms and hugs her tight, sobbing. "No!", she sobbed. "JOANA!"

#

Sue sat in a chair outside of the hospital room, her head low in sadness.

Joana, her best friend, was dead. Never to be seen again.

She was broken like her heart was ripped from her body. It was painful, but none as painful as how her son would react.

His reaction would mean the end of the world.

The end of *his* world.

Sighing, Sue brings her hands to her face, feeling defeated. Or so she thought when the sound of footsteps was heard. "Aunt Sue?"

Sue raises her head up to find her "sort-of nephew", Dominic Mitchell, standing before his dread-headed best friend and biracial girlfriend. "Dominic", Sue said, rising from her seat, before walking up to me. "Dominic, there's something I have to tell you."

I raise my brow. "What?"

Sue lowers her eyes in sadness. "It's Joana."

I blink. "What about her?"

Sue's eyes lower in sadness, much to my shock. "No"

"Dominic, just listen-"

"No!"

"Dominic!", Aunt Sue calls from behind as I enter the hospital room, where my mom is found lying in bed.

She was still, as still as a vegetable.

I approached the bed, her eyes closed but smile present. With tears welling in my eyes, I knelt on the floor. "Mom?", I whisper. "Momma?"

I took her hands in mine, her icy, cold fingers intertwining with mine as I sobbed. "Momma, I'm sorry. I'm so sorry!"

With that, I leaned my head onto Mom's hands and cried.

Little did I know, Amari, Amanda, and Aunt Sue were watching from behind, tears welling in their eyes. It isn't long before I'm comforted by each and every one of their touches.

It was nice, but it would've been better if it was a mother's touch.

My mother's touch.

But not tonight. Tonight, it was just my friends and me.

At that moment, that's all I needed.

#

Three weeks later.

The morning dawned hot in St. Mora, and Griffin Manor sat proudly on the hilltop, which was as perfect as it was the first time. Although, for some, it was the last time.

"Hurry up, guys!", said Amanda in her grey cap and gown. "We're going to be late!"

"Yeah, we'll be right down, Amanda!", Amari said up from the staircase.

Amanda was downstairs admiring herself in her grey cap and gown before a pair of feet approached her from behind. "Mrs. Griffin?", Amanda turns her eyes back to Butler Barry, his smile big. "The limousine is up and running, we'll be departing soon."

Amanda smiles happily. "Okay."

"You and the boys can come down now."

"Thanks, Barry. I'll let them know. Um, Sue Anne!"

"What's up?"

"Make sure to check up on Dominic. See if he's ready?"

"Yeah, sure."

With that, Amari makes his way down the corridor hallways of the house before stopping at the door, one which he quickly knocks on. "Dominic!", he said. "You in there?"

Suddenly, the door opens wide, revealing Aunt Sue to exit, much to Amari's shock. "Oh, Sue Anne."

"Hello, Mr. Jenkins. I see you trying to see about your friend Dominic?"

He nods. "Uh, yeah. Is he in there?"

"He is", Amari said, crossing her arms. "But he's not happy."

"What do you mean? Is he okay?"

He shook her head. "He's not in the best shape. He won't even get into his cap and gown."

"He doesn't."

"Nope, he's pretty bummed out."

"Well, then, let me talk to him. Surely, I can help him out."

Amari scratches her head. "I don't know. I've already tried, but he won't budge."

"Well, he can with me! Move aside, kid!", Sue Anne protests, walking past Aunt Sue and to the door.

Without a second thought, Sue Anne takes a deep breath and twists the doorknob, entering the room. "Dominic, it's me. I just wanted to know how you were doi—", Sue Anne's words were quickly cut off as he found a grey cap and gown lying on the bed next to a young, curly-haired boy sitting on the bed, with his head low. "Dom?", Amari said, making his way to the bed. "You, okay?"

I look down to the floor, sad as ever before speaking. "No"

"What's wrong?"

I sigh, my eyes still looking to the floor as Amari sits next to me. "What are you holding?"

Aunt Sue notices the picture frame of Mom smiling. "Oh, it's Joana?"

I nod. "I just can't believe she's gone."

"Yeah, neither can I, man. But let's not try to be so stuck on the past and try to make this a good graduation day?"

"I'm not going."

"What? What do you mean?"

"I barely made it through Mom's funeral. Does it look like I can survive my high school graduation? Especially when…", I place my hand on Mom's photo, my lips quivering as I turn to Amari, "she's not there."

Sue sighs, placing his hand on my shoulder before bringing me in for a hug. "I know it's hard. I know this isn't easy, but I'd really like to see you attend graduation with us. That's what I want; that's what *she* would want."

I lower my eyes back to Mom's framed photo, causing me to turn back to the cap and gown lying on the bed. "Alright. I'll be out in a minute."

Sue nods. "Okay", he rises from the bed, leaving me alone with the photo of Mom before heading out of the room.

Amari stood outside the door; her arms folded as Amari shut the door behind him with a sigh. "How is he?", she asks.

She sighs. "He's still upset, but can you blame him?"

Amanda sighs, nodding. "Yeah, getting over a death isn't easy, especially if it's someone you were close to."

"Yeah, it's trauma."

The sound of a car beeping was heard, causing Amari and Amanda to turn heads. "That's Barry. We better go."

Amari nods, turning back to the door before sighing. "Yeah, okay"

#

I remained in the room, his fingers clenching the purple envelope in his hands. This was a note Aunt Sue had given to him the day of his mother's funeral. He just hadn't opened it yet. She said when he was ready, he could, and now he was.

Without a second thought, I peeled off the sticker and opened it wide, where a set of words presented itself:

Dear Dominic,

If you're reading this, it means I'm gone. But I don't want you to be upset. No, I want you to be joyful, joyful because I'm free. I'm free from all the pain and all the suffering I've ever endured. There are millions of people in this world right now who are suffering from terrible illnesses. Some make it out, and some don't. People who don't are considered, the "unlucky ones" but that's not how I see it at all; that's not how I see death. Death isn't scary, nor is it painful; it's peaceful. Safe. Comforting. Like the warmest blanket wrapped around your body, shielding you from the coldest winters. It's what gives our lives meaning, a reason to see another day, which is exactly what I want you to do. To live every day like it's your last, cherish everything and everyone around you, no matter how angry or resentful you may feel towards them. Be forgiving, and never hold a grudge. 'Cause at the end of the day, who would even care?

I nodded, a tear falling down my cheek as I flipped to the next page to a second smaller paragraph.

I don't have very much time left, so I'm sending you off with something I think you'd like very much. When I was a little girl, my grandfather would often tell me something that really got me through some things. In some of my darkest days, I'd hear his voice and recall these words. He said: There are times in this life, when you're going to laugh and times when you're going to cry. At first, I didn't really know what he meant being so young. But now, having lived a little, I finally did. Even though there was more crying, then there was laughing. I regret not laughing more. But I am now, and it's in the most beautiful places I've ever seen, more beautiful than Earth itself. Someday, you'll be in this place and be happier than you could ever imagine. Don't throw this letter away; keep it close to your heart, and don't forget a single word that was said. Have it with you at all times, so in your saddest days, I'll be right there beside you. I'll always be right beside you.

We'll see each other soon, baby. I know it.

Sincerely, your momma, Joana.

P.S.: For the love of God, stop leaving your shoes outside in the rain! It's getting on my last damn nerves!

That got a laugh out of me, something I hadn't done in a long time, and it felt good to do it. Wiping a few tears from my eyes, I brought the letter close to my heart and squeezed it tight—like I was hugging my mother, and she was right here next to me. "I'll see you again, too, momma. I promise."

With these words, I fold Mom's letter into a square and slip it into my pocket. Then, I turned my eyes to the grey cap and gown lying beside me. A happy smile formed across my face, causing me to reach for it without a hint of regret.

#

"Are you sure you don't want to drive with us?", Amanda asked her mother and father, who were standing before her. "No, dearest. Your mother and I figured it would be best to drive alone. Besides, it is too cramped with all of us riding together"

Amanda raised her brow, confused. "It's a limousine, Dad, it wouldn't be too—"

"Amanda!", Mrs. Griffin snapped, looking dead at her. "Your father and I will be riding to the graduation alone! End of discussion!"

Amanda flinches. "Yes, mother."

"Mind your mother, dear. Just get to the car with Mr. Mitchell."

"He's not here."

"Not here. Well, where is he?"

"Right here!"

With that, Amanda and Amari walked down the hallway, leaving the door. Or so they thought, once the door opens wide, revealing a shadow figure. "Guys, wait!"

Amanda and Amari stop dead in the hallway, their heads turning back to find me standing in my grey cap and gown. "Don't forget about me", I laugh.

Two big, happy smiles formed on Amanda and Amari's faces, causing them to run right up to me, embracing me with a happy hug. "I knew you'd come, man."

"Of course, I would. You didn't think I was going to let you graduate alone, did you?"

Amanda kisses me on the cheek before taking my hand in hers, leading the three of us down the hallway. Soon, we were descending the steps of Griffin Manor and into the limousine. "To Summit High! Step on it, Barry!"

"Yes, Ms. Griffin?"

Beside Barry was Aunt Sue, popping her head out of the driver's seat, smiling happily at her nephew. "Is my graduate ready?"

"I sure am, Aunt Sue. Thanks for getting me back out here."

"That's what Aunties are for."

With that, the limousine steps on the gas, causing the limousine to move out of the Griffin Manor parking lot and out of the road. Amanda spent the last few minutes staring out the window before I took her hand in mine, causing her to turn back to me with a smile.

She shrugged. "I guess it does", Amanda kissed me on the cheek before wrapping her arms around me, her head resting on my shoulder. As for Amari, he raised his fist up at me, his smile present. "We cool?"

I nod and raise my fist. "Yeah, we're cool."

With those words, Amari and I made a quick fist bump, and our friendship was now rekindled. I spent the last few minutes staring out of the window, thinking of *her*.

I may not have Mom, but I still have my best friend, my girlfriend, and my Aunt Sue. I still had a family.

My family.

If I didn't have that, then what did I have?

With that said, I gazed out the window of the limousine, smiling, now exited for graduation.

EPILOGUE

"Robert?", answered Mrs. Griffin, entering the front door of her home. "Robert?!"

Evelyn's voice echoes throughout the house, as the door closes behind her. "Robert, I've been waiting in the car for about thirty minutes now. Are you ready to go?"

From up the stairway and through the halls, Robert was found in the bathroom, staring at his reflection in his mirror. Suddenly, he looked down at his hands where his Taurus-92 pistol was cuffed in his hands and brought it to the side of his skull. But before he could shoot, a second gun was pointed at the back of his head. "Not so fast, Robert."

Shocked, Robert's gun slips from his fingers and falls on the bathroom floor. Robert then puts his hands up in the air, his eyes wide with horror at the pepper-bearded man staring at him from the mirror.

Evelyn walks up the staircase, her head looking at the floor. "Robert, seriously, this isn't funny. Come downstairs or el—", Mrs. Griffin's head jumped up as the sound of a gunshot went off. "Robert!?", she called out in distress.

There was no answer, making her scared.

"Robert!"

Evelyn was now running up the steps, her heart beating out of her chest as she made it to the last step. In doing so, she runs down the hallway. That's when she found the door to the bathroom cracked open. With her heart now in her stomach, Mrs. Griffin slowly opens the door and speaks. "Robert? Are you in here?"

With the door now wide open, Mrs. Griffin's eyes widen as her husband lies bleeding out on the bathroom floor, with Octavius staring up at her.

Evelyn's eyes widened in shock at the man's nasty scar and knew. "You."

"You", he said back.

Without any hesitation, Evelyn runs past the bathroom door and down the hallway. As for Octavius, he stops dead at the door, watching her run. In doing so, a sinister smirk forms across his face as the sound of sirens is heard in the background.

Evelyn descended the steps, her heart racing at the speed of light as she did. She was scared, more afraid than she had ever been before. Was this it? Was her life going to end in the hand of a gun? Or worse?

She didn't know, except she needed to save herself before things got worse. Within seconds, she made her way to the steps, where there was a series of blue and red lights. Evelyn saw this and became confused, but from the situation she was in, the police were the best thing. "Oh, thank goodness, help!"

With these words, Evelyn ran towards the door, opening the door wide. "Please help me!"

Evelyn's words were stopped by the sight of a row of police officers lined up before her, their guns drawn directly at her. "HANDS ON YOUR HEAD, NOW!"

"What?"

"HANDS UP, NOW!"

"What did I do? Hey, wait!", she shouted as two policemen ran up toward her, handcuffing her. "Evelyn Griffin, you're under arrest for the murder of Robert Griffin! Anything you say can and will be used against you in the court of law!"

"Let go of me. I didn't do anything!"

Evelyn continued to shout as a mysterious figure in black watched the helpless woman be taken away. Octavius Mitchell stood there with absolute happiness.

"I guess revenge really is best served cold."

The End

Made in the USA
Columbia, SC
09 January 2025

51465870R00248